Praise for

ALL THE MEN I'VE LOVED AGAIN

USA Today Bestseller

"I adore second-chance romances, and Christine Pride's *All the Men I've Loved Again* is the ultimate! Pride weaves a deliciously twisty, heartwarming story that spans decades, tempts fate, and is wildly relatable to anyone who's ever found themselves lost in 'it's complicated' love. An unputdownable debut!"

—Tia Williams, bestselling author of *A Love Song for Ricki Wilde*

"*All the Men I've Loved Again* is a sweeping coming-of-age novel that explores hope, healing, and the heartache that lies between. With a raw, emotional depth, it captures the complexities of love and loss in a way that is both tender and moving."

—Sadeqa Johnson, *New York Times* bestselling author of *The House of Eve*

"A fascinating exploration of love, fate, and personal agency, *All the Men I've Loved Again* is a second-chance romance to devour in one gulp. The characters are relatable and complex, and the ending is more satisfying than I thought possible."

—Annabel Monaghan, bestselling author of *Nora Goes Off Script*

"Brave and devouring, *All the Men I've Loved Again* is the kind of satisfying romance for anyone second-guessing a second chance at love and life. Her sweeping adventures of self-discovery ultimately treat us with a tender and intimate saga that will wash you with restored hope."

—Xochitl Gonzalez, bestselling author of *Olga Dies Dreaming* and *Anita de Monte Laughs Last*

"A deeply heartfelt, poignant novel about the journey of love in all its beautiful agonies. Christine Pride made me hope, dream, fear, and then sigh knowing everything turns out as it should. This masterpiece reveals that our hearts are smart enough to find their way if we let them."

—Nancy Johnson, bestselling author of *People of Means*

"Equal parts clever, heartwarming, and unnervingly perceptive, *All the Men I've Loved Again* had me captivated from the first pages. Christine Pride delivers a fresh take on second-chance romances, proving you can never have too many opportunities for love; life is best when it's complicated; and '90s references will *never* die! Pride masterfully creates a story and characters that make you feel seen—the true mark of a great book!"

—Catherine Adel West, author of *Saving Ruby King*

"Christine Pride's sweeping, relatable, and bold *All the Men I've Loved Again* took me on a journey through the complications of love, growth, and self-discovery spanning decades, bolstered by a cast of lovable characters who feel real enough to touch."

—Shirlene Obuobi, author of *Between Friends & Lovers*

"The passionate love scenes and strong Black supporting cast will make this a hit with fans of Jasmine Guillory and Tia Williams."

—*Publishers Weekly*

"Coming-of-age moments, true friendship, first loves . . . this book has it all. A story of fate, choices, and second chances."

—*Woman's World*

ALSO BY CHRISTINE PRIDE

You Were Always Mine (with Jo Piazza)

We Are Not Like Them (with Jo Piazza)

ALL THE MEN I'VE LOVED AGAIN

A Novel

CHRISTINE PRIDE

ATRIA PAPERBACK

New York Amsterdam/Antwerp London
Toronto Sydney/Melbourne New Delhi

An Imprint of Simon & Schuster, LLC
1230 Avenue of the Americas
New York, NY 10020

First Atria Paperback edition June 2026

Interior design by Davina Mock-Maniscalco

Manufactured in the United States of America

1 3 5 7 9 10 8 6 4 2

Library of Congress Control Number: 2024055031

ISBN 978-1-6680-4953-2
ISBN 978-1-6680-4954-9 (pbk)
ISBN 978-1-6680-4955-6 (ebook)

Dedicated to
all the men I've loved; you know who you are
and
my dad, who set the highest bar

Each time you love
love as deeply
as if it were
forever.
—Audre Lorde, "For Each of You"

prologue | CORA HAS TO MAKE A CHOICE

December 2021

Cora's father always told her the most important decision she'd ever make was who she let herself love. "You'll have jobs, houses, friends, but it's who you give your heart to that's going to make all the difference. Make that choice carefully, baby girl."

God, how she's trying.

Lincoln. Aaron. Lincoln. Aaron. Lincoln. Aaron.

"Have you decided?"

The manicurist's voice snaps Cora out of her agonizing, even if at first she thinks this stranger is demanding an answer about her love life.

"She'll have this one." Neisha thrusts a bottle of neon-blue nail polish at the woman.

The color, Gotta Do Blue, is way outside Cora's comfort zone of various shades of neutral, mauve if she's feeling wild, but she's happy—grateful even—to defer to her best friend on this decision and most things. Cora can count the times she's said no to Neisha throughout the entirety of their twenty-year friendship on two hands.

So she nods, and they follow the manicurist to two plush pink chairs that face a boardwalk of sorts. Only in Los Angeles can you get your nails done in front of a bank of open floor-to-ceiling windows facing the sun-dappled expanse of the ocean and let the breeze dry your polish. Every time she visits Neisha, who moved across the country to this land of hikes and eternal sunshine and boba tea ten years ago, Cora wonders if the wildly erratic East Coast seasons she tells herself she loves are overrated. It's three days before Christmas and seventy degrees; it feels so good and so wrong.

When they're settled into their chairs, and the opportunity presents itself, Cora finally spills. She tells Neisha everything. It takes six minutes, half of what it would have taken if she'd talked in a normal cadence and not a breathless rush. There was another full minute of silence while Neisha held her hand up in the air. "Not another word, I need to process."

Then.

"Okay, well, I gotta say, this is a curveball I did not see coming." Neisha sucks her teeth and then adds a shake of the head to make sure there's no question about the level of her disbelief. They both know she's referring to the fact that Cora Rose Belle is about the last person you'd expect to find in a reality-show-worthy love triangle. And twice.

"It's the déjà vu that gets me. How did you up and do this *again*?"

Cora doesn't bother trying to summon an answer she doesn't have because Neisha plows right on along, happy not to have her usual animated monologues interrupted.

"Why does everything need to keep coming back around? Chokers. These biker shorts I probably have no business being in. What's next? Shai reuniting for a comeback album? Actually, I wouldn't be mad at that. Remember how fine that Garfield was? Too fine for that silly-ass name. Is he even alive still? Sad I have to keep googling to see if folks are dead or not. RIP, DMX. We old . . . anyhoo, back to you. I mean, who knew our little Cora could be so damn messy?"

Over the top as ever, Neisha suddenly grabs a thick nail file and pretends it's a microphone. "And now, on tonight's final episode of *The Love Triangle*, we'll find out . . . which man will win Cora Belle's heart?" She imitates a knockoff Chris Harrison (calling to mind their many *Bachelor* marathons over the years) and waits for Cora to laugh. Neisha is the kind of friend who routinely forces Cora to act out pivotal scenes from *The Color Purple*, but right now it's too much.

The stakes are too high. *Who will Cora choose?* It's a question days, months, years, decades in the making; all the history and memories and regret and second guesses have accumulated like the infinite particles of nail dust coating the salon, everywhere you look and just as impossible to wipe clean.

Cora turns to look at Neisha, whose eyes are boring into hers. The soft wrinkles sprouting around those eyes and the fullness that's crept into her friend's face often catch Cora off guard, same as the marks the years have made on her own face sometimes do, which makes for the occasional jarring moment when she catches her reflection and thinks, *Wait, is that really me?* But all Cora has to do is squint sideways at Neisha to see the reed-thin girl who bounded into their freshman bio study group with a purple Afro and a family-size pack of Chips Ahoy cookies tucked under her arm. She'd plopped down next to Cora, neither of them aware that two decades later, they'd still be sitting side by side, having witnessed every part of the other's journey to this point—a whole lifetime.

"Do I need to dig out a quarter? 'Cause you might as well flip a coin. But you need to do something. Like yesterday. You can't keep stringing that man along—he's about to ask you to *marry* him, Cora!"

Leave it to Neisha to make everything seem easier than it actually is. Or maybe it's that Cora makes everything harder than it needs to be—that's entirely possible.

Cora thinks of the email sitting in her drafts folder, the one she wrote and rewrote, then deleted and started again from scratch. Her heart begins to pound so hard, she suspects the woman applying polish with such care can feel the pulsing in her fingertips. The pounding escalates when Cora thinks of the gold floor-length dress she's already bought—well, borrowed from Rent the Runway—to wear Thursday night.

She'll show up in it or she won't.

She'll send the email or she won't.

But time is running out either way.

Finally, Neisha abandons her attempts to be glib or stern and shifts her whole body toward Cora. "Okay, sis, real talk. What's it going to take for you to decide once and for all?"

That's the problem—she doesn't know. All Cora has at her disposal is her so-called maturity. She is, after all, staring down forty, a grown-ass lady who should be able to follow her gut, make up her mind about nail polish colors, and decide who she should spend the rest of her life with. But trusting herself has never been one of Cora's strong suits, even after the self-help books and therapy, all the auditing, healing, self-care, and that one hot-yoga class that almost killed her, which did, at least, make it something of a spiritual experience.

She gazes at the Pacific laid out before her like a glittery blue blanket. Watching the waves slows her heart and her breathing as if they're trying to match the rhythm of the ocean. Maybe it's the exact way the light glints against the water that pierces her with a sudden clarity. Or maybe it's the way Neisha put it: It's not who she will choose, but *how*. It starts to dawn on Cora that she's been going at it all wrong. *To know where you're going, you have to understand where you've been.* It was another well-worn piece of advice from her father—ever the history teacher.

"You know, I have all the letters Aaron wrote me back then."

"Damn, I really hate that the early aughts was 'back then,' and I hate that word too, *aughts*. Who came up with that? But, yeah, no surprise you kept the letters."

"No, I mean I have them with me. Here." Cora looks down at the canvas tote at her feet, bulging with the past.

"You packed a pile of letters?"

"Yeah, I've been meaning to read them again. I just haven't been able to go there."

"I hear that. Do you think Aaron kept the ones you wrote him too? Probably stored in some old Birkenstocks shoebox?" Neisha has cracked herself up and is unfazed by Cora's glare.

"What! I mean, a Black dude wearing Birkenstocks? Come on. Guess he pulled it off, though, because here we are."

"Oh God, Neisha, I hate to think of rereading my letters. I can't even imagine how young and naive I sounded."

"I sure can! I was there! Remember, I was the one who convinced you that you wouldn't die of toxic shock syndrome if you dared use a tampon?" The manicurist has to wait for Neisha to stop laughing or risk slathering polish all over her cuticles. "But, hey, I'm not one to talk. We were all young and dumb. I mean, that time I broke my hand Rollerblading . . . drunk? Oh, let's not forget Kim's Lisa Bonet phase? That girl, I tell you."

A wistful somberness creeps in when Neisha says *That girl*, so subtle only Cora would notice it, and she does but just barely because she's lost in thought. A revelation, really. *I have to go backward before I can go forward.*

That's how she'll get the answers she needs. She must relive it all, retrace her steps—*their* steps, really, hers and Aaron's and Lincoln's—

and it will help her find the way. Like a turn-of-the-century explorer painstakingly cataloging miles of waterways and inlets to locate the source of a river, driven by faith that these discoveries will have broader implications and tangible applications. Her own trip down memory lane will surely reveal something important about how the world—and her heart—works. It will offer a map leading her straight to the right man, the right life, *the right choice.*

"You know what? What's past is prologue, Ne-ne."

Again, Cora barely registers what Neisha mumbles: "Ah, shit, you're over here dropping some vague Shakespeare mumbo jumbo? If anything, you need to be summoning Oprah right about now . . . or Jesus."

She doesn't—can't—respond because she's already floating years and miles away. Cora Belle has gone back to the beginning.

PART ONE

THEN

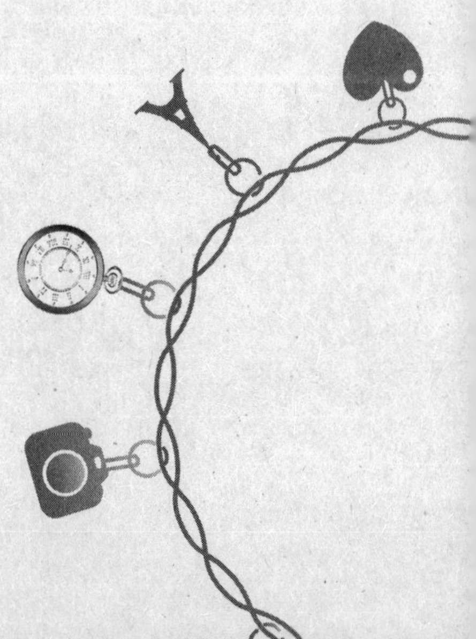

CORA DOESN'T KNOW WHAT TO DO WITH HERSELF

August 1999

Cora Belle arrived at college determined to conquer her fears once and for all. There were many: spiders; thick soups with unidentifiable ingredients; failure; getting lost, both physically and metaphorically; being late; being early; being alone; getting cancer.

Love.

Her plan was simple: She would completely transform herself into someone who was brave, confident, chill, and knew how to pull off a smoky eye. She would use her time at Hamlin to put herself together like a puzzle, take all the fledgling identities, fragments of personality and haphazard aspirations, and assemble them into a coherent version of herself, ready for the daunting task of adulthood. Also, improve her posture while she was at it.

She was not off to a good start. On any front.

Standing with slumped shoulders in the long, snaking line in the Hamlin University bookstore, Cora faced a more urgent concern: trying not to burst into tears in front of hundreds of other students who'd set about procuring mountains of textbooks in the early hours of a hot, bright late-August morning.

She looked around with wild eyes and barely concealed panic—what was she even doing in this place? Never mind that Cora had actively participated in all the steps to get here: printing out applications, taking the SATs, writing essay after essay about riveting topics like "a time you've faced a challenge," and tearing at the big white envelope from Hamlin Admissions when it arrived. Not to mention carefully packing sweaters and CDs, a stack of pristine Moleskine notebooks, and the stuffed Snoopy she'd had since she was a baby, currently stashed in the freshly unpacked duffel under the bed in her dorm room. Hidden, but close.

Had Cora ever been away from home before, she might have known to steel herself for the homesickness that consumed her as soon as her father grabbed her by both shoulders last night, trained his wide brown eyes on her, and said, "Well, I'd best be going now, Cora. You're going to be good, you hear? I know you know that even if you don't fully believe it yet." But she was bowled over by the unfamiliar feeling when Wes hugged her goodbye and had the audacity to drive away.

After watching the lights of her father's Acura until they faded from sight, Cora scurried up four flights of stairs (thereby avoiding the packed elevators) to her single room, the one she'd scored on account of exaggerated allergies, even though it was the prospect of living with a complete stranger that made her break out in hives. In the privacy of her closet-size dorm room, she sobbed into a pillow as quietly as possible waiting for the tears to stop, or the sun to rise, whichever came first. It was a close race. By 7:00 a.m., before anyone else in the dorm seemed to have stirred, Cora slunk to the communal hall bathroom, where she patted cold water on her puffy eyes and brushed the teeth that four long years of braces had wrestled into place. She smiled into the mirror for a full thirty seconds because she'd read somewhere that it could change your mood even if it was fake.

Cora attempted this strategy again now, grinning maniacally at no one and everyone in the packed bookstore that was brimming with the giddy energy of fresh starts, new adventures, and infinite possibilities. It was really quite oppressive. Especially when you factored in the body heat.

There was a second there where Cora thought she might be okay; she even relaxed a little, shook out her tight shoulders, looked at a flyer on the wall inviting new students to "Come Kick It at Kippen Field" for a meet-and-greet picnic, and thought, *Maybe?*

And then, just as she shuffled a few feet forward in line, an image came to her: her father, at home a hundred miles or so up I-95, opening the *Washington Post* and vigorously shaking it out, then folding the pages just right and going to read to her as he always did before realizing that she wasn't sitting across from him eating Frosted Flakes. Cora had been so focused on missing him, she hadn't stopped to consider how much he would miss *her*. Who would remind him to grab his travel coffee mug that he never failed to forget every single morning?

Her eyes welled to dangerous levels as she thought of that stupid steel mug. And the sound of her father humming while he sorted the mail. The green shag carpet in her bedroom. The row of *World Book* encyclopedias on the shelf above her desk where her pencil holder, stapler, and framed baby picture were lined up in precise order. The pumpkin-shaped cookie jar in the kitchen that held stray dollar bills and spare keys. The list went on and on, and with each item (her towering piles of *Seventeen* magazines!), Cora was ratcheted up to an increasingly wretched state. She glanced frantically around searching for an escape, if not from the bookstore itself than somehow from the anxious vice grip of her mind, and that's when she saw him.

Standing a few feet away, having materialized out of nowhere, was one of the most striking people Cora had ever seen. He stood out partly because he was so tall (at least six two) and partly because he was one of the only other brown faces around, but mainly because he was so . . . hot. Cora's extensive vocabulary was a source of pride but her addled brain couldn't come up with a more eloquent adjective to describe this stranger. She watched as he leaned over and dragged a sharp blade along the top of a large box at his feet. For whatever reason, this action played out in her mind in slow motion, such that she could see the subtle quivering of his forearm muscle as it flexed and released. When he stood back up, she zeroed in on the gold name tag attached to his bookstore uniform, a bright green polo: Lincoln Ames.

Cora whispered it a few times under her breath. "Lincoln Ames. Lincoln Ames. Lincoln Ames." She hadn't before considered that a name could be attractive. But it was, along with so much else about him. First, his skin. For this, she *was* able to summon just the right SAT word: *luminous*. Cora had only heard that term applied to women and only in makeup commercials, but it was the perfect description. It was like someone had taken an ideal human form and poured the silkiest, smoothest dark chocolate over it. Everything about him was long; each of his limbs stretched an extra inch beyond the factory model. His eyes were as jet black and shiny as piano keys. But it was his lips that nearly did her in. Full, pillowy, and smooth in a way that called to mind clouds and mangoes. These lips were responsible for sending Cora stumbling into the person in front of her, who'd been aggressively nodding his head along to whatever was playing on the Discman clipped to his jeans.

Guys like this, like Lincoln Ames, didn't exist in Cora's world outside John Singleton movies or the imaginary crushes she'd conjured that were all some version of a young James Earl Jones she once saw in one of the vintage *Ebony* magazines her father collected. Never in the flesh. It was as if she were in an elevator that had dropped too fast. There was a sudden, overwhelming wooziness and a warm heaviness deep within her, almost like vertigo but not quite. What she was experiencing was, of course, attraction, but Cora Belle was so unfamiliar with the concept and sensation, it registered mainly as confusion.

She lost herself to the mesmerizing distraction of watching Lincoln stack stuffed teddy bears emblazoned with the Hamlin Huskies logo into a structurally sound pyramid, breaking his focus only to give coworkers fist bumps when they passed or greet customers like this was his store and he was welcoming people to his own personal back-to-school party. His whole affect—so upbeat, so affable—was the opposite of Cora's, which made her even more self-conscious to be the pathetic guest bringing down the vibe of the entire affair. But then she remembered that exactly no one, including Lincoln, was paying attention to her. In moments like this, Cora relished the fact that she typically felt invisible in most situations; it meant she could observe Lincoln in peace.

Until. She felt the hands of someone on her. One of the two girls standing in line behind her reached out and touched her hair, causing Cora to startle and jump much more dramatically than the situation called for and in a way that drew too many eyes.

Before spotting Lincoln, Cora had been eavesdropping on the girls' overanimated chatter, though they hadn't been so much conversing as squawking at each other like a pair of high-pitched birds; they exchanged the most basic biographical details as if each one was an astonishing twist of fate and destiny.

"You're from New Jersey? No way! My parents have a house in Cape May."

"Wait! You have an older brother? I have an older brother! We're three years apart too—crazy!"

Based on these *incredible* commonalities, they were on their way to becoming best friends by the time they got to the front of the line. One already had complaints about her new roommate ("You would not believe how loudly she *breathes*"), which made Cora all the more grateful for her single.

Cora reflexively swatted at the girl who'd touched her, the shorter one with a mane of shaggy curls swept up in a giant bedazzled butterfly clip.

"Whoa, jeez, sorry, I was just . . . you still have the tag on your sweatshirt, you know?"

"Oh, I forgot to cut it off, I guess." Cora assumed her dad had done it for her before he handed her the brand-new Huskies sweatshirt compliments of this store right here.

"Here, let me rip it off for you." The girl went to lift Cora's braids to remove the tag, prompting Cora to dodge her again.

"No! That's okay, I got it." Her tone was regrettably harsh. She hadn't meant to lash out like an alley cat, but the damage was done. Cora had thrown off her invisibility cloak and revealed the weird, fumbling girl she'd been trying to outrun. Worse than being invisible was being utterly exposed; it was Cora's curse to always find herself swinging between these two extremes.

She tore off the offending tag and, not knowing what to do with it, clutched it in her clammy fist while an uncomfortable silence enveloped everyone involved. The girls were polite enough to wait until they were out of earshot to talk about her, but Cora could sense them exchanging a look: *What's her problem?*

Good question.

Actually, Cora knew exactly what her problem was—or problems. She, like everyone, had her fair share and kept a running list because knowledge was power. One of them was her desperation to escape people like this (as unfair as it might have been to lump them all together): white girls. The two in the bookstore were a composite of all the girls Cora had gone to school with, tiny with wide eyes and white-blond highlights and Juicy sweatsuits, all the ones who called her "girl" and asked how often she washed her hair and even *how* she washed her hair, who "joked" that with the right amount of Hawaiian Tropic they could get as dark as Cora over summer break. Girls who were nice enough but always made her feel like a curiosity.

Shooting straight to the top of Cora's many aspirations for college was making friends—real and true girlfriends. Black girlfriends. The ones she dreamed of while watching reruns of *Living Single*. Cora wanted to, at last, get in where she fit in, which was the well-meaning but utterly useless advice her father gave her when it came to her social life, or rather the lack thereof.

Fitting in was all but impossible at Prescott Academy, the prestigious prep school she'd attended for the entirety of her school years, where her father taught history, where the hefty annual tuition was waived because of that, and where one of the only other brown faces she saw had her exact same nose. This experience—spending her formative years as the only Black kid in a sea of white ones—had saddled Cora with a very particular kind of chronic identity crisis. Though she looked the part with her dark skin and cornrowed braids—the same style since first grade because her father had his hands full without having to devote time to reckoning with the complexities of hair every day—Cora still couldn't escape the feeling of being some sort of impostor. This was especially intense at her violin concerts, the summers she took riding lessons, and the rare occasion she found herself at a party in someone's wood-paneled basement nodding her head awkwardly to the Dave Matthews Band.

Where *did* she belong?

The question brought a fresh wave of panic. Actually, it wasn't the question itself but the prospect of never finding an answer that caused a hard knot to lodge right in the tender hollow between her belly and her ribs. As a single bead of hot sweat rolled down her temple, Cora again debated fleeing the line. A full-fledged panic attack would be worse than tears, worse than not having any books for the semester. But she wouldn't need books at all if she called her dad and demanded that he come pick her up.

She was contemplating just how big a failure it would be not to make it even a full twenty-four hours on campus when she looked up and locked eyes on Lincoln Ames. Again. Only this time, he was staring right back. And smiling. The smile landed on her like the sun and heated her from the outside in, just like a strong ray of light. This wasn't the first time anyone had ever smiled at her, obviously, but it might as well have been, given the effect it had.

Cora being Cora, she immediately hid her face, but mere seconds later she glanced up again despite herself, and he was still right there. His expression said, *Yeah, you.* Then he dropped his smile and looked serious, as if he were asking, *You good?*

Was this pity because he'd seen that awkward exchange with the girls or noted her puffy eyes or nervous sweating? Or had she imagined it all? No, there was a warm place in her chest where the smile had left its mark.

While she'd been busy working all that out, Cora had neglected to move her own cheeks a single millimeter, had merely stared at him blankly. By the time she'd come to the glaring realization that she could—should—smile back and how simple that would be, it was too late. Lincoln had returned to his work, lining up a row of beer cozies. An elderly couple with matching fanny packs approached him and he waved for them to follow him down an aisle. And then he was . . . gone. It was absurd that Cora would find this so upsetting. Then again, the prospect that he would return and smile at her again left her just as stricken. That both of these sentiments could be true should have been confounding, but Cora was used to half her thoughts and feelings being in direct opposition to the other half.

Craning her head this way and that in an effort to spot him again, Cora considered an idea that was as audacious as it was intimidating, as out of character as it was thrilling. An act that would kick-start her transformation into the type of person she desperately wanted to be: If and when Lincoln returned, she would talk to him. *Hi. Wow, it's so crowded, huh? I like your name.* She tried out possibilities, each one more spectacularly lame than the last, but it occupied her mind until, finally, she reached the front of the line.

The weary clerk with the crooked glasses took her printed course list and ferried textbooks from the metal shelves behind him to a mounting tower on the counter. She didn't mind that he moved at a pace only slightly faster than the pet turtle she'd once had, since it bought time for Lincoln to reappear.

Except he never did. And Cora could only linger with the stack of books in her quivering arms for so long waiting for a second chance that never came.

It didn't matter—that's what she told herself. The moment had passed, but it had also served its purpose. Inconsequential as it might have appeared, that random, warm smile and that strange connection was anything but meaningless for Cora. In fact, she would always think of it as magical, even though she would never admit that out loud. And even decades later, in a salon overlooking the Pacific, when she turns this memory over in her mind and checks it for flaws and hyperbole, that assessment will hold up. Because in that fleeting encounter with a captivating stranger, Cora got what she most needed and least expected right when it mattered the most: a reason to cling to a wild, willful hope that she might just be okay.

CORA WINS AND LOSES

October 1999

Hope could let you down; that was the risk of the whole enterprise. But when it delivered on its promise, there was no more glorious feeling in the world—you hadn't been a fool after all to believe that things might work out in your favor.

Cora was reminded of this every time she was with her friends. Friends! It remained a stunning development, these new connections built from scratch and against all odds. (The odds being Cora's personality, pessimism, and historical patterns.)

By the time Cora's dad arrived for parents weekend that October, Cora was positively bursting to show them off. Where there was once empty space, presto, behold Kim and Neisha, her very own Khadijah and Maxine, just like on *Living Single*. At the "Welcome, Hamlin Families" picnic, Cora gestured theatrically, a magician presenting an extraordinary trick. "Dad, here they are!"

"Well, well, now, I've heard so much about you two." Her father was as blatantly thrilled for her as she'd hoped he'd be.

Wes put a heavy hand on Neisha's shoulder. "You must be Neisha. I was told your hair was purple, though, young lady."

Neisha stretched a tight coil into her field of vision as if she'd forgotten what color she'd dyed her ends. "Oh, yeah, this is new."

"And how do your parents feel about green hair?"

"They hate it. It's like I'm torturing them. Watch, when my dad gets here, he's gonna whip out the bottle of Tums always rattling around his pocket and complain about the ulcers I give him. 'This one here will be the death of me.'"

Neisha imitated her father's low voice and heavy Ghanaian accent with dead-on—and hilarious—accuracy. She always joked that her dad never met a proverb he didn't like, and he trotted them out with great solemnity. When he'd seen her hair the night before, he'd muttered something about how the ax forgets but the tree remembers, even though no one knew what that had to do with hair color.

To be fair, the dyed 'fro *was* a shock. Cora might have even dropped her jaw when Neisha arrived at their first study group, thirty minutes late, greeting everyone with a "What's popping, y'all?" then proceeding to whip out a bag of Chips Ahoy that clearly was not for sharing. Though Neisha was largely silent during their study session except for a thoughtful question or two and the chomping, everything about her was somehow loud—her bright clothes, her toothy grin, and an energy that radiated off her so strongly that Cora could have sworn she heard the buzzing of a live wire.

Cora hadn't known quite what to make of Neisha's hair, which then was the exact color of Barney, or the way she devoured an entire sleeve of cookies in minutes, or the look she gave Cora when they were packing up their books to leave. The unfamiliar-familiar nod, like they were already in some sisterhood Cora was oblivious to. The way Neisha rolled her eyes conspiratorially and whispered, "Why don't white boys have lips?," nodding at Jeff, slinging his JanSport over his shoulder. The way she broke out laughing as Cora was thoughtfully ruminating on the lip size of every white guy she knew and said, "I think we need some Chick-fil-A, homegirl, what about you?" It didn't even occur to Cora to say no and run back to hole up in her dorm room as planned; she found herself falling into step beside Neisha and walking to the restaurant right off campus as if it were already the weekly ritual it soon became.

Once they were settled in a booth with sticky vinyl seats, Cora proceeded to ask a lot of questions, a technique she'd picked up reading a paperback of *How to Win Friends and Influence People* she'd found in her favorite study carrel tucked deep in the dusty stacks of the hushed library. Smiling a lot was another of Dale Carnegie's techniques and an area where Cora had room for improvement, seeing as how she was prone to displaying "resting-bitch face" well before the expression got that name.

When Kim slipped into the Chick-fil-A booth a short time later, Cora had to work hard not to gape at her. Kim was the type of pretty that was almost painful to look at but you couldn't turn away. Neisha had told Cora all about Kim, how she was "real saditty but she pulls it off," how they met at the summer orientation for Black students that Cora chickened out of attending at the last second, how they'd decided to be roommates from there. Cora wished Neisha had warned her about Kim's beauty, though. It was so intimidating Cora might have run from the table if Kim hadn't also been so nice, immediately hugging her, and squealing, "Oh, a new friend!," as she scooted in next to her.

It was a relief (but also somewhat perplexing) that it ended up being so easy to make friends, but it was. All you had to do was open up and listen and laugh, which, when you thought about it was fairly straightforward and perhaps didn't necessarily require all the strategizing, analysis, and deliberation Cora had devoted to the prospect. When Kim stared down a French fry and revealed that her mother had been weighing her and feeding her SlimFast since she was six, and Neisha opened up about starting school in America in fifth grade and tripping a girl who'd asked if she had a monkey back in Africa, it dawned on Cora what was happening. Friendships were being born right there across a beige Formica table, and all she had to do was let it unfold. For some people it was a song or a smell, but for Cora, it was chicken nuggets and honey mustard that flooded her with nostalgia for the afternoon she'd met her day ones (even if she wouldn't hear that term for a decade or so).

Now, at the picnic, Kim extended her hand toward Wes with the perfect poise, impeccable manners, and lyrical southern lilt of the Memphis debutante she was to introduce herself. "And I'm Kimberly. It's so nice to meet you, Mr. Belle."

"Oh, no, don't you 'Mr. Belle' me, I get enough of that at school. You girls can call me Wes."

"Oh . . . okay, W-Wes," Kim managed to choke out with all the ease of someone who'd never once called an adult by their first name.

Kim even referred to her own father as "sir," a formality that put Cora on edge. And the dynamic was not much warmer between Kim and her mother. Kim had told Cora that she pictured her mom judging her behavior at all times—like God, but with way more of a personal investment and much higher standards. Cora thought Kim was exaggerating until she'd seen it for herself that morning when she joined Kim for coffee with Jacqueline and Malcolm Freeman. Jacqueline (whom Cora properly addressed as "Mrs. Freeman," of course, and always with a straight back) seemed to be constantly scrutinizing Kim—the way she sat, the way she sipped her coffee, even what she put *in* her coffee. "Do you really need all that creamer, Kimberly?" It made Cora self-conscious about what she ordered, so much so that she passed on the croissant she'd been eyeing.

Cora usually treated mothers like subjects in an anthropological study, keenly observing their customs and ways like a fascinated researcher. But that morning over their steaming mugs and against the backdrop of Mr. Freeman's impossible-to-follow rant about interest rates, Cora was careful to avert her eyes from Kim's mom, from her meticulously applied magenta lipstick and fearsome cheekbones, the severe beauty she wielded like a weapon. That this extremely imposing woman was somebody's mother, someone who took temperatures and made peanut butter sandwiches and drove carpool, was hard for Cora to wrap her mind around. Then again, to hear Kim tell it, Jacqueline never actually did any of those things.

Nonetheless, the very fact of Kim having a mom at all, not to mention such an elegant one, was enough to rouse the jealousy that Cora was all too familiar with and didn't bother to pretend she was above. She'd learned to live with those ugly flare-ups the same way she'd learned to live without a mother, because she had no choice. The sharp edges of Cora's envy were softened—a little—when she saw how miserable Jacqueline made Kim. Still, every time Kim complained about her, Cora rebelled inside. *At least you get to have a mother.* Then, before she could stop it, she'd be sucked deep into an excruciating mental maze with no exit or solution: Was it better to have a terrible mother or no mother at all?

At the picnic, an exuberant guffaw from Neisha snapped Cora back from this treacherous terrain. She leaned into her dad as the warm breeze sent loose leaves falling to the soft grass around them and let his physical presence be the usual reliable safeguard against those dangerous feelings. *You have this father. That's enough.*

"Those are legit leather elbow patches, huh, Wes?" Neisha had no trouble being on a first-name basis with, and ribbing, Cora's father. "Cora said you'd be wearing a tweed blazer even though it's seventy-two degrees."

"You've got a point there. Let me take this off." Wes made a show of removing his jacket to reveal the T-shirt that had replaced his usual short-sleeved button-down.

"Dad, is that . . . Tupac?" They all stared in surprise. Or maybe confusion. Or both.

"You like it? I figured I needed to step up my game and be the cool dad."

"I see you, Mr. Wes!" Neisha said, patting him on the back. "That shirt's da bomb."

Cora was ninety percent sure her dad couldn't name one Tupac song or even say if the rapper was alive or dead, given that Wes listened only to music made before 1965, on principle, and preferably in Detroit. But she was touched by the effort he was putting forth.

Cora had not seen this coming, that one of the best parts of having friends was that her dad would enjoy it as much as she did. All those years, they'd *both* missed out on the privilege of sleepovers where he'd make stacks of pancakes in the morning and tell corny jokes; of Wes carting giggling girls in the back seat to Summer Jam concerts, waiting for them in the car reading his favorite Walter Mosley novels; of Wes saying, "You girls," like a comically exasperated sitcom dad when they spilled glitter all over his good towels. But better late than never.

"And speaking of new looks, Neisha," Wes said as he ran a hand down Cora's hair, "I hear you're the one who encouraged my daughter here to . . . how did you refer to it, Cora? *Update* her hair. I hardly recognize my own child."

There was more emotion in his voice than a new hairstyle called for. And *update* wasn't precisely how Neisha had put it; what she'd said was "Cora, you need to get rid of those braids that have you looking like a knockoff Moesha." With that motivation, Cora had found an inspirational picture of Regina Hall in *The Best Man* and tracked down the one Black hairdresser in twenty miles, a woman who washed hair in her kitchen sink and set up a clunky hair dryer on her screened-in porch.

"But it looks really nice on you. You look five years older, Cora, a real grown woman."

Cora could have sworn her father's eyes were misty when he looked her up and down as if she herself was a magic trick.

Before Wes could also ask about her new clothes—oversize Guess jeans Neisha insisted on to replace Cora's array of corduroys (corduroys!)—they were interrupted by two people bickering loudly enough for the sound to carry all the way across the lawn in front of the redbrick Student Affairs building.

"Oh Lordy, here come my parents—late and loud. I gotta go. Jesus help me." Neisha shook her head as she watched the spectacle of the Appiahs trying to lift an unwieldy cooler onto a picnic table already filled with food her mom had made and packed in all sizes of Tupperware since they didn't trust white people's cooking. Kim's parents also had concerns about eating at the picnic, but that was because they were too bougie for hot dogs. They'd made a reservation weeks ago at the Red Lantern, the one restaurant in town with white tablecloths and a wine list. Kim didn't have the heart to tell them that the Red Lantern didn't need reservations weeks in advance—or at all.

"I have to go too, Mr. B.—I mean, er, Wes. I just stopped by to say hi since I couldn't *not* meet Cora's dad after hearing so much about you. I wish I had time to hear one of your famous jokes, but if I'm late to meet my parents, I'll never hear the end of it."

Seeing the dread that spread across Kim's face, you'd think she was headed to clean out all the slimy hair that had built up in the dorm's shared showers, not to dinner with her parents. Cora wasn't so naive as to believe that being rich and glamorous made you happy. There were enough miserable kids at her elite private school for that to have sunk in. But the Freemans had an eerie veneer of perfection, like they were cardboard cutouts of an ideal family—all costumes and clenched-jaw smiles and not one ounce of anything that could be taken as warmth. Cora wanted to grab Kim's hand and scream, *Stay here with us*, but the other thing she knew about family was that it was largely unavoidable. The trick was to have one you didn't want to avoid; the challenge was that you had absolutely no control over that.

All Cora could do was pull Kim into her arms and offer some meager reassurance before sending her off. Neisha did the same with Wes, throwing her arms around his shoulders. And then the four of them mashed together for a spontaneous, jumbled group hug, as unlikely and delightful as Cora could have imagined.

Kim and Neisha went on their way, leaving Wes and Cora alone together for the first time in months. An unexpected awkwardness ballooned around father and daughter as it hit Cora that she'd stopped calling him in tears every other night, that she'd flaked on their last two Sunday calls because Neisha had dragged her to the weekly roller-skate party that had become their thing, that she hadn't even asked him about back-to-school night at Prescott last week. Somewhere along the way Cora had been distracted from missing him and now this—her happiness, her fledgling independence, the unfamiliar distance that had grown between them—felt like a betrayal.

"Look at you, Ms. Thing. You've really grown up in just these quick couple months."

Cora could imagine what would come next because it was what usually followed her father's misty-eyed realizations that she was taller or older or had outgrown sippy cups and training wheels. Wes would pull her into a hug, tickle her, and make her promise not to grow up any more than she already had at six, twelve, fourteen.

But that's not what happened. Instead he settled down on one of the red picnic tables set up on the lawn and patted the seat next to him for Cora to sit. "I'm really proud of you, baby girl. I told you you'd be okay."

Cora wasn't one of those people who hated when others were right, particularly her father, who always seemed to be. In this case, she didn't mind an affectionate *I told you so* either.

"Hey, you remember when I dropped you off at nursery school for the first time?"

This was also classic Wes, always packed for a trip down memory lane. His remember-when moods came on as fast and intense as summer storms, nostalgia pouring like rain. But Cora didn't want to go on this particular journey at the moment. She'd sooner forget her single day in nursery school, where she sat frozen and silent for four full hours after her father left her with strangers. When he returned at lunch to check on Cora, she hadn't moved a single muscle except her bladder, which had released warm pee down her white tights.

Cora had been trying very hard to gain distance from her old self and fully invest in her reinvention campaign, and it was working! She didn't welcome the reminder of how she used to be—that shy, pants-peeing little girl who still lurked within. But of course, she indulged her dad in this memory. He asked her for so little.

"How could I forget? I'm glad that little experiment lasted only a day. I was better off coloring under your desk the rest of the year."

"Maybe, maybe not. I always wondered if I should have pushed you harder to go back. That's the thing with parenting—for every decision you make, there's a second one, and a third, a thousand different ones you wonder if you shoulda made instead."

She'd never discussed her upbringing with her father, much less heard him second-guess it. She wondered if this was ushering in a new era where they talked as adults, equals.

"Don't worry, Dad. It all worked out, okay?" Cora presented herself as proof.

"And so it did. Listen, I'm going to need you to do something."

"What?"

Wes reached over and jiggled her thigh. "Stop growing up, okay?"

There was a sensation that was the exact reverse of homesickness, where you ached with the tenderness of connection. When love felt like something you could swallow and hold inside forever. And Cora was overwhelmed with it.

Then something—someone—caught her eye over by the massive grill belching plumes of smoke. She might or might not have let some sort of yelp-like sound escape her, which prompted her dad to do precisely what she did not want him to do—follow her gaze to the man, or boy, with the pleated khakis, fleece vest, and a wayward Afro that was in a constant identity crisis. The front wiry half of his hair that was clearly from his Black dad gave way abruptly, mid-scalp, to smoother strands courtesy of his white mother.

"Friend of yours?"

"Who? Where? It's . . . no one!"

Neither Cora nor her father understood why she was yelling. What she wouldn't have given for a sudden interruption by a marching band or clowns or even some long-winded remarks by the university president. But there was no program for today's picnic beyond hot dogs and family time and therefore no way to divert her dad away from Chris Jones. Cora was convinced that Wes would be able to recognize by way of fatherly radar that the guy casually squirting mustard from a bottle was involved with another extraordinary recent development: Cora losing her virginity.

How she hated that expression. It wasn't something she'd misplaced, like keys. Nor was it something she mourned losing, like if her stuffed Snoopy disappeared. Cora had been *eager* to shed it as quickly and efficiently as possible and before she had to confess her lack of experience to Neisha and Kim.

So when she first saw Chris lugging his bass across campus, she'd sized him up and found him a promising candidate. A fellow Black orchestra geek out in the wild was a rare sighting and gave her just enough comfort to start a conversation. In their first couple of chats, he was too shy to meet her eyes, and seemed somewhat stumped by basic questions, such as, "Where are you from?" It might not have been the case for everyone—or anyone—else, but for Cora, his supreme awkwardness was a draw. She recognized a kindred spirit, for better or worse, and, quite possibly, a fellow virgin. Her suspicions about that were raised when she saw the Goonies poster in his room and when his hands shook as he handed her Ritz crackers, a block of fancy cheese, and an airplane bottle of gin when she came over that fateful evening to "study."

Reading Judy Blume's *Forever* approximately 367 times had given Cora some sense of how these things unfolded but she wasn't aiming for tender romance so much as . . . completion. She approached the mission with the same focus and productive urgency she applied to an academic assignment, which she routinely completed well before their due dates. A procrastinator she was not. So she downed a gulp of gin and kissed him barely minutes after the pretense of cracking their books open. Her wholly unprecedented boldness gave her even more of a rush than the kissing itself, which was much drier than she'd thought possible, considering it involved mouths.

The second Chris shimmied out of his pants, revealing legs that were so ashy they were almost white, he immediately started panting with such intensity, she didn't know if he was excited or hyperventilating. All in all, as awkward, bumbling, and fast as it was (so, so fast, though they came to a halting stop only because they seemed to run out of steam by mutual agreement), Cora had never felt more accomplished.

Chris was waving at her now, leaving Cora with no choice but to raise her hand back to avoid being rude. Whenever they crossed paths, they went out of their way to smile warmly at each other and trade enthusiastic *How have you beens*, which just felt like good etiquette for someone you'd been naked with, even if they'd both agreed (after one more similarly lackluster attempt) that they didn't need to do that again.

"So you *do* know him?" Wes said, taking in their pleasantries and looking at Cora like she was losing it. And she was, at this point, having been hit by an extremely ill-timed flashback of Chris struggling to open the condom wrapper that kept slipping through his sweaty hands. He thrust it at her and asked her to try, as if she had some expertise and it wasn't the first condom she'd ever opened or held in all its slimy glory.

Cora was also thinking about how you never got to have your first time again, and though she had no regrets (apart from saying, "Hmm, that's it?" afterward, then realizing too late Chris would take it personally), part of her wondered if she should have given that more thought in her rush to be done with it.

"He a crush of yours or something? Is that why you're trying to be all slick?" Wes asked, grinning, an eager coconspirator in whatever mysterious romantic intrigues might be at play here.

"What? No!" Cora laughed too loudly.

"Well, do you have one of those?"

"What?"

"A crush? I'm the cool dad, remember? You can tell me."

"Dad!" So much said in one long syllable that rose and fell like a melody.

Wes threw his hands up in surrender and Cora immediately felt bad for ruining his attempts to bond. It was just that she didn't want to think about crushes. Which was to say, she didn't want to think about Lincoln

Ames, whom she'd let occupy way too much space in her mind for someone she'd interacted with once, if you could call thirty seconds of eye contact an interaction at all. Cora had eventually given up looking for Lincoln in every classroom and around every corner of campus or casually dropping by the bookstore and roaming the aisles in search of a ghost. Which is what he might as well have been. Just last week, she finally decided that she must have imagined him, it, everything. So she was hardly going to say his name out loud now. Into the universe. Like a wish.

CORA HAS A NIGHT OUT AND TO REMEMBER

February 2000

"We're going out!"

These were not the words you would expect to usher in a complete change to the course of Cora's story, but life was sneaky like that.

When Neisha announced this on a random Wednesday night deep into February, the longest, shortest month of the year, Cora looked down at her flannel pajamas and then at the clock, confused.

"Nee, it's almost ten o'clock and eighteen degrees outside and I'm busy."

"Busy doing what, exactly?"

The truth was Cora had been mindlessly staring at the collage of photos she'd had printed at Walgreens and tacked to the ribbon-framed bulletin board above her desk in her dorm room—the triple she'd moved into with Neisha and Kim a month before. There was a photo of Cora on New Year's Eve with a *2000* party hat on and a red digital time stamp in the corner of 12:45 a.m. Her deranged smile probably had less to do with the fact that Y2K hadn't destroyed the world and more to do with the Boone's Farm strawberry wine coursing through her system. There was Cora, Neisha, and Kim huddled in a pile like puppies on Neisha's bed under one of the matching plaid Pottery Barn comforters Kim's mom had ordered for them. There was Cora on a road trip, her first ever, to Virginia Beach with Kim and Neisha, during which she'd belted all the lyrics to "It's All About the Benjamins," even Lil' Kim's rap interlude, which she'd memorized after hours of secret, determined practice.

Gazing at the pictures had become a nightly ritual. After that, Cora would look around at the rows of lights they'd strung throughout the room that made the space—and her chest—feel like it was filled with starlight. And then she would go to bed happy.

"I was going to study, then watch *Dateline*." Cora looked over at Kim to back her up, but Kim had already slammed shut the textbook she'd been casually skimming and was plugging in the communal flat iron, the hardest-working appliance in all of Johnston Hall. Kim knew protesting was no use. She also didn't need a reason not to study . . . or go to class. Getting a degree in business admin was largely ceremonial for her, since she'd been groomed to work at her father's real estate company since birth—or since he'd given up on having a boy after two girls. Kim had said more than once that she might as well focus on getting her "Mrs." and Cora could never tell if she was kidding or not. All of which was to say, Kim was always up for a night out.

"*Dateline?*" Neisha looked at Cora like she'd said she was going to organize her underwear drawer, which, to be fair, was also a possibility. "Well, spoiler alert number one, the episode is going to be about some pasty chick wearing way too much makeup who gets strangled in a suburban ranch house, and spoiler alert number two, her man did it. Now we can go? The trinity is going out, and we're all wearing red!" How Neisha loved a theme.

Cora made a half-hearted effort to crawl up to her top bunk but Neisha and Kim grabbed one leg each and pulled her down, tickling her feet as they did, so by the time she hit the floor in a fit of giggles, she'd fully submitted.

They forced her into a sheer red shirt and a black skirt from Kim's closet and demanded that she hold still while Neisha slathered on bronzer, eyeliner, mascara, and, of course, a precise outline of brown lip liner to complete the look. Taking in her reflection, Cora was, as usual, awed at the metamorphosis of her face but also of all the other changes that had made their mark. Sometimes it was hard to catch up with herself. Who was this Cora who sported miniskirts and thongs and a waxed lip?

Although she'd set her mind to transformation, Cora hadn't considered how she would have to keep getting used to each new tweak. It helped that she was no stranger to being a stranger to herself but it still made her sweat. Or maybe that was because their room had become an oven from the scalding-hot flat iron heating the tiny space. The smell of burned hair permeated everything, though they tried to offset it by dousing themselves in CK One before scrambling out the door.

They pretended they weren't shivering in their barely there sheer shirts on the walk downtown along the shoulder of the dark, winding two-lane road circling Hamlin's campus that three girls tottering along in three-inch wedges had no business being on. Should a car come careening around the bend, the headline would be "Young and Reckless," but that's exactly what they were and this was their window to be both of those things and get away with it.

The wind blowing through the flimsy nylon of Cora's shirt made her nipples feel like someone was stabbing them with icicles. She had resigned herself to not being allowed to wear a coat when they went out, but why didn't Neisha let her wear a bra at least?

As frigid as it was outside, as soon as they arrived at Lou's, Cora immediately sweated out her hair as they climbed the narrow stairs to the claustrophobic club above the dry cleaner's Lou also owned. Lou himself was an entire vibe—inch-thick gold chains, velour sweatsuits, bulky Nokia pager clipped to his waist, and not an ounce of self-consciousness about being a fifty-five-year-old man who spent most nights DJing for college kids from a plywood platform plastered with Run-D.M.C. posters. Cora couldn't tell if it was admirable or embarrassing that Lou seemed hard-pressed to let go of his iron grip on the good old days when he himself had gone to Hamlin ("One of the very first Negroes they let through the gates!"), tales of which he was happy to regale you with as he worked a toothpick around his mouth and held tightly to your shoulder. He would also tell you about how he opened the place because there wasn't a spot for "the homies back in my day to kick it together." He wanted different for the next generations of Black students at Hamlin, wanted them to have a sanctuary of bass, body heat, pheromones, and, most important, a safe haven to "get loose with our own peoples."

Lou's noble mission didn't extend to elaborate libations. The establishment offered exactly one single drink option: Juke Juice, a deadly strong concoction composed, as far as Cora could tell, of grain alcohol and red Kool-Aid and dished out from huge plastic tubs. You got a red plastic Solo cup at the door and could refill it as often as you wanted at three dollars a pop. It was a cheap and fast way to get drunk, and that helped you ignore you were in a place with all the ambience and humidity of a pet store specializing in reptiles.

After a few sips of warm punch, Cora could stop worrying that there were more people in the room than the fire code surely allowed and gave herself fully over to the pounding of the music. Her contribution to the exuberant energy was swaying her hips, albeit almost imperceptibly.

She thrusted them left and right a little more effusively when "Say My Name" came on because her hips were powerless against Destiny's Child. She even threw her head back and closed her eyes in a moment of rare abandon. When she opened them, her dance moves, subtle as they were, ground to a sudden halt. There he was again. There *it* was again, the smile. So she could be sure, Cora blinked, rubbed her eyes, looked away and back again. And still Lincoln Ames was right there, real as ever, with only a few feet of sticky parquet floor and a half a dozen sweaty bodies between them.

The room had been loud with pulsing music and people screaming over it, but all the background noise abruptly faded; it called to mind for Cora lying on her back when she went swimming with her dad as a kid and the water blocking out all the sound except for her own breathing, which she normally couldn't hear or didn't bother to listen to but that roared in her ears when she was half submerged. And now.

She brought her Solo cup to her chest in a way that she hoped could pass for alluring even if the real purpose of the gesture was to keep her heart from flying out of her body as Lincoln made his way toward her. There was a good chance her knees would give out before he closed the distance. He never stopped looking at her just as intently as he had in the bookstore that day. This time, though, Cora returned his gaze, not once breaking eye contact, or the spell.

In the span of time it took for Lincoln to get so close she could smell him (sweet and soapy), Cora went from shock to an utterly inexplicable sense of inevitability. Her whole body screamed, *Finally*. It wasn't the nerves or the rum making her jittery; it was imagining how close she'd come to not going out tonight. She had planned to be home at this very moment watching *Dateline* in her pajamas! It was staggering—terrifying, actually—to consider all the ways your entire life could shift course or spin out in an entirely different direction based on one tiny decision; how many possibilities (infinite!) there were if you decided to turn right instead of left, go to UVA over Hamlin, stay home and watch TV versus put on a sheer top and go to a bar.

It was enough to make you believe in destiny, or it would be if you weren't Cora and skeptical of anything you couldn't see, touch, or prove. There wasn't much time to interrogate the nature of faith, however, because there was Lincoln speaking to her.

"What's good, Cora Belle?"

He knew her name?

"Yeah, I know your name, girl. Cora Belle, from Fairfax, Virginia."

She hadn't realized she'd expressed her surprise out loud. "Okay, yeah, cool. I know yours too. Lincoln."

She announced it like she was giving the right answer on a pop quiz, then wondered how many times from this point forward she would say something to Lincoln that she immediately wanted to take back.

He leaned in to hug her like it was the most natural thing in the world. She wondered if hugs were something you could mess up by lingering too long. But she concluded she'd done an acceptable job and stayed nestled in his embrace, waiting to see what would happen next. Or maybe they would just stay this way until the end of time, which was fine by her. Lincoln pulled back enough to leave a few inches between her cheek and his chest, and she instantly missed the musky warmth of his T-shirt. A consolation was having him reach out his impossibly long fingers, circle her wrist, and tug her to follow him. "Come on, let's dance." It was a command, not a question, and that only added to its appeal.

Cora trailed him, pushing onto the crowded dance floor, where Lincoln proceeded to turn her around, press himself to her backside, and slow-grind his hips to the silky rhythms of "All My Life." He sang along with K-Ci and JoJo in her ear—"'I prayed for someone like you'"—and Cora pretended this song and these lyrics were directly meant for her, even though Lou played it every single night as an ode to the ex-fiancée he pined over. It was supposed to have been their wedding song, and the fact that Cora knew this and could see Lou's eyes misting up from across the dance floor suggested Lou had a real issue with boundaries. And closure.

Pressing her eyes shut against any other distraction, Cora fully melted into Lincoln, not because she was trying to be pliable or seductive but because all her bones and muscles had turned to liquid and she was no longer able to stand on her own. The condition worsened when Lincoln spun her around and leaned his face so close to hers that she was glad she'd brushed her teeth—twice—before coming out instead of counting on the crumbled Cool Mint Certs Neisha always had at the bottom of her purse.

"You know, I saw you at the bookstore way back when looking all sad, like you just dropped your ice cream cone."

"Yep, that was me. I was pretty pathetic that day." There was enough emotional distance between that despairing girl and the one standing here in glittering eye shadow that she could laugh at herself. "You smiled at me and, I don't know, I felt better."

"You did?" Lincoln seemed taken aback that he could have that effect. "Why didn't you come holla at me then?"

"I don't know. I was going to, but then you were busy working . . . "

"I would have stopped to take a break. For you."

The wink he added helped, but Cora was still impressed that she was able to recognize this as flirting, even though, as far she knew, she'd never actually experienced it.

"I—I thought maybe I'd see you again." She stopped herself from saying she'd later decided he was a figment of her imagination.

"I guess I can be a little hard to find. I live off campus, out on Park Drive with two other sophomore guys. I have another job too, loading trucks at the UPS depot out on Route 11, so I'm there a lot. And I never come here. Lou's isn't really my scene but it's my boy Andre's birthday so I had to make an appearance. Glad I did. You're hard to find yourself."

So shocked was she by that statement, Cora barely had enough air to choke out a response. "You looked for me?"

"For sure. I've had my eye out—the girl with the red headband. No more braids, though." Lincoln paused to run a hand down her hair.

She'd forgotten all about her red headband so it was all the more astounding he remembered she was wearing it that day.

He continued to stroke her hair, causing a sound to spill from her that was suspiciously close to a purr but was, thankfully, hidden by the music. "I didn't know this is where you've been hiding. Of all places," he said in his own version of a low purr.

"I wasn't hiding. I wanted you to find me." It was Cora's turn to attempt to flirt, even trying out a coy little smile, but she was also just stating the plain truth.

"Well, good, then. Because I did."

It was beyond *good*. But Cora was too stupefied to reach for a more accurate adjective, if one even existed. She laid her head back against Lincoln's chest and let herself go, following the motion of his hips, their bodies swaying with the motion of a boat rocking on a gentle sea. This lasted for two more blissful songs before Lou ruined it with the blast of an air horn and a jarring and unwelcome switch to "Back That Azz Up." The influx of bodies streaming to the dance floor to do what the song called for undermined the romantic mood, as did the massive sweat stains under Lou's arms as he raised his hands like he just didn't care.

Cora was suddenly aware that Neisha was eyeing them from across the way with equal parts suspicion and pride. She mouthed something Cora couldn't make out but assumed was a version of *Well, looky, looky here*. Her arched eyebrow said it all.

"That's one of your girls, right?" Lincoln asked.

Cora had never heard it put like that. Yes, Neisha was one of *hers*.

"She gonna let you get out of here with me?"

It was a roundabout way to the invitation Cora had been secretly hoping—and fearing—was coming.

"I'm grown and can do what I want." Sometimes you had to say the words out loud to make them true. Or to realize it.

"All righty, then, let's bounce."

All Cora had to do was nod and take his hand.

CORA IS UNPREPARED BUT SO READY

February 2000

Cora's urge to turn and watch Lincoln sleep was so strong, her neck ached from the restraint. What if he woke up to find her staring at him? Instead, she turned to the thin line of weak sun sneaking around and through the crooked window blinds and decided to use this time to sort herself out before he woke up and she had to face him in the light of day, naked and with morning breath. This would also give her a chance to recap the twelve hours since they'd left Lou's in her head, sifting through and cementing all the details that were so overwhelming, it made the entire night feel like a dream and a memory at once.

In the replay unfolding in her mind, Cora took the liberty of editing out all the awkward parts, like when she tried to kick off her underwear with a sexy little flick of the heel but tripped over her own feet. Or when she went to climb on top of Lincoln during sex (Neisha had told her about "cowgirl") but got so nervous she didn't know whether she should face forward or backward (she cursed Neisha for not being more specific) and so stopped to ask him. He shrugged gamely and said, "Let's try both." But she didn't know in what order. She opted to start with "backward" since it had the bonus of ensuring that she didn't have to be concerned about what at least one body part—her face—was doing in that position.

It must have been painfully obvious to Lincoln that it was only the third time she'd ever had sex, even though Cora had made every effort to hide her inexperience. It helped that she could respond to and act on her own pleasure to guide her, whereas during her first two times, it was all stilted movements and clumsy mechanics with all the sensuality of a game of Twister. But with Chris, Cora hadn't been preoccupied with what he thought about her; her single-minded goal (*Lose virginity now!*) distracted her from her perpetual self-consciousness. With Lincoln, it was another story. She was currently well on her way down a bottomless spiral wondering about the quality of her performance. As with all things, Cora wanted a score, a grade, so she'd know where to improve. She thrived on feedback. *More thrust, less tongue.* But she couldn't exactly request an evaluation. She would take his moaning and writhing—the memory of which made her wobbly inside—as a sign of a job well done.

Another memory, another shuddering jolt—when Lincoln whispered, "You're so beautiful and you don't even know it," as he traced his hand across her bare shoulders. She didn't know that bones could burn, but where he touched her clavicle, a fiery heat spread wide and deep.

Lincoln was right; she didn't know she was beautiful. Cora had had reason to doubt that, starting in fifth grade when Devin Bryant called her ugly in such a matter-of-fact tone it stung more than the insult itself. Cora told herself it didn't matter—sticks and stones and all—but the comment stayed with her like a fingerprint pressed into soft clay that hardened around the hurt. From that point on, Cora was happy to stay under the radar of the white boys at Prescott, who rarely gave her a second look anyway. She never knew if their disregard was because they didn't find her attractive or because her being a Black girl made her looks irrelevant. Maybe they didn't find her attractive *because* she was Black. In any case, she spared herself from even trying to vie for their attention the way the other girls did.

Which was how she'd never bothered to fantasize about what it would be like to have someone look at her the way Lincoln had last night. It would have been like trying to comprehend black holes. It was thus an incredible, disconcerting shock to experience someone's desire. To experience *Lincoln's* desire, specifically. It was a high more powerful than all the drugs she was too afraid to try and undoubtedly just as addictive.

Cora was vaguely ashamed of how good it all felt. As a feminist, or at least a budding one (which Cora considered herself to be thanks to reading a lot of Audre Lorde), she worried it was problematic how much it meant to her that Lincoln (who could get any girl, surely) was choosing her. And the way she wanted Lincoln to want her—with an edge of desperation—could be a sign of weakness. She was supposed to be above such things.

Also, further complicating matters, Cora's head was overflowing with countless strategies and commands for how to get and keep a man that she and every other woman who breathed air had been bombarded with since birth: *Laugh at his jokes, don't be too eager, show interest in his interests, be easy to be with, smell good, show skin*, but also *Just be you!* As much as Cora loved rules, now that she had the opportunity to apply them in a real-world setting with an actual (naked) man six inches away, it was an overwhelming prospect.

Another rule, Cora recalled with a sinking feeling now, was *Don't sleep with him too soon.* That time frame was rather vague, but she was pretty sure six hours after they'd spoken their first words to each other qualified.

Whether it was feminist reasoning or fatalist (or both), Cora refused to accept that *when* they slept together would change the entire course of their fate. And anyway, Cora could no more have stopped herself from having sex with Lincoln than she could have reversed the direction of rain. She embraced this powerlessness, as it was an excuse to give in to herself and chalk it up to the pheromones. One look from Lincoln had sent her inhibitions crumbling. The wall could not be rebuilt.

In Cora's defense—the ironclad one she was mentally assembling—it wasn't like they'd just come home and done it. They'd cuddled up on the saggy sofa under a flashing neon sign reading THE POUND, the nickname Lincoln and his roommates had given to the shabby brick ranch they rented from a former professor who'd retired to Nags Head. They had the living room to themselves while Dre and Julian were still at Lou's, and they'd talked and talked. Or, rather, Lincoln talked and Cora listened, which was an ideal scenario. He clearly liked to hold court and his slow southern drawl made her lean in close like every deliberate syllable was a string pulling her toward him centimeter by centimeter. Or maybe that was just Cora's excuse.

She was a rapt audience as he bounced between any number of topics.

His hometown: "A little dot of a place in Mississippi you'd never heard of and would never wanna go."

His major: poli-sci.

His thoughts on Clarence Thomas: "Total sell-out. Black Republicans are like chickens voting for KFC."

His food crush: "I could eat only Red Lobster cheddar biscuits for the rest of my life and die happy."

His musical tastes: "Okay, don't clown me, but I got a soft spot for girl groups. En Vogue, SWV, TLC, Destiny's Child. Even those skinny Spice Girls. TLC is probably the only one that can go the distance. Gonna be winning Grammys in twenty years, calling that now."

His ultimate life goal: "You're looking at our first Black president. Calling that too."

Cora wasn't sure how seriously to take that part. Coming from anyone else, it might have sounded like a little boy's foolish, grandiose dream, but coming from Lincoln, who radiated an unnerving level of focus, it sounded . . . probable. Believable. After spending all of two hours with him, Cora could easily picture him yelling into a megaphone or standing behind a podium or strutting across stages at political rallies like the ones Wes had dragged her to since she'd been able to hold a JESSE JACKSON FOR PRESIDENT sign, which she'd wielded with such earnest dedication, you'd have thought that the entire 1988 presidential election rode on her tiny shoulders.

Lincoln had just launched into outlining his five-year plan with an intimidating level of detail when the oven timer dinged, announcing the DiGiorno's they'd put in to cook was ready. Cora really could have used a swig of liquid courage from the half-full bottle of vodka sitting on a stack of *Vibe* magazines but Lincoln didn't drink alcohol. He didn't smoke weed either.

"I don't mess with any of that. I'm dark as a coffee bean and from the Deep South; I got enough working against me, I got no room to slip up," he'd explained when she eyed the bottle and hinted she was thirsty, then he offered her a Snapple—delicious but no help with nerves.

They settled in to eat pizza and watch, or pretend to watch, *Fight Club* while scooting closer and closer until first their shoulders, then their thighs were touching. There was an exquisite torture in not knowing what was going to happen and also anticipating the inevitable at the exact same time. Finally, when Cora couldn't take it anymore, Lincoln turned, his face inches from hers, his breath like a blast of summer air coming through a rolled-down car window, and said, "I really want to kiss you."

To which she replied, "I really want that too." It was perhaps the first time Cora Belle had ever said the exact right response, one delivered with no hesitation, second-guessing, or regret.

Now, lying in bed, Cora continued to alternately quiver and cringe as the snapshots of their night played on. Especially one. She'd never had a penis in her mouth before, and she'd managed it for only a squeamish minute or two before deciding blow jobs were out of her depth. And then she'd gotten distracted by the unintended pun and the sudden memory of a sex ed video they'd watched in fifth grade, both of which made her break out in ill-timed giggles. The look on Lincoln's face told her you should never laugh with a man's dick so close to your mouth. She stopped to explain what was funny, doing her best imitation of the solemn narrator of the video *Where Did I Come From?* earnestly describing how the "male's penis gets bigger because it has a lot of work to do." At this, Lincoln started laughing too, but possibly for different reasons. "You're really something else, Cora Belle," he'd said with an amused shake of his head.

Lying on a man's chest was also entirely new territory for Cora, but it felt much more natural. She'd mastered it out of the gate, finding the ideal soft, warm blanket of skin to lightly rest her head and then holding herself frozen in that position without moving a single muscle so as not to disturb Lincoln as he drifted off, the same way she tried to breathe and even blink softly now. Cora had no idea what would happen when he woke up. Small talk? And what about the future beyond this morning? Would they have sex again today, next week? Go to the movies one day and hold hands? Get married? There were so many possibilities for what came next, she couldn't do a proper accounting.

That was enough to make her delirious, but it got worse when she was suddenly consumed by a desire to lean over and lick Lincoln. To run her tongue across his cheek or slowly down the velvety skin of his arm. That she had this weird impulse scandalized her. Was she altered forever? Could your first orgasm from sex change your very constitution? Cora wouldn't have been surprised if she'd looked in the mirror and discovered that her eyes were now another color.

She pressed her hands to her temples and vowed yet again to be as cool as the other side of the pillow, as her dad would say. Just as she had that thought, her stomach growled so loudly, it woke Lincoln up.

He rolled toward her and opened one eye. "Whoa girl, let me get up and make you some breakfast. Tame that beast you got in there." He sleepily pawed at her belly.

"Oh, no, I'm okay. Fine. It's all good."

"You have fun last night?"

"I did." She snuggled under his shoulder to underline this.

"Good, good, me too." It wasn't an actual grade, but Cora would take it. "It . . . wasn't your first time, was it?"

"No!" She tried not to sound offended, which she had no reason to be anyway.

"Okay, don't trip, I just wanted to make sure you were cool either way."

"I am, I am. Don't worry."

They lay there for a minute and she told herself it was fine—comfortable even—and that he wasn't secretly strategizing how to get her out of his bed as fast as possible.

"Man, I don't want to leave this bed but I should go fix you something. Eggs sound good? I could also whip up some French toast."

"Really?"

She felt bad that she was surprised Lincoln could cook. Stereotypes and all.

"What? You don't think I can cook? Don't sleep. I grew up middle of nowhere with nothing. If I didn't cook, I didn't eat. We always had chickens so I know my way around some eggs. Even had my own garden when I was a kid. You'd think I'da found a way to get to the moon, how proud I was when my first little tomato grew in, even though it was about as scrawny as I was."

"I can't cook at all. I mean, maybe some soup. Or cookies—I can definitely follow a recipe. But that's about it."

"Your mom didn't teach you to throw down?"

It was an innocent-enough question; the problem was Cora was so relaxed and off her guard that she'd forgotten to brace herself. She always made sure to do that in encounters with chipper salesclerks, well-meaning moms, and nosy babysitters who all seemed to be preoccupied with the subject of mothers in general and the whereabouts of hers in particular. Kids her own age were just as relentless, like when Sarah from YWCA camp took it upon herself to explain to the other campers that Cora was an orphan and they should all be especially nice to her because "that's so sad" as they organized to play red light, green light.

It wasn't even accurate, Cora wasn't an orphan; she had a dad, but it was as if that didn't count. What upset Cora the most, though, was the pity. There was a lot of that, given there was no more pitiable a creature than a motherless daughter. Who could fault Cora for not wanting to go down that particular rabbit hole at this moment, when she was so flush with hormones and happiness? She didn't want to risk clouding the mood or the moment with something as unfortunate as reality. It would be too much; fortunately, she'd had plenty of practice at deflecting.

"Eh, I'm more of daddy's girl. He's a great cook. Calls himself the Black Wolfgang Puck."

"Oh, yeah? A daddy's girl, huh?"

"You could say that." It was a massive understatement, but Cora had no idea how to convey how close she was to her dad, their sacred bubble of two. It was like doing justice to the relationship between rain and air.

"That's nice. Wasn't really ever close to my pops. Never got to know him that well . . . he's a long-haul truck driver, been out on the road since I was born with maybe a night or two home now and again that he mainly spent sleeping. Way my mom's always dogged him out, it's like he's not worth knowing. But I would have liked to find out for myself."

"You still can. It's not like he's dead . . . oh God, he's not dead, right?"

The laugh that erupted from Lincoln was surprisingly shrill, especially given his slow drawl. It catapulted into Cora's top five favorite sounds. She wished she had a way to secretly record it and listen to it anytime she felt the urge.

"Nah, he's alive. Far as I know, anyway. Doing some routes out west last I heard. Denver? Salt Lake City? Hard to keep track. I don't even bother."

The split-second lull in the conversation made her panic—Cora couldn't bear awkward silences. There was also the possibility that her stomach was gearing up to grumble again, and she rushed to cover it.

"Well, you two still have time. So, uh, where did the name Lincoln come from?" On some level, she knew she was supposed to stop and let him answer, but her nervous jitters took over and there was no stopping her mouth from moving. "I'm named after Cora LaRedd—you probably never heard of her. She was a dancer in New York in the twenties—my dad did his dissertation at Howard on the Cotton Club, and she performed there. I've always wanted to go. My dad would read his research texts to me as my bedtime stories—multitasking, I guess. I can tell you a lot more than you ever wanted to know about any Black person who picked up a trombone or recorded an album between 1921 and 1939, but I might have liked to hear *Charlotte's Web* or something like everyone else, though my dad thinks most classic children's books are all a little bit racist anyway—"

Like having to pee so bad that you can't stop once you give into it, Cora's stream of babbling showed no signs of slowing down. When she paused just long enough to take a quick breath Lincoln raised his finger to her mouth.

"Can I stop you so I can tell you something?"

She nodded. His warm finger against her lips created a current of electricity that made even her gums tingle, along with other soft places.

"I like you, Cora. I'm glad you're here."

His directness was disarming, a powerful floodlight pointing right at her. She squinted in the beam of his affection. Such a clear statement of fact laid out as easily as a picnic blanket. Cora was under the impression that romantic entanglements involved complicated subtext and analysis and confusion and games. She'd spent a full two hours last week with Kim and Neisha dissecting a fifteen-minute interaction Kim had had with a guy she'd hooked up with twice, and they were left with absolutely no conclusion about his feelings or intentions.

Given that, Cora was not prepared for it to be *this* effortless, this *straightfoward*. As she scooted over to tuck herself under Lincoln's heavy arm, she let herself believe that it was a sign that the two of them were meant to be. That it would always be as easy as this.

September 2, 2002

Cora, Cora, Cora . . . please don't get yourself all worked up, okay? Of course I forgive you, no begging needed. I understand why you didn't tell me everything. Don't get me wrong, it was all kinds of shady. :) But I get it. I hated to see you boo-hooing like that at the airport. Your "freak-out," as you called it. Especially since we didn't have time to get into it since that guy blowing his whistle like his life depended on it for you to move the car wasn't gonna let up. Not enough time. Feels like the theme of the summer, doesn't it?

Here's a confession of my own—I already knew about Lincoln. I overheard you talking to him in my studio one day before you noticed I was back from a shoot. I figured it wasn't really my business and you would tell me about him and what was up when you were ready. Didn't count on that being in the departures drop-off at Dulles before I left for four months, but timing is everything, as they say. I was . . . mad's not the right word, but I just needed a minute, you know? And I respect that "it's complicated." Always is. We're all trying to figure stuff out. Including me. You think I have everything worked out, but I don't. I'm just better at hiding it. Which you would call a skill—and some people might say is straight denial.

Look, Cora, for real, the last thing I want is for you to feel any pressure from me. You have enough of that. And you've had a lot going on with everything with your poor dad. That's why I tried to give you space this summer—I didn't want to come on too strong. But I also, well, I just wanted you to know how I felt. So maybe I'm the one that owes you the apology for dropping it on you on the way to the airport. I was never any good at basketball so makes sense I messed up shooting my shot.

I'm sorry for that (and for that lame joke), but not the feelings, just the timing. Whatever the case, you gotta know there was never any possibility

I wasn't going to write you back, so just put that thought out of your head. I'm still down to be pen pals like we planned—like Hemingway and Marlene Dietrich. I can't promise my letters will be as good as yours or have as many words. Also, I won't have fancy stationery like you do; those flowers are mad cute.

Man, it's hard to do Paris justice. I've been lucky to get to go to some cool places, since my parents are see-the-world types, but this city? Next level in a way that's impossible to describe. With words, at least. I've been trying to capture it with my lens, though, and I'll send you some shots if you want. The air, right now, stinks of garbage, actually. Hey, you asked for every detail, even what the air smells like. Sanitation workers are on strike again. Someone seems to be striking or protesting at all times here. I'm not mad about it. Power to the people and all that.

I have an attic apartment, five loooong-ass flights up—it's smaller than my old darkroom and hot as Hades, but it does the job. The sun streams in like the air is made of melted butter and if I angle my head just right out one of the tiny windows, I can see a slice of the Eiffel Tower. The place also smells like actual butter courtesy of the bakery downstairs and I'm not mad about that either. Got me over here dreaming about Mrs. Butterworth's every night. I mean, her curves. Haha.

I'm writing you now, though, from this dope café, Café de Flore. Baldwin used to hang here—it's where he wrote Go Tell It on the Mountain. *Maybe I'm even sitting at the same table as he did. Who knows? I'm telling myself that's the case and the creative juju is still on the table. I need all the inspiration I can get—fellowship starts tomorrow.*

Ya boy who dropped out of college has one of the most prestigious art fellowships in the world. I hate it when I think, How'd that happen? *Because why shouldn't I be here? I've worked my ass off. And I'm good;*

I know I'm good. But it's hard as hell to quiet that voice, the one that says, Who do you think you are?

So, for real Cora, it means something you're proud of me, so thanks for saying that. People don't say it enough. Not even parents, even though maybe on the other side of twenty-five, I shouldn't need them to anymore. And I know they're proud. It's still nice to hear the words. I don't know about me being "wildly successful" one day or what that even looks like, but I'm going to make the most of this, I can tell you that.

You asked me if I had any regrets about this summer. Only one—that you didn't let me photograph you. One day. Okay, actually, I have another one: that I didn't tell you how I felt about you sooner. Would it have made a difference? Maybe that's better left unanswered.

Write back, Cora Rose. And I'll do the same. Promise you that.

x, Aaron

CORA FALLS HARD

April 2000

That Hamlin's campus looked like a college brochure come to life was part of what drew Cora here; she could project all of her college fantasies onto this idyllic backdrop of whitewashed brick buildings with sweeping green carpets of grass, knee-high immaculately trimmed hedges, and wide ponds of flower beds that always seemed to have fresh dark mulch. Aside from the stately charm and the school's reputation ("liberal arts gem"), there was also the critical fact that it was mere hours from her childhood home. Cora had been too scared to even consider going any farther, though occasionally, deep in the night, she'd wondered about that limit she'd placed on herself; she'd contemplate an alternative world where she'd chosen Tulane or Brown, tentatively testing the level of her regret as one might dip a toe in a pool.

But not today. Today, everything—the cheerful birds chirping, the spring buds about to burst—conspired to make Cora feel like she was in just the right place after all. As she bounded into Professor Keane's cramped office, it wasn't the rushing that had her breathless but the sensation that her life was a musical and the memory of Lincoln's husky voice saying, "See you later, Bella," when she'd pulled herself from his arms fifteen minutes ago.

"Looks like someone's in a good mood," Keane greeted her from his perch in a wooden armchair in front of a floor-to-ceiling bookcase overflowing with ancient, dusty hardcovers that made Cora feel like she had to sneeze just looking at it.

Cora collapsed into the matching stiff chair across from his desk, which put her at eye (and nose) level with a half-eaten tuna sandwich on a paper towel. She'd never been to his office when there wasn't a half-eaten tuna sandwich on his desk.

"I guess so, Professor Keane. But I'm also stressed about this project. I don't know if I should come up with some themes for the poem first or start with picking the poet and work backward."

For her Irish poetry class final, they were supposed to write an original piece in the style of a great Irish poet. It wasn't due for a month, but it was important to Cora to get it right because it was her favorite class, the only one that didn't involve bland lectures and tests, but the energizing intellectual discussions she'd always pictured taking place at college (thanks to watching *Good Will Hunting*).

Cora had signed up for the class by accident, not realizing it was a graduate-level course. On the first day of class, so electrified by the discourse, *actual discourse*, Cora forgot all about her shyness and her intention to sit quietly and listen all semester and thrust her hand in the air to make a point about protest poetry and the thematic link of fatalism connecting Claude McKay's "If We Must Die" and Pádraig Pearse. Afterward, in the hallway, Professor Keane told her that he had planned to insist she drop the course but her astute observation changed his mind and he welcomed a "keen brain" like hers. It was a relief, because she'd been ready to beg him to let her stay.

Irish poetry! Who knew it would speak to her like this? Cora felt a little disloyal falling in love with all these pale poets. Her previous favorites were the ones her dad had read to her when she was little—June Jordan, Gwendolyn Brooks, Claude McKay. She rationalized that she was diversifying her reading to include more . . . white men. When she read Yeats, she was awash in the same poignant ache and yearning she felt when she read Langston Hughes. That testament to the power of transcendence spoke to her as much as the verse itself.

"You're overthinking it, Cora. Onerous little habit of yours, eh?" Keane smiled to show he was teasing her. "You're more focused on the process itself, the how of this exercise rather than the why of it. The why of things is almost always more interesting."

"Well, I think I know what I want to write about—"

He put his hand in the air to stop her. "Let me guess: Love?"

Was she that much of a cliché?

He continued on before she could defend herself. "I couldn't help but notice that a lot of the poems you've picked lately have leaned toward the . . . amorous, shall we say?"

Each week they had to memorize a poem for class—a woefully lost art, according to Professor Keane—and he'd randomly call on someone to recite their selection. This past week, Cora had recited Samuel Beckett's "Cascando," one of the most romantic poems she'd encountered. Her best efforts at a strong projection were undermined by the nerves and emotion that caused her voice to quiver as she recited the lines, but poetry was supposed to move you so she decided not to worry about it.

If you do not love me I shall not be loved
if I do not love you I shall not love

The ability to convey so much emotional clarity by arranging a few words filled Cora with awe. And the way Beckett evoked a certain obsessive agitation and fear alongside the passion . . . let's just say, Cora could relate.

It captured how she'd felt the last two months (*months!*) that she and Lincoln had been together (*together!*). Cora couldn't even fathom what had occupied her thoughts before. The weather? Her classes? Cereal choice? It was incomprehensible. Lincoln was on her mind when she opened her eyes in the morning, when she walked to class, when she sat through class, when she made attempts to study, when she showered, when she pretended to be listening to Neisha and Kim, when she waited to fall asleep, and then in her dreams if they came. It wasn't entirely comfortable to feel this out of control; it wasn't entirely pleasant for her days to have this intense, feverish quality. It was also, however, the best feeling in the world.

She wondered if she should be concerned about the amount of space Lincoln now took up in her body, her brain—even in her toes and the roots of her hair. Would she ever get to the point that she cared about anything but Lincoln again? It seemed doubtful.

So yes, she couldn't deny Professor Keane's suspicions. "I guess love *has* been on my mind," Cora conceded with a shy smile.

"So let's begin there. It's where most poetry does, after all. We've talked a lot in class about the way all art draws from the personal. Every poem exposes a piece of oneself and therein lies its power. Consider that as a starting point, perhaps. Is there a meaningful memory or an image that you can call on for inspiration?"

"I have been thinking about this time when I was a kid . . . my father took me clamming in this super-secluded cove he found along the Chesapeake Bay. We had to scramble over all these rocks to get there. There was no one else around. It felt like one of those movies where you're just lost on an island, the last two people on Earth." It occurred to Cora that that right there also represented how she felt about her father and her childhood, but she could handle only one weighty metaphor at a time.

"We stayed for hours digging around in the wet sand. And then, suddenly, the tide came rushing in and the tiny patch we were standing on started to disappear—fast. I think it stands out because it was the first time I remember seeing my dad scared. And the way he was clearly trying to hide it made it even more terrifying. The frothy water was already at my knees when he scooped me up and ran over to the slippery rocks just as the cove filled with water and became totally inaccessible."

Cora's feelings for Lincoln had come on like this tide—hard, fast, and furious. And just like the rush of water that day, it felt as exhilarating as it did perilous. These were the sentiments Cora was trying to wrangle from this memory and symbolism but she could never adequately arrange the words into verse. She reached for metaphors that in her mind sounded, well, poetic but somehow when they made the leap from her brain to the page, they transformed into silly clichés. She was, alas, no Samuel Beckett.

"That sounds like a lot to work with—some strong imagery. You might want to consider Seamus Heaney for the assignment; he uses a lot of naturalism in his work."

"But Professor Keane, every time I try to write something, it sounds like it comes from some melodramatic teenage girl." Horrifyingly, as Cora lamented this, her voice went up two octaves at the end of her statement, just like an overwrought teenage girl's.

"Well, I don't know about the melodramatic part, but you are a young woman, and there's nothing wrong with that."

So why did it feel like everything was wrong with that?

"I just want to do it right."

"Oh, Cora, my dear, poetry is like life. There's no way to do it 'right.' Which is the bad news, I suppose. But the good news is, there's also no way to do it wrong."

It wasn't as clear-cut an answer as Cora would have liked, but nothing ever was.

"Look, Cora, my advice is trust yourself to complete this assignment in stellar fashion. I certainly do. And now, it's a beautiful Friday evening . . . go be young. That won't last, you know. And let me get home to my lovely wife who's trying a new recipe she described to me as 'curry-Cuban fusion.' Heaven help me."

Professor Keane loved to play the part of the long-suffering, put-upon husband, but the loving way and the frequency he talked about Matilda told a different story, as did the poems he wrote for and about her and sometimes shared with his students.

"I'm going out with my boyfriend tonight." Cora put an awkward emphasis on *boyfriend* since she still wasn't used to saying it. At least she resisted adding, *Our first real date!*

It did feel like an occasion, though. Thanks to a Christmas gift card from his boss, Lincoln was taking her out to dinner at a real restaurant, Lucien's, where you got to select and cook your own meat at a big communal grill, and they served a Sweet Skillet, a massive chocolate chip cookie presented in the hot cast-iron pan it had been cooked in with ice cream on top.

This was a notable departure from their usual, eating Subway on the floor in Lincoln's room or hanging out in the living room at the Pound where she tried to ignore his roommates playing *Resident Evil* on PlayStation. Or, on recent warm-enough nights, they would sit in the broken-down plastic lawn chairs on the concrete slab out back that did its best impression of a deck and play rounds of Would You Rather. *Stomped by an elephant or mauled by a tiger? No tongue or no fingers? Transported back to one day of your choosing in the past or a random day in the future?* All the while, in Cora's mind was the most important question of all: *Would you rather be with me here or with anyone, anywhere else ever?*

Sometimes they would borrow Julian's car and drive aimlessly on the narrow roads lined by overgrown bushes and the occasional lonely fruit or vegetable stand that snaked through the valleys around Hamlin. They didn't need the radio, which went in and out, because Lincoln would talk for hours, and Cora, happy to be a captive audience in the passenger seat, laughed or asked questions at just the right point to make it clear how interested and entertained she was.

In rare stretches of quiet, they would look out the windshield without speaking as the landscape blurred by until Cora felt an inexplicable pressure build inside her to blurt out personal details to break the silence. In this way, she told him that she'd lost her mother when she was a baby, skipping through it as quickly as possible and taking care not to leave room for follow-up questions before she moved along.

Mostly, Cora spent these drives plucking random anecdotes from her life and offering them up like you might hold a gem to the light to see if it was the least bit valuable. Many of these memories she was sharing for the first time, since she finally had someone to listen to them. She wasn't just sharing recollections with Lincoln; she was piecing together the Story of Cora. She was, in real time, shaping a narrative of who she was for him but also for herself, editing and revising and reconsidering the heroine's tensions and motivations along the way, which gave her an objective sense of control over her story that she did not feel in her actual life. It was a comforting illusion that she could make her past anything she wanted it to be.

She had a free couple hours before meeting Lincoln, so when Cora left Keane's office, she walked back to her dorm at a leisurely pace, appreciating the fresh air (that much more refreshing after the smell of tuna and dust) and laughing at how every white guy she passed was already wearing shorts even though it was still early April and barely above sixty degrees. It was as sure a sign of the arrival of spring as the baby buds on the cherry trees. Cora loved the change of seasons, especially spring, which, every year, arrived like a reward for enduring something difficult.

The window of their dorm room was visible from the sidewalk and Cora was relieved to see no lights were on. She'd have the place to herself, a rarity, to get ready for her date. The first thing she noticed when she threw open the door and flipped on the lights was her favorite red Moleskine open on her desk. She knew she'd closed it; she always did because she'd be mortified if anyone saw the List. But Cora could see it was open to the page where she'd been keeping a running catalog of her favorite things about Lincoln.

The way he always looks up and to the left when he's concentrating

The random patch of moles scattered across his left shoulder like little pen marks

His knobby knees

When he asks me to read his homework to him

The way he says, "Hey, what's good man" to every single person he meets

He's always nodding his head to a beat only he can hear

How he always brings me sweet snacks

She didn't have time to fully process the violation of her privacy before registering Neisha quietly crying on her bed. Neisha was never quiet. And she never, ever cried.

"Ne-ne! What's going on? Are you okay?" Cora rushed over and dropped to the floor at her feet.

"Yeah, I'm fine." Neisha almost literally brushed off Cora's concern, coming close to knocking her over as she barreled passed and busied herself pulling out a duffel from their overstuffed communal closet. "Just some drama at home."

"What happened?"

"Nothing."

"Neisha. Obviously something happened. You can tell me. Please?"

"Well, if you must know, my dad caught my mom cheating."

"Wait a minute—your mom is cheating on your dad?"

That couldn't be right. Deidre Appiah, with her orthopedic sandals and amber-stained fingers from making vats of groundnut curry stew, didn't seem the type for adultery. From Cora's limited experience, adulterers were specific types—men, for one. Or at least, they weren't the kind of people who spent hours organizing their prized and shockingly extensive Beanie Baby collections.

Neisha stopped snatching underwear from her drawer long enough to glare. "I don't know who else she would be cheating on, Cora." She reined in her agitation with a deep breath. "He caught her a few weeks ago. They were gonna try and work it out. But she called me just now and said he's threatening to kick her out of the house. I mean, what she did is messed up, but he can't put her on the street. She doesn't have enough money to get a place on her paralegal salary."

Cora had watched the Appiahs hold hands at parents weekends. They solved sudoku puzzles together and called Neisha three times a week without fail, always together, talking loudly into phones from two separate rooms while BBC News blared in the background. Cora wasn't an expert on signs of marital trouble, but she would have expected them to be more obvious.

How did Mrs. Appiah meet a person to have an affair with? How long had it been going on? Was Neisha's father going to forgive her mother? Was their thirty-three-year marriage ending? Cora's thoughts spiraled with a panic that was an ironic counterpoint to Neisha's relative calm. The idea of anything you assumed was solid breaking—a vase, a vow—filled Cora with dread.

But she knew better than to ask for more details. She'd gotten just about all she was going to get from Neisha, who was throwing clothes in the bag like she was enraged at her jeans.

"So you're going home?"

"Yeah, in the morning. I can miss some classes, and then it's spring break anyway. I'm just gonna go see what's what. Get them on *Montel Williams* or something, I don't know." The joke was as flat as Neisha's affect.

Shocking as this development was, at least it explained why Neisha had been extra-temperamental these past few weeks. Neisha could be hard to figure out on her best days, and Kim and Cora devoted many hours to dissecting her unpredictable moods in hushed whispers, applying various rationales and theories drawn from Kim's Psych 101 class. They were always promising they'd tell one another everything, but Neisha maintained a force field of mystery. She constantly seemed to be withholding the full story, dismissing any innocent follow-up questions with a breezy "That's my business" or when they pushed too far, a decidedly less breezy conversation-stopping glare. The invisible boundaries Neisha put up were like an electrified fence, designed to deliver a cruel, sharp shock when you unknowingly got too close. Cora sometimes believed that the goal—and reward—of their friendship was to find a way over or around these emotional walls. Or become immune to the stinging zaps.

Ever the hard worker, Cora appreciated this aspect of their relationship, that it required something of her—effort. It was as gratifying to accept someone else's flaws as it was for that person to accept yours. She'd reminded herself of that the previous night when Neisha's cold simmer erupted into downright hostility. Cora had been trying on outfits for tonight's dinner with Lincoln and had counted on Neisha to weigh in whether she asked her to or not. Instead, Neisha complained about the pile of discarded options piled on her bed and huffed that it was "just clothes, Cora." If that had been the end of it, Cora could have swallowed the sting, but out of nowhere, Neisha accused her of being "so whupped you can't see straight. Unless it's Lincoln's ass in front of you. Obsession's not cute, Cora."

After casually slinging this little barb, Neisha had slung her backpack over her shoulder and was out the door before Cora had time to close her dropped jaw. Kim, who had been filing her nails like nobody's business, jumped up to hug Cora. "Ignore her, she's just jealous." Which didn't make one bit of sense; it was like the moon being jealous of a streetlight.

Cora was hurt by Neisha's comment and what it said about her, but even worse, she worried Neisha was right. Obsession *wasn't* cute.

Cora deferred to Neisha and Kim to guide her in just about everything, letting them dress her and choose how she should wear her hair and decide what music she should listen to, because she trusted they knew best. She'd been flailing and turning in circles before Kim and Neisha grabbed her and stopped her from spinning. "This way," they said, pointing her toward herself. She'd happily let them shepherd her through her first relationship. If she was messing this up, she wanted to know; she wanted to head off disaster and correct course. She wanted to make sure she didn't lose Lincoln . . . but she didn't want to lose herself either. And if her friends didn't keep that from happening, who'd be responsible? Cora? No, that didn't seem right. A relationship was too much to take on alone.

Cora had assumed there would be time for a follow-up conversation in which she could clarify what exactly Neisha meant by *obsession*. Where was the line and how would Cora recognize it? But now wasn't the moment—obviously. She went over to where Neisha stood by Cora's desk and forced her into a hug. With one extended finger, she reached behind Neisha's back as discreetly as possible and flicked her notebook closed as she spoke into Neisha's soft curls.

"I'm so sorry, Ne-ne. What can I do?" Cora, feeling woefully inadequate, needed clear directions. Neisha being pissed at a professor who'd told her she should be more articulate, Cora could handle, but when it came to her friend's parents' marriage falling apart, she was out of her depth.

"Get drunk on sake with me and Kim tonight at Yum's. Unless you have plans . . . "

Neisha was well aware Cora had plans; the purple Abercrombie dress she'd settled on had been ironed and laid carefully across Cora's bed.

"Yeah, remember, I was going out with Lincoln? Lucien's."

"Oh, yeah. Well, do what you gotta do." Neisha pulled away and returned her attention to her duffel on the floor. This was clearly a test, one Cora was determined to pass.

"No, no, I'll cancel. It's okay."

"You sure?" Neisha's surprise was so forced, Cora almost changed her mind. Her clear assumption that Cora would cancel on Lincoln burned and that Neisha skated right over her sacrifice without so much an ounce of acknowledgment or appreciation made the flame that much hotter.

But no matter the heat rising to Cora's cheeks, Neisha needed her and was offering an opportunity for Cora to prove her dedication and worth as a friend. That required showing up. And selflessness. And swallowing your irritation. Sometimes all of the above. And you got to bank the goodwill because you were bound to need it in return—that was friendship math.

"Yeah, it's no big deal. Let me go call Lincoln to let him know. I'll be right back. Then I'm all yours."

She was at the door when Neisha called out. "That's number one of the two hundred and thirty-six reasons I love you, Cora."

CORA DOESN'T GET IT

April 2000

Church was a surprise on many levels. First, that Lincoln went every single Sunday; next, that he wanted her to join him. Cora had found a way to beg off just about every week, but today she'd had a change of heart. Maybe it was to compensate for bailing on their Lucien's date a few days before to be there for Neisha or because she was leaving for spring break in forty-eight hours and wanted to spend as much time with him as possible, but that morning, Cora found herself sitting on a hard wooden pew in a floral wrap dress she'd borrowed from Kim and clutching the leather-bound Bible the Appiahs' had sent Neisha to college with. Cora grabbed it at the last minute in case it was a bring-your-own situation.

She hadn't told Lincoln that she'd been to church only twice in her life or that she was, like her father (because of her father), an atheist. Wes told her he'd stopped believing in God when he witnessed a white cop curb stomp a fellow Howard student, shattering the whole left side of his face, during the 1968 riots. "Any god who could allow our folks to be treated like this is no god of mine." Being a history teacher didn't help when it came to the matter of faith either. "Once you've researched and taught all manner of colonialism, genocide, and war, it makes it harder to believe someone or something's out there allowing all this."

Not to mention his and Cora's extreme personal tragedy; that too.

You couldn't argue with his reasoning, so even if Cora had been inclined to believe or curious to go to church, she saw it as a betrayal of her father's beliefs. Her loyalty was to Wes, not Jesus.

But Lincoln hadn't asked Cora about her beliefs. Though he might have sensed her apprehensions, judging by the pep talk he launched into when they pulled into the gravel parking lot of First Baptist.

"Just so you know, I'm not some Holy Roller. It's just . . . church was my quiet place growing up, the place my family was together ever really when I was little. And, I don't know . . . I liked it there. It was a place to escape, where the preacher told cool stories and was chill at least a couple hours. Couldn't help to grow to believe in the power of God. For sure, I wouldn't be anywhere close to where I'm at or who I am without something bigger. So, being here . . . this"—he waved at the pretty white-shingled chapel with a storybook-looking bell tower—"brings me peace and makes it feel like . . . there can always be more for me. Someone's looking out, you know? God's got me. But don't trip, no one's gonna speak in tongues or ask you to hold a snake, so don't look so nervous." Lincoln squeezed her hand as they crossed the gravel parking lot.

"You know they have those here?" He nodded at the Bible in her hand, laughing.

As promised, there were no mysterious languages or slithering creatures, just a small but very boisterous choir and a slew of handheld fans in flapping wrists. There wasn't even a lot of talk of God, at least at first. The pastor, who had the plastic complexion and dull shine of a doll, was more focused on the outcome of the Redskins-Eagles game happening that night than on scripture. It didn't seem right to Cora to pray for a team's victory over all the other problems out there—say, help for Kosovo refugees. But she preferred it to the fire-and-brimstone warnings that came next. Pastor John settled into the meat of the sermon, which was "Staying on the Lord's Path." Cora hadn't expected to hear a long list of reminders of all the ways you could stray from said path on a detour straight to hell, with fornication being at the top of that list. She glanced nervously at Lincoln during this particular section. He appeared unfazed.

When the collection plate came around and Lincoln dropped in three crisp twenties, Cora tried to hide her surprise. The generous sum must be to offset all the fornication, she thought with a smile before an image of white-hot flames licking at her toes chased it away.

After the service, Lincoln suggested they stop at Sweet Briar for hot doughnuts on the way home; it was a little like getting a lollipop after going to the doctor's office.

"I just want you to know how much I appreciate you doing that, joining me this morning. I know it's not your thing."

"Well, I'm never going to turn down a hot glaze, but you know you don't have to thank me. If something's important to you, it's important to me."

They'd settled in side-by-side swiveling stools at the retro counter to wait for their order, and Cora reached out to rub the jagged scar where a box at the UPS depot had flipped off the conveyor and left a four-inch gash in the valley of skin between Lincoln's wrist and elbow. She was becoming an expert at this, finding a reason to touch Lincoln. A hand, an ear, a hurt.

"Do you think prayer really works?" Cora tried and failed to keep the skepticism out of her voice. She couldn't make it make sense, that you could just direct requests to a higher power and they were granted (or not) in some arbitrary manner that defied logic. Though Cora recognized logic wasn't the point, she kept tripping on it and didn't see a way around that stubborn hurdle. Faith eluded her, a sensation she couldn't access.

"Of course," Lincoln said. As if the answer were as obvious as the smell of sugar in the air.

"And all the sinning that everyone does . . . everyone just gets forgiveness?"

"If you ask for it."

"That seems awfully easy."

Lincoln shrugged. "Just the way it works." A thousand years of Christianity boiled down to its essence.

"So just believe, pray, sin, repent. You don't think it's all just . . . too simple?"

"I think that's exactly the point, Cora. Give it time, okay? Faith's a journey. Not something you cram for overnight."

Cora hadn't been aware that her one visit to church was the start of a "journey" in Lincoln's view. It was hard to tell if the slight quaking in her hands was apprehension or the sugar rush from the first bite of the doughnut hitting her.

"Come on," Lincoln said, "we gotta go. If I don't get his car back in time for his shift, Julian's going to be the one raining down hellfire."

Julian did look capable of some biblical-level wrath when they pulled up to the Pound fifteen minutes later where he paced up and down the driveway. "You tryna get me fired, Link? This is the third time this week you've been late with my ride."

Lincoln threw him the keys with a half-hearted "My bad."

Irritated as Julian was, it would be forgotten by the time he drove off.

As Cora followed Lincoln up the wooden steps and through the tattered screen door, she traded her thoughts about religion to equally baffling ones about friendships, specifically guys' friendships.

She'd seen Lincoln and his friends sit side by side and barely say a word to each other for hours. The only time Neisha, Kim, and Cora were quiet for that long was when there was tension, like when Neisha intentionally recorded over a message from Kim's "latest buster" (Neisha's words) that Kim had been saving on their answering machine and listening to obsessively. This was minutes after Neisha had accused Kim of being boy crazy. The chill thawed only after hours of conversation, displays of tears, and a peace offering from Neisha (Kim's favorite Warm Vanilla Sugar Lotion from Bath & Body Works). Cora couldn't fathom conflicts being resolved with a casual, "My bad."

She also couldn't fathom how Lincoln was friends with Julian and Andre in the first place; he seemed to have so little in common with them.

First, Lincoln didn't smoke weed, drink, or bring home a new "shorty" every other week like they did. This earned him the nickname "Choirboy," which mostly seemed affectionate but occasionally was more like a taunt when the guys were goading him to take "just one shot" and "just live a little, nigga."

Also—and Cora was reminded of this as she was forced to stop in the Pound's bathroom, cursing all the Diet Coke she drank at Sweet Briar—Andre and Julian had drastically different hygiene standards than Lincoln. He was a neat freak to the point of wiping down the soles of his shoes, but he'd given up on trying to get them to clean the bathroom to his standards, and grime, black rings, and tiny wiry hairs coating every surface was the result. Between avoiding this bathroom and all the sex she'd been having, Cora had had two UTIs in one month.

Eyeing the one crispy hand towel, Cora remembered asking Lincoln why he was friends with them, even though it was a silly question. She could hardly account for why she was friends with Neisha and Kim—an alchemy of timing, chemistry, and compatibility you couldn't predict, orchestrate, or explain. The beauty of friendship was that it just *was*. But Lincoln had answered her without even thinking about it. "I know these dudes would die for me—they proved that." This was a reference to some incident that had happened early in their freshman year that bonded them, but Lincoln was tight-lipped about it beyond an outspoken animosity against the campus security guards. "They're my boys for life."

His conviction was unwavering, and she'd said, "Samc, same," referring to her and Neisha and Kim, even though Cora wasn't capable of that level of certainty about anything.

Cora wasn't so much running toward Lincoln's bedroom so much as fleeing the filth of the bathroom when she stopped short at the sound of the voice spilling loudly from the speakerphone.

"Ain't that some grade A bullshit? I told those useless mofos that—"

As soon as Cora appeared in the doorway, Lincoln smacked the volume button on the side of the cordless phone, but Cora could still hear his mother's loud exclamations exploding out like sparks, quieter now but no less aggressive. Deb didn't seem to have any other register. She also didn't seem to have any other topics to discuss beyond whoever was doing her wrong, which was usually Lincoln's dad. "Out there on the road while I'm trying to keep up with all these kids and sending me 'bout enough to buy a pot to piss in and not much else." Or she'd complain about Lincoln's three younger brothers outgrowing their clothes as if the boys were getting bigger just to spite her or curse the rotating list of "heifers" who were out to get her. Despite all the eavesdropping she'd done, Cora couldn't figure out why Deb didn't seem to work while Lincoln had multiple minimum-wage jobs on top of going to school. Every call seemed to start or end with Deb asking for money. It pained Cora to listen to Lincoln make yet another promise now.

"Look, Ma, I gotta go, but yeah, I'll send it. Soon as I can."

He slammed the phone on the bed hard enough that it bounced onto the floor. Cora sat on the edge of the mattress next to his slumped body and started rubbing his back in slow circles for lack of any other helpful consolations. "Is there anything I can do?"

She was desperate to fix this, the same way she'd been last week when Deb called after eleven p.m. demanding money for the light bill, and Lincoln had borrowed Julian's car so they could go to the Western Union where Cora watched him turn over all the cash he had in his scuffed wallet, save a ten-dollar bill. On the way home, they'd stopped at the twenty-four-hour ShopRite and she'd followed Lincoln through the aisles as he did mental calculations for what his last ten bucks could get him, grabbing some items off the shelf and returning them for others like he was a contestant in some cruel supermarket game show. He'd ended up with a loaf of bread, a box of knock-off Cheerios, and some ramen. Cora had almost whipped out her emergency credit card to pay for his mother's light bill or the groceries or anything that would help lighten the stress Lincoln carried. She used it fairly freely, and her dad never objected to the bills; money showed up in her student account like magic. The only reason she hadn't offered to use the card was that Lincoln didn't know about it, and she feared what it said about her.

"Nah, it's the same mess, different day. She's saying she's out of money for the bus. You know my little bro is deaf, well, he goes to a special school, and we have to pay for a bus to take him the one hour each way. She hasn't paid, so he's been missing school. I gotta come up with the money—he can't just sit at home and play video games."

Cora hated that her first thought was *That sixty dollars you left in the collection plate would have come in handy.* Her second thought wasn't much more helpful: *Why doesn't your dad give them more money?* It was clear that particular subject was off-limits. Cora respected that; she had her own subjects she preferred to avoid when it came to family.

"That's hard. I get it."

A hard-to-classify sound—something between a ragged laugh and a scoff—from Lincoln put her on edge.

"Well, no, Cora, you actually don't. 'Cause you've never been broke. Or had siblings that you had to take care of."

The statement—delivered as a matter of fact—was an insult and an accusation and an indictment all at once. Cora was shamed speechless.

"You understand my family's poor, right?" Lincoln said. "Not just I'm-here-on-a-full-scholarship poor but like ketchup-sandwiches poor." He spoke more slowly than usual, as if he were speaking a foreign language that he wanted to make sure she was comprehending but also like he was conveying a truth as simple and immutable as a state capital or the time. "And so, no, you don't get it, you can't get it because you've never struggled. And that's not your fault, but you can't pretend to get it. At all. Okay?"

There was no point in responding; there was no defense for her privilege. It was undeniable—she'd never struggled. Neither of them saw a reason for her to confirm this out loud. But in her frantic silence, she confronted an even more horrible truth. Not only had she never struggled, she'd never even known someone who had serious financial hardships. Cora had done volunteer projects at school, had dutifully cleaned out her clothes and toys once a year and taken them to Goodwill, but everyone she interacted with on any sort of regular basis—like all the kids at Prescott—had *more* money and resources than she did. They certainly never worried about having enough *food*. She'd never even thought about money, how much her dad had or didn't, where it came from, where it went, if there would be enough or not. It was mortifying. She loathed what it said about her, even if she had no control over her circumstances, much less any idea how to make up for her luck, her naïveté, her undeserved good fortune. An apology couldn't compensate for it, but it was all she had to offer.

"You don't have to apologize for not being broke, Cora. *I'm* sorry. I'm just frustrated with the situation, not you."

Cora took this as permission to scoot closer to him on the bed and lay her head on his shoulder. Lincoln closed his eyes and clasped his hands, which made Cora wonder if he was praying. Every time she caught him doing it, she was unsure what she was supposed to do. Wait? Join in? Mute the TV? Stop reading? She watched him, his eyes fluttering behind his closed lids. It was a problem, how good he looked when he was upset.

His dimples were more pronounced the more he frowned; his lashes seemed to grow even longer the sadder his eyes were. It was a little unseemly, how drawn she was to him in this state, vulnerable and distant, the twisted ache of longing it gave her. In that moment, Cora doubled down on a single galvanizing quest: she would be the one to save Lincoln from all the hurts he'd experienced or would ever experience. It was that simple.

She'd start small; she began playing with his earlobe the way she knew he liked; rubbing the silky skin was as soothing for her as it was for him. He slumped against her with almost his full weight. His heaviness wasn't a burden, though; it felt like an anchor.

CORA WANTS TO TAKE IT BACK

April 2000

Cora had always been terrible at goodbyes, building the stakes up so high that she became overwrought, a word that also described her mental state on the eve of spring break. She would be separated from Lincoln for all of eight days, but it might as well have been forever in her fevered heart. This explained why she was struggling to tear herself from being spooned against him, reclined between his legs on the saggy sofa.

"You sure you can't stay?" Lincoln murmured, pecking Cora softly on the neck, pulling up her T-shirt ever so slightly, and trailing two fingertips around her belly button and down and across the waistband of her low-slung jeans. For weeks Cora had immediately, reflexively sucked in her stomach every time he did this—until she realized with liberating clarity that it didn't matter. He didn't even notice. Or care about the illusion. Lincoln was barely thinking about anything with the blood rushing from his brain. She could feel him growing harder and harder against her back, which never stopped being a full-on biological wonder.

"I wish." Cora further burrowed herself against Lincoln to underscore this sentiment while grabbing his hand so it didn't meander any lower, past the point of no return. It was going to be hard enough to leave him; it would be impossible if they ended up naked in the next fifteen minutes.

There was a brief period where she'd entertained the fantasy of inviting Lincoln to join her and Wes on their trip. But that was ludicrous on many levels, starting with trying to picture the three of them sauntering through a hotel lobby together. She couldn't even let her mind venture toward sleeping arrangements. Even if she could brave those mental gymnastics, it didn't matter—Lincoln had already signed on to spend the break doing inventory and stock clearance at the bookstore for extra money. She hated that he would be laboring in a dank basement while she was lounging poolside at a five-star resort in Sea Island.

Wes didn't play around with their annual vacation, splurging every year for a week at a resort so swanky and decadent that the other guests raised their eyebrows when they saw there was a kid there—a little brown girl at that—until they realized that Cora behaved like the grown-ups around her, reading her Mildred Taylor novels by the pool and quietly sipping (virgin) daiquiris. When Cora told Lincoln about this tradition, he'd said, "That sounds real nice, Cora," in a way that made her realize Lincoln might never have been on a vacation.

And that was before their recent conversation that had left her feeling like some sort of naive spoiled princess (with the pink canopy bed in her childhood bedroom to prove it). Now she had all the more reason to keep Lincoln from seeing her through the lens of marble lobbies and oceanfront terraces.

But the biggest reason she didn't—couldn't—invite Lincoln was that her father didn't know he existed. Cora had yet to work out why she hadn't mentioned a word about him to Wes or when she would.

"I can almost feel you thinking." Lincoln tapped softly on Cora's temple. "You always got something going on in there. That must be exhausting."

It was, but it wasn't like jumping jacks—you couldn't just stop when you wanted to. "Just thinking about how much I'm going to miss you."

It was one of the rare times they were completely alone in the living room at the Pound, with the place to themselves. Julian and Dre had left at the crack of dawn to drive to Atlanta for spring break without bothering to clean up any of the empty bottles or the weed ash that dotted the coffee table. It was as if they'd partied until the second they'd hopped into Julian's Honda and left town.

"So why don't you bail on Kim tonight and show me how much?" Lincoln dragged her hand down to his crotch, which was ten degrees hotter than the rest of his body. With each pulse Cora felt through his jeans, her temptation to do just what he asked notched that much higher.

How she regretted volunteering to be a wing woman tonight at a party where Kim was scheming to run into her latest crush, a guy everyone called Rabbit. The nickname might have come from his high-school track days, his two protruding front teeth, or because he'd "run through every girl on campus." The last one was Neisha's theory. If Neisha were there, she might have been able to talk Kim out of going, but Neisha was back in Raleigh dealing with her family drama, and Cora didn't have the heart to try, even though it was likely that Rabbit wouldn't even show and Cora and Kim would just hole up in the corner with warm drinks and worry over Neisha, who'd gone radio silent since she'd left for home.

Cora nuzzled into Lincoln, ignoring the clock—she couldn't cancel on Kim but she could be a little late, and if there wasn't enough time to get naked, there were at least a few precious minutes for Lincoln to stroke her hair. "So, what, I just stay overnight and my dad picks me up here at the crack of dawn?"

"Why not? Then I'll get to meet him."

She sat up and turned to face him. "You want to meet my dad?"

He looked surprised that she was surprised. "Sure. You talk about him all the time. Seems like he'd be cool. Why not? Maybe not at six a.m., I guess, and with you coming straight from my bed, but at some point."

Lincoln wanted to meet her dad. It took some processing. Especially after Cora had confessed her fantasy of inviting Lincoln on vacation to Neisha, who had screamed, "Are you crazy? It's way too soon for all that! You're going to send that dude running."

"I mean, you want me to meet your dad, right? So he can see how lucky you are."

Lincoln's fingers crawled down to the soft flesh in the middle of her side, the pressure point he knew would send her into a fit of giggles. Through her twisting and squirming, she assured him she did want that to happen. Thrilling as the prospect was, however, it also left her mildly panicked, which, fortunately, she could hide behind her laughter.

"I gotta pee. Be right back." She got up, then leaned over to kiss him because even just leaving to go down the hall was a sad sort of goodbye.

Cora's destination was not the filthy bathroom, however, which, per usual, she intended to avoid at all costs. It was Lincoln's room, where she planned to leave a note tucked in his running shoes, a hiding spot she'd already scoped out, for him to find while she was gone.

Lincoln's neat-freak tendencies were on full display in his bedroom. There wasn't a single wrinkle to be found on the bedspread, pulled taut and tucked into tight corners; his sneakers were lined up in a straight row under the window; textbooks were neatly arranged on crates under a row of posters tacked to the wall—the space was as spotless as usual. Lincoln had snapped at Cora once, early on, after she'd left a trail of granola-bar crumbs across his desk; later he explained he was just particular about his personal space because creating order around himself, even if it was just a few square feet he could control, gave him a way to fight against the chaos he'd experienced growing up.

As Cora looked around, she regretted her uncharacteristic lack of preparation. She should have come armed with the note already written or at least with a pen and paper hidden in her jeans. She didn't dare rip a page out of one of his carefully stacked spiral notebooks, labeled by class, so she rooted around in the trash can and found a Subway receipt that would have to do. She grabbed a pen on the table by his bed and started scribbling.

I haven't even left yet and I miss you already. And by the time you find this note, I will be missing you even MORE. But we'll already be that much closer to being back together! It's only a week, but it will feel soooo long being apart. I love you.

She stepped back and stared at the note in disbelief. *I love you.* It was right there in her neat handwriting. It was almost as if someone—something, an inexplicable force—had taken hold of her hand. It was too much, too soon. To be in love at all, but worse, to admit it.

Looking at those words made her feel like her skin was on inside out. She wasn't even sure when this had happened. There wasn't a specific moment she could point to; she'd slipped into this state as easily and quietly as falling asleep.

She could hardly cross out what she'd written now; it would cause even more curiosity about what was beneath the dark scribbles. So she dived back into the trash can and frantically rooted around for another piece of paper to start over. Just as she heard Lincoln's footsteps coming down the hall, she opened a crumpled letter she found in the bin.

> Dear Lincoln Ames:
>
> We're pleased to welcome you to the Congressional Progressive Caucus summer 2000 internship program . . .

When Lincoln appeared at the door, she'd forgotten all about her note; she was far more concerned with why this paper was in the trash and why Lincoln had kept this news from her. "Lincoln! Why didn't you tell me you got the internship?"

Only forty of the most promising college sophomores and juniors from across the nation were accepted into the highly competitive program. He'd mentioned that he'd applied with such calculated nonchalance that it was obvious just how much he wanted it.

"What are you doing rooting through my trash?" Lincoln snapped, snatching the letter from her hand.

"I was . . . I wasn't . . . I just needed a piece of paper. But, Lincoln, this is an incredible opportunity and would be great for your law school applications. What's going on?"

"Yeah, it's an honor and all, but it doesn't matter since it doesn't come with housing and I can't afford to live in DC all summer. It's all good. I'll make way better money working at the new Amazon warehouse back home." He crumpled the letter up as if he were returning it to its rightful form and slammed it back into the trash can for good measure.

"Did you tell them no yet?"

"Nah, not yet. I don't have to say until May first. Maybe I was hoping there'd be a miracle between now and then, and He'd come through. You never know."

It took Cora a second to work out that Lincoln meant Jesus, but it was Cora who was determined to save the day. An idea was forming, one solution that would solve two problems—Lincoln not having a place to live in DC, and Cora and Lincoln being eight hundred miles apart for a whole summer, which she'd been dreading.

"That's right, you never know." Cora stepped forward, picked up his arms, and wrapped them around her, a peace offering and a distraction.

He pressed against her, still as hard as ever, which wasn't a surprise. Lincoln was always hard—when he woke up, when he made peanut butter sandwiches, when he went to bed. She wondered if he was even hard at work. He wasn't the least bit self-conscious about it either, like it was some wayward cowlick, a feature that couldn't be tamed and was more than a little adorable for that fact.

"Hey, can I bring this shirt with me?" she asked.

"Which one?"

"The one you're wearing."

"You literally want the shirt off my back?"

She gave him her most endearing smile; she'd had plenty of practice. "Yes, please."

He stepped back, raised his hand behind his neck, pulled it off in one fell swoop, dropping it warm in her hands.

"You know that's my favorite T-shirt, right? My pops gave it to me—brought it back from this jazz place he loves in LA."

That part she hadn't known, but now it made sense why Lincoln was always wearing it. Cora loved it precisely because it was so soft and lived-in that the threads had to work together and hang on tight for it to still be wearable.

"I'll take good care of it." She grabbed his prized bottle of Cool Water cologne from the dresser and sprayed the shirt with it so it smelled even more like him, then she buried her face in it as she'd done dozens of times to his shirts in the past and planned to do dozens of times over the next week when her father wasn't looking.

"Do not spill ketchup on my shirt, Cora Belle." Cora had a bad habit of spilling ketchup, among other things, down shirts. It was why Kim and Neisha barred her from wearing certain items in their closets. And from wearing anything white.

"I'll just wear it to bed."

"And pretend I'm next to you. Or, better yet, inside you." The gruffness and Lincoln's naked lust sent a wave of desire crashing over her, drenching her. He grabbed the back pocket of her jeans and pulled her over so that she was pinned against him and they both faced the mirror on top of his dresser. He thrust his hand down the front of her jeans and let his fingers crawl around until one settled into a slow circle just where and how she liked it. Cora watched herself in the mirror, barely recognizing the stranger who was arching her back and squirming with pleasure, biting her bottom lip and moaning softly.

She often struggled to make the connection that the throbbing between her legs, the way in which she gripped and guided Lincoln's hands, and the sounds that escaped her were happening in and to the same body that she, Cora Belle, inhabited. But there she was in the mirror, one and the same person. The same Cora Belle who'd once furtively sought a book in the library about how to masturbate, read it as quickly as she could in a bathroom stall, then replaced it before the librarian who always loved to ask Cora what she was reading could do just that.

At the moment, every inch of her body was screaming at her to stay, and she was close to actual screams as well—but if she did, she would be even later than she already was to meet Kim, her hair would be a mess, and she'd smell like sex. Reluctantly, she wrenched Lincoln's hand away, shimmying a little as if to shake off the currents shooting down her body, and gave him the quickest of pecks goodbye so as not to risk getting sucked in again or becoming even more distraught over their separation. It was only for eight days. She started counting down as soon as she walked out the door.

The next morning in the car with her dad, Cora could not for the life of her get the vivid image of Lincoln's hand down her jeans out of her head and, worse, the feeling of him pressing hot and hard against her back. The more she tried, the more persistent it was. She rolled down the window. She fidgeted with the seat belt. She manhandled the radio, careening between stations. She let the silence in the car bloom for sixty-some miles of the particular blandness that was I-95. Finally, neither she nor Wes could stand the quiet.

"Okay," Wes said. "What is going on with you, missy? You're like a corn kernel in hot oil. What's got you so out of sorts this morning?"

Neither of them expected the next two developments. First, Cora's sudden proclamation: "I'm in love, Daddy!" And then the flood of tears, like a shower turned on full blast.

She hadn't cried this hard since her first night alone on campus back in August. The release of all these pent-up emotions left her lightheaded with relief. It reminded Cora of when she'd come home from school with so many feelings stuffed so far down that when her dad asked her how her day had been, they exploded out in the form of tears, like air escaping a freshly opened can of soda.

"I don't knoooowww," she would lament when her father asked why she was sobbing.

It had been true then, and it was true now. Sometimes Cora just needed to cry. And, knowing this, Wes took it in stride as she told him about Lincoln. Through the hiccupping sobs, it all came rushing out, all the way back to the first smile. As soon as she finished talking, the waterworks stopped as abruptly as if someone had closed the tap.

Wes was prone to long silences, his pondering pauses, he called them. "People are too quick to talk," he always said. "Sometimes you just need to think. There's a difference between reacting and responding, Cora." His students were used to the prolonged thoughtful lulls. Cora had always found this habit excruciating and never more so than right then. Finally, he spoke.

"My baby girl's in love. Heaven help me."

He performed an animated impression of Redd Foxx clutching his chest on *Sanford and Son* that would have made Neisha proud. It was a well-worn comic antic, but it was all theatrics—in truth, it was almost as if he had been expecting this news. It made Cora think of the day she'd looked down to see a brownish-red streak in her underwear. Even though, at almost twelve, she vaguely knew to expect her period, she was still shocked and had no idea what to do next. She brought her underwear to her father, an act that never failed to mortify her every time she thought of it, but she'd felt like she needed to offer some sort of evidence, to avoid confusion. Wes, unfazed, calmly led her to the linen closet, where there was an unopened box of maxi-pads tucked on a lower shelf behind the hot-water bottle and first aid kit. Her father always seemed to be more prepared for what was going to happen to Cora than she was.

"I have a lot of questions about this young man," Wes said now. "Well, first his name, let's start there."

"Lincoln. Lincoln Ames."

Wes repeated it deliberately, as if he were trying it on for size. "Does he, this Lincoln, have a good head on his shoulders?"

Cora nodded so hard, the tiny hoops in her ears swayed.

"And he makes you happy? I want to hear you say it." Wes took his eyes off the road and stared at Cora long enough that it bordered on dangerous.

"Dad! You're going to drive us off the highway!"

"That's not an answer."

Cora could tell her father about the way Lincoln lit up every time he saw her as if he'd just discovered her; she could tell him how Lincoln always said Cora was the smartest person he knew or how he automatically opened cans of soda and bottles of juice before handing them to her, but it was much more efficient just to say yes.

"Okay, and you know I have to say this, Cora: I hope you're being safe. You have your whole future ahead of you. I don't want anything to derail you, least of all a baby, okay? I'm not having that. For you or for me. Being out here raising a grandbaby at my age? That's not in the cards for either of us. You hear me? I plan to take up golf any minute now and that's going to keep me very busy." Wes had been on the verge of taking up golf for years now.

"I know better than that." All the sacrifices her father had made for her—she wouldn't do that to him, never mind to herself. But having reassured him, she had to steer this conversation to less awkward territory as quickly as possible.

"So, Dad, Lincoln got accepted to a super-prestigious internship in DC, on the Hill, this summer but he can't afford the housing. I was thinking that—"

"If you're about to suggest that this young man I learned about all of two seconds ago move in with us, the answer to that is: Have you lost all your good sense?"

"No, I know better than that, but I was thinking he could he stay in one of the apartments? Is one of the units empty?"

Wes owned two side-by-side multiunit row houses in DC's Shaw neighborhood, where he'd spent a stint as a community organizer after undergrad at Howard. When Cora was a kid, she used to go with him to collect rent money while Wes held forth on the importance of investing and property ownership and "always making your money work for you." The small apartments were nothing fancy—they had modest living-room sets from Sears, popcorn ceilings, and beat-up cabinets Wes and Cora had spent one entire month sanding and painting—but it would work for Lincoln. And he'd be close. Not as close as the guest bedroom downstairs in their house, but mere miles away across the Potomac.

"Come to think of it, yeah, Simon, the kid in two G, is finishing up at GW next month and heading back to Korea. So that timing could work. But Lincoln needs to contribute something. Pay his way somehow."

"Dad! I just told you he can't!" Cora was rarely whiny or rebellious; there was never door slamming or feet stomping. Apparently, she'd had one tantrum in all her life. But, on occasion, she resorted to a shrill pleading, a particular tone she'd only ever used with exactly one person, and reverted to now.

"He can, Cora. He can find a way to pay me something—we can say a hundred dollars a month, and he can cut the grass. God knows, I don't want to be out there in that sun sweating all summer like John Henry. And I'm sure if he's the type of man I want for my daughter, he doesn't want to be a freeloader. It'll be good for him—and his pride—to contribute. Trust me."

That particular command never came with much of a choice.

"More important, we need to talk about what *you're* going to do this summer. You're up here all concerned with this boy's—excuse me, this man's—plans, but what about yours? Tell me that."

"I'm going back to Perry's." For the past three summers, Cora had worked scooping ice cream at Perry's Confectioners in Old Town.

"Cora, it's time to be more serious about your future . . . " And so began a redux of a recent lecture that was already taking on familiar notes from their weekly calls. She was smart, she was focused, she had so much potential—she needed to start zeroing in on what she was going to do with her life. It was time she had a plan, or plans, plural. A, B, and C.

What Cora's father didn't understand was that it took so much wherewithal and effort just for Cora to contend with the present. All those hours she had spent practicing her violin, making study flashcards, and memorizing debate points were intense, but at least there was an immediate gratification. A grade, a performance, an item crossed off the list. You could never cross the future off the list; it was vast and unyielding and went on forever.

It also had no structure or guidelines, no guardrails. And on top of that the guideposts were always moving. Her dad had been proud of her for getting herself hired at Perry's after he'd told her she had to have some sort of job once she was old enough to get a work permit. But now Perry's wasn't enough; she needed internships or fellowships. And then, after that, "real jobs" that required suits? She had to somehow chart a whole career, one that would make her happy and be satisfying and provide her with a "good living," whatever that meant and whatever that salary was.

"Can we just drop it for now, while we're on vacation? I promise to think about it."

"Okay, well, you're saved anyway, because I need to use the little boys' room. I'm going to pull into the rest stop over here."

Cora ignored the sudden pressure on her own bladder, which probably signaled yet another UTI, because finding a pay phone to call Lincoln and tell him she'd answered his prayers was more urgent than getting to a bathroom.

"Meet you back here in ten," she said as soon as they parked, and she dug a handful of quarters from the console.

The phone booth was hot, claustrophobic, and smelled like sweat. The black pockmarked handle was so grimy, she almost couldn't bring herself to touch it. Using the edge of her sweatshirt as a barrier, she held the phone an inch away from her face, which made Lincoln sound even farther away when he answered.

"Yo."

"Hey! It's me, Cora."

"Hey, you. You just caught me. 'Bout to head to work."

"Cool—so guess what?"

"You love me."

She could barely make out the smile in his voice over the rush of white noise filling her ears as she remembered the note she'd forgotten to throw away or flush or burn. At the realization of what she'd done—left her heart out on Lincoln's scuffed plywood desk—Cora had no other option but to squeal loudly and slam the phone down like it was on fire.

September 20, 2002

Dear C—

Okay, I'm trippin' out that you thought I was gonna be a white guy when we first met! That's pretty hilarious. I thought you were staring at me like that because I had food in my teeth or something, not because you were trying to make sense that I was melanated. I can see how the twists and goatee would throw you in that case. Hey, you threw me too, even though I didn't know what to expect when you walked into Busboys and Poets that day. I try not to have too many of those—expectations—and let life surprise me. And there you were, answering my Craigslist ad.

You did seem a little nervous, but it was a job interview, I suppose. Though it never felt like one. And there was zero need for you to try to impress me with how smart and qualified you were—it was clear the second I met you that you were way above digitizing thousands of photos and helping me organize my chaotic studio. But when you explained your situation, I felt for you, hard. I would have hired you for the gig no matter what. Even if other people had applied. Ha-ha.

I already decided it was yours before I invited you back to the loft to see my work, so no, that wasn't some sort of test (why do you think everything's some sorta test?). But I did want to see your reaction to my stuff in a way I can't explain. I wasn't expecting you to have any . . . how did you put it—"Clever thoughts about composition and lighting" and whatnot. It was enough when you said, "Oh my God, these photographs are beautiful!" It was enough just to see the look on your face taking them in. When I asked you which one was your favorite—well, okay, I was testing you there. And you passed. "Glory Girl" is my favorite too. As you could probably tell when I went on and on about what I was trying to do with the juxtaposition of the little girl holding that sparkler against her dark skin in front of the tombstone of a Confederate soldier and how it was an homage to Jamel Shabazz. I was probably boring you; I can get carried away when it comes to that stuff, so sorry about that.

What I remember most about that day, though, is how we just jumped right in. We must have spent, what, like, four hours at that little table talking and taking turns peeing because of all the tea we were drinking and pissing off the waiter, who kept saying, "Ready for the check yet?" No, dude, we'll let you know. We may never be ready. I don't know how it happened; I was supposed to be the one asking the questions, but there you go, somehow getting me to pop off about all my damn business! How I got into photography, my dyslexia, how school was so hard for me, teachers writing me off as another dumb, distracted Black boy. My parents getting me that first Nikon for my thirteenth birthday that changed the game. How I lost my virginity to my twenty-five-year-old math tutor (no idea how we got on that subject!). How I was always embarrassed growing up that I couldn't—and still can't—hoop. If you couldn't play sports, it automatically meant you were gay. Period. And then if you liked art on top of that—forget about it. I might as well have had a bull's-eye on my back. Those gymnastics lessons my parents made me take sure didn't help either! (I see your horseback-riding lessons and raise you a skinny cocoa-brown kid in a unitard.) Luckily, I don't much care about what people think of me. I don't know if that's a superpower, as you called it. But maybe. You're not the first person to say I'm hard to read, by the way. That's a li'l bit intentional. I think you lose something when people think they have you all figured out, you know?

You're one to talk anyway. :) Not exactly an open book. Are you shy or mysterious? Still haven't put my finger on it. But if I asked the right questions, I could get you to open up too. It was like having the right combo to a lock. So, yeah, I had to get creative—my specialty—and ask all my "Aaron questions." What can I say? I wanted to know you. Still do. If I said that to your face right now, you'd look all shocked and say, "But why?" As if I need a reason.

But if I do . . . I don't know, there's something about you. You're so sheltered (that's not a dis) but also so worldly and book-smart. Never met a girl who could hold her own talking about so many things—Shakespeare and all the types of clouds there are and shit. You're so serious, but then you'll just drop some sarcasm, sharp as cheddar. You're always in your head but not self-absorbed because you stay concerned about other people. You've been through this brutal ordeal this summer and still manage to smile. Selfishly, I hope I had something to do with that. You wrote that you felt bad that you let me be your escape, like you were using me for a distraction from everything going on. And maybe you were, but it was okay because I was happy to be there for you. I agree people come into your life for a reason—oldest, truest cliché there is. Means there's a reason for us. That's what I believe anyway.

x, Aaron

CORA WAITS FOR IT

May–June 2000

It shouldn't have mattered who said it first, and yet Cora hated that she had laid her feelings bare before Lincoln did. But that ship had sailed, much like the boat she was on in the middle of the choppy waters of the Atlantic, fishing with Wes, on their last day of vacation. He kept glancing over at Cora like he was worried about her and didn't know what to do with all the angst she was radiating so strongly, it was probably scaring off the fish. Usually, he would have asked. He regularly used the expression "Penny for your thoughts?" earnestly, like some sort of Victorian Englishman (or nerdy history teacher), but he knew somehow better to ask that now. Cora was unaccustomed to opening up about anything to do with her love life, mainly because she'd never had one before, and she was hardly going to admit that she was torturing herself imagining what would have happened had she not hung up on Lincoln. If Cora had given him the chance, she wondered if he would have said, *I love you too, Bella.*

Unless he didn't love her. In which case, she'd made the right call by hanging up before he could say something devastating like *That's nice* or *Thank you.* Eventually, she'd convinced herself that love was something to be *experienced*, not proclaimed. Her dad rarely said *I love you*, but Cora never doubted that he did. Following this promising line of reasoning, it didn't matter if Lincoln ever said it; Cora could *feel* it. At least she thought she did. Of course, she'd have preferred unequivocal confirmation, the way you could sense it was going to rain but felt assured of your instincts only when you had the proof of the fat drops themselves.

All she could do now was believe Lincoln loved her until firmer evidence materialized. Maybe Cora knew something about faith after all.

Upon their reunion the next day, Cora practically dove into Lincoln's widespread arms as soon as he opened his front door, then stepped back and scanned him from head to toe, looking for all the ways he'd changed in the 192 hours (she'd counted) they'd been apart. He said, "I missed you." Which may not have been the three little words she was looking for, but they were nice too.

They were wasting no time still standing in the open doorway when Cora announced the incredible news she'd intended to tell him on the phone: He could accept the congressional internship and live in her dad's rental.

Lincoln grabbed the door frame in shock. "For real, wow. No one's ever done anything like this for me, Cora." He pulled her to him. "Wow, I . . . I . . . "—Cora held her breath, thinking this was it—"appreciate you so much. You have no idea." It was so close. Though her "You're welcome" was tinged with the slightest hint of irrational disappointment. She deserved an *I love you.*

"I wish I'd gotten to meet your dad this afternoon so I could have thanked him myself."

Cora did too but Wes had to rush back home for an emergency meeting at Prescott. Just before vacation, he'd assigned his students to research Virginia slave archives to look for their ancestors, both white and Black, and present their findings at the end of the year. Some of the parents were up in arms about this project—presumably worried about what side of history and the Confederacy their relatives had landed on—and were demanding to be heard on the matter. It didn't feel like much of an emergency, given that this "hoopla," as Wes referred to it, happened almost every year over this particular assignment, which was part of its educational point.

For that reason, Wes wasn't too worried about it. He had the full support of the head of school, who shared Wes's belief that, as a pedagogical argument, "We don't want our kids to feel bad" failed to hold water. But Wes still had to show up at seven tonight and face an auditorium full of agitated parents where he would ask them why they were so afraid of history.

"You'll get to meet him soon enough!"

In just six short weeks. Cora was already thinking of it as her Summer of Love and had an ongoing mental montage of the memories they would make and things they would do together—tour all the childhood landmarks that were important to her, roam the Smithsonian and the National Zoo, paddleboat in the Tidal Basin—all of it set to a soundtrack heavy on Brian McKnight. As she studied for finals, she played McKnight's version of "Crazy Love" on her Sony boom box so often that Neisha and Kim finally banned it from the rotation. But the melody unlocked something in Cora, and she credited it for inspiring the poem that helped her nail her Irish poetry final. She'd ultimately selected Eavan Boland for her homage assignment, deciding it was important to pick a woman, since most of the poets they'd studied were men; Cora could feel good about the feminism, if nothing else.

The roommates belted Boyz II Men as they packed up their dorm room, even though Neisha groaned that having "It's So Hard to Say Goodbye" on a continuous loop was as bad as "Crazy Love." "Is everyone on their period this week or do y'all just want to be sad for no reason?"

"It *is* sad that we're leaving. Our first year of college is over forever." Cora ripped down a row of string lights and hugged them to her chest.

"Jeez, Cora. You realize we have three more years to go, right? And we'll find a way to hang out this summer."

That would be next to impossible though. Kim was going on a monthlong cruise with her family and then to their summerhouse on Martha's Vineyard. And Neisha was spending the summer in Ghana with her grandmother while her parents "worked on their marriage," which as far as Neisha could tell involved her mother cooking her father elaborate meals and desserts and being more deferential than usual. Cora thought making amends for an affair seemed to require more than almond cookies, but what did she know?

They wrangled everything into bags and boxes and pretended it wouldn't be three months before they were all in one place again, which allowed them to hold it together enough to say goodbye to their empty, echoing dorm room and to one another.

And to the people they had been nine months ago.

You had to go some distance before you could truly measure how far you'd come. For Cora, that became clear as Wes drove her away from campus in his Acura, packed to the gills with her belongings, making the reverse journey of nine months ago. When the tears came this time, at least she could appreciate the irony.

As soon as Cora unpacked her toothbrush, she threw herself into the preparations for Lincoln's arrival. He would be in DC in just over a week after a quick trip home, so their goodbye, in front of a Greyhound bus heaving exhaust fumes, wasn't as fraught. Now, she scrutinized her childhood bedroom, ruthlessly discarding anything that made her look silly or immature. She wrestled the frilly pink canopy off her bed and dragged it to the curb just in time to watch it be scooped up by a Virginia waste management truck and disappear in a satisfying, grinding crush. Also discarded were the cluster of stuffed animals on her bed (except Snoopy) and the stack of *Seventeen* magazines that had continued to pile up. The most recent issue featured Selma Blair on the cover, a "Who's Hot, Who's Not" survey, and a love quiz titled "Is It the End or Can It Last?" Cora almost grabbed a pen before thinking better of it.

On the day of Lincoln's arrival, Cora's room was in acceptable shape and she'd put together a welcome package complete with a map of the Metro and a potted succulent. The whole drive to National, Cora chewed on the inside of her cheek, a nervous tell she didn't bother hiding. By the time they'd parked and were waiting at the gate for the arrival of Flight 1252, the corners of the little sign Cora had made (WELCOME TO DC, LINCOLN AMES, for lack of anything catchier) were wilted by her sweaty hands and she had a raw spot on the inside of her left cheek. It rubbed against her teeth as her face broke into the widest grin at the sight of Lincoln emerging from the Jetway.

Cora wanted Lincoln to sweep her up and rain kisses down on her, but at the same time, she was relieved he opted for a chaste peck before throwing his shoulders back and thrusting out his hand to her dad. "It's nice to meet you, Mr. Belle. Thank you for this opportunity." Lincoln appeared alarmingly close to saluting Wes for no reason.

"Relax, son, you haven't arrived at boot camp. It's nice to meet you too." He grabbed Lincoln's bag with one hand and slapped him on the back with the other. "Packing light, eh?"

Lincoln had one small duffel bag and a backpack. "Yeah, didn't figure I'd need too much, I s'pose." His southern lilt was noticeably heavier after a few days at home. The dregs of the agitation he'd seemed to have the couple times Cora had talked to him while he was in Mississippi this past week were there too. It wasn't obvious, but she noticed, and she liked what that revealed about their intimacy. She *knew* him.

"You got a suit in there?" Wes asked.

Lincoln's sheepish shrug tugged at her heart.

"Well, no doubt you're going to need one or two. I would let you borrow from my closet but something tells me it wouldn't be the best fit." That "something" was the robust belly that Wes patted now. Cora had eaten her fair share of pizza that year, but it was her dad who'd gained the freshman fifteen. She hadn't been sure he was aware of it until this acknowledgment.

"Tell you what, let's drop Cora off at home and I'll take you over to Men's Warehouse straightaway and get you squared away. Give us a chance to get to know each other. What do you say?"

Everyone understood the question was rhetorical.

The idea of Wes and Lincoln alone together for the afternoon barely an hour after Lincoln had arrived was enough to send Cora gnawing at the inside of her cheek again, but she relaxed in the car once they settled into easy banter about the Orioles' prospects for the season, Carolina barbecue versus Memphis-style, and, improbably enough, Napster (which involved Lincoln patiently explaining it and Wes looking perplexed. "I don't need a computer science degree to play my albums. I know that's right"). Fifteen minutes into the car ride, Cora couldn't remember why she'd been so nervous in the first place, the story of her life.

When they pulled up in front of their redbrick house, Wes didn't even park the car; he just motioned for Cora to get out. "Don't give me that look. He's in good hands. We'll get some suits and then I'll drop him off at the apartment. Y'all have the whole summer, let the man have the evening to get settled in."

It felt like her dad was taking her boyfriend hostage, but Lincoln didn't seem to mind. He slid into the front seat as she exited it, giving her a little kiss on the cheek as he passed and whispering, "I got this, Bella. Let me do my thing."

What could Cora do but pace the house, alternating between being annoyed that she wasn't spending Lincoln's first hours in town with him and fretting about what he and her dad were talking about?

When she heard the garage opening, she bounded to the side door like a puppy left home for the first time. She was standing in the kitchen when Wes came in and flipped on the lights.

"You've been sitting here in the dark?"

Cora had been oblivious to irrelevant details like the setting sun. "Well?"

"Well what?" Wes ambled over to the fridge and pulled out a bowl of grapes.

"Dad! You know what. How was it? Did Lincoln like the place? Did he get suits?"

"Whoa there, baby girl. Give a man a minute to breathe. Course he liked the place—"

"Did he see the plant I got him?"

"Yes, yes. I'm sure he appreciated the homey touch. And we got two new suits. Can't believe he was going to wear jeans on his first day of work." Wes shook his head at this tragedy and took a seat at the kitchen island where he'd graded approximately three thousand papers over the years and Cora had done as many math problems, where they'd had the most casual and also most intense conversations of their lives. It was unclear which this one was shaping up to be.

"Look, I like him, Cora. I know that's what you really want to know. I do."

Cora actually clapped her hands. "I knew you would."

"He's got a good head on his shoulders, like you said. He wouldn't have gotten into this program otherwise. Maybe a little cocky, but a man needs to have confidence if he's going to get anywhere, especially a Black man, so I'll allow him some swagger."

There was a pause. Cora sensed a *but* floating around in there that sent her reaching for a glass for a gulp of water she'd poured hours ago and forgotten about.

"Look here, sometimes you gotta find out what's driving folks in life. Are they running fast as they can toward something or away from something? Often, it's both. But it's just helpful to know. Lincoln strikes me as the type who's got something to prove, and that can be tricky. Too early to tell how that restless spirit'll play out. Y'all think you're grown, but you're just babies. You're still deciding who to be, and you can't see or imagine all the ways you'll change and grow."

Wes seemed to be one step away from trotting out a proverb like Neisha's dad.

"The takeaway is, he's a fine young man and I like him for you. I can see he's bringing you out of your shell. You just always gotta be careful though, Cora. It's a little like what I told you about playing with matches. Sometimes they're a tool to give you all the light and warmth you need, and sometimes you end up burned and with scars for life. Far as I can tell, that's how love is. Especially first love. Okay, I'm worn out with all this meet-the-parents stuff. Your old man needs some shut-eye stat." He kissed her on the top of her head.

He was at the staircase when he turned back around; Cora was busy contemplating heat and flames.

"I will say, Lincoln looks sharp in a suit. I told him he should wear it and take you out for your birthday. I was surprised he didn't know it's next week. What's up with that?"

"I didn't want him to feel pressured to plan something." And she could avoid disappointment if he didn't.

"Well, I told him to take you somewhere nice. And it'd be my treat."

"Wait, what about our tradition?"

Every year since Cora turned three, they'd gone to IHOP for her birthday to have breakfast for dinner, and Cora would eat as many pancakes as the age she was turning. (Her stomach maxed out when she got to double digits.) Then they came home and watched *The Little Mermaid*. Neither Wes nor Cora gave any thought to when they would grow out of this long tradition, a willful denial. It was easy to think things would always be as they had always been.

"I'm not a betting man, but I'd put this house up that you'd rather hang out with Lincoln than your old man this year. How about we do pancakes for lunch, then you and Lincoln can have dinner? And maybe we skip *The Little Mermaid*?"

It was bewildering not to be able to tell if you were gaining something or losing something or both.

It was just as bewildering when you experienced the present and future at once, as Cora did when she laid eyes on Lincoln the night of her birthday. She gasped a little, much as she had when she saw him for the first time in the bookstore. Standing there in his suit, the crisp white shirt tucked into his pants just enough that the cloth pulled over his taut stomach, the pale pink tie popping against his dark skin, Lincoln looked as sharp as Wes had said. But more than that, he was transformed in Cora's eyes into someone who had to attend important meetings (not classes), someone who had a money clip (not a literal paper clip) around his cash, an expensive leather briefcase (not a backpack), and a sleek silver sedan (not a Metro card). In other words, he looked like the man he would one day be.

Meanwhile, Cora looked like Cora . . . in a dress.

Lincoln cocked his head and struck a pose when he spotted her waiting outside the Metro station. "This suit is all that, huh?"

"You look great. The shoes are a nice touch too."

He looked surprised to find spanking-new Air Jordans on his feet. "Oh, yeah, some of the other interns and I went to the mall the other day after work, and these called my name from Foot Locker."

"They look good," she said, although what she really meant was *They look expensive*, especially given his meager stipend.

"Well, you know—gotta look the part, right?" he said, taking her hand for the short walk to the restaurant.

She nodded, even though she was unsure what "the part" was.

"And see here, birthday girl, I asked for the best table."

They settled into a corner booth next to a massive wall of windows where they could watch the golden orb of sun drop closer and closer to the Potomac River. The Kennedy Center was aglow across the rippling water. "I wanted to take you somewhere legit. I saw this place when my boss took me to the Channel Inn last week—that's where all the Black bigwigs in DC go. Mayor Williams was there. And Maxine Waters. I know she's older than my mama, but I gotta say, she's fly."

"So is Maxine Waters your hall pass? I can live with that."

"You better watch out. I saw her checking me out, just saying." He playfully pulled at the collar of his shirt to emphasize his irresistible desirability.

"I bet she was. Well, for real, thank you for bringing me here, Lincoln." Cora carefully unfolded her napkin, placed it on her lap, and sat up straighter, trying to shake the feeling that she was pretending to be a grown-up. It didn't help that other diners glanced over at them like they were out of place; whether that was because they were so young or the only brown people in the dining room (except for the servers), she couldn't tell. She doubted that Lincoln had ever been to a restaurant like this—white tablecloths, gilded sconces, fifty-dollar steaks—and yet he seemed very much in his element, poring over the massive leather menu he held upright in front of him.

"You thought about your birthday wish yet? 'Cause I'm already eyeing this molten java cake with anise icing, whatever that is."

"Not yet—I have some ideas, though." In fact, she had exactly one. A singular blinding wish that tonight was finally the night.

"You look nice, by the way. You should wear dresses more. I'm into this look, legs all out and proud."

"Oh, this, it's so old." That was technically true, though it also was brand-new. The white wrap dress had been hanging in her closet for years, taunting her; she'd bought it secretly thinking she would wear it to a Prescott dance one day, but she'd never made it to one. Now Cora indulged in some revisionist history, telling herself that she'd actually been saving it for another special occasion—tonight.

"You need to stop with that."

"Stop with what?"

"Deflecting compliments. It's like you live to sell yourself short, Cora. You're always saying you're silly, downplaying everything you do, and acting like your girls know everything about everything and you don't. Like how you said Professor Keane gave you an A for your final project only because you went to office hours every week and not because your poem was straight fire."

"How would you know it was good? You never read it."

"Because you wouldn't let me. But I don't need to read it to know that it was, because it's you—everything you do is next level. You got a three point eight this year barely cracking a book. You gotta start claiming your power or whatever Iyanla Vanzant would say."

Seeing Cora's raised eyebrow, he explained that one of the secretaries at work had a stack of Vanzant's books on her desk, and he might have dipped into one or two.

"You're special, Cora. You're, like, the real deal, okay? I wouldn't be with you if you weren't. And I'm going to call you out every time you forget that."

Cora had no idea if Lincoln had gotten her anything for her birthday, but as far as she was concerned, this validation and the way he looked at her now was gift enough.

"Well, thank you."

"Hey, you never have to thank me for stating facts. But you do have to thank me for this." Lincoln dug in the interior pocket of his suit jacket and produced a delicate chain that he threaded through his fingers.

"It's new, I promise, it came in one of those velvet boxes but I thought it would be bulky in my pocket and you would see it, and I wanted to surprise you—so, surprise! I was going to give it to you later, but why wait? It's fitting now, see, because . . . "

He held up the necklace so she could see the charm dangling from it—the word *Believe* spelled out in cursive. It looked like Carrie's necklace in *Sex and the City*, which Lincoln secretly watched.

"Don't worry, I don't mean Jesus!" Lincoln let loose a quick laugh before turning serious again. "I want you to believe in yourself, Cora. So every time you wear it or see it, it's a reminder."

He slid out of the booth and over to her to help with the clasp. For the rest of dinner, she couldn't stop touching the necklace as if it were an amulet and wearing it would protect her from unknown dangers.

When the cake came and she leaned in to blow out the candle, the charm hung over the flame, catching the light. It burned a little when it flipped back against the delicate skin of her neck in a way that reinforced her sense that it was enchanted.

"Okay, let's get outta here so I can give you your other present." The way Lincoln bit his bottom lip left no confusion as to what that was, and Cora felt the usual flutter low in her belly and the wetness between her legs. It never stopped being disconcerting, this bald expression of her desire, the way her body responded with little input from her mind.

Cora was usually too self-conscious for PDA, but it being a special occasion and all, she let Lincoln rub her thigh on the Metro; his hand reached so far up her dress that his pinkie grazed her damp panties. They started frantically making out before they got through the door of Lincoln's apartment, which she thought people did only in the movies. Her dress slid off as soon as they were inside, and they never stopped kissing, which was a feat of mechanics and coordination.

Lincoln tore himself from her only long enough to press play on the Keith Sweat CD on the stereo and jog over and turn on the window-mounted AC unit in the living room so the space could cool from 110 to 90 degrees. She met him on the couch, where she was already splayed out in her bra and underwear. He stopped to study her, illuminated from behind by the sliver of light that came through the window in the otherwise dark room. It was probably from a streetlamp, but Cora chose to think it was moonlight. She sat back on the itchy fabric and stared up at Lincoln, zeroing in on those inches of him standing at attention directly in front of her face.

He looked down. "It looks nice."

For a split second, Cora thought Lincoln meant his penis, but he reached out and fingered the thin gold rope around her neck and then continued trailing his finger slowly up, across her chin, and around her lips. She wanted to say thank you—for both the compliment and the necklace—but she had no ability to speak, and that was even before Lincoln dropped to his knees and buried his face between her legs. So overtaken was she with shock and pleasure feeling Lincoln's tongue against her that she let her body flail around, her hips writhe, and strange sounds escape her. And when she had the most astonishing orgasm of her young life, she clutched Lincoln's arm so hard, she left a small indentation from the mood ring she wore on her middle finger. (It stayed there for days. She loved that she'd left him . . . marked. It was how she felt as well.)

Before she could recover, Lincoln was inside her. She pressed every inch of herself against every inch of him so there was no air or light between their bodies, and still he wasn't close enough, so she pulled him closer. Even though she hadn't picked up her violin in over a year, her hands had been strengthened by a decade of playing, which made it easier to grip Lincoln's broad back. She willed them to be strong enough to never let go.

He came quickly, and while he seemed sheepish about it, it made her feel powerful. It was hard for her to fathom that she had the ability to make someone feel this good. When he whispered, "I hope you enjoyed your birthday, Bella," it had the opposite effect: She trembled with weakness.

Lying on her back with Lincoln on top of her, his head heavy on her chest, their sweat mixing together in a pleasant slickness, she was hard-pressed to think of anything that would have made this a better night, and that's when it happened.

Lincoln's voice vibrated against her chest when he spoke: "I love you, Bella." The words melted over her literal heart.

"What?" She'd heard him, but she'd waited so long; Cora wanted—needed—him to say it again, if only to prolong the moment. How many times could she ask him to repeat it?

"I love you." This time Lincoln angled his head up to face her, and the intensity of his eyes almost made her look away. But she didn't. She couldn't. She wouldn't. Maybe ever.

"I . . . I . . . love you too." She stuttered through it and lost steam toward the end but that was because she was overwhelmed by the gravity of what was happening, not from any lack of conviction.

"I know." The smile. It never failed her.

Even though on some level she understood that love didn't work this way, Cora was convinced that saying it out loud made the condition permanent—there could be no take-backs once such a profound sentiment was voiced. This was, and would always be, the first time a man said he loved her. She tucked the moment into the pocket of her heart with the hope that it would stay preserved for eternity and that every time she wanted to recall it, she could as easily, and vividly as if she was reliving it.

Lincoln had already started drifting off. It was astonishing how fast he could sink into a deep sleep, especially after sex; it was if he vacated his body every night and then sprang back into consciousness in the morning. It would be greedy—and incredibly weird—to wake him up and ask him: Why? Why did he love her? But she was curious about the specific reasons, if Lincoln kept track like she did. Cora still added to the List every day—it had become a ritual and she feared cosmic consequences if she stopped. Or it could be taken as a sign that she'd run out of reasons when in fact they just kept coming.

Cora didn't need to know the specifics, but she did need to know one thing, and it couldn't wait. She shook him gently awake.

"Wassup?" Lincoln shimmied a little, readjusting himself against her so they fit together perfectly again but with a different configuration of body parts tangled together.

Cora said the next words to herself, the same as she had her birthday wish. "Do you think you'll always love me?" Then she gathered herself to repeat it out loud. "Will you . . . will you always love me?"

"Yes, Cora, forever."

She believed him.

CORA DREAMS OF GOING THE DISTANCE

August 2000

"Nothing lasts forever, baby girl."

As if Cora needed this reminder from her dad while she lamented the end of what would forever and always be the best summer of her life. So rare was it that reality lined up with your most romantic visions, Cora knew even then to have the proper reverence when it did.

Wes had dropped his gem of wisdom while he brushed hot, freshly baked scones with butter. They were waiting for Lincoln to arrive at the house for one last brunch before the two of them headed back to school.

Baking was one of many new hobbies Wes had taken up over the past year, and his commitment to the pursuit had reached zealous levels during his free time over the summer, which likely accounted for all that extra padding around his middle. His other favorite pastime these past few months had been bonding with Lincoln, a project he approached with the same delighted devotion as he did trying his tenth frittata recipe that morning.

Wes and Lincoln had a standing weekly date, meeting every Tuesday at the National Air and Space Museum to have lunch at its cafeteria-style restaurant they both loved for mystifying reasons that must have gone beyond the astronaut ice cream. This happened while Cora was at Perry's scooping real ice cream and obsessing over what they discussed week after week.

When she'd asked Lincoln, he'd said, "I don't know . . . stuff."

Her dad's answer was similarly elusive. "We chop it up about this and that. I'm just trying to be there for him. Seems like Lincoln could use a father figure in his life, someone to talk to. You wanted me to like him and I do, but now it seems like you want me to back off?"

It wasn't exactly that. Cora couldn't understand why she found these lunches so unsettling until she'd overheard Wes on the phone with his best friend and Cora's godfather, Tony, last week, two scotches in, telling him that Lincoln was the son he never got to have.

Cora happened to be walking down the hall past his office just then and she stumbled, not just over the notoriously loose floorboard but over the gut punch of that statement. She'd long ago accepted their circumstances with a maturity of which she was proud—so much so that it felt like blasphemy for her to wish it were any other way. Wes wanting a son was like her wanting another parent, a different parent, as if these were roles to be swapped in some sort of cruel Faustian bargain. A most twisted *would you rather*. A son in place of a daughter? A father instead of a mother? However irrational, she took it as a betrayal that Wes could even contemplate anything beyond their bubble of two.

Lincoln missed the edge in Cora's voice when she'd told him about what she'd overheard. He was too focused on how flattered he was by what Wes had said. "See? I told you to let me do my thing and your pops would be all in on me." It was no surprise Lincoln took this as a positive development for many reasons. And it was, she wanted her father and her boyfriend to be close, of course she did. Cora just had to remind herself of that, which she did when Lincoln arrived for brunch and greeted Wes with an elaborate dance of an eager handshake turned half hug, and culminating in effusive back pats.

"My man, my man," Wes said over and over, pulling a bottle of champagne out of the fridge. "Now, I know you don't hit the hard stuff, Lincoln, and y'all are too young to be imbibing anyway, but I'm gonna offer up a couple sips of some bubbly, since celebrations are in order. I've been looking forward to toasting your big news."

Lincoln had made such an impression during his fellowship that on his last day yesterday, Congressman Wilkens offered him a role in his office next summer. As much as Lincoln had complained about his boss, his halitosis and micromanaging, he'd worked hard to ingratiate himself with him, even going to church with Wilkens and his family every Sunday at Metropolitan AME, where DC's Black political elite went to rub elbows as much as praise Jesus. Lincoln was not only about looking the part that summer, he was about "playing the game," a concept that was just as vague to Cora but apparently worked.

"Here's to Lincoln and all his success!" Wes raised a glass, then shook Lincoln's shoulder so hard, the liquid inside sloshed over the rim.

"I also want to toast you two little lovebirds. It sure was nice to spend time with y'all this summer. I enjoyed having you around and having my favorite daughter back under my roof. Cora was just saying how fast this time went. Boy, does it ever. Days, summers, life."

Cora blamed the champagne for her father's sudden sentimentality, though it never took much.

"My little girl's gonna be gone soon." Wes shook his head hard and slow against this reality.

"I'm just going back to school, Dad, down the road. I'll be back."

"Oh, I don't just mean school. I mean you're gonna be *gone*-gone soon. Off living your life. Which is what I want for you, don't get me wrong. But I'll have to find yet another hobby to fill the Cora-size hole. Probably 'bout time for golf."

"Hey, Wes, you ever thought about getting back out there?"

Cora nearly choked on her champagne while her dad expressed his utter confusion. "Out where?"

"Dating, you know. There's this new thing, eHarmony?"

"E-what, now?"

Lincoln had recently learned about internet dating thanks to the same secretaries at work who schooled him on Iyanla Vanzant and he described how it worked to Wes, who looked like he was hearing about time travel. Cora was similarly exasperated as she recalled how Lincoln had recently said, "Your dad's not a monk, Cora. He has needs."

This was as jarring to contemplate as the idea of Wes longing for a son. It forced Cora to awaken to the uncomfortable reality that he was not just a dad, her dad, but a man with interests, dreams, regrets, and, heaven help her, those needs that she could have done without Lincoln mentioning. Cora had as much trouble wrapping her mind around that as Wes was having with the concept of eHarmony.

"So let me get this straight: There's just pictures of women on the World Wide Web and you look at them and then reach out? Sounds like a mail-order bride sort of thing."

Lincoln offered up a smile equal parts patient and indulgent. "Nah, it's not like that. You answer all these questions about yourself and the women do too and you get matched because you have stuff in common. Then you send messages to each other and can meet up in real life for dinner or a movie or whatever."

"So the computer just knows who's right for me?" Wes said this was the incredulity of someone who also didn't believe in these newfangled cell phones. ("I shouldn't be able to get a call in the grocery store—it's just not right.")

"Something like that."

"I can't say I'm ready for all that, Lincoln. It's been a minute since, uh, I had someone in my life."

Wes squinted out the patio window into the backyard as if conjuring a far-off memory. Simultaneously, Cora reached for her own hazy recollection of a woman who had the shrill, singsongy voice of an animated character—or maybe that was just how she spoke to six-year-old Cora. But the voice was as much as Cora could recall about her—she didn't even remember her name. All that she had truly registered about the woman was the most salient detail—that she wasn't her mother.

"Yeah, I get that, I guess. My aunt never got remarried after losing my uncle Ron, and that was before I was born. He died of cancer too."

Wes froze but for his eyes, which darted to Cora, confused. She didn't know how or why Lincoln had assumed her mother died of cancer, but somewhere along the way he'd mentioned it, and she hadn't corrected him because it was easier to let him believe that.

Cora blinked at Wes, the only response she could muster. Their communication remained entirely silent, which was fitting, since they never, ever spoke about her mother. At one point, she thought Wes avoided the subject to protect her, and then somewhere along the line, when Cora learned to suppress her questions and curiosity, her thinking shifted to believing that he didn't mention her mother, didn't so much as say her name, to spare himself pain. Finally, Cora came to understand the silence itself was the reason they never broached the subject. A conversation at rest will always stay at rest.

Lincoln must have sensed the sudden shift in the barometric pressure of the room. "Sorry, sorry, my bad, I didn't mean to bring up hard memories."

"All good, son!"

"It's fine!"

Wes and Cora rushed to talk over each other and busy themselves with every distracting task within arm's reach.

Mercifully, Lincoln could be counted on to just keep talking. "Congressman Wilkens and his wife have been married fifty-six years. He's worried her memory is going, but he's the one who's told me the story of how they met and how she had the best legs in all of Cleveland at least twenty-two times and I gotta pretend it's the first I've heard it. Tears up every single time too."

"Well, that's another thing that happens when you get older. Doesn't take much to make you all mushy and sentimental. And forgetful."

"I told Wilkens that was gonna be me. Us. Cora and me. College sweethearts. Telling our li'l meet-cute when we're all old and gray." Lincoln leaned forward over the counter like that could give him a head start on the future. "I—we—got it all planned out."

Lincoln had laid out his vision a few nights ago as they cuddled in the bed of his stuffy studio, sticking to the sweaty sheets and trying to remain still enough that the weak trickle of air-conditioning from the creaky window unit cooled their hottest body parts. (Cora was so sweaty, Lincoln made a joke about her boobs crying.) Listening to Lincoln unspool what lay ahead was like hearing a fairy tale. *There once was a girl named Cora who went to college, met the love of her life, got a cute one-bedroom apartment in an exciting city and a job that progressed from a cubicle to an office with a door, and went to the farmers' market on Saturdays to buy fresh flowers, and the two of them lived happily ever after for all their days.* It had once seemed so hard! The story of their future soothed and settled something inside her, just like the best bedtime stories do.

That was pillow talk though, dreamy musings; Cora wasn't ready for Lincoln to share any of this with her dad, but there was no stopping him.

"Cora's gonna take a couple extra classes this year and next, and with all those AP credits, she can graduate with me, since I'm a year ahead, and then Wilkens already said he'd help me get into his alma mater—University of Chicago—for law school. So we'll hit Chi-town."

"Oh, wow, that's a lot, now." Wes was addressing Lincoln but staring at Cora. "Graduating a year early, huh?"

Cora just nodded.

"And what's *your* plan for Chicago?" Wes stopped even the pretense of washing dishes; his eyes bored directly into hers. But it was Lincoln who answered.

"Grad school? Or with a communications degree, a marketing job. PR, maybe. You know your daughter can do anything."

"I'm well aware of Cora's talents, yes. Also her need to focus them."

"I know, Dad. I'm going to figure it out. I will."

"Look, you two, I love a plan, as my daughter well knows. And far be it for me to stand in the way of romance. But it's my fatherly duty to remind you that the last thing y'all need to do is rush anything. You've got to get to know yourselves and grow into yourselves if you have any chance of growing with each other. Life comes at you fast enough—you'd best pace yourself if you're going to go the distance."

There was a note of warning in Wes's tone and in the way he pointedly looked at each of them. It conveyed that this would be a serious challenge, not one to be undertaken lightly, and success was not guaranteed. Wes, of all people, knew this.

Two years. Twenty years. *Fifty-six years.* It was an intimidating span of time, so much room for so much to go wrong. It also wasn't something you could race through, like a book. But Cora didn't have a time machine or a magic wand to give her control over when she met Lincoln. She couldn't delay it until they were older or more mature or could take into account all those ways they might grow and change. They couldn't put their relationship on hold for five or ten years and pick it back up like pausing a movie. The universe had put them together now, and that had to mean something.

So she raised her glass and said, "Here's to going the distance." A toast. A safeguard. A dream and a plan all at once.

The few sips of champagne did the job of drowning out the darker thoughts, the worrisome *what-ifs?* It would do Cora no good to try to steel herself for all the ways they could be derailed between now and happily ever after.

It wouldn't have mattered anyway—she would have been wildly off the mark.

CORA REFUSES TO BELIEVE IT

October 2000

Cora eyed the trash can across the room and debated whether she could make it. It was worth a try; either way, she risked leaving a pool of vomit on the classroom floor. Swallowing hard to hold her gut in check, she shuffled across the paint-flecked tile and got to the metal bin just as the heaving began.

She had had extended bouts of nausea as a kid, but then it was because she was stressed about something—an upcoming recital, the annual Presidential Fitness Test, the girl down the street who bullied her every day of sixth grade. But Cora couldn't figure out what she was so wound up about now, when everything was going so well. She was loved! And though she didn't want to keep coming back to that as the defining feature of her life, it was. Love had that effect on you. It convinced you that it was the only thing that mattered.

It wasn't enough, however, to spare you the misery of your stomach turning itself inside out. After another round of heaves, Cora wiped her mouth with a paper towel and settled back on the creaky stool in front of her easel. It was a saving grace that she had the studio to herself at eleven on Friday night; she could both paint and retch without prying eyes. Of course, Cora would much rather have been back in her dorm room, tucked under her Pottery Barn comforter, but Kim wanted the place to herself while she "entertained" her latest prospect—her third frenzied fling in almost as many months that fall. Fabiene was an exchange student from Florence who had wildly crooked teeth that gave him the most improbably charming grin, but he always left the faintest trace of BO in his wake. Kim was already convinced that by Christmas, spring break at the latest, she'd be invited to gallivant around Italy with him. She'd started tying her hair in silk scarves like Grace Kelly in preparation for her seat on the back of the moped she presumed Fabiene owned.

Cora leaned toward the canvas before her as if it held secrets. All that white space waiting for something, waiting for her, made her heart race. It was not unlike the blank page she had tried to wrestle words onto for last year's poetry assignment this pressure to make something from nothing with only her own mind to draw upon. She could swear the canvas was staring at her expectantly, like *Well*? Or maybe that was just the voice in her head.

The first slow drag of the brush was the most satisfying, the soothing friction and the streak of scarlet it left, like she'd sliced through flesh. So Cora did it again and again, trailing the brush from top to bottom, until thick rows lined up like fence posts. Her paintings—the three she'd completed for this beginner's art class so far this semester—were objectively terrible, clunky, flat, and amateurish. She might as well have been scribbling fat rainbows like she'd done as a kid. But for once Cora didn't care about doing something perfectly or right, and that was the miracle of this particular discovery; once she let go, she abandoned herself to the surprise of what leaped from the far reaches of her brain onto the empty space before her. Even if it was nothing more than . . . stripes.

Part of her abandon was due to the fact that she genuinely enjoyed painting and part was because the professor, who told the students to call him Sketch, announced on the first day of class that everyone would get an A. This went against university policy, but you could tell he was the type (see nickname, long hair, vintage Pink Floyd T-shirts, screeds about fighting the establishment) to relish such a thing. Cora could relax knowing that her performance in class, which was to say her artistic talent or lack of it, wouldn't affect her pristine GPA.

She was focused on unraveling what this particular piece could become when hot bile erupted once again, sending her gagging over the bin she'd dragged to sit at her feet. Little flecks splashed onto the bottom of the canvas, sticking to the wet red paint—a sure sign that she should call it a day and go home. Her only hope was that if she walked slowly enough, Fabiene would be gone by the time she arrived. Or maybe he'd take the hint and leave. If only Neisha were around. She'd have no qualms about kicking out "Funky Fabiene," but Neisha was five thousand miles away.

Perhaps this was the source of Cora's nausea: how much she missed Neisha, who had abruptly dropped the shocking news, barely two weeks before they were due to return to school, that she'd be studying abroad at University College London for the entire year.

Why London? Why didn't you tell us? How could you leave us? Neisha did not feel compelled to offer any satisfying answers or explanations throughout a tense and tearful three-way call. She did at least, finally, apologize for leaving Cora and Kim to scramble to find housing together, since they'd been booted from their coveted triple once Neisha withdrew. The Freemans were able to pull some strings—by all accounts, one of their favorite activities—and Kim and Cora ended up securing a stupidly large suite in Earl Grant Hall, one of the oldest buildings at Hamlin.

When they moved in, Kim's dad said, "Just think, a hundred years ago you'd have been in bondage cleaning these rooms, and now I give this school enough money to have my daughter in the best room on this campus—even if the building is named for some cracker Confederate hee-haw." He said this with a showy satisfaction, like he was making a point to those hee-haw ghosts and not to Cora and Kim, who were busy trying to hang art—a framed *Starry Night* poster—on the exposed-brick wall. Cora started to point out that Earl Grant was actually a Union soldier. Ever the history teacher's daughter, she'd looked up several of the names and statues on campus, but she stopped herself from sharing this because Malcolm Freeman was not a man who liked to be corrected. Especially while he was standing in the palatial digs he'd procured for you.

Besides, Cora chose not to think about history and slavery as they'd unpacked and instead focused on all the details that defied everything you'd expect to see in a dorm room: ornate tin ceilings, the three large south-facing windows that overlooked the prettiest corner of campus, and—the best part—an actual fireplace that was bigger than a bathroom stall. The chimney had long ago been blocked off, presumably so a drunk student didn't burn the century-old building down, but Cora and Kim filled the hearth with oversize pillows with fat tassels from Pier 1 Imports that made the little nook feel exotic and made them feel sophisticated, like they were the type of women—not girls, *women*—who'd been to Marrakech or other exotic locales.

They called it "the Nest" and decided this was where they would solve any and all of life's problems, though so far, they mainly sat there and talked about Neisha and how quiet it was without her—so many fewer dance parties, cookie crumbs, and impromptu fashion shows. Their lingering annoyance paled against how much they missed her. Leave it to Neisha to be larger than life, even in her absence.

Fall that year came on as hard and strong as Cora's queasiness. It wasn't right for it to be thirty-six degrees in October, but the digital thermometer above Whitting Hall, home of the meteorology program Hamlin was known for, confirmed this in neon-red digits.

After complaining about the cold snap all week, Cora was grateful for it as she opened the heavy metal door of the fine arts building and stepped out into the steely night. The bracing air was as close as she could get to the feeling of the cool washcloths Wes dabbed her forehead with when she was sick. The walk back to her room through the shortcut behind Whitting, with its whitewashed stone facade, was one Cora had made uneventfully dozens of times, her body leading her across campus with such autonomy that she often didn't even remember the trip. But that night, she stopped abruptly on the empty path and stared up at the heavy moon as if it had called out to her.

Sure, Cora appreciated the daily miracle of a hazy orange sunrise and the imposing cut of a mountain range against a blue sky as much as the next person, but she was not the communing-with-nature type. She liked trees—who didn't?—but she had no desire to hug one. And yet she found herself craning her neck to take in the silver sliver hovering low and obscured by a thin line of wispy clouds. All around it was a flurry of stars, like glitter thrown up against the sky. How had she ignored them night after night, and why was she all choked up looking at them now? She was suddenly consumed by the idea that there were as many possible paths for her life as there were stars above her.

There was no explanation for Cora's sudden existential awe, no reason why she turned in slow circles, her face to the sky, contemplating her staggering freedom and everything that might one day happen to her. She could live to be eighty. She could die in a car crash tomorrow. She could live abroad. She might own a dog. She might lose a limb. There could be a war in her lifetime. There was a real possibility she could be First Lady one day. Imagine that. Oh, and what about the lottery? Who was to say she wouldn't win Powerball? And then there were all the experiences she *wasn't* going to have, because she'd get only this one chance to do it all.

Suffice it to say, Cora Belle was having *a moment.* Out of nowhere, on an unremarkable Tuesday.

She realized she was crying only when the wind chilled the tears on her face. She decided she needed to get to bed as quickly as humanly possible before she found herself howling at the moon or singing Sarah McLachlan.

Or vomiting on the bronze statue of Hamlin's founder on her left.

She arrived to find a message on the dry-erase message board of their door that almost made her start weeping again, this time with relief: *Ended up going back to F's. See you in the morning. Hope you're feeling better!* This was followed by a long string of hearts, because no message from Kim was complete without a long string of hearts.

There were twelve hours and seventeen minutes between the mercy of Cora slipping into her warm bed and waking up to find Kim hovering over her. Twelve hours Cora had spent in a rare deep and dreamless sleep. (She would later consider this a waste, since those might have been the last truly innocent hours of her entire life, and she'd lost them to unconsciousness.) As soon as Cora opened her eyes, she felt Kim's face inches from hers.

"You look terrible."

"Good morning to you too, Kimmie. You look like . . . you had fun last night." Cora nodded at the faint Florida-shaped hickey on Kim's neck. "Why are you back so early?"

"It's almost noon, Cora. And I brought you this."

Kim thrust a white CVS bag at Cora. She dug inside it gratefully, expecting to find crackers, Gatorade, or some Pepto. Instead, she found a small white box.

A deranged guffaw erupted from Cora. "Kim! There's no way. Did Neisha put you up to this?"

"Yes, she made me promise to get you a test. I swear everyone was looking at me all side-eyed, even though I put some chips and two lip glosses in my basket too. I wanted to be like, 'This EPT isn't for me!' but everyone tries that trick. Anyway, what do you mean, there's no way? Of course there's a way. Please don't tell me I need to tell you where babies come from. Just rule it out. Okay?"

But it was impossible; it had to be impossible. Or maybe it was incomprehensible, but there was no point in splitting hairs. Cora didn't waste her energy on doing the calendar math, or pinning down her erratic period, or thinking back to the few times she and Lincoln had "slipped up" because those facts were irrelevant against a larger crucial truth: There was simply no way Cora Belle could be pregnant. So adamant was she that she could bend this reality to her will, she grabbed the box and marched down the hall to the bathroom. She had to confirm this truth as quickly and thoroughly as she could.

"Good luck!" Kim's voice floated down the hall behind her.

"I don't need it!" Cora yelled over her shoulder, ignoring the ever-so-slight hiccup of her heartbeat.

Cora didn't bother reading the directions; she just sat on the toilet, staring at the terrazzo floor tiles with chunky, chipped grout, and peed on the stick, and all over her hand too, gross but unavoidable.

If she had prepared herself even a little bit, if she'd stopped to allow the hint of possibility to seep into her mind, if she hadn't so deliberately and thoroughly leaned into her denial, Cora would not have slid right off the toilet seat onto the ice-cold floor when the two red lines appeared, so fast that she hadn't even wiped the warm pee from her thumb.

When she screamed, Kim came running as if she'd been waiting right outside the bathroom door, which she probably had been. She pulled Cora to her feet, ignoring the drops of pee that transferred from Cora's hand to her own because that was friendship. They stood staring at the test and then at each other in the mirror.

Cora collapsed again, and Kim slid down beside her on the floor under the belly of sink basins.

"What am I going to do?" It was as simple and sincere a question as Cora had ever asked. And as futile. Kim wouldn't have the answers. She would hug her a lot and hold her trembling hands and stare at her with her big brown deer eyes, like she did now, but that wasn't helpful. It was Neisha who Cora needed, who she could count on to take charge and tell her what should happen next. This was why you had different friends. Like different shoes, they suited different occasions.

"I guess you start with telling Lincoln and take it from there?"

Lincoln! It was strange how little thought Cora had given to him in the past ten game-changing minutes. Now he came slamming into her mind so hard that she had an instant pounding headache. If Cora had managed to have some semblance of calm (shock in disguise) before, it vaporized at the mention of his name.

When Cora was twelve, she'd stolen the answer key to an algebra test. It was a dumb thing to do on many levels, not least of which was that she probably would have aced the final anyway. But it was right there, sitting unattended on the teacher's desk, and Cora snatched it almost without meaning to; it would be an insurance policy against failure (aka a B). In the end, she didn't use it, couldn't bring herself to look at it at all, but that didn't matter since her algebra teacher—who was also one of her dad's favorite colleagues—figured out she'd taken it and told Wes, who immediately summoned her to his classroom. The longest walk of her life.

While she waited for her father to speak, to gut her with his disappointment, all she could think was, *This is it, this is when he could stop loving me.* On some level, deep and primal, she knew her father's devotion to be unconditional, but she had also never tested it, or considered the devastating possibility that your actions could cause someone to doubt, second guess, or even retract their love. In that moment, despite her dad's understanding and almost immediate forgiveness, she recognized that the only way to protect yourself from this possibility, from being forsaken, was to never let anyone down and never, ever fuck up.

And now she had fucked up. Royally.

Objectively, Cora understood her predicament wasn't (entirely) her fault, that she wasn't (entirely) to blame, that this (she couldn't even give name to what "this" was) wasn't a moral failure, but none of it mattered. She was in trouble—in so many senses of the word.

The shame of it filled her like hot liquid from a never-ending fountain—thick, molten, and oozing everywhere.

Kim jumped up, wet some paper towels, and dabbed at Cora's sweaty forehead. This was as effective as holding a plastic bag over your head in a monsoon.

"Do I really have to . . . to tell him?"

"Um . . . yeah, I think so."

She didn't, though—she didn't have to tell anyone ever. Cora allowed herself this magical thinking for a solid six minutes before she finally got up, trudged to her room, picked up their phone that was shaped like a red patent leather high heel shoe and paged Lincoln: *911*.

An hour later, they met at the little public park just off campus where Chris, who was a local, had told her he used to play tag in elementary school. *Chris.* She hadn't thought about him in months. It had been a year since she'd lost her virginity to him, but it might as well have been ten. Or never happened at all. It was disconcerting how something that had seemed so pivotal then was already merely a blip on the screen of her life.

Lincoln found her doubled over on a bench.

Cora couldn't bring herself to say the actual words, so she just pulled the pregnancy test out of the back pocket of jeans and thrust it at him. Then she squeezed her eyes shut so she could avoid registering his shock and then fear and then anger and then whatever came after. If she never saw his face in that second, there was no risk of having his expression permanently etched on the stone wall of her mind.

Finally, when the apprehension became too much, Cora opened one eye, tentatively, like she was watching a horror movie and squinting to see if the machete-wielding killer had jumped out of the closet yet. Lincoln was staring at the swings on the playground like they had answers. She was frantic for him to say something, *anything*.

Is it mine?

How did this happen?

What are you going to do about it?

All her reference points for possible reactions were straight out of Afterschool Specials. "The more you know," all right.

Cora braced herself for every response except the one that came. Lincoln dropped to his knees in front of her like he was about to propose. He grabbed both her hands in his. “Okay, okay . . . this is no big deal, we got this.”

No. Big. Deal.

The rage that bowled Cora over was as unprecedented as the circumstances, a meteor exploding into fiery embers that could burn her up from the inside out. But perhaps it wasn’t actual rage but the hormones that had clearly been ravaging her (and that explained not just the nausea but why the moon had made her cry the night before) because it disappeared just as fast, replaced by hard, hiccupping sobs. Lincoln held her and let her tears and snot pool across his thighs while she wailed into his lap, muffled and incoherent.

“No big deal? It is! It is the biggest deal! What about going places? Law school?” Cora became increasingly shrill as she blurted out random phrases. “The plan! Too young! Diapers! My dad!”

Notably absent from the spoken list but as loud as ever in her mind was *my mom.*

“Bella, Bella, calm down. Seriously, it’s going to be okay.”

Lincoln had never lied to her before.

“I can’t . . . have a . . . ” She couldn’t say the word.

Cora had never even babysat! She’d had zero interest in taking responsibility for someone else’s child, even if all it amounted to was warming a bottle or reading a book while the parents went to the Cheesecake Factory for an hour. The one infant she’d held belonged to Ms. Hayes, the Prescott school nurse. She was a friend of Wes and had brought the red-faced child around to meet him, and suddenly Cora found the tiny floppy body in her lap and Ms. Hayes beaming at her. “You’re a natural. Look at her, Wes.”

Cora was not a natural; she was stiff and timid and, if she was being honest, more than a little grossed out by the infant acne dotting the baby’s face. She was also extremely uncomfortable when Ms. Hayes smiled at her beatifically and said, “Just wait until you have one of your own and can know a love like this.”

Even at the age of eleven, Cora recognized this was a presumptuous statement—she wasn’t even in middle school yet, so why was this woman talking to her about becoming a mother? It was as preposterous as Lincoln talking about it now. Cora didn't want a baby now. Maybe not ever.

Lincoln's life plan included two or three children who looked adorable in glossy campaign ads; Cora knew this in the same way she knew he wanted to be the kind of man who palmed large tips into valets' hands and ordered custom tailored suits—without him saying so. But this was a conversation they weren't supposed to have for *at least* five years. Not now. Cora had thought she had time, plenty of it, to confront the fact that she never intended to become a mother and face all the reasons for it.

Cora got some air into her lungs—a struggle—to steady herself so there was no question or confusion about what she said next. "I can't have a . . . baby." She barely got the word out and vowed never to say it again.

"What do you mean, Cora? It's not like we really have a choice." She caught Lincoln's gaze floating to her abdomen and fought not to cross her hands over her middle.

"Actually, we do . . . " That choice was left unspoken but it was there. Right there. She met his eyes for the first time that afternoon.

"No!" Lincoln leaped to his feet and walked away so fast, she thought he was leaving. He abruptly turned, strode a few feet back toward her, then pivoted away again, muttering the whole time. "No way, Cora. That's not an option. It's wrong. Period."

"This isn't about right or wrong. I just can't do it." It was impossible to make this more clear. If throwing herself on the cold asphalt would have helped, she'd have done it.

"You can. Plenty of girls do it. Aretha Franklin had her first kid when she was like, thirteen. She had four kids by thirty and that didn't stop her from living her best life."

Aretha Franklin? That the Queen of Soul had entered this conversation was such a level of stunning irrelevancy that Cora came close to exploding into laughter. Or maybe that was also the hormones.

"And my mom was twenty when she had me."

As far as role models went, Deb Ames was even less helpful.

"Lincoln, I—"

"What if my mom had decided to abort me? Huh, Cora?"

"Lincoln! That's not fair, I—" She ran out of steam before she could even begin to counter that argument.

"Look, Cora, I know this isn't what either of us planned, but you never know what's going to turn out to be a blessing."

A blessing.

This was what broke her. That her life being upended could possibly be "a blessing." That Lincoln had already accepted a baby as a foregone conclusion, practically before the pee on the stick was dry. Then there was the way he'd said, "Plenty of girls do it." The way he had the audacity to turn his lips up into something precariously close to a smile. It was probably meant to be reassuring but had the exact opposite effect.

Cora couldn't tolerate it. Any of it. Somehow she'd assumed they'd be on the same page, even if she hadn't known what exactly was written on that page, but instead, Lincoln was asking her to choose. Not intentionally and not directly, but the realization that he would never go along with—or forgive—her having an abortion hit her with the strength and bite of a slap in the face.

Mere hours before, Cora was marveling at all the ways her life could unfold, all of the possible options and outcomes before her, and now everything had narrowed to making one stark, life-altering choice. Actually, two viciously intertwined choices—becoming a mother or not; losing Lincoln or not. Unless . . .

An alternative solution started to form, a drastic one. It might allow her to keep Lincoln, but she could lose something else . . . herself.

CORA DOES WHAT SHE DOES

October 2000

If you really put your mind to it, you could convince yourself of a lot—including your own essential goodness. It just required enormous effort, especially when all evidence would point to the contrary.

Cora exhausted herself justifying her actions: She was sparing Lincoln from compromising his morals. She was saving him from being involved in a decision that could haunt him for life. She was protecting the plan. She was doing this for him as much as for herself. In that light, Cora was able to rationalize that she was acting selflessly. If Lincoln ever discovered what she'd done, he would surely understand that.

But also, that could never, ever happen.

That was Cora's last thought before she nodded solemnly at Kim to pick up their red stiletto telephone. Whoever designed this ridiculous object obviously did not imagine anyone having a conversation more serious than ordering pizza.

Kim nodded back, took a steadying breath, dialed Lincoln's number, and spun the story they'd rehearsed. Cora had had a sudden miscarriage. Kim had taken her to the doctor to be checked out. She was fine now and just needed to rest, et cetera.

It was just as well that Cora couldn't hear Lincoln's reactions on the other end. Kim, having delivered the performance of a lifetime, hung up. "He's on his way."

This was inevitable and yet Cora still wasn't ready to face him, the hardest part of this whole harrowing ordeal. Harder even then walking across the parking lot this morning and facing down the wild-eyed protester who spat at her, *"Baby killer."*

"Thank you for doing that, Kimmie."

Cora had doubted her own ability to be convincing so she'd accepted Kim's offer to make the call on her behalf, cowardly as it was. Now she had that to feel bad about—letting Kim do her dirty work—on top of everything else.

"That's what friends are for," Kim said, coming over to sit on the edge of Cora's twin bed, opposite her own.

It wasn't true, though. Friends were there to lend you clothes or money, to listen to you complain about your family, and, yes, hold your hand after your abortion. Maybe even give you a kidney, but you should be responsible for your own lies.

"Oh, Kim, what have I done?" Cora wailed and pulled the covers over her head. She didn't know if she meant the abortion this morning or the lying now, but both filled her with the dread of absolute finality; there were no take-backs. "I'm not a terrible person, right?"

"Oh, Cora, nooooooo, no, no, no. You're doing what you need to do. It's just hard. Really hard. That doesn't make it wrong."

Kim had had to remind Cora of this at least once a day over the past ten days, starting with the moment Cora fled from Lincoln in the park and returned to their dorm room with a tear-streaked face, wind blown hair, and a sheer, billowing panic in her eyes that anyone who'd ever felt like they were out of options would recognize. She'd told Kim what she intended to do before there was time to let doubt creep in, demanded promises for absolute *to-the-grave* secrecy, and followed that with the first of many distraught pleas for Kim not to think she was a monster.

Kim had immediately pulled her into the Nest and laid her head on Cora's thin shoulders. "You couldn't be a bad person if you tried, Cora."

"Well, I'm giving it a real go."

"Oh, hush. I'll be right back." Kim had left Cora cocooned in a pile of faux silk floor pillows, too distracted by contemplating what a massive mess she was in to wonder why Kim had bounded off. The mystery was solved when she returned lugging the four-inch-thick Yellow Pages that lived on the dorm lounge's communal phone stand.

"Okay, let's do this." She flipped a few pages to *A*—and just above Automotive Parts, they found one clinic in the area.

"It's only like an hour from here. I can get us a taxi there and back. My treat. I can also help you pay for . . . the procedure . . . if you need help?"

Given that Cora felt completely hollow inside, it had been a challenge to wrestle herself up from the floor, but she'd stretched to reach the phone and felt even sillier than usual bringing that stupid heel to her ear. "Let's call now." It was important to keep up that momentum, a rushing river she could surrender to that would carry her along from here to there.

There being Lilac Women's Center at six o'clock this morning, where Cora had sat next to Kim in the cramped waiting room. It had all the trappings of the reception area at a dentist's office—*People* magazines and medical posters, a pile of clipboards holding various forms. Even a candy dish. But Cora had never seen a woman crying waiting for the dentist, as the blond woman in the corner had been. She was old, at least forty (Cora couldn't tell how old most adults were and so just assumed they were forty), and Cora found this surprising—she'd pictured being in a roomful of distraught teenagers. Everyone politely ignored the woman's sobbing, including the man next to her.

Lincoln, had he been here, would have at least taken Cora's hand. Or brought her Kleenex from one of the half a dozen boxes scattered about. But Cora couldn't give Lincoln the chance to come around, to be the guy who filled out the forms and brought her a little paper cone of water from the waiting room's cooler, because the risk was too great he wouldn't. The trick was not to set people up to let you down—it was easier to need forgiveness than offer it. Also, crucially, she was protecting him. She kept telling herself that.

It was Kim who was holding Cora's hand so tightly her nails beds turned white when the nurse came through the door that had a four-inch metal bolt, which, along with the inch-thick bulletproof Plexiglas around the reception desk, was another feature you wouldn't find at a dentist's office. Cora was summoned to a small, freezing room, where she floated through the motions of changing into a faded gown, settling onto crackling paper on the exam table, placing her feet in stirrups, splaying knees. Obeying the doctor with kind eyes. *Just a little wider, hun. Can you scoot down for me? Another inch more.*

It was odd what your brain focused on to distract you and then held on to—the lone red balloon drifting through the air at a funeral; the commercial jingle in the background when you got the call. For Cora, it was the doctor's wire glasses, how they were askew on her face and how much Cora wanted to reach out and straighten them as she waited for the anesthesia to sweep her into temporary oblivion.

When she woke up, alone, a few hours later, on a stiff cot in the recovery room with dim lights and a scuffed little table stocked with cookies and orange juice, Cora held her breath, waiting for whatever emotions would show up like unwanted party guests. The guilt she'd expected, but it was offset, somewhat, by the profound relief. The surprise was the newfound feeling of fortitude. Cora had made an impossible decision, one that would affect the rest of her life; she'd summoned resources and wherewithal she wasn't aware she had, and, though she knew better than to admit this, she was sort of proud. Going through this crucible had allowed—forced—her to prove something to herself: that she was *equipped*. There was simply no way to know if you were (or could learn how to be) except by facing down an ordeal you wouldn't choose for yourself in a million years. So, although Cora wished none of this had ever happened, obviously, she clung to this unfamiliar, fledgling sense of resilience the way you would grip a life raft in the open ocean, understanding that it had the power to save you.

A nurse smelling faintly of baby powder, a scent that was lovely and wrong, entered the room. "You doing okay, sweetie? You can go whenever you're feeling ready." She extended a wrinkled hand and Cora took it and sat up, a movement that made her wince with a dull pain blooming from her belly.

"This'll help." The nurse handed her a bag with thick pads and a bottle of prescription-strength ibuprofen. "Do you have someone who can stay with you the next few days while you take it easy?"

"Yeah, my friend Kim's in the waiting room."

"Good, good, a friend like that is priceless. You'd be surprised the number of women who show up here all alone. We have volunteers to take them home, but I can't imagine anything lonelier."

Nor could Cora.

"It's important you have someone to talk to. You did something difficult today, and you should open up about it if you need to." The nurse rubbed her back, and Cora, who'd managed to keep it together all morning, came close to ruin at one shattering thought: *This is what it would be like to have a mother.* She blamed the lingering effects of anesthesia for allowing her thoughts to betray her.

Lying in bed now, trying to absorb Kim's words—"It's just hard, not wrong"—Cora remembered another protester, a frail woman with a shock of white hair. She was waiting in the clinic's parking lot when Cora and Kim left and could barely hold up her sign, which featured an alien-looking fetus and the words I'M NOT A CHOICE. The old lady looked at her with an almost comically intense frown and said, "I'm sorry you felt like you had to do that." And Cora met her eyes and said, "Me too."

Truer words had never been uttered as far as Cora was concerned.

Kim squeezed Cora's arm now, transmitting one last burst of reassurance. "Look, I'm going to go before Lincoln gets here so you can have some alone time. I'm headed to Fabiene's with about nine hundred condoms. You're like a billboard for birth control. No offense."

Laughing intensified the cramps but the fleeting moment of levity was worth it. "None taken." Cora grabbed Kim's hand. "Thank you again."

"Will you please stop saying that! Friendship means never having to say thank you."

"What about I'm sorry?"

"No need for that either. You have nothing to be sorry for, Cora."

It wasn't the hormones that brought tears to Cora's eyes. The brightest silver linings of the darkest situations was that they revealed who you could count on and which people would show up for you. It tested and strengthened your relationships and made whatever you were going through almost worth it for that fact alone. Cora had lost a lot of tears, a lot of weight, and her mind these past weeks, but she'd gained something too, a new understanding of friendship, the way it constantly stretched and grew to hold and heal you.

"Oh, shoot, I almost forgot!" Kim strode across the room and started digging in their overflowing communal closet. "Neisha sent this for you. I'm supposed to give it to you today to cheer you up."

Kim held up some sort of garment with an array of brightly patterned swatches stitched together in a chaotic fashion.

"Is that a . . . sweater?"

"I think so? Or something like it. Homemade."

Neisha had recently abandoned her pre-med major and was now studying fashion design, much to her parents' dismay.

Cora reached over for the sweater and held it up. "Um, it's . . . kinda hideous, right?"

"Oh, definitely. With Neisha's sewing skills, it's probably good she isn't gonna be a surgeon after all. She better see you wear it, though." With that, Kim leaned over, pecked her on the forehead, and headed out the door.

Cora's uneasy twists and turns to find a comfortable position in bed mirrored the acrobatics in her mind. She remained in full physical and mental disarray when the door swung open thirty seconds later.

"The paperwork!" Kim hollered. They'd left the clinic's discharge instructions on Cora's desk. Kim snatched the papers and ran back out the door. "I'll keep them in my bag!"

Not ten minutes later, Lincoln arrived, out of breath, armed with hot cocoa, cookies, and concern. He was still in his bookstore uniform, complete with sweat stains from his dash over. Cora had carefully timed the call for when he'd completed his shift that day, a small courtesy she would never get credit for.

"Oh, Bella. Are you okay?"

Absorbing Lincoln's naked worry and love was her penance. He climbed in bed with her in his khakis and green polo and spooned her, rubbing her back in slow soothing circles. The kindness was so much more harrowing than anything that had happened that morning.

When he jumped up and went to fill a Ziploc bag with warm water from the hall bathroom tap to create a makeshift hot-water bottle, Cora slipped into silent, ashamed tears, which she let him mistake for sadness when he returned.

"I don't deserve you," she whispered into his neck.

"I know, but you get me anyway." Lincoln poked a little at her side as he teased her, sending a live wire of pain radiating deep into her abdomen, which she relished, because that—that she did deserve.

"Oh, sorry, I didn't realize you were in pain. Need these?" Lincoln picked up the bottle of prescription painkillers on the floor by her bed and read the label. "Lilac Women's Center? What's that? You didn't go to student health?"

Here was another lesson: Lies required more lies.

"Yeah, um, no, Kim had a bad experience there, so she insisted I go to a fancier place she knew about—you know how she is."

The way Lincoln immediately accepted this with a little shrug while Cora's heart felt like it was going to explode in her chest made her wonder if she would survive her lies or drop dead of deception.

Lincoln leaned over, kissed her neck, and let his soft lips move against her skin as he spoke. "I'm sorry this happened, Bella, but it's for the best, I guess. You're going to be okay."

He was always so certain of that. Lincoln was always so certain of everything.

He pulled her face toward him so his nose was touching hers. The rest of their two bodies converged, their noses, their chests, their hips; even their feet were coiled together. There was no space between them physically. This should have been comforting, but instead, Cora was smothered by the heat and tangled limbs and intimacy. Her sense of suffocation wasn't physical, though; Cora was being smothered by the weight of her actions.

As close as Cora and Lincoln might have been or would ever become, the lie lived wedged between them now, as real and permanent and altering as—a child. Staving off regret was exhausting work; Cora drifted off in Lincoln's embrace, realizing only later that she'd mumbled something like *Can you ever forgive me?* in her drug-induced, guilt-laced haze. In the restless dreams that followed, he always said yes.

CORA GOES SOUTH

November 2000

Her goal had been to be able to look Lincoln in the eye by the time they drove to Mississippi to spend Thanksgiving at his mom's, but Cora wasn't quite there yet—she worried she might need years, decades. For the next nine hours, though, she would have a reprieve from making eye contact with Lincoln as they sat side by side in Julian's borrowed Honda, which shook and shuddered when forced to go above sixty-five miles an hour. If they stopped only twice, which was Lincoln's food and bathroom allotment, they'd arrive by sundown.

Listening to the Fugees' "Killing Me Softly" with Lincoln's hot hand keeping the beat of the music on her thigh and the miles passing in a soothing monotony, Cora could almost forget everything that had happened over the past few weeks and what she'd done. Almost.

The thunderstorm that had followed just behind their taillights across North Carolina finally caught up with them just as they crossed into Tennessee, unleashing a torrent of rain that sent thick sheets of water sluicing off the windshield. It was around this point in the trip that Lincoln's mood took as ominous a turn as the weather had.

He'd gotten all worked up about his Latin American history professor, whom he was convinced wasn't reading his papers and just giving him (and the three other Black kids in class) a C no matter what. Lincoln was planning to write *I know you're not bothering to read this, you racist* in the middle of a paper to prove his point. Gradually, though, right around the time they saw the very first sign marking the miles to the Mississippi state line, Lincoln got quiet. With just the rhythmic whoosh of the windshield wipers as white noise, Cora thought about how many different types of silences there were—comfortable, fraught, tense, expectant, and so on—until she found herself in the unbearable category.

"Are you okay?"

"Yeah, yeah, I'm cool."

Cora hadn't expected a different answer; she knew better at this point. When these moods descended on Lincoln, it made it worse if she tried to pull him out of it instead of pretending that everything was fine. Although Cora had never been good at make-believe. It was the reason she'd never bothered playing with dolls.

"Hey, let's get some barbecue!" Lincoln was suddenly animated, like this was the brilliant solution to an unnamed problem. "I know a place off eighty-five. Smokies. I think I can find it again." He was already swerving to the exit, passing so close to a hurtling eighteen-wheeler that Cora braced for impact.

Cora's life had barely stopped flashing before her eyes, when they heard an explosive popping sound and the car started shuddering violently. Cora held on to the dash as Lincoln guided the shaking vehicle to the gravelly shoulder of the empty back road.

"What was that? The transmission?" Not that she knew what a transmission did or what it sounded like when it conked out.

"No, I'm guessing a flat tire. I'm gonna check it out." Lincoln opened the car door, letting in a blast of cold, damp air, and hustled around to the back. When he returned, he brought in more chill along with bad news.

"The back tire's completely blown and there's no spare. I should have checked, Bella. That's on me. But freaking Julian . . . who doesn't have a spare? I'm going to run back to the gas station where we turned off the highway and get someone to come fix it."

"I'll go with you."

"Girl, are you crazy? No. It's still raining. You'll get soaked. I can run and it'll be faster." He was already bundling up and tightening his shoelaces like he was setting off on a marathon. His jack-in-the-box energy served him well in a crisis—he was wound tight and ready to spring into action. "Be right back!" He went out the door without kissing her, which she had the nerve to notice.

For lack of anything better to do while she waited, Cora got out a book that she'd tucked in her bag in case conversation ran out and they needed some help—*1,001 Essential Questions for Couples.*

It was not meant to be a solitary activity but she considered it a productive use of her time to think of responses to *Describe your first heartbreak* (an easy one—she hadn't had one, lucky her!) and *What does your partner think is the sexiest thing about you?* That was as hard as the previous one was easy. Cora finally settled on her . . . toes? Lincoln once called them sexy, which was ridiculous; they were knobby and took up too high a percentage of her feet overall, but his assessment helped her hate them less. It was funny how all the parts of you that you thought fell short—the gap in your teeth, that weird birthmark, the bump in your nose—could be made over completely in someone else's eyes. From hideous to hot with one easy compliment.

A giant pickup truck sped by so fast, it set the car shuddering, and it occurred to Cora, stranded all alone on the narrow shoulder with nothing but a field of marshy weeds beyond, that her present circumstances were a setup for a serial-killer movie. Fortunately, Lincoln returned before she could replay the scenes from *Fallen,* which they'd rented at Blockbuster the night before and that she'd gotten through only by picturing Denzel Washington naked.

Lincoln slipped back into the car smelling damp and musty. "They didn't have anyone who could come now. We just have to wait until their guy—Gus—comes back. Shouldn't be too long, but who knows. I don't want to risk the battery by keeping the car on. You warm enough?"

Her shivers answered for her.

"Come on, let's get in the back where we can cuddle. It'll be cozy."

To avoid the rain, they climbed, clumsily, over the middle console and settled themselves in the back seat, with Cora lying in the snug wedge between Lincoln's thighs. The windows were so steamed up, they couldn't see anything beyond the faint red flashing lights of the hazards that created an eerie light show. It *was* cozy and chased away her thoughts of being murdered. Or at least, if they were murdered, they'd have this last moment. Lincoln's hot breath on her neck sparked another sort of shiver, little explosions that crackled through Cora's body before settling in her white-hot center. He reached up under her sweatshirt and tugged her bra aside, and his cold finger landed on her nipple like an ice cube. It responded by getting hard before he moved on to the other one. Cora arched against him and he pulled her shirt over her head, which gave him more room and purchase to paw hungrily at her breasts. Her exposed skin felt even hotter with the cool air and Lincoln's rough palms against it.

Cora had gone on the birth control pill as fast as possible, but she still had trouble letting go and giving in to sex the two times they'd tried over the past few weeks. It didn't help that Lincoln was so tentative with her, like she was fragile and would break if he pressed the wrong place. He'd asked her if there was permanent damage from the miscarriage, to which she could answer, honestly, no.

But today, the conditions allowed them to escape their inhibitions.

Cora wiggled out of her pants and underwear, climbed on Lincoln, and straddled him so that he sank deep inside her. They stayed still for a long time, not moving at all apart from Cora's muscles squeezing involuntarily against the fullness in her. Finally, she started rocking slowly, head thrown back.

Lincoln always kept up a constant stream of chatter during sex. "Do you like this?" "Does this feel good?" "Tell me how much you want it." It had taken Cora a very long time to register that these questions were rhetorical and it was okay if she didn't answer each one. Today, though, she did.

"Yes, yes, you feel so good." She repeated it for emphasis. And when he hit just the right spot and rhythm, she moved on to an impassioned command. *"Don't stop, don't stop, don't stop."* She braced herself against the window of the car, leaving one single handprint above his head in the fogged glass. When she came, her whole body quivered so much, she could have sworn she set the car rocking harder than the passing F-150 had.

Here was the wonder of sex—it was like silences; there were so many different types. Sweaty or soft, fast or slow, and you never knew and couldn't control how it was going to be. The vibe was something that developed outside of you, a vortex of its own, and you just had to go with the flow. Which was pretty much the only time Cora could succumb to anything so out of her control.

It also served so many different purposes. Sometimes it was just fun, sometimes it was because they were bored, sometimes it was a means to an end. That afternoon in a steamed-up car on a rural roadside, it was a way back to each other. After the strain and stress of the past few weeks, she felt something give way, if not between them, then at least inside herself—a loosening, a reprieve from the burden of her remorse. To test this, Cora stared into Lincoln's eyes, as steady a gaze as she had been able to hold in weeks.

"What?" he asked. "You wanna go again already?"

The sudden blare of a loud horn inches away from the car sent them on a comedic mad dash to put on their clothes, though it was suspicious when they both emerged from the back seat. And on top of that, Cora's shirt was inside out.

Cora fixed her shirt and hair while Lincoln set about becoming Gus's assistant. When they were done changing the tire, there were enthusiastic handshakes and they said goodbyes like old friends.

Lincoln got back in the car with muddy knees and a trace of grease on his cheek. "Real cool dude, that guy. He helps with Formula One cars over at the Charlotte Speedway."

Reason number 172 she loved Lincoln: He could always find a way to connect with anyone who crossed his path. Even a white man twice his age with two missing teeth and a tight T-shirt with a bald eagle on it that exposed two inches of hairy belly.

Cora had hoped to arrive in Shannon, the small town Lincoln was from, while there was some light so she could get a sense of the surroundings and orient herself. Instead they were met with a darkness like she'd never experienced, an inky black drape over everything. Not a streetlight to be found or a star to be spotted in the cloudy sky. Occasionally, their headlights swept over a broken-down wooden structure on the side of the road or caught the glowing eyes of some small animal she couldn't identify. It was hard to tell how Lincoln knew where to go absent any road signs or landmarks. He was a homing pigeon.

Finally, they turned down an uneven dirt road that sent the car jiggling, and the Honda's headlights illuminated a scattered semicircle of three trailers around a patch of gravel and crabgrass; one of them had the faint blue glow of a TV screen flickering in the window.

Cora fixed her face to hide her distress at the angle of the mobile home and the unsteady cinder blocks that acted as stairs. The whole structure was noticeably tilted to one side, so Cora cocked her head to make it look even, something the foundation itself couldn't do.

"Yeah, it's not much, but it's home." Lincoln shrugged. "Come on." He might as well have added, *Let's get this over with.*

"It's great!" she said in a voice approximately six octaves higher than usual.

The cigarette smoke was an immediate assault on her nose and lungs, even her tongue; she could taste it. Much to her dismay, Cora started coughing before she could even choke out a hello to the woman sitting in the corduroy armchair holding the stub of a burning cigarette and mesmerized by a chirping host on QVC.

"You need some water?" Deb asked, suspicious and skipping right past hellos.

"No, no, I'm fine." Cora patted herself on the chest to have something to do with her hand. "Just happy to finally be here. We got held up with a flat tire and . . . " She looked around for Lincoln to pick up the story but he'd disappeared with their bags after a quick "Hey, Ma."

"It's nice to . . . " As Cora continued her nervous greeting, she stepped forward and leaned over to hug Deb, but she could see she'd horribly miscalculated; Deb glared at her in confusion. Cora stumbled back and thrust out the box she was carrying. The rest of the sentence came out as one long word: "Meet-you-I-got-you-this."

When it was clear Deb wasn't going to reach for the floral box, Cora placed it on the metal table next to her.

"What is it?"

"Uh, a candle?" A pricey lavender soy candle Cora had gotten at the fancy gift shop where she'd bought the couples' questions book and that she now wanted to swallow and make disappear.

"What for?" The question seemed so genuine that Cora felt compelled to come up with a sincere answer.

"Oh, just to . . . I don't know. Relax?"

Lincoln returned, rescuing Cora from any further explanations about self-care.

"Bummed I missed the boys. They been asleep long?"

"Yeah, stayed up as long as they could. They'll be up early in the morning. You can deal with 'em then."

"Cool. All righty, then, good night. Come on, Cora."

That was it. As she followed Lincoln down the tight hallway, Cora counted on her fingers how many words they'd exchanged with his mother. The idea of sharing a whole strained Thanksgiving meal tomorrow made her want to run straight into the pitch-black night.

They passed a room without a door where Lincoln's three brothers were sleeping, all tangled on one mattress together.

"We're gonna sleep out here. There's blankets and a space heater, so it should be okay."

A rickety screen door on the back of the trailer opened onto a makeshift indoor porch. The space heater was alarmingly ancient with a frayed cord. One look at the thing and Cora knew she was going to have to stay up all night vigilantly monitoring it for signs of malfunction and potentially saving everyone from burning to death in a tin can.

They stood for a minute squinting into the shadows that expanded everywhere outside the window. There was an outline of a building a few feet away. "What's that?"

"Oh, the old chicken coop. Remember how I told you I'd get fresh eggs in the morning when I was a kid? I'd reach under a hen and practically catch the egg as it fell out. And over there, you can't see it, but that's the stump where we'd kill 'em. Lock its head in a little wire, and then I'd take an ax and . . . " Lincoln made a sick whacking sound.

"That's horrible!"

"Says the girl who downed chicken nuggets on the way here."

"But you had to do it yourself—kill something. I could never . . . "

"Eh, I'm a country boy, goes with the territory."

"I'm just glad our turkey tomorrow is coming from a store. It is, right?"

"No, we're going hunting for it in the morning."

"Lincoln!"

"Calm down, I'm kidding. Come on, let's go to bed."

Bed was half a dozen itchy blankets that they fluffed into a pile thick enough to resemble a mattress. Cora pressed herself against Lincoln to get as much body heat as possible. As usual, he had no trouble falling into a deep sleep, leaving Cora alone for a long, restless night.

Morning announced itself with a loud chorus of insects and a mist rising from the damp earth. As soon as there was the barest hint of sunshine breaking through the window slats, there were three gangly boys screaming and jumping on them.

"Get off us, you hooligans!" But Lincoln just pulled his brothers closer into the pile, raining fake punches on them, and giving them noogies. They roughhoused so much, Deacon's right hearing aid popped out, and everyone stopped to look for it on the wooden planks.

The break presented time for introductions.

"Y'all, this is Cora. Cora—Deacon, Elliot, and Lawrence." Lincoln pointed at them one by one; they'd naturally sorted themselves by age and size order. Little Lawrence was missing two teeth, and his tongue filled in the space when he grinned. He belonged in a Cheerios commercial.

Cora had never seen Lincoln use sign language before but his long fingers were well suited for it; he looked like he was conducting an invisible symphony. He and Deacon, who had the lanky awkwardness of a teenager growing into his limbs, communicated for a minute before Lincoln turned to translate. "He says you're pretty. I told him hands off."

"How do I say thank you?"

Lincoln showed Cora how: bringing his hand to his chin and then extending it out in front of him.

Deacon signed something back that she took to mean *You're welcome.*

"Can you ask him if he'll teach me more?"

"Yeah, yeah, but first things first. We gotta get stuff to make a meal today. No doubt the fridge is empty, huh?"

Ten-year-old Elliot nodded solemnly.

"Okay, then, y'all come on with me to the store. Let's let Cora and Mama rest."

The boys scrambled to get dressed while Cora's brain scrambled at the thought of being left home alone with Lincoln's mother, though he assured her she'd probably sleep in.

Cora made instant coffee she'd found in one of the chipped cabinets, drank it black so she didn't use the last inch of milk, took a shower, and dried herself with one of Lincoln's T-shirts, since she wasn't sure where to find a spare towel or if she was entitled to one. Her hair was a disaster from all the rain and back-seat sex but she slicked it into a respectable bun. She put on her Thanksgiving Day outfit, beyond relieved that she'd talked herself out of wearing a dress. Even in her striped button-up, she feared that every time Deb looked at her, she'd be screaming *This uppity li'l so-and-so* in her head.

In the living room, Cora tiptoed around like the trespasser she felt like, looking for clues to Lincoln and his beginnings. There were two framed pictures sitting on a metal TV tray in a corner. One was of Lincoln's parents on their wedding day. In it, Deb was smiling or something close to it, which was likely the first and last time that happened. It looked out of place on her face, even in her white dress with puffy chiffon sleeves that encased her tiny shoulders like cupcake frosting. The other photo was of Lincoln when he was about Lawrence's age; he had an almost identical gap-toothed smile and was holding a snake. Cora wanted to pick up the picture to examine it at length but she was too terrified to disturb the thick blanket of dust that surrounded it, so she leaned over for a closer look. It was still hard to believe, despite this clear proof, that Lincoln had ever been this young. Or that he'd had to grow up so fast.

Next to the cracked frames was a heavy black telephone. She longed to call Wes, who she imagined was just starting to make his "world-famous" pecan pie to bring over to their neighbor's house for Thanksgiving dinner, but she had no way to pay for the long-distance call ahead of time, and she could see Deb losing it when the bill came in.

Two more steps and Cora had covered the whole living room. She stopped to look out the main window through a film of bird poop and fingerprints. The two other trailers looked empty; the whole area seemed empty, desolate. Stretching in both directions was nothing but red-brown dirt and towering trees as thin as they were tall. She wanted to find it serene, but instead it felt ominous. Rattlesnakes and hunters and swampy marshes and ghosts. Cora had never felt farther from civilization, or at least her idea of it, which, sadly, involved malls and McDonald's. There was no way there was a Kroger anywhere close by, so she couldn't imagine where Lincoln was getting groceries. She pictured an old-timey general store with hard candies at the register. (And a vintage WHITES ONLY sign.)

There were two chairs in the living room. Deb had been sitting in the one closer to the TV, so Cora knew to give that one a wide berth. She settled in the other one, sitting upright and formal, ankles crossed, hands in lap, lest Deb appear and think that she'd gotten too comfortable. Not that she needed to worry—Lincoln's mother didn't emerge from her bedroom until the thick of the afternoon, after the boys had returned with brown bags of groceries and Lincoln had set to work on the meal. Deb shuffled to her place at the kitchen table in a nubby bathrobe and held court, bossing the boys around and grumbling about everything from her bad back to how the satellite dish kept falling right in the middle of *Wheel of Fortune* and could Lincoln climb up and have a look.

At four p.m., as if an invisible clock struck, Deb ambled over to the kitchen sink in her slippers and reached under it for a clear unlabeled bottle with a few inches of brown liquid. Two refills in, she offered Cora some, and it would have been rude not to accept it even though just the smell wafting from Deb's glass was enough to burn Cora's nostrils and make her eyes water. Cora got down a sip without coughing and it was the most accomplished she'd felt all day. Even Deb appeared impressed, if surprised. That look of respect disappeared faster than the moonshine down Deb's throat.

"So, you don't cook?" Every question Deb asked came out like an accusation. Cora forced down another swig, wondering if a personality was something you could get used to, like this whiskey.

"Leave her alone, Ma. I told her I got this."

Lincoln was putting the finishing touches on whatever he had brewing in an enormous cast-iron pot that looked to be from the Civil War era.

A bowl of corn-bread batter was coming together on the side. He poured grease from a tin can on the back of the stove into a hot skillet.

"Can I set the table, though?"

Everyone looked at Cora as if she had two heads—everyone except Deacon, presumably because he didn't hear her offer.

"Just chill, Cora. It's all good." Lincoln turned and signed something to Deacon, and he came over and sat next to her. "You said you wanted to learn sign. Deacon's going to teach you the alphabet."

Cora mastered letters *A* through *F* pretty easily but her hand stumbled over the hook of the *G*. "Wait, like this?" She turned to Deb to include her in the conversation.

"Don't ask me." Deb threw her hands up, communicating her disregard as clearly as if she'd said it in ASL.

"You don't know sign language?" It was Cora's turn to make an accusation disguised as a question.

"They're supposed to be teaching that boy to *speak* at that fancy school so he can get along out here."

One didn't seem to have much to do with the other but Cora was hardly about to point that out. Same way she wasn't going to say a word about how Deb's wig kept slipping farther and farther to the left. Instead, she turned to Lincoln. "Food almost ready?"

"Yep, let's eat."

Lawrence passed out plastic bowls and they all lined up at the stove for Lincoln to ladle them full. Cora grabbed the empty bowl in front of Deb to fill it for her, and the smack to her hand was a shock. "I got it, girl. I don't need you touching my soup." She pointedly stretched around Cora to give the bowl to Lincoln. "Fill that up, boy."

They settled around the metal table and the steaming bowls. Cora gulped a big spoonful before she realized everyone was grabbing hands for grace.

Deb reached her nicotine-stained fingers for Cora's hand with obvious reluctance. "Go on ahead, Link."

Lincoln bowed his head and spoke for a longer time than Cora would have expected about the blessings of food and family and God's generosity. "In His name, all things are possible. Amen."

Everyone started sipping soup, quietly, as if they were waiting on something, which they were—for Deb to speak.

"This is good, Link. Real good." Deb slurped, oblivious to her wayward hairpiece.

"Thanks, Ma."

"I raised a good boy here, Coral."

Maybe it was a power move or maybe Deb was too drunk to remember Cora's name, but it didn't matter. Cora decided to let Deb call her Coral forever, since she wasn't brave enough to correct her and it was already too late.

"You did." Cora was ready to gush about how she felt about her son but decided restraint was in order. *Less is more* seemed to be Deb's motto when it came to affection, conversation, and heat. (Cora was freezing.)

Before they could clear the plates, Deb had nodded off with a lit cigarette in her hand, its inch-long ash hanging precariously close to a pile of dirty napkins.

"Should we help her to bed?" Cora asked as Deb's head slumped ever closer toward the table.

The boys were putting leftovers in old margarine tubs, and Lincoln didn't so much as glance his mother's way. "Nah, she'll be all right. Can y'all finish the dishes?"

His brothers said they would, and Cora followed Lincoln back to the porch. They lay down, and the space heater at their feet burned their toes but left the tip of Cora's nose ice cold. She angled her head to rub her nose against Lincoln's.

She missed his warmth when he abruptly rolled away from her onto his back.

"Was tonight okay, Bella?"

"Yeah, of course, more than okay. It was nice." It was what she needed to say and what Lincoln needed to hear. And it *was* nice—meeting Lincoln's mother (for better or worse) and being in this place he was raised, she'd glimpsed something fundamental about him—the source of his drive, his defiance, his resourcefulness. You couldn't truly know someone until you understood where and who he came from.

"I don't know if you were expecting matching towel sets or cloth napkins or something, but this is it, Cora. This is where I'm from. And don't get it twisted—I'm not ashamed of it. It's made me who I am."

It was like he was challenging an unspoken assumption she'd made.

"Of course you aren't ashamed, Lincoln."

He was quiet for a long time, but Cora had learned to wait. If she didn't rush to fill the silences, sometimes Lincoln would. Her patience was rewarded.

"You know, Lawrence once asked me—dead serious—if our mom loved us. Like it was a real question with a straight-up yes or no. I tried to explain that she loves us the best way she knows how: by being angry—even though she's angry at the world for being what it is. All her bluster . . . her hardness, she's just trying to prepare us for it, toughen us up. She was always so terrified we were going to be soft. That was the worst thing we could be—weak."

Lincoln's voice got strangled at the end, like the words were getting caught in his throat, which made Cora's own throat ache. This was the vulnerability she was always craving from him, and now she saw why it was almost impossible for him to show it.

She didn't dare move so she wouldn't spook him. After a beat, he went on.

"I'm gonna do it all different though, Cora. First off, I'm gonna be there for our kids, day in and day out. And I'm gonna hug and kiss 'em all the time and tell them I love them so much they'll get sick of hearing it. And I'm going to buy them everything I can afford, and I don't even care if they're spoiled, because it's way better to be spoiled than go without. The only people who don't think so have never woken up on Christmas with no gifts. I'ma let you be the tough parent, with the rules and the discipline. You'll be good at that."

Lincoln closed his eyes like the matter of their future children and parenting styles was decided.

It was her turn to open up, if for no other reason than this would always be the moment when Lincoln wondered why she didn't.

"What if . . . what if I don't want kids, Lincoln?" Posing it as a hypothetical allowed her some mental space to maneuver.

Lincoln reached out and actually patted her head. "Like ever? Come on, Cora. You're just saying that because of . . . what happened. It's too fresh. And, whatever, we don't need to think about that now. We have time. It's all good."

"You make everything sound so simple, Lincoln. It's not always like that."

"Isn't it, though? You get a hand, you play it. When you don't have a lot of choices, it keeps things pretty simple. You just gotta go with what's in front of you and make the best of it. Your problem is you make things harder than they need to be. You've always had everything you ever needed or could possibly want. All options are available to you . . . clothes, food, colleges. When things are that easy, there's no sense in trying to make them harder. Doubting and overanalyzing and whatnot."

You've had everything you ever needed or could possibly want. Lincoln really believed this to be true, and on top of that, he resented her for it. It was enough to send Cora rolling over across the dusty wooden planks away from him. She needed space. She needed to be facing the wall of blackness of the backyard if she had any hope of getting out the words, fighting hard to be swallowed back down.

"What the—you okay?" Lincoln sat up, perplexed by Cora's sudden agitation.

"You think I've just had this cushy, ideal life. But it's not like that . . . my mother didn't die of cancer, Lincoln."

"Wait a minute—what?"

"Yeah, she killed herself, okay?" She wasn't sure Lincoln heard her because she'd choked this out in a hoarse whisper, the highest volume she could manage. Her mouth moved, gaping like a hooked fish's, as she struggled to go on. "I don't really know why. I don't know if you can ever know why. My dad . . . he never . . . well, we don't talk about it. Ever. But maybe it was something with having me, like postpartum depression? I don't know, but she . . . " Cora had said it once and that was hard enough. "I was almost two. Just old enough to think I remember her singing to me and the way her bangs curled over her eyes but not really be sure of it. So, yeah, it *is* simple for me to say I don't want to have kids, because I don't want to end up like her. And anyway, what would I even know about being a mother since I never really had one. So . . . "

Cora tested the idea of forging ahead, telling him about the abortion, with the hope that he would better understand now, knowing this, her ugliest truth. But then, though she should have known better, Cora looked over her shoulder and saw Lincoln's face. The look he was giving her—the one that said she was damaged, tainted, pathetic—was too much. Cora quickly calculated what she could withstand, an assessment she was constantly making lately. Her psyche was a raft and she was vigilantly measuring what weight it could take without sinking. Cora's current calculus led her to press her lips shut and curl into a fetal position. Lincoln's care, shock, and pity (which was difficult enough to endure) would transform into something else (rage?) if she told him the rest of it, and that would be too much. The equivalent of being simultaneously hugged and strangled.

"Whoa, Cora. I don't know what to say." She'd managed to leave Lincoln Ames speechless.

"There's nothing to say. It's why I don't talk about it. So don't bother trying, okay?" Though it wasn't that she didn't want Lincoln to say anything; she didn't want to risk him saying the wrong thing. Something ruinously, irrevocably wrong.

"But . . . but maybe you do need to talk about it?" He reached out to touch her, and she flinched so quickly she hoped he didn't notice.

"What, like with you? A therapist? My friends?" An idea so preposterous she scoffed, which she also hoped he didn't notice. But of course he did.

"Don't act like it's so crazy. That's a lot to carry, Bella. A lot."

Even in the shadows of the porch, she could see that expression was still there. She couldn't bear to have him look at her like that another second, much less forever.

"I'm fine, okay? I don't need to talk about it and definitely not tonight. I just . . . I just wanted to tell you."

Lincoln grabbed her pinkie, understanding that was all the contact she could tolerate. The vulnerability made her wild-eyed and panicked, like a wounded animal hiding under a bush, terrified of anyone, no matter how well-meaning, approaching.

"Well, it's good you did, Cora. I don't want us to have secrets."

Dread pulsed through her so savage and toxic, her whole body shuddered. It was another critical juncture—Lincoln could always come back to this, to right now, as the moment when she also should have come clean about the abortion. *No secrets.* But she couldn't tell him. Or wouldn't. There wasn't much point in trying to distinguish between the two.

"It wasn't a secret. Like I said, I just don't like to talk about it. It was a long time ago. I never even knew her."

"Cora. It was your *mother*. You knew her, even if you didn't know her."

She'd been terrified of what Lincoln would say, but this softened her. They took long breaths together, an accidental meditation. Cora was relieved when it appeared Lincoln had drifted off so she could concentrate on getting each of the six hundred rigid muscles in her body to release in turn. She started with one hand, although both were balled into tight fists, but Lincoln's voice sent her tensing up again.

"Can I just ask you one thing, Cora?"

"Okay." She braced herself for *How did she do it?* or some other gruesome inquiry, but she should have given Lincoln more credit. He asked the one question she welcomed.

"What was your mom's name?"

Cora whispered it, sweet and rare on her lips, like a candy you craved but denied yourself: "Adriana."

She would forever be grateful that Lincoln let that be the last word.

October 5, 2002

Oh, man, C. I'm sorry to hear that you're having such a hard time. I can see how getting your diploma in the mail would send you spinning. I bet this is going to happen from time to time, especially as the adrenaline you've been burning through in crisis mode keeps wearing off, and what you've missed out on (like crossing the stage in your cap and gown) hits you. Sometimes I wonder what it would have been like to cross the stage myself, but that's mostly for my folks' sake. I know deep down they wanted a son who would do that, one whose GPA or honors or whatnot they could brag about. I guess they're good parents for pretending otherwise. But sorry, sorry this isn't about me. I wish I could help you.

I feel a little helpless being so far away. All I could think to do to cheer you up was make you a CD. I spent hours at the Virgin Megastore on the Champs-Élysées trying to find all the right tracks. Cheesy as hell. But music helps me. When I'm down, I play Sam Cooke. Maybe it's because his music reminds me of my parents playing it on the eight-track in our car on the long drive to Michigan to see my grandparents while my sister and I fought over whose turn it was to pass Dad a soggy ham sandwich from the cooler or who was better at I Spy. (Can you even be good at I Spy?)

Got off track again, bad habit. The point is, when you're feeling down, it helps to get your mind to a place where it feels safe, and music does that for me. Transports me. Lately, I have track two of your CD on repeat: "Next Lifetime." Erykah Badu can be my spiritual guru any day.

I also tried to get you a book that'd indulge your self-help addiction. Though you know I doubt that you can figure out anything about real life from a book. It's a learn-by-doing thing, as I see it, but there's no swaying you. My little bookworm. Maybe I'm just a hater, since books and me never jived too much. They didn't have anything good (in English) at

Shakespeare and Company, this legendary bookstore here, but it was a good excuse to go. Books may not be my thing, but bookstores are, which is a little weird, I guess. They're just peaceful and I like seeing what other people are into. Saw a dude reading a whole book about seahorses! Least as far as I could tell from the pictures—my French still isn't that great. I did find you the fancy notebook enclosed here, though, since I know you love those. Like you love your lists—maybe you can write down all the things that bring you joy? Or journal? Purging all those emotional demons with a pen could help. Or maybe you can get back to painting? Try a little exercise? (Don't roll your eyes—it's not like I expect you to run a marathon, but a walk around the block never hurt anyone.) Or sometimes you just need a pity party—I'm here for that too.

One thing I'm sure of . . . your friends haven't forgotten about you. Friendships just have ebbs and flows. (Says the introverted loner. :)) But I know what you mean, that feeling you described where your life is like a truck driving right by you and you're jumping and waving your hands but you can't get it to slow down or stop. Or like when you're on a train that's standing still and another train next to you starts moving and there's an illusion you're going backward when you're actually not moving. It can feel like everyone and everything is moving on without you—but just like the train, it's an illusion. Your life's not biding its time; it's not waiting to begin, Cora. It's happening right now. You're living it. Every second. That's so easy to forget—try not to do that, okay? Maybe you should go to the trellis to get some fresh air? It's a stretch for me to think of it as "our spot," since I only took you there that one time. My parents would have lost their minds if they knew my favorite place to hang as a kid was the abandoned, overgrown railroad track behind the Mormon temple. At least I wasn't drinking or drugging it up, which, judging by all the empty bottles there, other kids were doing on the regular.

Okay, confession: I wanted to kiss you that day (and a few others).

I thought it might happen. Our pinkies were touching as we lay on the grass and it felt like an invitation. But like I said, I didn't want to come on too strong. I don't know—was I imagining all those secret glances and "accidental" touches, the charged energy between us? I don't think so.

But the moment never came. That stupid fox ruined it. I've never heard anyone scream so loud. It was like you'd seen someone charging at you with a chain saw, not a ten-pound furry thing walking along, minding its own business. But it gave me a chance to comfort you. And to hear that story about how you tried to nurse a sick chipmunk when you were a kid, keeping it in a shoebox under your bed until it died, and you were too scared to tell your dad who only found out when it stunk up the place. I'm sorry I laughed—it was funny, even though you were still sad about failing Alvin.

When the fox "charged" us (your word, though that might be a stretch, ha-ha), you had the same look on your face as you did when I suggested we walk out on the bridge. You surveyed the rotted wood and rusted metal like you were an engineer. That's part of the rush, though, the rickety planks and looking at the water a hundred feet below—so far we couldn't even hear the faint splash when you accidentally kicked a piece of ancient railroad tie off the side—and knowing that you're on the edge and feeling that surge of adrenaline and the wind in your face and thinking you could die but probably won't.

Another rush was squeezing your hand and saying, "I got you."

The biggest rush of all was that you believed me.

So I'll say it again now: I'm sorry it was such a rough day, but I got you, Cora. I got you.

x, A

CORA DOESN'T SEE IT COMING

February 2002

Cora was always asking herself if she wanted time to speed up or slow down. The answer was both and neither, the sort of entangled thinking that gave her a headache.

As hard as she'd worked to graduate early, now, with the end of college bearing down on her in three short months, she could have used more time. For what exactly, Cora didn't know; she just had a general sense that she wasn't ready.

It was why she'd delayed turning in her grad-school applications, much to Lincoln's frustration. There was now only one program in Chicago she could still apply to for the fall. The fat sealed envelope with all her materials sat on her desk, ready to be sent off. All she had to do was slip it into a mailbox.

She vowed to do it today, before the impending storm hit and they were snowed in. She'd promised Lincoln she would do it by Saturday, their two-year anniversary. The momentous day Cora had traded *Dateline* for destiny.

But first, she needed toast. The only problem was that Neisha was on the kitchen phone screaming at her father, and Cora wanted to avoid having a front-row seat to yet another blow-up. Though, with the way Neisha's voice came barreling down the hall of the off-campus apartment they had all moved into together, Cora might as well have been two feet away.

"Well, I'm sorry I'm such a disappointment, Father, but you know what? You're not winning any Dad of the Year awards either! How about that?"

They had the same argument over and over. Neisha's father thought he could bully her out of her "silly" dreams of a career in fashion and into letting the hair on her bald head grow back. Neisha thought she could bully him into breaking up with his new girlfriend and out of his insistence that he knew what was best for everyone. It was, of course, impossible to browbeat someone into becoming a different person, but that was a reality neither of them seemed willing to accept.

They'd tried full estrangement for nearly a year but had recently traded that for explosive screaming matches. The former was quieter, at least, if no more effective.

Neisha had returned from London last May (with the shaved head, a vaguely British accent, and a habit of calling fries "chips") and told Kim and Cora that she had run off for the year because her parents had decided to divorce and she wanted to be far, far away when it happened. She'd avoided awkward holidays, tense standoffs, and having to choose sides by putting a whole ocean between herself and her parents' drama. By the time she'd shared this development with Cora and Kim—declaring herself "over it"—the papers had been signed, her dad had moved into the back room at his storefront accounting office, and he had met Misty. Neisha focused on her stupid name as if it were an unforgivable fault, but that was mainly because Neisha refused to meet her, so there wasn't much else in the way of ammunition.

After a beat of silence, Neisha screamed, "I'm done with this. With you! Don't call me again unless you have something supportive to say for once!"

At the loud slam of the phone in its cradle on the wall, Cora counted slowly backward from five. At "two" she heard the aggressive slam of Neisha's bedroom door, and only then did she slink down the hall to their bright galley kitchen. In the adjacent small sunken living room, Kim reclined on their couch in an emerald-green silk robe her dad had brought her from Japan flipping through an *Essence* magazine.

They all had their own bedrooms in this apartment, a fantasy they'd dreamed of when their dorm rooms and intimacy felt claustrophobic, but Cora sort of missed when they were within sight of each other at all times.

"Welp, that seemed to go well," Cora said in response to Kim's rolled eyes.

"Right? It's funny how she can't stop calling him stubborn. Who's going to explain pot and kettle to her?"

"Not it," Cora said, turning her attention to the dozen plastic grocery bags taking up the whole counter. "Do you think you got enough food, Kim?"

"I just got the staples—ramen, salt-and-vinegar potato chips, Rice Krispies Treats, batteries. And this . . . " She waved to the stack of poster boards, magazines, and glue sticks on the coffee table, supplies for them to create yet another round of the vision boards Kim was obsessed with. Kim placed a lot of faith in the effectiveness of cutting out pictures from magazines. Cora knew better—you couldn't will your desires into being with glossy photos from perfume ads—but she dutifully participated and nodded her head every time Kim said *manifesting*, the same way she did when Kim expressed her strong belief in the power of jinxing.

"You got a full gallon of mayo, Kimmie. It's not like we're going to be trapped for days."

"The mayo is for masks! And we might be! They're saying this could be the worst blizzard to hit Virginia in decades. See, it's already started."

Cora stepped over the sliding glass doors that overlooked a small square of parking lot. The sky was a menacing swirl of grays, and the chill pouring in from around the edges of the windows was especially sharp. A blast of wind sent the glass shrieking, causing Cora to stumble back a few steps. She didn't hear Kim leave the room, but when Cora turned around, she was alone. Except for the foreboding that had been keeping her steady company. She blamed this angst on the relentless ominous weather reports and hysteria around the "monster" storm that would stretch from North Carolina to Pennsylvania. It was preferable to blaming it on the real source.

Cora might have tried to talk to Kim had she not disappeared, but then again, she didn't know if it would help or hurt to give voice to her unease: *Things have been weird with Lincoln.*

It was probably pointless anyway because she knew what Kim would say: *You're being silly.* It was what Lincoln had told Cora on New Year's Eve, which she kept coming back to as the moment when something had shifted between them. Or maybe it was the day she lied to him about having a miscarriage. Or maybe it was when she told him about her mom at

Thanksgiving last year. Or maybe it was when she'd decided to spend the previous summer in Richmond with Neisha working at an art gallery while Lincoln went back to DC. He'd said, "You're just going to leave me like that?" when Cora wasn't the one leaving. Or maybe it was when she'd discovered that he'd quit his UPS gig but hadn't told her for weeks because "It didn't seem that important."

It was easy to spot a canyon; much harder to spy a tiny crack. Neisha had fractured her finger in December (a combination of Rollerblading plus ice plus lemon-drop shots) but didn't know it until, after her hand had stayed purple for an alarming amount of time, Cora and Kim forced her to go to student health. You could walk around with a part of you broken and not even know it.

This was what had been on Cora's mind on New Year's Eve when Lincoln found her sobbing uncontrollably in his bedroom under a pile of coats just after midnight. The guys had had a party at the Pound and she drank too much, mainly because she was on edge. Too many people she didn't know, too many girls paraded in front of her who knew how to dress and dance and enjoyed hanging all over Lincoln and the other guys while she busied herself rinsing empty bottles and refilling the Brita so people could stay hydrated. Cora was the one who dealt with the neighbors when they came to complain about the noise and kept covertly turning down the volume of the stereo in the living room every time someone turned it up. She felt more like an uptight den mother than a girlfriend, and Lincoln being so distracted all night didn't help. At 11:51 p.m., she started looking for him in the crowd packed into the living room and spilling over to the rickety back patio but couldn't find him anywhere. She stopped trying when the countdown to midnight began. Just as the crowd of drunken revelers screamed, "*One!*," Cora burst into tears, alone in the hall outside of Lincoln's room.

When Lincoln found her in his bed, buried under a mound of coats, he was clearly coming from outside because he was wearing the North Face parka Wes had gotten him for Christmas. He seemed to appreciate Wes's gift more than hers, which was a painting. Even though she wasn't in Sketch's class anymore, he let her use the studio whenever she wanted. He'd told Cora that she was talented, that she had potential if she'd accept that she didn't always have to color inside the lines, and he'd connected her with the Warren Gallery for her summer job. Lincoln had only half smiled when he ripped open the meticulously gift-wrapped canvas. "Oh, cool, cool, I'll put it up above my bed." He hadn't yet. The painting was right there, leaning against the wall beside a pile of Nikes. Cora added this to the list of reasons why she was sobbing. Also, perhaps, the six rum and Cokes she'd downed.

"What are you doing, Bella?" Lincoln slipped out of his jacket and threw it on the pile.

"Where were you?" Each syllable was pathetically elongated, especially the *yoooooouuuuu*.

"What do you mean?"

"I tried to find you and I couldn't."

"I was outside . . . I just stepped out for a minute. I lost track of time. I'm here now."

"But it's too late!"

This didn't make a lot of sense but it captured Cora's apprehension that time was slipping away and they'd missed something important.

"Too late for what?"

"We weren't together to kiss at midnight!" Cora wailed. It was, she worried, a sign of something. Though she was aware she'd sound insane if she tried to explain that.

"Oh, Bella, I'm here now," he repeated.

"Are you, though?"

She still wasn't making much sense, but she knew what she meant.

That's when Lincoln had told her she was being silly. "You just drank too much is all."

Kim bounding back into the living room was a welcome distraction from this memory that Cora had worked over too many times.

"Well?" Kim sashayed toward her like she was on a runway, dressed in a bright magenta ski suit with flaming orange stripes across the chest and knees and matching magenta goggles.

"Why are you dressed like a Black Picabo Street?"

"Winston's never seen real snow before. We're going sledding!"

Kim's new boyfriend was from Jamaica. He'd lived in Miami since he was fifteen, but Kim treated him like he'd arrived in the United States yesterday and she was his personal cultural ambassador, exposing him to every formative touchstone he might have missed out on—*Family Matters*, Chia Pets, Dairy Queen. She'd already gotten them tickets for the Orioles' opening day to "introduce" him to baseball. It was as if Winston were a transplant from Mars or a time traveler rather than a guy from the Caribbean, where, Cora was pretty sure, they had sports and sitcoms. But he seemed to genuinely appreciate Kim's efforts and Kim herself in a way the Rabbit and Fabiene hadn't. (Exhibit D for despicable: Fabiene broke up with Kim not twenty-four hours after returning to Rome, by email and *in Italian*; having to translate it added an extra and unnecessary layer of indignity.)

Cora found Kim's romantic exuberance endearing—and relatable. She understood why Kim framed and displayed an excessive amount of pictures of herself and Winston: Sometimes you needed the proof of your happiness around you. *It's real—look!*

"You and Lincoln should come sledding too!"

"Maybe later, if it's not too bad out, but now I need to stop in the computer lab before it gets too bad."

Classes had been canceled for the day in anticipation of the bad weather but Cora was planning to print out the study guide for her Spanish midterm so she could make use of her time trapped inside.

"I can't believe you're that pressed about classes. Oh, wait, I can."

"Don't be jealous of my stellar study habits."

"No one in the history of the world has ever been jealous of *study habits*, Cora." Kim groaned affectionately as she left the living room.

Layers were the key to winter dressing. Cora pulled on item after item—long underwear topped with her heaviest Champion sweatpants, two sweatshirts, two mismatched scarves, gloves, and hat—so that once fully outfitted, she couldn't drop her arms to her sides or bend her knees. Kim looked like a glamorous Olympian while Cora looked like the marshmallow man from *Ghostbusters*. But at least she was warm. At the last second, she grabbed her grad-school application to slip into the mailbox.

Stepping outside was like entering a snow globe—heavy, wide flakes swirled around in blasts of frigid wind that couldn't seem to decide which way they wanted to go. An especially feisty gust slammed the building's door hard behind her, dislodging a pile of snow from the eaves above her that fell smack on top of her head. As with a lot of things, snow was considerably more appealing from a distance, not when it was whipping around you and stinging your cheeks.

Cora hoped her dad wouldn't try to shovel all the snow that was coming himself. Knowing Wes, he would think he could, especially after he'd announced over Christmas break that he was getting into shape following a sobering admonishment by his doctor at his last physical. He'd transformed the upstairs guest room into a home gym, and stocked it with a top-of-the-line rowing machine, a ThighMaster (still in the box), and an inconceivable number of brand-new weights that filled the space with the scent of neoprene. Wes proclaimed he was going to get "ripped" like Hulk Hogan, which was the sort of hubris that would let him believe he could shovel four feet of snow. Cora didn't want to have to go home and tend to a father with a broken back.

She didn't want a broken back of her own either, so once she was in the computer lab, she slowed down and took deliberate baby steps in her snow slick boots. She could have just settled at the closest monitor—they were all free, since no one else was foolish enough to be here—but she walked all the way over to her favorite carrel near the row of printers. She liked being close to the bulletin board so she could peruse the random listings for gently used mountain bikes and pottery classes and other eccentric hobbies she could take up. Cora tried on the idea of salsa dancing while waiting for the clunky monitor to boot up.

It still seemed silly, the whole concept of electronic mail. Her freshman class had been the first to get email on campus, and though the university, and her Spanish professor, seemed really excited by the cutting-edge technology, there was some general confusion about who they were supposed to be writing to online and about what. Cora had reconnected with one of her old camp counselors who had email at her HR job and sent her a few weird chain letters, but other than that, Cora didn't see much point in it.

So her inbox was about as empty as usual: One message from campus officials with a weather alert. One message from her Spanish TA with the study guide. And a third from a sender she didn't recognize, ConcernedFriend23@aol.com, with the subject line *You Should Know . . .*

As far as mysterious teasers went, this was irresistible. Cora clicked without pause.

I hate to have to tell you this, but your boyfriend cheated with my friend and I think you should know. Lincoln did you both dirty and that's not cool.

It might as well have been written in code or disappearing ink for all Cora could comprehend from this jumble of words. She blinked slowly, counting every time her lids opened and shut, then tried rereading it, but the two sentences remained incomprehensible.

She closed the email with a different strategy in mind: pretending it didn't exist. Cora calmly dragged the mouse across the little square pad it rested on, navigated to the message from her Spanish TA, and sent the study guide to the printer. The machine roared to life, then stopped and the only sound to be heard was the thunderous rush in Cora's ears. There was a streak of fresh blood on the beige keyboard that Cora traced to the hangnail she'd ripped off her thumb. The red stain and the ache were a surprise. Cora looked up to find some guy with such large snowflakes in his dark silky hair that they looked like giant flakes of dandruff was talking to her—also a surprise. "You okay?"

"Yeah, fine."

Cora's tone, apparently, was not convincing. Nor was the way she didn't look at him but continued to stare into the middle distance, thinking of all things, about a video they'd watched recently in her geology class about the explosion of Mount Pinatubo—the largest volcanic eruption in history. She wanted to explain the abject shock she experienced watching this video to the stranger taking a seat a few carrels over. *One minute you're tilling rice fields and the next you're engulfed in a pile of fiery rocks.* But he was already looking at her suspiciously enough. "Um, you don't seem fine."

Cora had a vague plan to sit frozen in this chair forever, digging into the raw skin around her nail, and never having to deal with the snow and the cold . . . or anything else. But the way the guy was staring at her, like he might try to engage her more or call campus security propelled her to her wobbly feet and out the door, abandoning the still warm pages nestled in the printer.

The numbness in her calves made for slow going but she hoped it would take over her whole body. She picked up a handful of hard snow and held it against her chest, willing it to have the same effect. It did nothing but leave a wet spot over the place where her heart banged hard against her ribs.

The park wasn't where she thought she'd end up, but that was where her legs carried her. Everything was buried except for the top of the metal slide, the one that Lincoln had insisted they go down together one day last fall. They kept getting stuck and falling into fits of laughter mid-slide, and eventually a six-year-old appeared and asked if they could please get off so he could have a turn.

Besieged by gusts of snow and memories, both equally sharp and painful, she decided going to the park had been a terrible idea and what she needed was a nap. She sweated through all her layers speed-walking to the safety of her room. Normally Cora refused to put even her backpack on her clean bed, but now she crawled under the covers in her damp and dirty clothes and willed herself to sleep, well aware that she was delaying the inevitable.

It was déjà vu when she awoke to Kim, still in her ski suit, hovering over her, worried. "Cora Belle taking a nap? I've never seen you nap before. You sick or something?"

"No, no, I'm just tired, I guess." She wasn't trying to mislead Kim, but Cora still wasn't ready for the email to be real. She leaned into the logic that a development of this magnitude was like a tree falling in the forest when no one was around to hear; if your best friends didn't know, it hadn't happened. It offered a temporary reprieve. "What time is it?"

"Four . . . you missed sledding. Lincoln called while you were out. I just got home and checked the machine. He said he's scooping you up at five, so you better get up. I just came back to grab some stuff to sleep at Win's. No idea where Neisha is. She didn't leave a note."

"Oh, okay."

Why she put on a turtleneck sweater dress and tights, Cora didn't know. Some inchoate notion that getting your heart broken was serious business, so she should be professional about it. It certainly wasn't like she was trying to look nice to prove something. She had the good sense to know that none of this was about her appearance. That did beg the question she'd been putting off all day: Why, then, Lincoln, *why*? Because she knew what the email revealed was true. For one, Cora doubted some anonymous person would concoct such a lie. But there was also her gut. In this instance, it screamed with a certainty. It was a twisted sort of solace that there was at least one thing Cora could still count on—her intuition. *Things have been weird.* The words she never dared say out loud from some childish belief that saying them would make them true. As if you could jinx your relationship.

But Cora already decided the *whens* and *wheres* and especially the *whys* didn't matter, because what reason would be acceptable? She had also already decided she wasn't going to cry. Not out of any sense of pride but because if she started crying, he would try to comfort her, and it was too perverse to be comforted by the person who was the cause of the pain. And also because if she started crying, there was a real risk that she'd never stop.

While Cora struggled to remember how to execute the simple task of putting on a bra, Kim buzzed around, her giddiness infecting Cora with lethal levels of bitterness. Cora was supposed to be the happy one. If one of them was going to be dating a cheater, it should be Kim—she was the one who was always picking losers! It was, hands down, one of the most despicable thoughts Cora had ever had, but given the circumstances, she gave into it. Her silent resentment was a victimless crime.

"You and Lincoln can't be going out anywhere tonight. Everything's gonna be closed. Why are you so dressed up? And, wait, isn't that my dress?"

"Yeah, I just wanted to look nice, I guess."

Lincoln was also understandably confused by her attire when Cora slipped into the passenger seat of Julian's Honda. "Why are you out here in some tights? Your legs must be freezing."

"I don't know." It was the truth. Cora didn't know anything anymore. Whatever she'd thought she'd learned about love and trust and loyalty was all gone. Or, if not all gone, all wrong.

"You okay? You seem off."

"I know what you did."

"What are you talking about?"

"I got an email today."

"Email? From who?"

"I don't know."

"You're not making any sense . . . "

Cora needed to get to the point; she was only prolonging her agony. "You cheated on me."

Lincoln braked hard in the middle of the road and the car skidded a few feet across the icy pavement. He stopped and turned to her and said, without missing a beat, "It was nothing."

This was a small mercy, that he wasn't going to deny it so they didn't have to bother going through the charade—the further insult—of his lying about it.

"It was just twice, okay? Two times, that's all. Three, tops. And it was dumb. I . . . I don't know . . . I got caught up. But like I said, it was nothing. I mean, it meant nothing."

It meant everything, Cora corrected him in her head.

A car honked behind them, Lincoln started driving again, seemingly relieved to have something to do. "Say something, Bella."

She was pretty sure he was the one who was supposed to be doing all the talking: *I'm sorry, I'm a worthless monster,* et cetera. For her part, she had nothing. It was possible that she was doing this wrong, that the occasion called for screaming, wailing, crying, panic. Instead of shocked hysterics, though, she'd opted for detachment. Her heart was as frozen as the ground outside.

"I don't have anything to say," Cora said, pressing her face to the frigid glass of the passenger-side window to cool her hot cheeks.

"Let me explain, okay?"

They both knew he couldn't no matter how hard he tried. But he was going to give it a go anyway.

"First, this happened a while back, so I don't even know why this is coming up now. But, look, Cora, it was . . . I don't know, kinda heavy between us there for a minute, you know? Not just us . . . everything. Applications for law school and planning the move and how fast it's all happening . . . it just got real and—"

"That made you *fuck* someone else?"

It wasn't that Cora didn't curse just because Lincoln didn't curse, but she'd never thought that dropping F-bombs was something she could pull off, so she'd done it about twice in her life. Deploying one now, at this choice moment, was incredibly satisfying. The hard consonants on her tongue and Lincoln's surprise.

"No, I don't know . . . I started thinking about the future and everything. And how you maybe don't want to have kids—"

"Hold on." Cora had to reach out and do the same with the dashboard. "You had sex with this person because you want to have kids with her?"

"No, no! No way. Just meaning, yo, like . . . I started questioning everything. Are we right for each other and all that. Do we want the same things?"

"Well, last I checked, we *wanted* to move to Chicago in four months. We *wanted* to celebrate our anniversary at Lucien's. We very much *wanted* to be together."

"Nothing about that has changed."

He stopped at a red light, which was an ideal place for the streetlamp to illuminate Cora's face. And for Lincoln to take it in. The outrage spoke for itself.

"What I mean is . . . this stupid . . . slipup is ancient news. It doesn't have to mess us up. It doesn't change the way I feel about you. I just freaked out or something. I've only been with, like, three other girls, ever, before you. It was dumb. Just some . . . fun."

She gave him credit for realizing that *fun* was a terrible choice of word even before she yelped like she'd been Tasered. Actually, Cora would have preferred being Tasered and wished she'd had the choice.

"Okay, not fun! I don't mean fun! I mean, you and I have fun. I'm not trying to say you're not fun. It was just different, a distraction or whatever."

His desperate defenses had started to sound to her like the teacher from the *Charlie Brown* cartoons she used to watch: *mwah-mwah-mwah*. The words had little power to comfort her, but they also couldn't hurt her. "Can you take me home, please?"

They'd made it only as far as the roundabout in the center of town that anchored the main drag. Cora could see the gift shop where she'd foolishly bought Lincoln's mom a forty-dollar candle, now with a hand-painted CLOSED sign swaying in the window.

The road was lined with idling salt trucks and snowplows whose headlights captured swirling snow. Despite everything, Cora could still appreciate the striking beauty of a backlit snowflake hanging in the air. This was a welcome surprise and offered something like hope. There was a chance, slim as the point of a needle, she wouldn't be completely and totally annihilated by this—even if it felt that way right now.

"Bella—"

"Don't, Lincoln. There's truly nothing you can say."

He turned the car around and they drove in silence—the torturous kind. While she'd been sincere in telling him there was nothing he could say that would make a difference, it nonetheless destroyed her when he stopped trying. She had let him off the hook, even if that wasn't her intention.

When he pulled up to the little white gatehouse at the entrance to the apartment complex, Cora reached up and unclasped the necklace he'd given her the night of her birthday, the night he'd said *I love you* for the first time. The gold glinted in her hand as she let it dangle across her palm. She believed that he did love her, and she'd already begun the futile, excruciating process of deciding whether that had been a mistake or not. The necklace made a soft clang when she dropped it in the cup holder between the seats. If a sound could shatter, the two of them would be in as many pieces as there were flakes piled around them.

The car door groaned loudly when she threw it open, echoing in the snow-muffled evening. The skies had opened up, as if shedding all the tears that Cora refused to. The storm had been an omen after all. But that was the problem with omens—the warning was blazingly obvious only after the fact, when it was too late to matter.

Cora gently pushed the door closed behind her. It latched with the sharp snap of something breaking apart.

CORA ~~TRIES~~ FAILS TO KEEP IT TOGETHER

February–March 2002

Cora's herculean composure and improbable calm lasted eight days. What ended up breaking her was the smallest thing: finding Lincoln's favorite T-shirt in her laundry. It was the last Saturday of the month, so laundry day, and motion and routines were the delicate strings holding her life together. Cora had innocently enough dragged her plastic hamper down the hall to the cramped room with two washers and two dryers shared by the other apartments on the floor. She'd started dumping the contents into the mouth of the washing machine when the offending object tumbled out. She'd forgotten about this stupid T-shirt buried deep under her dirty underwear.

Had she just thrown the shirt into the washing machine with everything else, Cora might have been okay; her mistake was bringing it to her nose and taking a big sniff. Even though she was the last to wear it and even though it had been mixed in with less freshly scented items, the smell of it remained so unmistakably and uniquely Lincoln—Cool Water and musk—that she fell to her knees clutching it like she was in some sort of soap opera scene.

The dam gave way, flimsy little twigs against a raging river, and finally, there Cora was with a couple of dirty white Maytags bearing witness as she collapsed into the heaving, sobbing, snotty mess everyone—including herself—expected her to be.

In a way, the agony, when it came, was bracing, clarifying. Liberating, even. There was relief when the worst thing happened—you could stop fearing it. Except this time, Cora, for once, had forgotten to fear something. She'd let herself get swept away; love had made her complacent, smug. Recognizing her hubris sharpened the pain. She should have been more vigilant. She should have known better. She should have expected heartbreak and prepared for it like they had for the blizzard. Had she done that, she could have avoided being blindsided. Her fears had always protected her, and she had let her guard down. The great surprise was getting a boyfriend in the first place, not losing one.

It was like the time she'd spent hours making a sandcastle on the beach in Ocean City. She'd applied an industriousness at odds with the relaxing day. Her final product was exquisite—people wandered over to gape in awe. But Cora had miscalculated the distance to shore. A large wave came in and, just like that, her masterpiece was . . . gone. It was strange because she'd known it wasn't going to be permanent, yet she was still stunned by its abrupt destruction. Cora remembered all the tears she'd shed, leaving dark marks on the sand, and her dad embracing her to ward off despair. "Ahh, I'm sorry, kiddo. You'll build another just as beautiful."

But she couldn't—it wouldn't be the same, and it, too, would be washed away, so what was the point? It was a lesson that made Cora feel wise and mature beyond her nine years. And terribly sad. Why did those feelings so often go together? And why did you have to learn some lessons again and again? She was too good a student for that.

Actually, she wasn't a good student at all anymore—when Cora finally succumbed to her broken heart, she stopped going to classes in favor of locking herself in her room and giving in to every single cliché of heartbreak: eating pints of Ben & Jerry's Phish Food, allowing herself to be overtaken by spontaneous crying jags, replaying the highlights of their relationship in her head like the world's saddest slideshow, and listening to the pathetic breakup mix 24/7 on the MP3 player she'd gotten for Christmas.

Toni Braxton could truly comprehend what Cora was going through, the yearning for someone to unbreak her heart. Céline knew what it was like to be all by yourself. But it was Whitney that did her in every time: "Didn't We Almost Have It All?" Every time Cora got to the part about how "the ride with you was worth the fall," she unraveled, mainly because it got directly to the heart of her agonizing. Was it all worth . . . this? She looked at the stained sweatsuit she was living in as a symbol of "this," her broken, forsaken state.

While she believed that these R & B divas understood, if not her specific heartache, the general misery of lost love, there was an unbreachable gulf between herself and the real people she interacted with outside the confines of her headphones. The loneliness of being newly single was bad enough, but it was compounded, cruelly, by the isolation of being trapped in a cycle of grief while everyone else went about their lives. (Cora tried to be thrilled when Kim booked a flight to go to Jamaica with Winston for spring break, but they both knew she'd failed.) At least the sun cooperated, not showing its face very much that spring, as if in solidarity. Cora spent many grayed-out afternoons staring at the white wall next to her bed, wishing she had a way to get answers to the questions that tormented her: *Why does the pain get worse at night just like a cough? Where does all the love go? How long does it take to get over someone?*

She'd actually asked Kim and Neisha that last one, expecting a real answer. Instead, Neisha jumped up from the couch where she'd been oiling Kim's scalp and grabbed Cora with two greasy hands.

"That's it. You've been moping around for weeks. Get up!" Neisha pulled her to her feet. "We're going to lunch. To CJ's. You love CJ's and you're going to get your favorite grilled cheese and tomato soup and you're going to have some wine and let me make you laugh."

"And then what? What's that going to do?"

"And then maybe you talk to Lincoln? Hear him out, at least?"

Cora threw herself back against the couch with such force, she knocked over a lamp; it fell and gouged the floor, leaving a scar. Fitting. "No! No way. And you broke the rules—you know you're not allowed to say his name."

Neisha and Kim exchanged a look over her head. "Cora. The dude has called here four hundred times a day for weeks now. I can't even be in this room without sneezing from all the flowers he's sent." She gestured to the bouquets in water glasses in varying states of decay that Lincoln had dropped off when Cora wasn't home or was hiding in her room. "Yeah, he fucked up. Big time. But he's sorry. Clearly. Maybe just hear him out at least? Curse his ass out. Make him grovel."

"Why do you even care? It's not like you liked him anyway." Cora glared at Neisha, daring her to deny it.

"Damn, Cora. That's not fair. I care about *you* and I hate seeing you like this. My opinion about Lincoln doesn't matter."

"Ha! That is rich. Since when is your opinion not the only thing that matters?"

Heartbreak was like the flu; every day a new symptom overtook Cora, and today, apparently, it was bitchiness.

But she spoke the truth: Neisha didn't bother pretending she liked Lincoln. Cora had tried to come up with a specific reason why Lincoln and Neisha never vibed but eventually she gave up and accepted that sometimes, inexplicably, two people could repel each other. That it was two of her favorite people had made her sad, but it didn't matter now.

"And how you're always going on about how 'they all cheat'? I guess you were right."

To think, Cora had pitied Neisha for her cynicism. To think, Cora had been annoyed that Neisha didn't give Lincoln enough credit, that she didn't understand he was different, *special*.

"I'm such an idiot." Cora said it with finality, the last word on the matter.

Kim got up to move from the couch she was on to the one opposite, where Cora was sprawled in stained sweats, head hidden under skinny arms. Cora looked up and stopped her with a scowl, and Kim sat back down and spoke to her from across the coffee table.

"You're not an idiot! Lincoln's the one who should be ashamed. He's the idiot to do this to you. But is there a world where you can see past this? Last week, Winston totally forgot I had that huge case study to present in my business admin class. He didn't say a word, even though he knew how nervous about it I was. I mean, you didn't either, but I give you a pass because you've been a hot mess. I yelled and I cried, but then he said he was sorry, and I got over it. Forgiveness is important in a relationship."

The outrageous comparison sent Cora to her feet; she punched a hole through the living-room wall while screaming at the top of her lungs, *"Are you kidding me!"*

At least, that's what happened in her mind. In reality, she robotically stood up so she could leave the room before she did do something that unhinged. Not for another single second could she take Kim's sanctimony or Neisha sitting there thinking *I told you so* or being subjected to what felt dangerously close to an uninvited and unwelcome intervention.

"I'm going back to bed."

Neither Kim nor Neisha stopped her.

Later, Cora ducked out to go to the bathroom, and found a bag of carryout from CJ's by her bedroom door. Spooning the lukewarm soup into her mouth, she realized she'd forgotten all about food. She put the empty cardboard bowl on top of the stack of new books on her bedside table.

The only time Cora had left the house the past two weeks was to go to the Borders in the mall, an act of desperation. She'd made a beeline for the self-help aisles and perused as many books on healing from heartbreak as she could find, aching for help in the form of research, practical advice, and expert recommendations, books with titles like *You Can Heal Your Heart.*

Yes, please. How? Cora bought five hardcovers with her emergency credit card and stayed up all night reading and highlighting line after line as if she'd be quizzed in the morning.

Meanwhile, her textbooks remained unopened. The Bs she would end up getting in poli-sci *and* geology would mar her GPA, but she didn't care. In fact, she appreciated that they would serve as permanent evidence of the extent of her despair: *See how bad it was?* Not that it mattered much anyway; it would all be over soon—the semester, her time at college, and, she could only hope, the heartbreak.

The next day, or maybe days later, who could know, Cora sat on the nubby carpet in her bedroom and stared at her reflection in the full-length mirror. She was supposed to be giving herself a pep talk—today was the day she showered, or left the house, or made herself a meal—but instead she took in the bonnet she'd been wearing so long it might as well have been permanently attached to her head, her sunken eyes, and her ashy elbows and thought about how she'd come so far to go nowhere.

Then the door to her bedroom flew open, and standing there was the last person Cora expected to see.

"Dad?"

Neisha was right behind him, in Wes's literal shadow.

"What are you doing here?" She turned to Neisha. "Did you call him?" The question had an accusatory bite.

"No one needed to call me, Cora. You haven't returned my calls in weeks. I know when something's wrong with my daughter. I woke up this morning and got in the car." With some effort, he knelt down next to her. "Now, what's going on?"

"Nothing."

"Well, my eyes say otherwise and they're not lying." He turned to Neisha, who was lingering in the doorway. "Could you please give us a moment, Neisha."

She left, shutting the door behind her, and Wes looked around, taking in the half-empty wine bottle she'd been swigging from, the empty Lean Cuisine boxes and ice cream cartons and the clumps of tissues scattered about. Cora could sense his increasing alarm.

"Don't do this to me, Cora. I mean it. If you're in trouble, we can get you meds. A therapist. You can come home if you need to. I'll take you right now. We can get in the car this minute."

The panic in his voice was palpable and it wrenched Cora out of her malaise. Of course he would be utterly terrified seeing her like this, and that wasn't fair. She could pull herself together for him; she had to.

"No, Dad, it's okay, really." She stood up with straight shoulders and made a show of smoothing her mangled hair to try to prove this. "I'm sorry, I'm sorry. I didn't mean to freak you out. I'm just sad. Very sad. But I'll be okay." In her urgency to convince her father of this, she was able to persuade herself too. It was like being trapped in a well and suddenly noticing a ladder you'd been blind to; it was possible to climb out, however many rungs, however slow going. "I promise."

With loudly creaking knees, Wes got up, and they both settled on the bed as if to regroup. "You can't worry me like this, Cora. I always need to know you're going to be okay."

"I know, Daddy. I know."

"Now, what happened and what can I do?"

"There's nothing you can do . . . Lincoln and I broke up."

"Oh, baby girl, baby girl." Wes pulled her face to his shoulder and held her tight. "I'm so, so sorry to hear that. You guys have been through a lot."

"What . . . what do you mean?"

"I don't want you to be mad, okay? But Lincoln told me what happened last year. You having a miscarriage. All you've been carrying. It was bound to catch up with y'all one way or another. That's a lot for a young couple."

"I can't believe he told you!" Cora tried to pull away from her dad, but he only tightened his hold in response. Had she been able to wriggle free, she would have run out of her room, out of her apartment, across campus, across the state of Virginia. She never would have stopped, and she still would not have been able to outrun her mortification.

"I'm sorry, Daddy." The words were muffled against the soft fabric of Wes's sweater.

"Oh, honey, you have nothing to be sorry for."

It was torture to bear all this care and concern when scorn and judgment would have suited her better.

"I did the one thing you told me not to do. I almost ruined my whole life." The same gut-wrenching panic resurfaced, like it was yesterday. It was not unlike having flashbacks to a genuine brush with death, the stomach-plunging adrenaline and fear that the future you'd expected was gone, instantly. You could never forget how close you'd come, no matter how hard you tried. And, oh, how she'd tried.

"Oh, Cora, you didn't ruin anything. You'd have been fine. I'm going to see to it that you're always fine, long as I'm around. Stuff happens and you can't be too hard on yourself. It does you no good to beat yourself up—it doesn't change a damn thing about what happened or what will happen. Like I said, I just wish you'd have called me. It's my failure that you didn't feel like you could come to me."

"It's not you. It's me. I was too ashamed. And Lincoln shouldn't have told you. It wasn't his place."

"That may be true, but he was just struggling and needed some advice about how to support you. He was all torn up when you lost the . . .

the pregnancy. Even if it was for the best. Do you think you need to talk to someone?"

"No." Maybe, but not about the abortion—about this, all these layers and levels of treachery. "I just . . . I can't believe he did that." She wasn't sure which betrayal she was referring to.

"He wasn't trying to hurt you by telling me. I know that for sure. He was worried about you is all."

"Just like he didn't mean to hurt me by cheating on me?"

Wes unlocked his grip on her and nudged her away in shock. "Say what, now? He cheated on you? Damn that boy! What was he thinking? He wasn't thinking, that's the problem. Or thinking with the wrong part of his body."

Wes was talking to himself as much as to Cora, but then he seemed to remember his audience. "Oh, honey. I'm so sorry. Boys are immature. They haven't gotten control over their . . . manhoods yet. I don't want to be crass, but that's the truth of it. Every temptation calls at that age, so loud you can't think straight. I'm not making excuses for him, but Lincoln has a lot of growing up to do, just like you."

"You're always talking about character. Well, lying and cheating is bad character. Period."

"I can't argue with that. But character's one of those things that you work at, that you fine-tune through life experience. Sometimes people need a chance to build it. I've done some things in my past I'm not proud of. We've all hurt people. Even me."

"Don't start talking to me about forgiveness, okay?"

"Well, I might have to, Cora, because it's an important life skill. Fact of the matter is people are going to mess up, kiddo, even people you love. And you're going to have to dig deep in your heart over and over again to decide if you're able to see past those disappointments. I'm not saying that's what you should do here, but just in general, this isn't the only time someone is going to let you down, sadly. Only you can decide if you're up and willing or able to give that person a second chance or not."

"Could you forgive him?"

"For hurting my favorite daughter? I don't know. But what I would or would not do doesn't matter one bit. I will say this, though, if we cut everyone out of our lives for messing up, we'd all end up real lonely."

"This is partly why I didn't want to tell you. You love Lincoln like he's a son. And—"

"Oh, no, no, no, stop with that right now. Let there be *no* confusion. You're my daughter. I'm Team Cora all the way. I have a good mind to ground you for the very first time for even letting that thought cross your mind. But I'm not gonna lie, I do hate this. For both of you. I was looking forward to taking you two out to dinner at graduation next month. And what about Chicago? What about grad school?"

"None of that is happening." Her plans for the future had disappeared faster than a sleeve of Chips Ahoy cookies in Neisha's hands.

"Graduation is absolutely happening, young lady. I've been waiting twenty-one years to see you walk across that stage. I'll be damned if anything gets in the way of that. But the rest of it . . . well, there's time to sort that out. You have so much time. I'm just gonna keep making sure you understand that."

"It doesn't feel like it."

"I know, I know. That's the hard part. It never does."

"Daddy?"

"Yes, baby girl?"

"Could I come home this summer? I mean, I'm not going to Chicago anymore, so . . . "

"Cora Rose Belle, look at me."

Her father was blurry through her wet eyes. "You never have to ask to come home. Never. Now, come here." He pulled her back into his tight embrace, making her feel like the little girl she had once been and sometimes wished she always could be.

"It hurts so much, Daddy." Cora surrendered to the wails she'd been holding in; streaks of snot ran down her face. Her father wiped at them with his bare hands.

"You're going to be all right, Cora. It's not always going to feel this bad."

"I'm never going to let this happen again. I'm never going to let myself love someone again, not Lincoln, not anyone."

Deciding never to open her heart again might have been extreme, but, extreme in the same way you might have to saw off your arm to get out of a trap. It was what you had to resort to to survive.

"Oh, honey, you feel that way now, but it's never a good bet to turn your back on love. Take it from me."

Cora went limp against her father, drained of the sadness he'd let her pour into him. "No, I mean it. Never again."

CORA HAS NO IDEA

April 2002

The tattoo was a terrible idea.

But that was part of its appeal, so Cora let Neisha talk her into it. It would be small and tasteful and hidden, and it would symbolize something. The weight and pressure to determine where and what paralyzed Cora, as did the dozens upon dozens of options laminated on a long wall in front of her.

This mission—marking her body permanently—called for significantly more preparation than she'd done, but had Neisha given her more warning than she did (twelve hours), Cora would have talked herself out of it entirely. The spontaneity was another part of the appeal, but it meant that right now she had to identify an image that meaningfully represented her whole life and self. It was a lot of pressure to put on a butterfly or an infinity sign.

Finally, Cora settled on a compass on the back of her left shoulder with some hazy notion about it reminding her to always find her way. But really, the selection was made in haste because the guy with the sleeve of snake tattoos up his arm was impatient for her to choose something, anything already so he could get to other customers. And Neisha, who'd decided to put her lucky number—13—on her ankle with much less agonizing, insisted that they had to be done by five p.m., in time to make it for the two-for-one margaritas special at Rio's.

Afterward, peeking at the freshly inked skin under the slimy gauze, it wasn't that Cora regretted the tattoo itself—which would have been pointless anyway, since there were no take-backs—but she hated the symbolic power she'd invested in it. Having a tattoo didn't magically imbue her with all the qualities she'd assumed the type of person who got a tattoo would have. When would Cora accept that she couldn't merely dress up as a persona to make it so? You could wear all the leather you wanted; it didn't make you a biker chick . . . or a cow.

Nor did the compass have the power that Cora had hoped it would. After it had oozed and peeled and started to heal, Cora was no less lost about what came next, as directionless as ever.

There were signs of progress, however, since the day last month she would think of as rock bottom, when her father had shown up and spoon-fed her vanilla pudding and washed and changed her sheets. She'd reasoned it would only be up from there, and it was.

She regularly showered again now, and she hadn't cried in five full days, not even when she'd come across the ticket stubs she'd saved from the first movie she and Lincoln ever saw together (*Erin Brockovich*). Memories didn't have the same ability to destroy her as they'd had mere weeks before. And another positive sign: Cora had laughed, belly-laughed, when Neisha told her she'd gone on a date and ripped her pants all the way up to her butt as she was getting out of the guy's car, and as if that weren't bad enough, it exposed the ugly granny panties she'd worn to head off sleeping with him in case she was tempted. Cora used these moments as glue for all her broken parts.

By the time the spring career fair rolled around, Cora had just enough emotional wherewithal to put on her best Limited suit and the black blocky heels she almost never wore and set about a Hail Mary attempt to come up with a plan for the next one to five years of her life.

Under the soft petals of cherry blossoms floating from the trees surrounding the lawn, Cora too floated from booth to booth set up across the quad, all of which featured glossy corporate placards, out-of-place streamers, and corporate representatives offering firm handshakes and come-join-the-team energy.

Could she work as an account manager at State Farm? The title conjured nothing for her about the work itself, and insurance sounded deadly boring, but the representative said the "benefits package" was "solid" as if it were an offer Cora couldn't refuse.

There was a mile-long table framed by a massive balloon arch for Accenture and a small army of corporate representatives passing out branded tote bags like the keys to success were in them. Cora walked by as quickly as she could without making eye contact.

She was momentarily intrigued by a guy with tufts of unruly blond hair who made a convincing case about the glamour of advertising. "There's a reason you know all the commercial jingles! Getting people to want to buy stuff is powerful." He added that his firm was big on affirmative action, so she'd probably be a shoo-in for an entry-level job. At that point, Cora handed him back his brochure and speed-walked as fast as her uncomfortable shoes would allow to the booth where they were offering free doughnuts.

She plopped down on the wide steps at the entrance to the building that housed the career center and advising offices and ate her chocolate-glaze, letting crumbs fall onto her blouse. She thought of going upstairs to see her adviser, Ms. Reardon, who just last week had given Cora a copy of *What Color Is Your Parachute?*, which remained unopened in her backpack but ultimately decided it wasn't worth the effort to climb the four flights to her office in these shoes on the off chance Ms. Reardon was there to offer a generic pep talk about Cora's "considerable promise."

But the copy of *What Color Is Your Parachute?* remained somewhere in her bag and she dug for it now, hoping to find some insight that would motivate her to return to the career fair and arm her with enough wisdom to direct her to the right industry and company. The glossy cover was promising, or at least bright, and that gave her hope, but she didn't get much beyond that before she heard it. Or, rather, *him*. The slow southern drawl.

"There you go, with your nose in a book. Some things never change."

This day had always been looming. Running into Lincoln was one of those dreaded but inevitable ordeals that you could be spared for only so long, like losing your wallet or getting in a fender bender. For weeks after the breakup, Cora felt her heart lurch every time she spotted a tall Black guy (few and far between), but eventually she managed to be out and about without having nervous palpitations. She took comfort in remembering all those months her freshman year that she'd longed to see Lincoln and never ran into him and was now grateful for those mysterious forces that kept them apart. Curses, blessings—such a fine line between them that depended so much on how you held them up to the light.

Cora had to crane her neck to look up at Lincoln now, and even then, she couldn't make out his features because he was backlit by the sun. Well, that wasn't true—she could make out one feature: his mouth, that smile.

"Hi?" Cora wasn't sure she wanted to commit herself to even a greeting.

Lincoln looked like he was carefully considering whether he should open his mouth again, unsure if she'd run off if he started talking, which was fair. She didn't know either. But he couldn't just stand there holding her with his eyes forever, so he spoke.

"What are you doing over here?"

"I was at the career fair and just, I don't know, stopped here for a minute. My feet hurt."

"How was it? The fair?"

"Fine." She discreetly slid the book back into her bag and stood up, signaling she was leaving.

"Wait, Cora. Please, don't go."

She'd started down the stairs but now stopped, awkwardly straddling the two steep steps but unable to make a decision about where her feet should be.

"I was here getting all my financial aid stuff." He stepped in front of her. "For law school. I got into Chicago. Got the official letter a couple weeks ago."

"That's great." She believed in Lincoln so much, she'd had no doubt this would happen, so she couldn't muster the proper excitement. Also, she had no energy to spare; all of it was devoted to not throwing herself at him, which she was utterly dismayed to discover she wanted to do.

"Okay, well . . . I gotta get going." Cora tried to pass by him on the stairs, but he stopped her with a brush of the hand; it was so fast, so light, so subtle, and yet she felt a white-hot current charge all the way up her arm and then all the way down her spine.

"You headed home? I got my own ride now. Piece of junk, but I'm hoping it can make it to Chicago. I can drive you. You say your feet hurt. Let me save you the walk."

All these months, all her resolve, and all Cora had to do was move her head barely an inch up and down, and they were headed for . . . what? She didn't know. A reunion? A reckoning? Or maybe just a ride home—her feet *were* killing her.

"Okay, good, good. This is good. We can—we can talk."

Chitchat would be unbearable, but Cora didn't want to just dive right in to the heavy stuff, so there was nothing to do but make a show of fussing with her seat belt and wait.

Lincoln busied himself with the ignition and the AC before speaking. "Your dad coming up for graduation?"

"Yeah, he told me he got an air horn for the occasion called the Earsplitter, and I'm not sure he's joking."

"That sounds like Wes, all right. He's proud of his baby girl. Nothing wrong with that."

In the version of graduation day that was supposed to have unfolded, Wes would have taken them to dinner at the Red Lantern and gushed about how proud he was of both of them. There would have been toasts and tears—all Wes's. As it stood now, her father barely mentioned Lincoln's name. He used to cautiously ask about him, but he'd stopped abruptly one day, as if he'd reached a deadline on the calendar.

"Is your mom going to be able to make it?" Cora asked.

"Probably not. But all good. I want to try to find a way to pay for the boys to get here—get them bus tickets. We'll see if I can swing it. I want them to see it's possible for them too."

Their familiarity was like quicksand; Cora felt it overtaking her inch by inch.

"I've been waiting to talk to you for so long, Cora. I appreciate you hearing me out." The *finally* was implied. The sign for her street came into view; Lincoln clearly recognized they were approaching not only her house but a point of no return. It was now or never.

"Look, Cora, I know what I did was wrong. Big-time. And I'm so sorry—you have no idea. But the way you just cut me off like I was gum on your shoe or something, like what we had didn't mean anything after *years* together . . . I don't know, Cora, I think I deserved a chance to explain, at least."

"What about what I deserved, Lincoln? Like not being cheated on or lied to? I wasn't trying to punish you. I just didn't know what to do.

There didn't seem any point to us talking. I knew I'd never get over it, get past it. Why put us through that? What would you even have said?"

"What I'm saying now: I'm sorry. I've prayed every day I'd get another chance with you. If I had known I would lose you forever just like that—" He snapped his long fingers loudly.

"But why would it be the risk of losing me that would keep you from not hurting me? Like, it would be okay for you to sleep with someone else if you knew I would just forgive you and move on? I'm not Jesus, Lincoln. I'm a human girl with feelings. You had to know I was going to be destroyed. That's the worst part—you did, and you did it anyway."

Lincoln dropped his head so low, his chin grazed his broad chest. "You're right. I deserved to lose you. Maybe I never even deserved to have you."

She refused to let him make her feel bad for him. They were idling in front of the gatehouse at her apartment complex, which brought an unpleasant wave of déjà vu. They sat there staring at each other for a long time, long enough for her to watch Lincoln's eyes slowly well up but not so long that a tear could escape.

"Okay, then." Cora's eyes were drawn to the dashboard clock as she prepared to leave the car. It seemed important to know what time it was: 4:32 p.m. It might be the last time she'd ever in her life see Lincoln Ames.

When Cora pulled on the door handle, she suddenly felt like someone was stepping on both her head and her lungs. She held on to both sides of her seat and tried to catch her breath.

"What's wrong, Bella?" Lincoln's hand on her shoulder wasn't helping this out-of-body experience.

"Nothing, nothing. I don't know. I had Indian for lunch." She closed her eyes against the wave of dizziness.

"You know curry upsets your stomach."

"I know, I know." Lincoln knew this about her and so much more—the exact temperature she liked her hot cocoa and that she couldn't stand it if different foods touched on her plate and the shape of the birthmark on the inside of her thigh. Each of these was a scalpel. The devastation that no one would ever know her like Lincoln did—intimately, thoroughly, deeply. That this was because she wouldn't let it happen didn't make it any less horrible.

The flip side of this, which sliced as deep but in the opposite direction, were all the things Lincoln *didn't* know—she had a tattoo now! She'd gotten a new bra. She'd watched the finale of *their* show alone, and neither of them knew how the other felt about the twist at the end. Her life had gone on, just without him to witness it.

Most tragic of all—the realization of how much she missed Lincoln. So much it was clearly making her physically ill.

Cora went about her second attempt to get out of the car but it was half-hearted and Lincoln seized the opportunity to grab her hand. Her other hand was on the door, which gave her the feeling that she was literally being pulled in two directions.

"Cora. Please, if you want me to beg you, I will. Please let's try again. In twenty years, this will be a blip on the radar screen. I will have had all that time to make it up to you. You have no idea how much I've missed you—miss you. My boys keep clowning me that I'm so whupped and I just need to keep it moving, but . . . I can't. There's been no one else *but* you since we've been apart. That's gotta count for something."

There'd been no one else for Cora either. But what *did* that count for? What did that add up to? There wasn't a comforting, precise algebraic formula that she could apply: the amount of time that had passed plus the amount of contrition minus the severity of the betrayal multiplied by years together equals—forgiveness? A second chance?

"Come to Chicago, Cora. You still could. It's not too late."

"We haven't talked in months and you want me to just move to Chicago with you like nothing happened?"

"What can I say? I think big."

Was it possible that Lincoln's teeth had gotten even brighter or was it the way the light was reflecting off the windshield? She couldn't pinpoint why his grin was even more dazzling. She missed it as soon as he turned serious again. "It was our dream. Just think about it, Cora. That's all I ask."

The problem was, she couldn't think clearly with Lincoln's body, his smooth skin, his magnetic spark so close to her. Pulling at her. His beautiful fingers curved around the steering wheel made her think of all those times he'd wrapped them around her wrists and pulled her toward him. All those times he'd kissed her forehead for no reason. All the times he'd said, "You're such a nut, Cora, you know that?" while stroking the curve of her jaw with his thumb.

The only way to escape the screaming white noise of her longing was to get out of this car as fast as possible, like it was on fire, which it might as well have been. "I'll . . . I'll let you know."

There was a phenomenon where you're consumed by an irrational urge to fling yourself into the abyss when looking out over a great height. Cora struggled to remember the name of it, but whatever it was called, it was similar to the intense, irrational impulse seizing her right now: To run back to Lincoln's car and say, *Yes, yes, yes!* To throw herself into his lap and kiss him and let the past be the past.

That she was even considering this was troubling, given what it had taken for Cora to move on—the sheer willpower required to distance herself from him. Was her shaky resolve a sign of the strength of their connection or her own weakness?

The only way to know was to sleep on it. Or, if not sleep, spend the night staring at the ceiling and hoping the answer would come to her. If she felt the same way in the morning, Cora would call Lincoln, agree to lunch or a walk. A baby step, not a leap.

She never got the chance.

CORA FACES THE ABYSS

April 2002

It never occurred to Cora that her father could die. It would have been like contemplating the sun falling out of the sky.

But she was forced to face this incomprehensible prospect as she stared at him lying in the ICU at Inova Hospital. Ashen, weak, unconscious, and attached to multiple tubes and wires. Almost more inconceivable than her father dying was that he could be this fragile, this vulnerable.

Wes had had all of one cold that Cora could remember, years ago. It was a big deal that he'd had a substitute teacher for three consecutive days, the first and last time that had happened in his career. Cora found it exciting that she got to bring him tea and take his temperature. It was all fun and no fear because she had no doubt he'd get better.

Now Cora experienced a sensation beyond fear—a cold, dark dread that left her dazed, dumbstruck, destroyed. She was at the far boundary of an emotional landscape she could barely contemplate—a barren no-man's-land where she staggered around, struggling to piece together the past few hours, which came to her only in incoherent fragments.

One second she was sitting with Lincoln in a hot car talking about second chances, and the next, she was walking in a daze back to her apartment and there was screaming from Neisha or Kim or both. "Oh God, there you are. Something's happened, Cora."

Then she was in a car driving very fast on a highway for minutes or hours. There was music, or there was Kim saying, "He's going to be okay, I'm sure he's going to be okay," over and over. Or maybe there was panicked silence.

"He could be dead by the time we get there." Cora remembered saying that or at least thinking it before her mind went black.

Then: Harsh fluorescent lights. Neisha holding one of her hands, Kim the other. A doctor with a red turban talking slowly and seemingly from a great distance. *He collapsed in his classroom. A student with a contraband cell phone called an ambulance. Stroke. Midbrain ischemic. Bilateral thalamic. Rare. Touch-and-go.*

The doctor had at some point became flustered, like a comedian bombing at a show. "It's a lot to take in—any questions?"

Cora had one. "What time? What time did this happen?"

The doctor skimmed through the chart. "Looks like the 911 call came in at four forty-two, so I suspect right before that? Four thirty or so."

It had been 4:32, Cora knew, when she'd clutched herself in phantom pain. She'd been sitting in a car with Lincoln thinking about her stupid, irrelevant love life while her dad's brain exploded.

Another detail: the doctor's white Crocs. The click against the floor as he rocked back and forth in them, increasingly anxious to leave. Cora thought, *Me too.*

His desperate exit strategy: to pass the baton. "I'll send the social worker to talk to you. Anyone else you can call? Your mother?"

Cora didn't know if she responded; she didn't know if she still had the ability to speak.

"She has us." Neisha had stepped toward him defensively, which only seemed to increase the doctor's eagerness to escape.

"Okay, great, well, you can go see your dad, but just you and just for a few minutes."

The memory loop squeezed closed and spat Cora out here in this awful, windowless, freezing room.

Even just standing, an act that she'd not previously given much thought to, required a level of concentration and intention that depleted her. She didn't see a chair in the tight space around Wes's hospital bed, so she stood next to it, looking everywhere but at his limp body after the nurse said she'd leave them alone for a little bit. The right thing to do would be to touch him, to grab his hand or kiss his forehead, one of the few places where she could reach his soft wrinkled skin, but Cora simply couldn't do it. It was the worst failure of her life.

She frantically looked around, wondering what had happened to Neisha and Kim, before she remembered she'd sent them back to campus. There was nothing they could do and nowhere they could stay, and they had nothing with them. They'd rushed out of their apartment so fast, Neisha was still wearing a plastic shower cap over the deep-conditioning treatment she'd had on her hair when the headmaster at Prescott called, interrupting *The Oprah Winfrey Show,* which would have been comical in any other circumstances.

The world of deep conditioners, talk shows, *What Color Is Your Parachute?*—that was all gone now.

The size of Cora's universe shrank to the hard plastic chair outside her father's room, from which she could pop up like a gopher and look at her dad through the window while the medical team went about their mysterious interventions, and her father's bedside, where she sat for as long as she could before the nurses gently suggested a bathroom break or coffee. Cora quickly came to realize that her round-the-clock vigil was not protocol for visitors, but the busy nurses and staff had taken pity on her and allowed it.

There was no sense of time, weather, news, anything at all outside the hospital walls; there was only Cora talking to Wes in a nonstop stream-of-consciousness chatter of memories and observations and random facts because the doctors said it was likely he could hear her.

Sometimes she broke up the talking with singing, even though her dad had always teased her about her tone deafness and imitated a dog howling whenever she started in on a few notes of a song. Remembering this, Cora would tear up while trying to match Minnie Riperton's soaring octaves in "Lovin' You," willing him to wake up and laugh at her.

She discovered a stash of books outside the pediatrics unit, including some of her favorites from when she was a kid, like *The Runaway Bunny,* and she started reading to Wes each afternoon, blinking back tears that, despite her best efforts, dripped onto the page, leaving puckered spots. At first, Cora worried that reading her dad children's books was too patronizing—this was a man who regularly contributed op-eds to the *Washington Post,* who routinely quoted Frederick Douglass, who could tell you the name and tenure of every Black person elected during Reconstruction—but she decided Wes would embrace the nostalgia, the poignancy of reversing the roles on all those nights he'd read to Cora and she'd begged for one more story.

The only time Cora left her father's side was when one of his friends or Prescott coworkers came by. She would meet them in the cafeteria and give them inconclusive updates about his condition and then bear their pity and platitudes before insisting she had to get back.

People who hadn't seen her in years would make comments that were all variations of *My, how you've grown*. It wasn't just that Cora had grown up—though she did feel she'd aged ten years overnight—it was that she was *reconfigured*; her very atomic makeup had been altered. That was what her dad's coworkers saw—her new self, a stranger to them all, Cora included.

On the fourth day, Cora finally got up the nerve to touch her father and reached for his limp hand. Now that she'd felt his warm skin, his hand in hers was not nearly enough. Cora gripped his arm below his IV and buried her face in his once broad but now sunken chest, in the valley between tubes and wires, unleashing the emotions that she'd tried to stuff away until she was filled to this bursting point. Through anguished heaving wails, she was reduced to outright begging.

"Please, Daddy, you can't leave me. You have to get better. I haven't learned everything I need to from you yet. We need more time. We need more time." *Please, please, please, please.*

In the end, Cora lost track of who she was pleading with. Her wails turned to whimpers; her piercing pleas turned to fervent prayers. If only she had listened more when she went to church with Lincoln or asked him to teach her to pray, because she wasn't convinced that she was doing it right. There had to be more to it than begging God, *Please let him wake up*. He answered some prayers and not others, and she wasn't sure how to make sure hers was in the former category. If intensity helped, she had that.

No doubt the head nurse had witnessed histrionic scenes like this before, but Cora still felt that she had been caught in the act of doing something unseemly and furtive when Birdie walked in. It was the wild nest of a straw-like hair that had inspired Cora to give her the petty nickname, that and Cora's irrational animosity toward the woman after running into her cheerfully buying bottles of wine at the 7-Eleven next to the hospital. How dare she have the nerve to clock out and go about her merry evening, planning to enjoy some Barefoot Moscato and giggling, *giggling*, with the cashier, when Cora's father, Birdie's charge, was in critical condition?

Birdie barreled into the room with crossed arms and an attitude, paying no mind to the abject unraveling she'd come upon.

"There's a large man at the information desk demanding to speak to you. Per hospital policy, I could neither confirm nor deny that your father was a patient here. Not that it matters anyway, because it's well past visiting hours."

"Is he still there?" Cora asked, but she'd already passed Birdie, flying into the hallway.

"I have no idea. I told him I'd call security if he didn't stop being so rowdy." Birdie's lips, pursed so hard they'd turned white, told Cora she was secretly delighted by the authority she was getting to wield.

Cora had no doubt that the "rowdy" visitor was a six-foot-two Black man and that he wasn't rowdy at all, that he was simply tall and dark-skinned and demanding. She practically sprinted down the hall, the most energy she'd mustered in days and found Lincoln standing quietly near the double doors she'd burst through days ago. She used her last rush of strength to throw herself at him.

"You're here. You're still here!" Apparently sometimes God answered prayers you didn't even make.

"Oh, Bella, of course I'm here. I wasn't leaving until I saw you. I'm sorry I didn't come sooner. No one told me. When I didn't hear from you, I came by your place. Neisha told me what happened, and I drove straight up. How is he?"

"I don't really know. They're waiting for him to wake up. When the swelling in his brain goes down, that'll mean he's out of the woods, I guess, and they can better assess how he's doing, if he'll walk and talk again. But . . . he's gotta . . . wake up. Oh, God, Lincoln, he's got to wake up." She'd turned to begging Lincoln, anyone.

He gently pushed her away, stepped back, and took her in. His alarm alarmed her. "Have you eaten or had any sleep or water, Cora?"

"A little?" Basic biological functions and needs had ceased to matter. She suddenly registered that the ripe smell she'd kept catching whiffs of was coming from her own body. A nurse had given her scrubs to change into and a little travel kit, the kind you'd get at a hotel. She'd brushed her teeth with the toothbrush in it, or she thought she had.

"Listen, I'm going to take you home, to your dad's place. You need to get some sleep and have a shower. We'll come back first thing in the morning, before the sun's even up. I have to get back for my shift anyway. It's after eleven, your dad's probably asleep for the night."

"He's unconscious."

"Okay, baby, okay, come on, we're going now." Lincoln grabbed her hand and didn't let go the whole way out of the hospital, to the car, and for the twenty-minute drive. He released her only to grab the towering pile of mail on the porch. They stepped over the fruit baskets that had been attacked by squirrels and a trail of decimated peaches and plums to get to the front door. The house smelled of emptiness and Pledge, a testament to her dad's obsession with dusting. Cora ran over, grabbed the silver travel mug on the counter, and opened it. The sour smell of five-day-old coffee filled the kitchen. "He forgot it."

Cora attempted to drink the cold, stale, bitter liquid from the mug, but Lincoln grabbed it. He poured the coffee into the sink and again firmly took her hand in his, this time pulling her toward the upstairs bathroom. There he sat her on the toilet, turned on the shower, and proceeded to undress her like a baby. When she was naked, he helped her to her feet and into the stream of water. It was as if it were the first shower she'd ever taken—blissfully hot but also confounding. What was she was supposed to do first? Soap? Face wash? She couldn't possibly deal with her hair.

Lincoln sat on the toilet, vigilant. He jumped up when she turned the water off and met her with a plush towel. He led her to her bedroom and rooted around in a drawer for pajamas, but she'd already climbed into her childhood bed, naked.

"Lincoln?" she whispered.

"Yeah, Bella?"

"Remember when you said my life was so easy?"

"Oh, Cora. I'm sorry. I shouldn't have said that. Pretty much no one's life is easy. That wasn't fair."

Nothing was.

She curled up in as tight a ball as possible. "What am I going to do?" She couldn't seem to speak above a whisper.

"What do you mean?"

"I mean . . . if he . . . "

"Cora, don't even say that. Wes is strong. He'll pull through. Just watch."

Cora forced herself to consider the alternative, though. She had to go there. Step into the abyss. By leaning into the unthinkable pain, she could save herself from it. Or so went her warped, anguished logic. She saw herself writing her dad's eulogy on one of his yellow legal pads, pictured her father in a satin-lined coffin in the navy suit he wore to graduation every year, imagined cleaning out his study.

This horrible mental exercise was supposed to prepare her, but it had the opposite effect. It left her with such a gaping void inside that she had to conclude that if her father died, she would too. She would simply cease to exist if he did. She'd vanish. Though on some level, Cora knew this was too much to hope for.

"Lincoln . . . Lincoln . . . I need you. Now." Her meaning was clear.

Lincoln slipped out of his sweatshirt and jeans and climbed under the covers next to her. His tongue slipped inside her mouth only seconds before he slid between her legs. Cora lay completely still while he moved gently on top of her. Every so often, he would lean over and catch a tear streaming down her face with his lips or tongue.

She barely registered that he'd slowly stopped moving on top of her. "You need to sleep, Bella."

"Okay, but don't leave me."

"I won't."

He stayed inside her, anchoring her, holding her to him and to herself. The last thing she remembered before drifting off was Lincoln quietly singing "All My Life." When she opened her eyes in the morning, Lincoln was singing softly, leaving her wondering if he picked up, or never stopped.

Cora jumped out of bed like she was late for something and threw on clean clothes. "Can you get me back now?"

"Yeah, yeah. I got you." He matched Cora's frantic pace in throwing on the clothes that he'd left in a pile on the floor.

They were in the car within ten minutes, Cora cradling Wes's metal travel mug. She'd decided it was a talisman.

Lincoln kept glancing over at her. "Do you think you're coming back to school?"

"I doubt it. The doctors say he'll need to go to a rehab hospital if—" She stopped, corrected herself. "*When* he wakes up, as soon as he can be moved, and who knows how long he'll be there . . . I'm going to talk to the dean, see if there's a way I can take my finals from here somehow. I don't know. Can you drive any faster?"

Lincoln sped up and stopped talking, and she was grateful for both. When he pulled up to the hospital's main entrance, Cora jumped out of his car without turning around and without acknowledging to Lincoln (or herself) how much the past few hours had affected her. She didn't have the time—or emotional stamina—for drawn-out goodbyes or to let herself wonder what this meant or when she would see Lincoln again. She bounded toward the glass double doors with no intention of looking back, but when Lincoln called to her through the open passenger-side window, she had no choice.

"Cora! Cora! I'm praying for him, okay? I've been praying hard. For him. For you. For us too, okay?"

The stubborn lump in her throat made it impossible to speak, swallow, or breathe. But there was no medical treatment—even in the state-of-the-art level-one trauma center she turned to enter—that could cure this particular condition.

In the ICU, Cora pulled the lone chair she'd dragged into the room over to the bed and settled in for another hours-long stretch of holding her father's hand, and it happened.

Wes's eyes finally fluttered open. She leaped up from her chair so fast, she knocked it over. It was vital that he knew that she was here, right here. And always would be.

If it had been just five minutes earlier, though . . . Cora shut down the haunting thought that she could have missed this moment; she let her father's eyes slowly find hers and focus.

"Ba . . . ba . . . "

"Baby girl! Yes, it's me! I'm here. Oh God. You're awake."

Cora would never, as long as she lived, comprehend what she'd done to deserve this moment, this mercy. Or how she would ever prove herself worthy of it.

October 21, 2002

Bonjour, C—

I do believe in miracles, yeah, but not so much God— I don't know if those two add up. It's no problem asking me about my beliefs—not sure why you were worried about that. You should know by now, you can ask me anything—nothing's off-limits. Especially in letters. It's easier to be open. And okay, that includes asking about other women so I don't mind you did that either. It might be a different story if I were seeing someone. Maybe I'd feel some type of way about opening up about that. But that's not where my head is. I'm just focused on making the most of this opportunity here in Paris and soaking up the city while I can. Hard to believe I'm already almost two months in.

On the female tip, there is one girl in the program who I'll admit might have caught my eye under different circumstances. She reminds me of my ex—but Olivia's my ex for a reason, so there's also something that says, Stay away, Aaron. *Tania is cute in that bohemian way, but she has that needy type energy you can just feel, you know? Like you'll never be enough or do enough to make a woman like that (or like Olivia) happy. With Olivia it was always like she was saying,* Why can't you be the person I want you to be instead of the person you are? *I don't understand the point of being with someone if your whole goal is to change them. And then she was all confused when we broke up, like we were some perfect match. She wanted to hold on to the fantasy she had in her head of me, I guess, and she wasn't going to be bothered with the "real" me—the guy who can do without bougie dinners and watching Bravo. (Among other things we fought about.) One thing I've never understood is why people seem to think it's so much easier to hold on than to let go. And not just relationships. But I guess that's just me.*

So, yeah, I don't know if I want what my parents have—a long, happy marriage that's easy as Sunday morning. (That's how my mom described it at their anniversary party last year.) I remember how you were so blown away that my dad always makes sure my mom has a full tank of gas, so she hasn't laid hands on a pump once since they've been together. Who knew gas could be so romantic? But there you were, swooning. Ha-ha.

I mean, it's cool they're so in love, don't get me wrong, but as crazy as it is to say, I kinda wanted them to have more drama. Like I thought to be a true artist, I needed to have this tortured childhood. Instead, I was eating Lunchables and getting state-of-the-art photography equipment for Christmas. It's embarrassing to admit that I wanted to struggle more—I know better now.

I also know better about marriage. Even though I've seen the "love story" up close and how it's done, it's made the bar even higher. Ironic that that shit feels more unattainable when you have a front-row seat. So I'm just not sure if the whole domestic picket-fence thing is in the cards for me—two parents, two kids, two Camrys . . . I have zero desire to fill my dad's sensible loafers. My mom mentioned grandkids to me the other day! I'm not even thirty—slow your roll, Patricia. I said I didn't believe in marriage. She couldn't tell if I was serious. Neither could I.

So, my turn. Am I allowed to ask you about your . . . status? What's up with your "unfinished business"? I think that's how you put it. What happened with Lincoln or what is happening—I don't even know which tense to use. Also don't know if I even want to know where things stand, if things are done with him or not. Is anything ever done? Now you got me feeling all philosophical. I take your point—first love may end but you never get over it. Also, I don't get down with absolutes like "Never again." Remember that night we were trying to roast s'mores over the hot plate in my studio (what were we thinking?) and you showed me the little scar on the tip of your finger where you'd burned your hand on a stove? (That was another time I wanted to kiss you, it, by the way . . .) Anyway, you explained that's how you thought of love—that you know better now. And I gotta say, I don't cosign that analogy. The scar on your finger proves it—you healed and that patch of flesh is even stronger. Don't get me wrong, I get being afraid, I just don't get not doing it anyway. Same rationale I have for skydiving. (Don't worry, I'll never try to convince you!)

Not to get all Psyche 101 (you're the smartie with the degree) but I guess it's the same fear that drives your compulsive need to know how everything's going to work out. It's as impossible as it is adorable. Like how you flip to the end of all those novels you're always reading to see how they turn out before you even get into chapter 1. You were so mad that time we saw Memento and you begged me to tell you what happens and I refused because what's the fun in that?

Instead I said, "How do you think this ends?" You didn't understand what I was talking about until you saw that I was waving my finger between us in the dark theater. I stopped you before you could answer because it was a trick question—who's to say this ever ends? We haven't even started. The question is: Will we start, you think? And that one's not a trick.

x, A

PS: Okay, one more question, it's related: How about you come visit me in Paris?

CORA IS THROWN

July 2002

Technically, she wasn't snooping when she found the letter; Cora's motives for rifling through her father's desk were fully aboveboard—the medical and physical therapy bills were becoming a crucible she couldn't ignore. Cora had been interviewing home-health aides to assist full-time when Wes came home from the rehab hospital, and the cost was astounding.

She needed to find information about their insurance policy and what it covered and also some sort of bank statements. Prescott was continuing to pay Wes's salary and there was still the rental income coming in from the Shaw buildings. Tony had sent a check for five thousand dollars tucked into a lame get-well-soon card, which Cora chalked up to guilt that he'd never made the trip from Oakland to see his sick best friend or his goddaughter, but it still helped. Otherwise, Cora was completely in the dark about their financial picture. She vaguely recalled mention of a savings account, but where that was and how much was in it was a mystery. She could only hope it was enough to cover the staggering amounts listed in the statements with PAST DUE splashed in red that arrived with relentless regularity.

Cora's quest became that much more daunting when she discovered that Wes's desk drawers were shockingly chaotic, with random papers stuffed in with no obvious order and piled over with stray knickknacks. She picked up a Bill Clinton bobblehead, and the letter was underneath. It was a woman's handwriting; that was immediately obvious, a delicate cursive without a single cross-out or smudge. Cora grabbed it greedily, turned it over, and zeroed in on the signature. She expected—and hoped and feared, in equal measure—to see *Love, Adriana*. But it was another name after a long string of *X*s and *O*s: *Renee*

The woman with the cartoon voice. The name clicked into place with a memory of her insisting young Cora call her Renee instead of Ms. Barnes, although Cora was never that informal with her father's friends. That should have been a clue Renee didn't see herself as just a friend.

There was no defense for invading her father's privacy, but Cora read the letter before stopping to consider the moral implications. It could only be described as a plea—a long one—for Wes not to let Renee go. *Your daughter has to be your priority, of course, but can't you have enough room in your heart for both of us?* There were many lines detailing all the ways that what they had was special and how she hoped to grow closer to Cora and eventually *love her as if she were my own*. By the end, Renee raised the intensity of her entreaties: *Please, Wesley, you deserve love* and *I bet your daughter would want you to be happy and not give up everything—me, us—out of some overinflated sense of parental duty.*

Then the last line: *I think you're going to look back and regret this one day when you find yourself alone, when you need someone by your side, when you realize you could have had love <u>and</u> been the kind of father you wanted to be. Please just think about what you're giving up and why.*

Cora dropped the letter back in the drawer and slammed it shut against what she'd just read, literally and metaphorically, with about as much success as Pandora had had.

Each question that besieged Cora was even more unanswerable than the next, not least because Wes could still barely speak.

Had Wes denied himself something as fundamental as love? Did he regret it? Which was to say, was his sacrifice worth it? Which was to say, was Cora worth it?

Another line of thinking emerged, just as troubling. What about what Cora's father had denied Cora? A woman who would have grown to love her. Someone who could have been here to help her with cutting Wes's toenails and interviewing nurses and tracking his meds. Someone to stay up late with Cora stress-eating Triscuits over the kitchen sink. Someone who could have stood at the edge of the black abyss with

Cora, gripping her hand, contemplating an inconceivable devastation that only they could understand. Someone who would have joined Cora when she collapsed against the vending machine in the hospital hall the day Wes woke up and wept with frenzied relief. Someone who would have happily shared the worry and the caregiving because of their united, singular love for one person. What Cora wouldn't have given.

Sitting in her father's study in their big, empty house with the stack of bills on the desk and the water heater racked by a disturbing clanging Cora didn't know what to do about, contemplating whether she had been enough—Cora was felled by an overwhelming loneliness she had, at one point, trained herself to get used to. She'd let the muscle get weak.

This, too, felt like yet another problem she had no idea how to solve.

Calling Neisha or Kim wasn't an option. She'd shut them out these past couple months, and even though she knew she was doing it—and hated it—she was powerless to stop. It was strange what they didn't know about her life when she was used to the three of them having a level of intimacy down to when she pooped. They didn't know that she'd cut her hair—herself, with scissors in the bathroom mirror, which would have given Kim a heart attack—or that she went through a period where she threw up everything she ate in the hospital bathroom or didn't eat at all until she saw that her arms resembled noodles and scared herself into making sure she maintained some basic nutrition.

Cora didn't want to be a burden; that was the main reason she didn't respond to her friends' well-meaning check-ins. But it was also that what she could hold in her heart and her head had shrunk to the size of the random single die on Wes's cluttered desk. There wasn't room left over to listen to a detailed account of Winston meeting Kim's parents for the first time or to dissect celebrity gossip with Neisha. *My dad almost died and who cares if Justin and Britney are breaking up or getting back together!* The distance between their world (drunken barbecues, new clothes, irritating parents) and hers (cold waiting rooms, MRIs, endless frozen meals alone at the kitchen counter) felt impossible to bridge. Though she had to trust at some point they'd find a way.

Often, Cora thought back to the doctor asking her, "Anyone you can call? Your mother?" and Neisha stepping up: "She has us." It was a declaration and a promise and even more than that, it spoke to a piercing truth: They were the closest thing to mothers she would ever have. They'd nursed her through illness and heartbreak, gone with her to get birth control, made sure she was fed, and told her when the pants she tried on were too tight. And during the worst moment of her life, they'd held her up—literally. But maybe the best way they'd mothered her was by reminding her that no matter what, they were there for her.

It took Cora a long time, longer than it should have, to be fully convinced of that, but now she could relax into the knowledge the way you could flip on your back in the ocean and trust the water to hold you. She had the luxury of accepting them as a constant and being able to take that for granted just as she would a mother's love. Whenever she surfaced again, she could count on the fact they would be there.

Cora next thought of calling Lincoln, who checked in constantly, partly out of concern about her and Wes but also because he wanted to know her answer. She never should have told him that she'd gotten into graduate school at the University of Illinois, since he took it as a sign and doubled down on his quest for their reunion.

She'd told him she couldn't make any decisions at the moment—there was too much up in the air. But he was incapable of accepting that, and Cora didn't know what to do about his increasingly insistent overtures. Before they got off the phone last night, he'd said, "Just tell me, what's it going to take?"

She had no clue. It was beyond her to be able to untangle the layers of grief that had knotted themselves into a net she couldn't escape—her father's stroke on the heels of her heartbreak. She'd had no space to think about what she wanted or needed, which was why she kept putting Lincoln off.

And anyway, there was someone else Cora could call right now. Someone else Cora *wanted* to call right now: Aaron.

They'd known each other for only two weeks; it didn't make sense. But neither did her reaction when she walked into the café they'd agreed to meet at after she'd answered his Craigslist ad. Neither did the way thoughts of him infiltrated a securely walled-off corner of her mind since then and made themselves quite comfortable.

Cora had stumbled on the post about a part-time gig "organizing and digitizing photo archives" late one night and thought, *Why not?* It was a way to make some cash, it was flexible, and it had the potential to fill the long, empty afternoons lined up like dominoes as far as the eye could see. Though she almost bailed on the interview, having been waylaid by traffic and tears after she'd left Wes's rehab hospital. She couldn't find a place to park and was one more circle around the block away from giving up when a spot opened right in front of Busboys and Poets. Inside the too-hip café, she instantly spotted the green paisley shirt Aaron had said to look for to find him—how could she not? It was a blinding neon lime color. Except it didn't belong to the old white man she'd pictured from their messages but a Black guy maybe a few years older than her.

Having to adjust that image in her mind wasn't what made her stop to collect herself at the hostess stand though. It was the way her body felt, a hot/cold tingle not unlike the first blush of a fever, as she watched him, the languid way he sat with one elegant hand draped over the back of his chair, legs crossed, as comfortable as a cat in the sun. He radiated a mellow, detached curiosity with an undertone of haughtiness that also reminded her of a cat. Not a house cat, though—a puma or a jaguar. Watchful, smart, curious.

The most unsettling part was that she said one word under her breath, or maybe it was just so loud in her mind, she thought she'd spoken it out loud: *You*.

When Cora got within feet of Aaron's table, they locked eyes and she spotted the same flash of recognition she'd had. Or maybe she was so far from what he had been expecting that he, too, was making instant mental adjustments.

"Mr. Wright?"

He glanced around with exaggerated confusion, then turned back to her. "Sorry, I was looking for my dad." His grin was generous and expansive but somehow still managed to hide his teeth. Perhaps to hide the little gap she spotted between his two front teeth when he spoke again. "Please, it's Aaron. You must be Cora . . . sit, sit."

In a flash of madness, Cora eyed the space right next to him in the booth before she took her place on the other side of the table. "You, uh, aren't what I expected, Aaron."

He blinked slowly, curious and unbothered. "That's why I try not to have expectations. It's nice to be surprised."

"I hate surprises, actually." Where this response came from and whether it was an attempt to flirt or open up wasn't clear to Cora at the time or later when she replayed and analyzed their entire conversation, looking for clues to solve a confounding mystery: What was going on here?

"Maybe you just haven't had the right kind," he responded, stirring his tea in a way that could only be described as seductive, even if that wasn't the intention.

There was something palpable in the air between them, and Cora wondered if it was possible for pheromones to be so strong they presented like steam, then realized that it *was* steam—rising into the air from his mug of tea. But the pheromones, they were there too, tangible in a way that blurred the senses. And yet Cora could almost taste them on her tongue as she spoke.

She could almost taste them again now as she dialed Aaron, or maybe it was just the anticipation of hearing his voice that released metallic-tasting adrenaline into her system.

"Aaron." When she said his name, it wasn't so much a greeting as a confirmation, an affirmation of something, his presence on the other end of the line. And her life.

"Look at that—I thought you up."

"What do you mean?"

"I was just sitting here thinking about the time you told me you'd dressed up like a bald eagle for Halloween one year. I'm watching a documentary about bird migration on Animal Planet. I'm going to need a picture of that costume, by the way."

Cora's fourth-grade Halloween costume was one of about twelve hundred facts she'd shared with Aaron over their marathon first conversation that stretched from hours at Busboys to hours in his studio surrounded by oversize prints of his photographs. Cora had made fascinating discoveries about Aaron too. For example, just after midnight, when he slid down to sit cross-legged directly opposite where she sat in the same position on the scuffed wooden floors, next to the mattress he slept on in the corner, she learned his eyes had the slightest hint of green that made surprising appearances depending on the tilt of his head and the glint of the light.

Those unexpected green flecks danced around in her head as they talked now. "It tracks that you're spending Saturday morning learning about ornithology," she said.

"Look at you with the SAT word. I'm impressed."

Cora wasn't trying to impress him. No, that wasn't true—she was trying to suppress the fact that she was trying to impress him. "Seriously, though, birds?"

"What can I say, I have a curious mind. A dirty one too, sometimes, but that's a different story. But speaking of minds, what's on yours? You sound down. Rough day?"

"A long string of them."

"You wanna talk about it?"

"Eh, not really, I'm just rethinking everything I thought I knew about everything and everyone . . . again." Cora twisted the phone cord around and around her hand until it was wound as tight as her insides after finding that letter.

"Oy, it's like that, huh? Full-on existential. How about I pick you up and take you somewhere?"

"Where?"

"A surprise. I know how you love those."

"About as much as I love sarcasm."

"Is that more than you dig birds?"

"Aaron! I don't love birds, okay? I don't know how I ended up in that stupid costume. Patriotism?"

"That's not much better."

"Anyway, I would love to hang but I'm supposed to go to the hospital this afternoon."

That afternoon and every afternoon. Cora spent more time at the rehab hospital than she did sleeping. She didn't want to miss a single one of her father's progress milestones. They were eerily similar to a child's development—walking, talking, feeding himself, a high five, guiding a shaky hand to snap a piece into place in the puzzle they'd been working on—and Cora cheered him on just as he had done for her, with something akin to a parent's pride. When he took his first halting steps at PT, Cora deployed the air horn that he'd planned to use at her graduation, an event that had come and gone without either of them registering it. Bigger fish and all.

Wes had defied all the most grim predictions, no surprise to Cora. The doctors could administer all the tests and read all the journals and studies, but they didn't *know* Wes, the man who'd taught himself to play trumpet when he was seventeen on a lark and who'd once decided to get a second master's in German. A man who'd withstood a devastating loss and raised a daughter completely alone. Cora came by her stubbornness honestly, which was to say, genetically.

He was able to talk in short bursts now, complaining that Cora was fussing over him too much, which she took as a good sign. He smiled his lopsided smile and rolled his eyes whenever she lectured him about doing his PT exercises, to which she'd respond, "I can see you want to strangle me, and you're going to need two hands for that." Wes's laugh was the only truly familiar trace in this new, somewhat diminished version of her dad, so she tried to make it happen as often as possible.

"I think your dad will understand? Missing one day. But no pressure. I totally get it. Another time."

"No! I want to go."

She did. Very badly. This was what Cora had been chasing when she picked up the phone to call Aaron—a reprieve from the prison of her mind, and her circumstances, if just for an hour.

"It's settled, then. See you in thirty minutes. Bring a bathing suit."

"Bathing suit?"

"You heard me. And no more questions."

"Hey, you're the one with all the questions! The first thing you asked me was 'Tell me everything about yourself.' What was that?"

When Aaron had said that to her, it was accompanied by a gaze so intense, Cora couldn't be certain that he wasn't peering directly into her mind, and what a nightmare that would have been because her thoughts had already strayed into all sorts of shocking territory. For example, she wondered what the curve of his back where it met his ass looked like naked. And what the skin behind his ear felt like. And what he sounded like when he woke up in the morning before he'd spoken to anyone.

"Well, Cora, 'Tell me everything' is technically not a question. More like a command. Or, as I like to think of it, an invitation. What can I say? It was a very thorough job interview."

"It felt like something else."

"A date?"

"I was going to say *interrogation*."

"I wanted to get to know you, Ms. Belle."

"Why?"

"Girl, I said no more questions. And let today be a surprise. I'm still trying to sell you on those. Now, go get ready. I'll see you soon."

Smiling felt so foreign to Cora as of late that she almost didn't recognize what was happening to her face.

She clung to the phone for too long after Aaron hung up, listening to her heart race. It thudded in the way it used to right before she stepped onstage for a violin recital, which was different—harder, firmer—than the way it raced when she was anxious, which was fast and light. One little heart and so many different ways it had to tell you how you felt.

All she had to do was listen.

CORA SAYS *AU REVOIR*

November 2002

She knew she was going to go to Paris as soon as Aaron asked, before she'd even folded his letter up back in the airmail envelope. Aaron would be in France only until Christmas, when his program ended; it was now or never. So there was no hedging, no doubting, no pros and cons list, just a sense of conviction like an invisible string tugging Cora somewhere—across an ocean. Even if she didn't exactly know what awaited her there.

Cora's one hesitancy was leaving her father for even just a few days. But when she casually mentioned she might want to see a friend in Paris, Wes had surprised her by picking up the phone and calling his travel agent, buying her a ticket right then and there. He'd said it was a thank-you for all her help and support over the past few months. But the gift was also an excuse and preamble for a long and serious conversation about how it had been more than six months since his stroke, and it was far past time for Cora to return to her life and stop letting her old man be a burden. He was sick and tired of all her fussing and wanted to get back to him taking care of her, "the right order of things."

Nothing felt more "right" than taking care of her father, but Cora took his point and his permission. And in twelve hours she would be on a flight—her first solo flight. The stiff blue passport on her desk was literally a pass to escape for seventy-two blissful hours—to spend time somewhere other than in doctors' offices with her father, at her deadly tedious temp job at an accounting firm in a drab office park in Tysons Corner, and in her childhood bedroom, staring at the pink globe on her desk that mocked her.

But first she had to tell Lincoln. He still called her every other night, so she felt obligated to tell him she wouldn't be reachable for the next few days. This meant preparing herself to have a version of the same conversation they'd had so many times Cora couldn't count them (she'd actually tried). Night after night, he came at her with the same observations, assessments, and arguments that started to take on the familiar chorus of a pop song.

Every call ended the same way as well—with Lincoln asking (or sometimes insisting) that she still loved him. *Right, Cora, right?*

Whether Cora did or didn't (she did), she couldn't decide if it mattered at this point. See *history*; see *heartbreak*. And see the question as old as love itself: *Was it enough?* That was not actually a yes-or-no question; it only pretended to be one.

Any answers evaded her. In a way, Cora was waiting for clarity to magically come to her. In the meantime, as overwhelming as his overtures sometimes were, Lincoln's attention and his attempts to win her back had become a steadying force in her life. A constant. It was like the blankie she couldn't live without as a kid. It didn't matter about the holes and stains; you couldn't bear to throw it away. Or lose it. Or have it taken away.

Ultimately, this left Cora trying to do the impossible—to both hold on and let go.

Or run away.

"Hey, random, but I just wanted to let you know I'm going to be away for a few days . . . Paris!" Cora had barely let Lincoln get in a hello.

"What now? How are you just going to drop a trip to Europe on me?"

"I know, it's sort of random. I just need to get away and clear my head."

"All the way to Paris! You could come to Chicago for a weekend for that. What's in Paris?"

More like who.

"As wonderful as I'm sure Chicago is, it's not Paris. You know, the Eiffel Tower, the Louvre, the Catacombs, et cetera, et cetera. That's what's in Paris."

Also, Aaron.

"You're going all the way to France solo?" Lincoln might as well have asked if she was planning to ride a unicycle across Europe; such was his level of incredulity.

"I'm gonna hang out with one of Neisha's friends from back when she lived in London."

It wasn't the worst lie Cora had ever told him.

"What about work and your dad? You're just leaving him?"

Given Lincoln's insistence that Wes was so much better now and didn't need her as a nurse, the trace of condemnation in his voice was ironic.

"Well, the beautiful thing about temp work is I can take off whenever. As far as my dad goes, he'll be okay. He's gotten settled in at home this last month and has his routine down. Alma, his favorite nurse, will stay here in case he needs anything. It's just a few days. He's insisting I go."

"Do you even have a passport?"

"Lincoln! I'm not a total idiot. Of course I have a passport. My flight leaves tomorrow at seven a.m."

"Tomorrow! So this has been in the works for a while, and I'm only just hearing about it?"

"Well, it was a little last minute. I got a rush passport."

"I wanted to take you there one day." Lincoln said this with the tone of a little boy denied his first-choice lollipop flavor.

"Well, that could still happen."

"Kicking the ball again. You're becoming the queen of *maybe one day*. I gotta say, Cora, I'm losing faith."

"I'll call you when I'm back, Lincoln. We'll talk. I promise."

To her credit, Cora didn't know that this would also turn out to be a lie.

For the first hour of her flight, Cora stared straight ahead, holding tight to both armrests and trying (in vain) not to register that it was the first time she'd been on a plane since the 9/11 terrorist attacks last year and attempting not to replay those scenes in her mind. She had huddled with Neisha and Kim in front of their little living-room TV, watching Katie Couric's solemn face as the Twin Towers crumbled to the ground, waiting to hear from her father, who was a full ten miles from the Pentagon but was still much too close to it for comfort. Cora remembered the dizzying sense that the world was ending—but their pizza delivery still came.

For the next hour, Cora distracted herself by rereading the letters Aaron had sent her since he'd left Labor Day weekend.

This led to an hour spent recalling their conversation the last time she'd seen him in person and trying to keep it together in the departures dropoff at National Airport.

AARON: "You should have told me there was someone else."
CORA: "I didn't think it mattered. I didn't . . . know how you felt."
AARON: "Are you sure about that, Cora?"

The next hour (possibly more) of the flight, Cora devoted to obsessing over whether or not she was making a mistake. Momentum and a desire to for once in her life throw caution to the wind had gotten her on this flight. But thirty thousand feet in the air, beelining into the great unknown, Cora's initial conviction faltered and she felt her joie de vivre burning away faster than the jet fuel. When her seatmate started looking at her with alarm, presumably because of the hyperventilation she was trying to hide, Cora decided to escape into a movie.

Watching *Notting Hill* took up two hours. Thinking about Hugh Grant and Julia Roberts and just how many chances any two people got at love took up a solid thirty minutes. Then she had a quick nap, and the next thing Cora knew, the plane was touching down at Charles de Gaulle.

She had Aaron's address written on a piece of paper tucked in the pocket of her jeans, and she took it out and checked it so often that by the time she handed it to the cabdriver, the ink was smudged.

Aaron had offered to meet her at the airport but she wanted to test her independence. Her global worldliness would be established only if she navigated through the teeming airport and got herself through customs (an unnecessarily intimidating process) and into a cab on her own and with just six words of French at her disposal.

Also, this way Cora could be alone in the back seat, free to press her forehead against the window and gape and gawk at the sights like the guileless tourist she was.

The taxi stopped in front of a limestone building with stacked rows of intricate wrought-iron balconies stretching up eight levels, like layers on a cake. There was a bustling patisserie on the ground floor pumping out the smell of butter and sugar like sweet factory exhaust.

Cora wrestled her purple American Tourister luggage out of the trunk with no help from the driver and lugged it up a small set of stairs to the shiny black door where there was a buzzer for each of the eleven or so apartments. Before she pressed it, Cora looked around, up and down the narrow street, watching cyclists whiz past. She caught the eye of a woman sitting at a patio table of the corner café holding an espresso cup with two delicate fingers. She gave Cora a nod, as if she'd read her mind and was saying, *Yes, you're really doing this.*

Cora *was* really doing this—she was meeting a man in Paris. The most improbable sentence of her life.

She was about to buzz Aaron when a tiny man with a white poodle exited the building and grandly gestured her inside as if it were his personal residence. And they said French people were mean. Once through the front door, Cora craned her neck up to take in the five flights of narrow, winding stairs that would have been intimidating enough without also lugging a forty-pound suitcase. Cora hadn't come this far to break an ankle or have a heart attack, but she also had come too far to turn back now. And so she climbed.

When, huffing and puffing, Cora arrived at the penultimate flight of stairs, she applied the same approach that climbers did before reaching the summit—taking a moment to collect themselves before the big triumph. For her, that meant opening her luggage on the cramped landing to find something to dry her sweat, a comb to rake through her freshly pressed hair, and her grapefruit-scented body spray to spritz liberally head to toe. This was supposed to be surreptitious so she'd arrive at Aaron's doorstep looking and smelling a bit less like a drowned rat.

She was sniffing her left armpit when she heard "Cora?" and looked up to find Aaron peering over the shiny wooden banister watching her. "Busted!"

"Hi." She waved because her arm was already in the air, applying deodorant.

Aaron bounded down the stairs, stepped over her open suitcase, and pulled her to him. "You're here."

He was suddenly kissing her. Not a little welcome peck, not a tentative hello, not an iota of fumbling hesitancy. No, Aaron stepped forward with authority and focus, and they were, within seconds, fully entwined, arms and lips, so naturally and with such passion, an observer would be surprised to learn this was the first time it had happened and wonder what had taken them so long. Both thoughts crossed Cora's mind as she felt Aaron's tongue against hers. Of all the scenarios Cora had played out on the plane and in the weeks leading to her arrival here, nothing came close to this passionate greeting.

A neighbor opened a door in the hall below them, and Aaron stepped back, tripping over her bag. Cora also teetered a little but had no luggage to blame for her unsteadiness. They stood there and stared at each other stupidly, dazed.

"I guess we should go up?" Aaron said, grabbing her suitcase in one hand and placing the other on the sweaty patch spread across the small of her back.

"I guess so." But Cora could have stayed on that stifling landing staring at Aaron for at least four more hours.

The tin ceilings were so low in the attic apartment, Aaron's head grazed them, making the tiny space feel like it was a cave or a secret clubhouse or the former home of hobbits.

Running through the center of the studio was a string stretched from one plaster wall to the other with Polaroids—self-portraits of Aaron in various Parisian backdrops—attached with clothespins. There was a twin bed on one side and, on the other, a counter that held a minifridge and hot plate, the entirety of the "kitchen." Straight ahead were two casement windows thrown open to let in the breeze along with the loud cooing of a fat mottled-gray pigeon perched on the concrete ledge.

"Aren't you afraid it'll fly in?"

"Him. That's Charlie. And I don't know—wouldn't be terrible to have a roommate."

"Well, this weekend, you have one, so Charlie can stay all the way outside."

"Go look out the window," Aaron commanded, smiling. "To the right."

Cora approached the window, much to Charlie's ruffled-feathered displeasure, and craned her neck out as far as she could. There was the Eiffel Tower, drenched in sun. It was impossible to be chill when life presented you a postcard version of itself, so she didn't bother. "Oh my God, Aaron. I truly can't believe I'm here!" It hadn't seemed real until she saw this view.

He stood behind her, wrapped his arms around her, and leaned his chin on her shoulder. "I can't believe you are either. It's a little surreal."

"How do you say 'I'm ready for anything' in French?"

"*Je suis* ready? I'm shit at languages, so my strategy is just to put a *le* or *je suis* in front of whatever English word I'm trying to say. *Je suis* hungry?"

"Starving."

"Good—I got this spread." He waved to a plate of sandwiches, grapes, cheeses, and chocolates on the counter. If a platter could say, *You're in France,* this one screamed it. "The woman who runs the patisserie downstairs makes the best bread in all of Paris. Which is saying something. I assume you smelled it on the way up?"

"It's just as strong now." The air was scented with butter even on the fifth floor. "I wish I could wash my hair in that smell."

"You're probably tired, huh? It's a long flight. Here, come," Aaron said, sitting on the narrow bed and patting the sliver of space next to him.

Cora curled up against his shoulder with the intention of kissing him again, but then she closed her eyes, "just for a second," and when she opened them again it was somehow completely dark, and she was sprawled across the bed, Aaron watching her from the other side of the room.

"Why didn't you wake me?"

"Jet lag's a bitch. You needed to sleep. And it was selfish. I liked watching you."

"But it's already so late! I don't want to miss anything! We only have three days."

"Relax, we'll get it all in, I promise. I have a big day planned for us tomorrow. Can we have a night in tonight, though? We have plenty of food and we can watch a movie. How does that sound?"

"Perfect. Even better if I can shower first."

"Have at it."

Twenty minutes later, Cora emerged from the airplane-size bathroom transformed. She'd wrapped herself in Aaron's terry robe, which was so comfortable, she couldn't even pretend to add a veneer of sexiness. "Is it okay I'm wearing this?"

"More than okay." He lay on the bed in polka-dot boxers with his laptop open on his bare thighs. "I just loaded up *Casablanca*. Have you seen it?"

"Oh, man, I would have expected *Jurassic Park* or something."

"Come on, give me a little credit for my cinematic sophistication. I got this from this old guy who sells bootleg DVDs at this flea market near Montmartre. He told me I had to buy it and that I would love it. But I'm pretty sure it's the only movie he had in English."

"I'm a sucker for old movies. Though not the time my dad and I accidentally started watching *Last Tango in Paris* on Turner Classic Movies. Neither of us ever fully recovered, even though we switched to *ER* as fast as we could find the remote."

"Why is there nothing more embarrassing in the world than watching a movie with your folks when a sex scene comes on? Watching with a special friend, however . . . "

"Special friend, huh?"

Aaron tugged on the ties of the robe to pull her down next to him on the creaky bed. "Let's see how much of this movie we get through."

Twelve minutes.

It was barely enough time to feel nerves or apprehension or awkwardness, but Cora didn't experience any of that anyway. They came together with the ease of the robe slipping past her shoulders and onto the floor.

"I've been wanting to see you like this all summer. Naked." The way he looked her body up and down sent a tingle blazing from the top of her spine, straight through her stomach until it finally settled between her legs, where it pulsed, hot and trapped.

Cora had previously understood sex to be about connection, attraction, and pleasure. But with Aaron, it was something else. As he moved slowly in and out of her, Cora had her eyes shut. "Look at me," Aaron said, and she obeyed, opening them and never once breaking eye contact as an indescribable energy built and billowed, enveloping the bed and the room and seeping into every hollow space in Cora. She could barely process what was happening to her body; let alone her mind. And that her . . . *spirit* seemed to be involved really threw her. It was beyond her grasp to comprehend that what was unfolding between them took them well beyond their bodies physically moving together. Whatever it was overwhelmed Cora so completely that she broke into tears as soon as she came.

Trying to hide this was not possible, since the tears streamed in warm rivulets through the field of wiry hairs across Aaron's bare chest.

"It's okay, it's okay, it's okay," Aaron assured her in the most tender whisper. This only made her cry harder and deepened her mortification.

Then he said, "I feel it too, Cora," and she couldn't tell if the violent surge inside her was something giving way or filling up, but whatever it was, the transformation was now permanent.

She forced herself to sleep for the purposes of recovery more than anything and also as a way to suspend this moment in time without saying another word.

The volume and intensity of Charlie's cooing was louder and more insistent than any alarm clock she'd ever owned, but it was nice to wake to the sounds of nature. Cora began the process of gathering her wits, getting her bearings, and pulling herself together, all of which were daunting considering how disoriented she was. She blamed the jet lag for this. That seemed safer than acknowledging the real reason she was so out of sorts was due to a total emotional and spiritual upheaval in the wake of one of the most profoundly intimate experiences she'd ever had.

Aaron wasn't in the bed next to her, but even with her eyes closed, she felt his presence nearby. She had the sense that he was watching her again and she let him.

After a few minutes, she turned over and scooted up in bed, wrapping the sheet just over her pleasantly sore nipples. Aaron was standing by the window, fiddling with one of the six cameras that lined a table.

"What time is it?"

"Almost eight."

"Wow. I can't remember the last time I slept ten hours straight."

"Guess I wore you out."

"Something like that." Cora's cheeks were as sore as her nipples, but whether from smiling or kissing, she couldn't tell.

"So, what should we do today?"

"We'll get to that, but first . . . " Aaron held up his camera and pointed it at her at the same time Cora shot up her hand to block the shot.

"No, don't! I hate having my picture taken."

"Come on, please. This lighting is too good to waste. Do you see that?"

A buttery yellow beam streamed across the slats of the wooden floor and bathed the bed in sunlight while Aaron's corner of the room remained shadowy. Aaron dropped the camera a half an inch and then brought it back up as Cora looked out the window to follow the light.

"Cora?"

She turned over her shoulder.

"Gotcha!"

"Aaron!" She yanked the sheets up over her head.

"You can't hide from me. Come on, let me get one more."

Cora dropped the sheet all the way to her lap, threw her head back, and smiled out the window at the whole city waiting for them to conquer it.

And conquer it they did. Every corner, every crêperie, every sight they could fit in. Long walks along the Seine, hours at the Louvre, a hike to Montmartre, a terrifying tour of the Catacombs—and all the while they were never not touching, especially deep underground surrounded by thousands of ancient skulls, where Cora gripped his hand even harder. It was like their bodies had become extensions of each other's. In the same way Aaron's camera was an extension of himself; he was always snapping, the click of the shutter became a soundtrack of their days, inspiring Cora to take in the sweep of Paris in the most captivating details as she followed the direction of his lens.

Night two, there was more sex . . . and more tears. And something else: Cora, who'd promised herself that she would just enjoy the moment, started thinking about the future. Visions and possibilities ballooned because it was true what they said: Wherever you go, there you are. Despite her intention to be Paris Cora and live in the present, she was also American Cora, always thinking about what lay ahead. About what all this meant. About whether she could bear not sleeping next to Aaron, something she'd gotten used to unnervingly fast.

The idea of parting ways was slightly less intolerable when Cora remembered Aaron would be returning home soon; she talked herself down from an overwrought goodbye with that in mind.

In the cab on the way to the airport for her departing flight (she let him join her this time because she had nothing left to prove and wanted to squeeze in every last second with him), she looked at his hand in hers instead of at the sights, letting the Arc de Triomphe pass by unnoticed.

"So the fellowship ends on the fifteenth, right? And you'll be getting back to Maryland just before Christmas?"

Cora felt Aaron's hand tense in hers, so subtly it could have been mistaken for an accidental twitch.

"Actually . . . I'm going to stay in Paris, Cora."

"For the holidays, you mean?"

"No, I mean . . . for a while. Maybe indefinitely. I really dig it here. I feel at home."

"Wait. You're not coming back? And you're just telling me this now, when we're almost at the airport?"

"I didn't think it would make a difference this weekend. Or maybe I was worried it would?"

"That I wouldn't have sex with you? Is that what this was about?"

"No! Cora, no. I think we have a connection. Obviously. And we owed it to ourselves to see that through. We can sort out what's next."

"What does that even mean? We're supposed to continue just writing letters, being pen pals, after . . . this?"

"And we can see each other sometimes."

"It's expensive to fly back and forth to Paris. And to talk on the phone long distance! I barely make any money!" Cora couldn't comprehend how she was managing to yell when there was no air in her lungs.

"Well, what . . . what if you spent some time here too?"

"Moving to Paris! Is that a real suggestion? What would I do for work? I don't speak French! And what about my dad?" It was a further medical marvel that she could continue to yell at such a shrill pitch when she had no way to breathe anymore.

Cora had pulled her hand away from Aaron's and now she brought it to her mouth to try to fight the feeling that she was choking. And stop her tears. And keep from flinging herself out of the moving car. How had she let this happen? This entire trip to Paris, this entire summer, was like looking in a funhouse mirror—nothing was what it seemed.

They rode the next fifteen minutes in silence, with the cabdriver peering at them in the rearview mirror every so often, nosy or worried or both. She wondered if he spoke English and could follow this conversation or if he was letting his imagination run wild wondering what these two lovers were fighting about. What *were* they fighting about? It was more what Cora was fighting *against*. And that was the voice in her head that asked, *How could you let this happen?* Then screamed, *You should have known better. This was too good to be true*. It was a battle she'd never win.

"I'm sorry, Cora. I didn't see this coming. I didn't think we had to have it all figured out today, now. I mean, don't you still have 'complications' to figure out, too? With Lincoln? We haven't even talked about that. So yeah, there's some uncertainty, but we can . . . "

It was only then that Aaron registered that she was crying, and only because the taxi driver threw a box of tissues over the seat.

"Oh, God, shit. Please don't cry. I'm sorry."

She dabbed at her face, determined to pull herself together before she had to traipse through a crowded airport. She wouldn't be that girl. "There's nothing to be sorry for. It is what it is. We had a nice time and now this is our thing, I guess. Bad airport goodbyes."

"But, Cora, this doesn't have to be goodbye. This doesn't have to be the end."

PART TWO

NOW

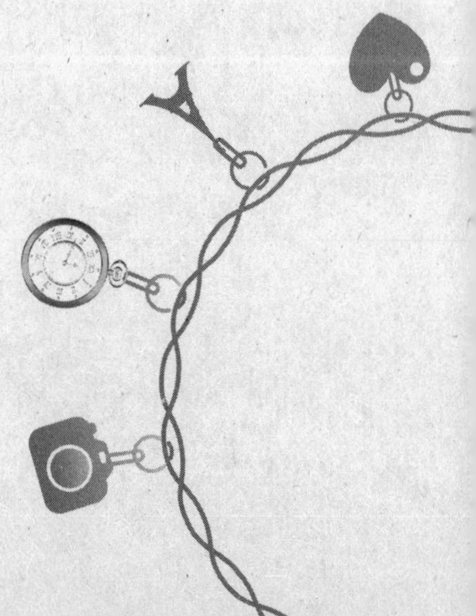

CORA IS ALL GROWED UP. OR MOSTLY, ANYWAY

August 2021

Cora never thought this day would come. Here she is, though—long silk dress, sleek French twist, gold strappy sandals with a too-high heel, pale pink nails in the same shade as the single peony she'll wear in her hair, which is, for now, chilling in the fridge along with a case of champagne. Everything is set and ready except, perhaps, for Cora herself, who wanders around her childhood home holding index cards with her notes for the ceremony in clammy hands.

She peeks through the window of her dad's study to survey the backyard one last time. The small semicircle of white wicker chairs sit hot and waiting in the ruthless sun. The flowers in the arch above the small altar set up where her yellow swing set once stood are already wilting in the humidity that's so thick, it's like the air itself is sweating.

An outdoor wedding is a horrendous idea weather-wise, but indoor gatherings are still problematic. There's a narrow window to make it happen between the midsummer COVID wave and the fall one that everyone knows by now is as inevitable as the August heat itself, so instead of postponing, they've seized the moment—and an auspicious date, 8/8—for a handful of guests to gather outdoors, masked and socially distant, with a few others joining by Zoom.

Cora remembers why she's in the study: to get the laptop and set it up on one of the chairs facing the altar. She eyes it suspiciously, the innocent sleeve of steel that's about to become a portal to the past. Dragging her slick hand along her dress first, she picks it up and opens it to confirm that it's fully charged to last through the short ceremony. The trill of the doorbell floats upstairs and down the hall—the first of the guests have arrived.

She rehearses topics for small talk with people she hasn't seen in ages, a skill that has gotten rusty over the past year of isolation and social purgatory.

Yes, this heat is insane. I haven't caught much of the Summer Olympics, no. I'm still working at Kids First, over eight years now. I know, I can't believe we're still in masks. It never ends. Let's hope the boosters hold.

Small talk is the least of Cora's concerns, though; being in the limelight is worse, but unavoidable. She tells herself that it's impossible to mess up the ceremony, but that's not true because nothing exists that can't be ruined in some way. For that reason, Cora was reluctant to agree to this—the pressure!—but how could she have said no?

Her therapist, Greta, is working with her on this—on saying no, but also on being aware of her inclination to focus on the worst outcomes. Cora has made the case that her pessimism is just her natural state of being, not to mention logical—just watch six minutes of CNN. Greta, however, is intent on persuading Cora that her tendency to catastrophize (there's apparently a term for it) is an unhealthy coping mechanism that's contributing to her anxiety, not an endearing personality quirk.

"Are you snooping, stalling, or hiding?"

The voice surprises her and she whips around so fast, a bobby pin comes loose, allowing a carefully contained curl to go rogue.

"Daddy!" A pause to take him in. "Wow. You look amazing."

Wes stands in the doorway, impossibly regal. Dashing, to put it in the language of the thick Regency romance novels that Cora's taken to devouring in the pandemic with the same fervor others have for their sourdough starters.

Tan suit, gleaming white Cole Haan sneakers, and a brand-new gold cane just for the occasion. Even after all these years, in the most illogical moments—like this one—Cora's mind will suddenly cut to an image of her father shrunken and slack-jawed in bed attached to all those tubes in that cold hospital room. It's a mental stutter she's never been able to shed. And when it happens, she's jarred by the man that exists before her, as lively and vibrant as ever. In the chasm between those two images is an entire miracle. The only lingering effects of the massive stroke he suffered almost two decades ago are a limp in his left leg, slurred speech when he's tired, and, for Cora, the vestiges of dread that make it so she can't, to this day, pass a hospital or even watch a medical drama without her stomach turning over.

Wes performs a showy spin in the doorway and then taps his cane with a flourish that would make Fred Astaire proud. "I clean up okay, I suppose. I'm glad you talked me out of trying to dye all this gray with Just For Men last night. I'm already sweating like a racehorse. Have me out here dripping black streams down my face like that fool Rudy Giuliani."

"The gray makes you look very distinguished, Daddy."

"Forget that mess. *Distinguished* is just another word for *old*. I don't want to look distinguished, I want to look like Idris Elba."

"Hey, in twenty years, Idris Elba is going to wanna look as good as *you* do right now. And he'll wish he was able to pull off a bow tie half as well."

"The bow tie *is* super fly, ain't it? What can I say, I had to do it for today. It's a big one. I think everyone's 'bout here. You ready for this, baby girl?"

"Forget me. Are *you* ready, Daddy? It's your wedding day. I'm just the officiant . . . and best woman."

One of those roles required Cora to get registered in Virginia as a civil celebrant and spend weeks writing and rewriting the perfect sermon; the other required her to help her dad pick out rings and now she has to keep them safe, since he often can't remember where he left his car keys, never mind a set of diamond wedding bands.

"That's something, huh? Your old man getting hitched after all this time. Since golf wasn't in the cards for me with this bum leg, I suppose taking up married life in retirement is a solid plan B. I just joked with Lorraine a minute ago that you know you're getting up there when you met your bride playing trivia on a Viking river cruise. We're gonna have to start lying and tell people we met on the computer; it's just too dang cliché. At least it was trivia and not bingo."

"Wait a minute—you saw Lorraine already? She's supposed to stay in the guest room until we start. That's bad luck!"

"Oh, nonsense. I done used up all my bad luck. Nothing left but the good. That stone-cold fox agreeing to marry me is proof of that."

"Luck had nothing to do with it, Dad."

"Hey, how many times I gotta tell you, you can't have love without luck. Those two go hand in hand, like pickles and bananas."

"How many times do I have to tell you that's a heinous combination."

"Whatever. I do me. Isn't that what you kids say? Anyway, we best get out there. I think everyone's about here. I appreciate you being the one to marry us today, Cora. I know public speaking isn't exactly your thing."

"Don't worry, Dad. I've got this."

"You always do. Also, I appreciate that you were okay with Lincoln joining in on the Noom or Vroom or whatever is. It's a shame he can't make it."

"What are you talking about, he can't make it?"

For weeks now, Cora has been fortifying herself for this, picturing Lincoln's face materializing in the two-by-two box on the screen, rehearsing the even tone she'd use. *Hey, Lincoln, long time.* And now he isn't coming? It was like spending all week preparing for a hurricane that swerves out to sea at the last second. All those boarded-up windows and adrenaline—such a waste.

"Sorry, I thought he might have texted you. He reached out this morning and said something came up with one of his cases. He better be making big bucks to be working on a Sunday and missing my big day."

The way that Cora's hand grips the laptop so tightly her knuckles hurt is at odds with her cheeriness when she responds. "Oh, no, he didn't tell me. That's too bad."

"Well, my man sent a five-hundred-dollar bottle of Macallan, so I feel better already."

Cora is supposed to feel better too, that she doesn't have to face Lincoln today after all, but the signals her body is sending her seem to be confusing relief with disappointment or vice versa. She recognizes it as the same chaotic roiling she experienced the last time she spoke to Lincoln. Eight years ago. The night before he married Naomi. A woman whom Cora had thought of as Lincoln's rebound . . . until she was his fiancée. That evening, the phone rang after midnight. Cora was climbing the stairs to her apartment after a bad date (because of course). She'd agreed, hastily, to meet up with Malik—a setup by her coworker—solely to distract herself from the fact that Lincoln was getting married in less than twenty-four hours, and she'd sworn to herself that she'd decide how she felt about that development by then, before it was too late. And yet she hadn't. The emotional limbo remained, a tightrope she'd walked for so many years now, she could close her eyes and balance on it.

That call, though, the timing of it, caught her off guard. Cora had had to sit down for the conversation, collapsing on her West Elm couch, the one that looked like it belonged in someone's parents' house and was the first unequivocally adult item she'd ever purchased (or, rather, paid for every month). She could barely hear Lincoln over the chatter and music in the background; he was talking into his cell phone in a low whisper, and yet his words were loud and clear. "I don't know if I'm making a mistake, Bella."

There was no reason for her to whisper, since she was alone in her apartment except for the flamingos looking at her, wide-eyed, from the whimsical wallpaper she'd spent twelve hours painstakingly hanging on an accent wall opposite the sofa, yet she responded in a hush that matched his. "I can't tell you not to marry her, Lincoln. If that's what you want me to do, I can't."

"I know. I just . . . I just always thought it would be you, Bella."

"Lincoln—" One word and Cora stopped cold. She was distracted thinking about that day, all those years ago, forty-eight hours after she'd returned from Paris, when she'd written to Lincoln to tell him that she'd finally made a decision. Whatever it was that they were doing at that point—was officially over. For real this time. She wasn't going to move to Chicago; she had to focus on herself and her own choices. She wanted, or, if not wanted, *needed* to be by herself. To go it alone. At least for a while, until she could prove to herself that she could. (Cora, naturally, left out any mention of the emotional whirlwind of her time in Paris and whether it had or hadn't influenced this somewhat impulsive decision so as not to confuse matters.)

It was cowardly to do it by email—she was no better than Funky Fabiene—but Cora couldn't face Lincoln. She wasn't convinced she was strong enough for the barrage of counterarguments that would come. An hour after sending the email, she received a one-sentence reply: *You're going to regret this.* Cora woke up every day waiting to see if he was right until it was too late to matter. The night before his wedding, Lincoln had asked her directly.

"Do you have any regrets, Cora?"

"So many and none at all—it depends on the day."

"Cora being Cora."

A high and light giggle came from somewhere near Lincoln, and Cora wondered if it was Naomi, the elated future Mrs. Ames, blissfully oblivious. "Why are you calling me, Lincoln?"

His sigh was so loud, she could almost feel his warm breath in her ear. "I don't know. Is that okay?"

"It's not like you, but yeah, it's okay. I don't know what you want me to say though."

"I just . . . wanted to hear your voice is all. It's been too long."

"Well, I'm glad you called so I could tell you I'm happy for you. Nerves or doubts before your wedding is normal, or so I hear. But it's going to be good, Lincoln. This is everything you always wanted." The depth of her sincerity came as a surprise to Cora and probably to Lincoln, and she decided that explained the catch in his voice as he ended their call.

"So I guess this is goodbye, then, Bella . . . again."

It wasn't goodbye, though, because they weren't capable of goodbye. There were texts over the years. And emails. One or two postcards. But, as Neisha said every time she and Lincoln were in touch, "Come on, Cora, you had your chance. You're no homewrecker—put the matches down." At the end of the day, though, Cora could no more cut off Lincoln than she could cut off the tip of her pinkie. The ache of loss would always be there, even if the injury didn't cripple her.

However, ironically, Cora hasn't been in touch with Lincoln since he *stopped* being another woman's husband. She found out about Lincoln's separation the same way she learned of many of the developments in his life—through her father, who became, with Cora's approval, close to Lincoln again during the long years of his recovery.

It was Wes who'd shown her a picture of Lincoln's newborn son, then the daughter who came soon after. She couldn't be mad at her father for subjecting her to this; she was bound to see the photos on Facebook at some point, but the way Wes thrust his phone in her face with a level of delight, like he was these kids' actual grandfather, was an unpleasant sensation she would have avoided staring at the pictures alone, in bed, which she did a few times before she hid Lincoln's profile altogether.

Wes wasted no time in reporting that Lincoln was "on the market again." He'd called to share this tidbit while Cora was in line at Sweetgreen to get a healthy kale Caesar for lunch, and after the call she was forced to divert to the Five Guys next door. Lettuce wouldn't do; her unsettled stomach cried for French fries.

She would kill for hot fries right now, the forever antidote for any unrest, but there is no time, and she will almost certainly get grease on her dress minutes before the ceremony. Also, today is not about her. Or Lincoln. Or the past. Or love. Actually, it is very much about love, her dad's turn at it. At last. He shouldn't have to share this moment with Cora's regrets and second-guessing.

"Come on, Daddy, let's get you hitched." Cora threads her arm through his and rests her head on his shoulder, which grows meatier every year. He kisses her forehead and neither of them move, as if nothing will change if they don't leave this study; it will be the two of them forever as it has always been. They'd stopped considering that it could be any other way, and they silently stand hand in hand, holding tight, reminding each other that whatever may come, this remains so. One last squeeze and Cora pulls them both forward into the day.

As she stands at the altar facing the dozen or so guests, Cora rethinks everything she planned to say about commitment, timing, destiny, patience, and luck—her index cards are packed with every thought about partnership and marriage she could find, heavy on quotes from Jay Shetty, Audre Lorde, Shakespeare, and even the Bible, because she's heard "Love is patient, love is kind" at so many weddings, it almost feels like a requirement. She even added, in an act of desperation, an Anita Baker lyric or two. It is a hackneyed, jumbled mess of ideas about love meant to substitute for Cora's own woeful lack of understanding of the subject, and it won't do.

She drops the cards and starts speaking, trusting herself to say something right and true off the cuff—a monumental risk. Her voice is shaky to start but she hits her stride telling the story of how her dad took her swimming every single Sunday for five years straight when she was little. Cora initially refused to go into the cold, chemical-smelling water at the indoor swim center, but eventually, Wes coaxed her in. Over time, he taught her to swim, and when she mastered that, he gave her challenges to complete—learn to dive, jump off the concrete high-dive platform into the deep end, hold her breath underwater for a minute, et cetera. Afterward, they went to McDonald's and she got a strawberry sundae for dessert if she had successfully completed the challenge. To this day, Cora associates the tang of strawberries with triumph.

"But this isn't a story about how I learned to swim—it's about how I learned what love is in that pool. When I refused to open my eyes underwater, I came to trust that I could reach out my flailing arms and find my dad. When the water was so freezing I thought my goose bumps would be permanent, I came to trust I would be warm again. When I thought I couldn't do another lap or face a higher dive or hold my breath another second, I came to trust that I could go on. That's what love does—teaches you, pushes you, challenges you, warms you.

"My dad has been singularly devoted to me for my entire life; I'll never be able to repay everything he's given up to raise me, the sacrifices I'm aware of and the many I'll never know about. Whether they be small, like him losing sleep, or—"

Wes interrupts her. "Sleep is no small thing, baby girl. You cried every night from two to six in the morning for a decade. And that's only a slight exaggeration."

Cora joins with the laughter, then waits a beat for it to die down, allowing herself time to control the quake in her voice and squash the memory of Renee and her letter.

"Okay, well, I won't even get started on the big ones, then. The point is, I like to think that the universe rewarded him by bringing him Lorraine. And for you, Lorraine—the funny, generous kind person you are—I like to think my dad is your reward too. After all, what greater gift can the universe offer than leading us to our perfect match. That's what you two are . . . just like pickles and bananas." Cora stops to wink at her dad, but it's an excuse to gather herself for the next part.

She closes her eyes, opens them, and recites Samuel Beckett's "Cascando." She hasn't said the poem out loud since her Professor Keane days, but every word, every intonation, is right there, nestled snugly in her memory. It never stops being a source of fascination and fear for Cora, just how many things there are to forget and to remember, the never-ending work of sifting out what to hold on to and what to let go of . . . memories, objects, grudges, fears. *People.*

Finally, Cora arrives at the end, and the tears she's managed to hold off will be denied no longer: "And now, it's my great honor to announce Wesley Lewis Belle and Lorraine Ann Kennedy are officially husband and wife. You can kiss the bride!"

Their embrace is a little passionate for Cora's taste. Watching her dad kiss his new wife (*wife!*) leaves her both thrilled and squeamish. Mostly thrilled, though.

Still, she looks away, bashful, as the kiss goes on and on. Her eyes turn skyward and this, along with the looming wistfulness, thick as the humidity, makes her think of her mother, whom she imagines floating around somewhere beyond the clouds. Cora's never outgrown her little-girl version of heaven—rainbows, clouds, white robes—even if she's never been quite sold on the idea.

It's nice, if jarring, to let thoughts of her mom wash over her without the reflexive resistance. She credits Greta for this. Therapy is supposed to help you overcome your mommy issues even when you refuse to cop to them, or maybe especially then. She still remembers how Greta's practiced placid expression cracked into a sort of shocked bemusement when Cora told her that her mother was a "nonissue" in her life ("It was a long time ago, I was so young," et cetera). Cora had sought therapy for a more pressing matter. Her breakup with Carlos.

Actually, it wasn't so much their breakup she wanted to understand or figure out how to get over (she was practiced enough at that by that point); what Cora wanted to get to the bottom of was why she was so devastated to lose someone she wasn't, in retrospect, convinced she'd truly loved, even after over four years together. Cora had decided she'd wanted to marry Carlos. She'd arrived at this decision for a lot of reasons, most of which had nothing to do with love and everything to do with the nine weddings she'd been to the year they met, the same year she turned thirty, and the inchoate dread born of a thousand cultural messages that there would be disastrous consequences if she didn't get herself down an aisle in the near future. The problem was, Carlos didn't agree they should get married, for reasons that also had nothing to do with love and everything to do with dreams of an acting career and his vague explanations about not being ready "for that type of stuff." Did he mean marriage? Adulthood? Dish sets? Cora could never tell. But it didn't matter after he said, "I can't do this anymore." All that mattered was that Cora was single again and she has stayed that way. She's stayed with Greta too, long after Carlos faded from being the most important person in her life to someone she used to know.

Week after week, Greta has taken a chisel to Cora's defenses and helped her accept "a big truth" of her life (Greta is a fan of "big truths"): Cora's mother's death has affected her in ways that she hasn't recognized or acknowledged, and the approach of "locking the topic in the trunk of my mind," as Cora described it, has not proven to be all that effective a strategy. This perhaps shouldn't have been as surprising as it was, but given that it upended everything Cora thought about her entire life, it has taken some processing. "The work," Greta calls it. Turns out a breakthrough in therapy offers a similar rush as a bright red A splashed across an exam or paper. Cora has now gotten to the point where she can think of her mother without a painful cramp seizing her heart; can forgive her father for being so overwhelmed by raising her alone that he shut down in many ways (a "trauma response") and unknowingly passed some of those emotional blocks to Cora; can fully appreciate how beautiful it is that Wes is opening up to another chance at love in the wake of such devastating loss. Her dad has always been big on lessons, and he is living one. It's as plain to see as the wide smile spread across his face.

Wes catches her watching him now. He nods as if offering an answer to a question she hasn't asked, raises a glass, and turns back to the scrum of well-wishers gathered around him. They're standing either too close or too far apart, since no one can remember how physical space works, and talking too loudly with the heightened, fevered revelry of people out of practice at it. Wes is in his element, holding court, hand in hand with his bride, flanked by friends, all back pats and *Did I ever tell you the story . . .* and *That reminds me of a joke, tell me if you've heard this before.* They've almost always heard it before, but they're hardly going to stop him.

Cora should be polite and mingle with the guests and indulge all the folks who are undoubtedly going to ask if there's anyone special in her life, the central focus of conversation with any single woman, especially at weddings. She should stop thinking of her mother and Carlos and how she recently asked Greta if there was something wrong with her for being single for so, so long (was that tied to her mother too?) and how Greta turned it around, as she was wont to do. "I don't know, Cora—do you think there's something wrong with you?"

And Cora most definitely should give more thought to what she's about to do but the champagne she grabs from an ice bucket will help with that.

She swigs quickly, directly from the bottle, as she makes way her into the house and down the hall to the bathroom, so by the time she perches on the edge of the tub, the tile like a block of ice against her sticky thighs, she has plausible deniability. Getting tipsy is a shield and an excuse to give in to impulse and do what she's known she was going to do for at least the past hour. Momentum also helps. Deliberating for too long about whether to eat another slice of cake or not cuts the joy with guilt when you end up eating the cake anyway. Better to dive right in. So though her mind is screaming, *Maybe this is a bad idea,* her fingers are already fumbling to pull the cell phone from the pocket of her dress.

She calls, immediately disconnects, and FaceTimes instead—she needs to see him. When Lincoln appears on the screen, she blinks slowly several times to register the fuller face, the thick salt-and-pepper beard, the higher forehead. She superimposes these features over the boy's she used to know like computer-aging software, then flips back and forth between them, fascinated by how handsome both versions are in completely different ways.

What's most striking is how familiar he is to her. The same way she can still vividly recall all the dents in the silver pot her long-dead grandmother made oatmeal in, Cora is willing to bet that she could still trace the patch of scattered freckles in Lincoln's left shoulder blindfolded.

And, of course, the reason she FaceTimed in the first place: that smile. Right there, so close she could touch it.

"What's good, Cora Belle?"

Those were the first words he ever said to her all those years ago. She doesn't believe this is intentional. He's probably used this greeting a thousand times. And yet the echo from the past hits her some type of way, like a rush of champagne bubbles to the head.

Time has lost all meaning lately, so it makes sense that Cora can't be sure if it's 1999 or 2021 or maybe both can exist simultaneously in some bizarre time warp. As she stares at Lincoln, it's yesterday, today, and tomorrow all at once.

A circle has always been her favorite shape.

CORA GOES BACK TO THE FUTURE

September 2021

What am I doing?

The answer eludes Cora for the whole Uber ride to the airport, the entire three-hour flight on an eerily empty 747, and the trip through rush-hour traffic in a black Mercedes town car to the sleek lakefront high-rise. But the second she steps on the elevator that will shoot her twenty-three stories up to Lincoln's penthouse, it's irrelevant, because it's done. She's here. So she'll also stop asking herself why. Or what she hopes will come of spending a weekend in Chicago with her recently divorced ex-boyfriend.

Cora, gamely, tried to summon a suitable answer when Greta asked this at their last session: "I just can't keep thinking there's unfinished business there," she said. Neisha got a variation on that: "You're making too much of this, Ne-ne. It's no big deal. Just meeting up with an old friend. What else do I have going on?"

This morning, at two a.m., staring at the clock, Cora indulged a melodramatic, and possibly more truthful, rationale: *Maybe no one will ever love me like Lincoln; maybe he was always the one; maybe you've always missed him. Maybe we're supposed to live happily ever after. There's only one way to find out.*

Together, these statements added up to a somewhat coherent explanation, the same way a pile of Popsicle sticks could be built into a house as long as you didn't push it too hard. Or try to live in it.

Lincoln's glossy mahogany door flies open before Cora can even knock. When he pulls her into a tight embrace, all the weirdness Cora anticipated melts into an ease and familiarity that's almost more disorienting than the awkwardness would have been. But at that instant Cora knows that coming here was the right choice, whatever the weekend holds, and with that, she decides to just let go and enjoy herself. Greta would be proud.

The night of her dad's wedding, she'd gotten off the phone with Lincoln long enough to say goodbye to the guests and see her dad and Lorraine off to their honeymoon suite at the Mayflower Hotel. Then she'd left the pile of dirty dishes and smudged glasses she'd promised to stay and clean waiting in the kitchen, crawled into her childhood bed in her silk dress, and called Lincoln right back. They caught up a bit more and Lincoln told her how bad he felt about missing the wedding before he said, "Talking to you is great, but I want to see you. I *need* to see you. And not on a screen. Check your email."

In her inbox was a first-class ticket to Chicago. "It's a weekend I don't have the kids. Will it work?"

It was as simple as saying yes. They agreed to get off the phone and wait to catch up properly in person, but that only added more weight and anticipation to this meeting, a buildup a month in the making.

Now Lincoln steps back and ushers her into the opulent foyer; there's so many gilded surfaces, she might need to put her sunglasses back on. "I'm sorry I couldn't pick you up at O'Hare; I just wrapped up my Zoom. Was the car okay?"

"The driver offered me Fiji Water and two warm oatmeal cookies. It was more than okay."

"I told him to come prepped! That sweet tooth of yours."

Cora runs her hands over the textured wallpaper of the hallway as she follows him into the apartment. "Um, is this . . . fur?"

"Yeah, pony hide. Ain't that a trip?"

They arrive in an enormous sunken living room backed by a dramatic wall of glass with a view of the city and Lake Michigan beyond. The water, a swirl of sun-flecked greens and blues, seems to start right at her toes, and stretch to the horizon, giving her the sensation that she could just float away.

"These views!" Cora swivels her head across the panoramic expanse, surveying the city laid out before her. She's finally here—all those years dreaming of a life in Chicago, and she'd never set foot in the city, but now she's face-to-face with the backdrop of that other life that awaited her once upon a time.

"Yeah, it never gets old." Lincoln crosses his arms and gazes on the skyline anchored by the looming Sears Tower and the glittering water beyond it with such pride, he might have built all the skyscrapers and dug the lake bed himself.

"Come on, let me give you the full tour."

"Do we have time for that? This place is huge."

"Four thousand square feet, but who's counting."

"You, apparently!"

"Well, my Realtor. She sold me on it by telling me both Michael Jordan and Common own condos here. Had to add Lincoln Ames to the illustrious roster, ya know?"

"I have to confess, I was kinda expecting a sad bachelor pad. I mean, the last place I saw you living in was the Pound—shoes in plastic crates and whatnot."

"I hired a decorator to help move me away from particleboard and Kobe Bryant posters."

Cora's eyes drift to the framed magazine cover, blown up to nearly life-size and prominently displayed on the living-room wall. It's Lincoln in full glossy glory, striking a similar pose to the one he does now, Superman stance, cocky smile, chin jutting. The bold headline grazes the top of his head: TAKING AMES AT THE CPD.

Cora read the *Chicago* magazine profile when it was published a few years back upon the record-setting, multimillion-dollar settlement Lincoln scored against the Chicago PD for racial profiling.

"Clever what they did there with the *Ames*. What's it feel like to be a cover model?"

"Not as good as it felt to make those thugs pay up."

They amble over to the slate fireplace and the row of frames on the mantel. Cora leans in and picks up a picture of his kids. She's supposed to eagerly proclaim how cute they are no matter what, but they truly are, in a way that makes her ache for so many different reasons that a lifetime on Greta's couch could never unpack them all.

The daughter, Laila, has Lincoln's eyes—jet-black, round, and wide like she's in a perpetual state of surprise or delight. And little Leon cocks his head the same way as his father, causing Cora to marvel at the astonishing power of genetics. She's glad there aren't any pictures of Naomi because her Noxzema-commercial beauty feels like a personal attack.

"Your kids are adorable. No surprise." She finds the phrase *your kids* sticky against her lips.

"They are, aren't they?" He shrugs like the good fortune to have two adorable, smiling, healthy children is all part of his destiny. "You know, Laila's middle name is Rose."

Cora almost drops the frame in her hand. She did not know this. Nor does she know what to do with this bombshell. "After me?"

"I don't know—maybe. Or a nod to . . . what happened. You know. It felt right. Or something I needed to acknowledge? I just sort of suggested it in the hospital room, and Naomi was into the name so . . . not that she would have made the connection."

There are long stretches of time—months, if not years—that Cora forgets about their "ordeal," as she always labeled it. It isn't that it's locked away like some shameful secret, because she isn't ashamed at all. Over the years, she has been ever more grateful that she even had the choice and never more so than when she periodically pondered what her life would have been like at various points—with an eight-year-old, a twelve-year-old, or, today, a nineteen-year-old. A nineteen-year-old! An alternative reality that never failed to leave her dumbfounded.

The relief that she'd had the ability—the wherewithal, the resources, and, most important, the access—to save herself from this path is as intense today as it was the day she'd left the clinic slumped against Kim. So when the shout-your-abortion hashtag became a thing a few years back, she almost did it even if she had tweeted all of twice in her life. She was this close before realizing that Lincoln might see it. She'd kept up the lie of her miscarriage for so long, it had nearly morphed into the truth by sheer longevity. And using that same excuse—the fact that so much time had passed—she'd decided that Lincoln never needed to know what she did. A rationale grounded in platitudes about letting sleeping dogs lie and water under the bridge and all that. Their current line of conversation threatens to force her to revisit this reasoning, so she pivots as fast as she can.

"So, uh, what else is there to see around here? Life-size gold-plated tigers?"

"Those are on order. But follow me."

They go down another wide hall lined with canvases of various sizes. She passes slowly, taking each one in like she's at a museum. She spots one and does a double take.

"Lincoln, you kept it!"

In front of Cora is the striped painting she gave him for Christmas all those years ago, which, to her surprise, is holding its own next to the other artwork.

"Of course I kept it."

"And put up right next to a Kehinde Wiley? Is that a *real* Kehinde Wiley?"

"Girl, please. Of course it's real. But I got this early, when there were a few less zeros in the price. You know his work?"

Since her summer working at the Warren Gallery in Richmond and her whirlwind trip to Paris and the museums she loved there, Cora has made an effort to learn about art. Not necessarily because she loves art itself—though some of it speaks to her—but because she wants to be a person who knows about art. Also, she finds museums peaceful. There are so few places where the point is to be quiet and alone.

"Yeah, I do, I'm a fan. He came on my radar when he did the Obama portraits. I got a postcard of his *Two Sisters* painting at the National Portrait Gallery gift shop. I don't have anything like this, though. Obviously." She stumbles back from the painting as if she could damage the canvas by standing too close. "You know, it's okay to hang my work in the bathroom or something. Not sure this is where it belongs."

"Get outta here. Your painting is right where it's supposed to be."

In a few more steps they're standing at the double doors that open to Lincoln's bedroom suite. The carpet is so white and soft-looking, she's worried it's made of actual rabbit fur. There's a king-size bed on a raised platform against a leather headboard that spans the entire wall. It's impossible to ignore it for many reasons—its size, its placement, its fifty-four pillows, its quiet beckoning.

They stand there, so close they can feel the heat coming off each other, watching the bed like it's going to perform a trick.

"Come on, let's get out of here. I want to take you somewhere before dinner."

With one last glance at the bed, Cora turns to follow him.

When they make it down to the garage, Cora has seen enough of Lincoln's world to know that the matte-black Ranger Rover is his even before the chirp of the alarm confirms it. With anyone else, this would all be insufferable: The two-inch-wide Rolex. The plain black sweatshirt that has *Balenciaga* splashed across it. *The pony hide.* But Cora forgives Lincoln of his flashiness because she understands its source. She sees through all the brands and bravado to the kid from the claustrophobic trailer oozing nicotine from its thin wood-paneled walls. The scrawny student who arrived at college on a Greyhound bus with his clothes in a black Hefty bag is going to make damn sure that everyone—especially himself—appreciates how far he's come. So Cora isn't put off by his puffed-up pride; she shares it. He has the life story that inspirational memoirs are made of. It's one thing to love someone; it's another thing altogether to admire him, and how can you not admire Lincoln Jerome Ames?

They drive down the famed Gold Coast, following the path of the Chicago River cutting through the city. The streets are packed with tourists wearing wool blazers and cashmere scarves against the fall chill that's already announced itself, even this early in September, undeterred by the dogged sun.

Lincoln turns up the stereo, and Cora can feel the bass pound through the heated leather seats and vibrate under her, intensifying the hot thrumming she was already experiencing and trying—and failing—to ignore.

"Okay, I'm just going to say it—they don't make music like they used to. You can't even understand what these young'uns are saying. They're just mumbling over a beat."

"You sound like my dad. You are aware you just said *young'uns*, right?"

"I sound like everyone's dad. That's what happens when you become one. I told a legit dad joke at work the other day. Wanna hear it?"

"I have a feeling I don't have a choice."

"You don't. Here goes: The past, present, and future walk into a bar. What's the mood?"

"I give up."

"Tense!" His booming laugh reminds Cora that she once wished she could record it and save it forever. Thanks to the iPhone in her bag, she now can. But she realizes she never needed technology for that; the sound is lodged in her mind, as recognizable and distantly familiar as the trill of the ice cream truck coming down her street and with the same ability to shoot her through with nostalgia.

"They should fire you for that. How is work, anyway? Do you still love it?"

"It's cool. Not what I thought I would be doing, I suppose—working for some old white dudes that look like the villainous overseers in every slavery movie ever made, but you know, those golden handcuffs. Once they finally promoted me last summer, it felt like a wrap. August 2020, I made partner. Coincidence? Cartwright and Company wasn't even thinking about that before then, even after I was on magazine covers. They were all 'Wait your turn and you still need to prove yourself; that was just one big case.' All that BS to avoid putting my picture in the partners' gallery. I had to call them out. 'Oh, so nooow I'm getting a promotion because George Floyd was murdered and y'all suddenly see fit to right some wrongs?' The equity partners are all in the boardroom around this stupidly big table and they're looking at each other like *This Negro, how dare he not just shut up and be grateful*? But they know by now, I'ma going to call a spade a spade. Then I asked for two hundred K more, because why not? Reparations."

"And they gave it to you?" He's acting like it's loose change, when it's more than twice Cora's salary.

"Yup. I come a long way from the kid who had to collect plastic bottles to pay for his braces, eh?"

"So what's it like to be rich?"

"Ha! Even better than I imagined. And definitely better than the alternative, I'll say that. People—especially white people—give you a little more respect when you have some money in your pocket. They like a couple of successful Black folks around so they can say: *See? Anyone can do it! Good ol' American dream.* But they also resent you too—it's always just under the surface. *How exactly did you get here?* They can't pinpoint it. It just don't feel right to them, ya know? Any way you cut it, you still can't escape their suspicion. The unique plight of the rich Black man." He stops to strum an imaginary violin and chuckle.

"For real though, the thing is that when you're poor, you're convinced money can solve all your problems. It just makes them easier to deal with, though, that's all. I can afford to send my mom to the fanciest rehab but can't convince her to go—no amount of zeros in my account can get the bottle outta her hands. Or get her to stop smoking, and now she has the COPD. In and out of the hospital all the time but you still can't tell her nothing. I haven't seen much of her. She refuses to come to Chicago for whatever reason—I think she's scared to fly and doesn't want to admit it—and Naomi always refused to go to Mississippi, which was just as well. They were like two alley cats anyway. I was fittin' to get heart issues being in the same room as those two, few times that happened."

Petty as it may be, Cora draws some delight that Naomi was as hard-pressed to win Deb over as she was.

"How's your dad and brothers?"

"Pops . . . he's been spending more time back home. He bought the trailer across from my mom. Probably about as close as they need to be so they can avoid killing each other. He pulls up every now and then with his hand out. Brothers are good. Deacon's by you, matter a fact. Teaching at Gallaudet. I funded a scholarship there in Dre's name. I had to do something."

Andre died six years ago—a sudden heart attack at his cousin's wedding—and when Cora learned that, she left work early and sat in a park and sobbed. It was an odd reaction, considering she wasn't ever all that close to Dre, and she hadn't talked to him for years at that point, but she'd spent many a night in college listening to him vent about girls while sitting on the saggy couch at the Pound, and she'd watched his life unfold on Facebook—his wedding, the birth of his son, starting his software business—and so had a distant but very real feeling of intimacy. He was also the first person her own age who'd died. That's death's real curse when it strikes close, not just the grief but the fear. *What if I'm next?* Andre had had so much more living to do at thirty-four and so did she, and only one of them would get to do it. The staggering unfairness and capriciousness of that sent Cora to the park bench, where the ducks watched her calm and unfazed as if they'd figured something essential about nature and mortality.

Cora had sent Lincoln a Hallmark card with a note about how sorry she was. She'd read somewhere that it was nice to include a personal anecdote in your condolences, so she wrote about how she always got a kick out of how much Andre cared about the two sad fish in the tank they'd had at the Pound, how he was so attentive to Biggie and Smalls, pinching just the right amount of fish food into the tank every night. It spoke to his nurturing spirit. Cora thought it was a nice sentiment, but as soon as she dropped the envelope in the mailbox, it bowled her over how inadequate it was. Feeding fish? The stupid mass-produced card with the somber floral print? *I hope you're doing okay?* What meager gestures in the face of an astonishing finality. In the face of losing your best friend, your boy for life. When she didn't hear back from Lincoln after sending the card, she assumed he agreed.

"Dre passing like that was rough. Some losses you never get over. Only thought that makes me happy is that the last thing he did on this earth was the electric slide."

"That's something. It'd be amazing if we could choose how we got to go, wouldn't it?"

"What would it be for you?"

"I don't know—eating, I guess. Let me choke on a French fry? At eighty-five, though. What about you?"

"Can I say in your arms?"

"Lincoln!"

"What? You think I'm playing."

"I am not touching that. Where are we going, anyway?"

"We're in Oak Park right now. That house right there . . . " Lincoln slows the car and points to a stately brick house with black shutters and a red roof. "That's a Frank Lloyd Wright. He did a bunch of houses in this area. I would kill to get one of them, but they never go on the market. One day, though." He stares through the window with a glint of determination before pulling off. "But I don't have a destination in mind. Just wanted to drive with you . . . like back in college. How we'd get in the car and go nowhere because it was all I could afford to do and that's only because we were using Julian's gas. I'd love to drive you up to Lake Geneva. Got my eye on a place there, right on the water. I'll take you next time."

Next time.

"We gotta get back for our dinner reservation. You'll love this place. Best Wagyu rib eye you've ever had, mark my words. I got you a dress to wear. It's hanging in the guest-room closet."

"What? This isn't *Pretty Woman*. I have something I can wear."

It's presumptuous for Lincoln to think that she didn't pack anything suitable, but then again, the Marshalls dress that looked so sophisticated and sexy (it was fitted and backless!) in her bathroom mirror now suddenly seems shabby and embarrassing and destined for Goodwill as soon as she gets back home. "Besides, how do you know it'll fit? I'm not college size anymore."

"None of us are. Even though I pay my trainer a fortune to make it so. All the money in the world can't turn back time, alas. In your case, a little extra meat suits you. But I got three sizes so you can see which fits best."

Sure enough, back at Lincoln's apartment, she finds three identical dresses hanging in the otherwise empty guest-room closet, like a rack in a high-end boutique. They are as beautiful as pieces of art—a velvety smooth black crepe fabric with intricate embroidered flowers, a halter neck, and a startlingly high slit up the side. Cora dares to look at the price tag: eight hundred dollars. More expensive than the dress she wore to her father's wedding. More than the bridesmaid dress she had to buy for Neisha's wedding, which was as much as she'd ever spent on a single item of clothing. Forget the matching heart necklaces split in two; that garment hanging in her closet is a testament to their friendship as much as anything—Cora's willingness to spend an entire paycheck on an asymmetrical dress the color of wet concrete that she'd wear exactly once.

Cora's still clutching the price tag when Lincoln appears at the door with a small box. "One more thing."

"Are you kidding me? The dress is already too much. What did I say? This isn't some *Pretty Woman* scenario."

"Cora Belle, just open it."

She obeys. Inside is a diamond tennis bracelet nestled in red satin. The diamonds are so brilliant, she reflexively squints looking down at it. "Lincoln—I can't accept this."

"Don't be silly." He takes her wrist and fastens the bracelet around it with ease. "Much better than that janky necklace I got you at the mall kiosk."

It isn't better at all. Truth is, Cora would have rather have had that back. It had probably turned all shades of green by now, if Lincoln had even kept it. Something tells her he did not, because he saw a piece of junk metal, not its true value.

"Okay, I'll let you get changed. We're leaving in twenty." It is only then that he lets go of his soft hold on Cora's wrist.

At the restaurant—an old mattress factory turned swanky steak house—the maître d' says, "Follow me, Mr. and Mrs. Ames." They don't correct him and Cora allows herself to try on being Lincoln's wife for the walk to the dark booth in the back corner, which, actually, is not unlike imagining herself as Julia Roberts in *Pretty Woman*.

Just as they arrive at the booth, she feels a finger run along her back, just below her shoulder, where the skin is exposed at the edge of the delicate fabric.

"Well, well, well, what's this?"

It's easy to forget her tattoo is there; much harder to forget when and why she got it and that Lincoln hasn't seen it before.

"Oh, a tattoo. I got it back in college, actually, after we broke up."

Lincoln looks at her like she's pulled a rabbit from under her dress. Or a bag of meth. "Whoa. Who woulda thought. What's it mean?"

"It's silly . . . a compass, it was supposed to help me find my way? Something like that."

"Did it work?"

"Too soon to tell, I suppose."

"Still?" he asks, holding her eyes across the table as they sit down.

"I need a drink."

The cocktail she settles on is absinthe and six other ingredients she's never heard of. To her surprise, Lincoln orders a martini.

"Wait, you drink now? Who woulda thought?"

"On occasion. Hazard of the job. I got too many looks at firm functions when I didn't drink, like I was an alcoholic or addict they had to worry about. Ironic. I didn't care about peer pressure in college, but my boss says, 'Oh, come on, surely you're not turning down a Glenlivet,' and next thing you know, I'm knocking back scotches to fit in. Still don't love it but it helps when I'm nervous."

"You're nervous?"

"Li'l bit, li'l bit."

"Why?"

"I don't know, Cora. Because you're here. Finally. And I don't want to fuck it up."

"You curse now too?" Cora makes a show of clutching her imaginary pearls.

"Here and there."

"It's sexy, I gotta say." That may or may not be the absinthe talking.

"Well, I'll sure as hell have to do it more, in that case."

"So, Choirboy, are you no longer thinking about running for office at some point?"

"Eh, I don't know. Maybe. That other dude from Chicago beat me to first Black president. Second doesn't have the same ring to it. What about you? I'm proud of you for doing such good work—helping kids and all—but are you going to stay at Kids First forever? Or at least become executive director or something?"

"Who knows. My boss isn't going anywhere anytime soon, and I'm not sure I want to run the org anyway. It mainly involves asking wealthy people for money to support our work, and that's not my thing. But I feel good about what I do and that counts for a lot—especially these days with everything." Cora gestures widely to indicate the dumpster fire outside this dimly lit oasis of the 1 percent.

"Look at you, out here fighting the good fight."

"Me? I'm not the one with my picture on magazine covers."

"Yeah, I guess. I try to do my part. With my work, and writing fat checks. Take the kids to volunteer at a soup kitchen once a month. But it never feels like enough, you know? And sometimes I think I'm just doing it to feel good, and that's not the same as *being* good. You were always truly good."

"I don't know about all that."

"Same old Cora—can't take a compliment."

"You're right, you're right. Thank you for recognizing I'm basically Mother Teresa."

"Ha! I got some feet you could wash. For real, though, you ever want more?"

"What do you mean, more?"

"I don't know . . . you could start your own organization, run the Red Cross or something, get into corporate philanthropy, make some real money."

"I'm happy with what I do. I did five years at Accenture as soon as my dad was better—you know that. And I hated it. The politics and butt-kissing. The grind. The travel. People turning nouns into verbs. *Ideating*? Gross. Working at Kids First may not be glamorous but it's meaningful. It's enough."

"It's funny. We've always had such different ideas of *enough*. I was grabbing scraps to make a meal and you got a five-course dinner and you weren't even hungry. Guess that's how it works. I just look at you and see so much potential. That's also a compliment, by the way. You could have so much more if you were hungrier."

Cora tries to wash away the bad taste of this "compliment" with a swig of her drink, but the bitterness remains. Once upon a time, she would have been as thirsty for observations like this as a fragile seedling was for water—how would she grow without it? Lincoln—people—telling her who she was seemed like the only way she could figure out who to be. Turns out, that project can't be outsourced. Now that she understands that, Cora chafes against this critique disguised as encouragement.

"More? What does that even mean? Not everybody needs to have grandiose dreams to be content. Being a CEO or writing the great

American novel or getting a million followers on Instagram"—Cora has exactly 127—"why do we always have to be aiming for the next thing, to be the best, to make a mark? I'm not a bad person just because I don't want to hashtag conquer life or wake up at four a.m. every day to hack and hustle myself to death or whatever all those tech bros go on about in podcasts. Leaving Accenture for the nonprofit world *was* my wanting more, more peace for myself. And even if the money's not great, it's okay. I don't need designer clothes or a Tesla or . . . " She holds up her wrist. "Fancy jewelry."

As far as Cora is concerned, wanting too little in life isn't nearly as dangerous as wanting too much. It just isn't a popular opinion. America and all. But she can accept that she and Lincoln have different definitions of success as long as she doesn't have to defend hers.

"Naomi used to say that to me—'I don't care about money.' Had the nerve to accuse me of being flashy. Then she sure got used to it in a hurry. For someone who doesn't care about money, why's she demanding fifteen K a month in alimony? Riddle me that."

"Yikes. How is all that?"

"Divorce? It sucks, full stop. But marriage was no picnic either. I knew I shouldn't have married her. I was so lost in law school. I almost failed out my last year, trying to work full-time and study. Still trying to get over you." He pauses as if to let that sink in. "Meeting Naomi made a difference. What can I say—I always do better with a good woman by my side. But she just wasn't right for me. I knew that but felt like I owed it to her to marry her after all the time and support she put in while I did my thing, years waiting for me to be ready. I was too much of a coward to leave her by then. Especially since she was bouncing off the walls to finally have kids. It was easier just to go along to get along when she pushed for each next step. If she sensed my reluctance, she ignored it. That's one thing she and I do have in common—we're pretty single-minded. Or hardheaded, whatever you want to call it."

"So no regrets, then?"

"Nah. Divorce was the right thing to do. I hope it doesn't screw up the kids too bad. Then I remember how I was raised and I'm like, if I'm all right, they're gonna be straight. Anyway, no one ever won the game of shoulda, coulda, woulda, so not much point in playing. Amiright?" He raises his frosty glass, and Cora signals her agreement by sipping from hers.

"Now I'm supposed to flip the script and ask you about your love life, but you know what, Cora? I don't want to know a damn thing about that, so can I change the subject?"

"Please."

"Okay, good. You look beautiful."

"That's not a subject."

"You're right. I guess that's just a fact."

Another fact: Lincoln and Cora will sleep together tonight. If there was any doubt in her mind, it disappears as he feeds her the last bite of lobster mac and cheese and then reaches over to drag his finger slowly along her lip in pursuit of a nonexistent breadcrumb. When his hand makes its way to her inner thigh on the drive home, it's not so much an invitation as a confirmation of what's about to happen.

Cora hasn't been with anyone for years—not since Carlos. A shameful secret. She's let her friends believe she's at least had some random hookups via the apps or whatever, because she couldn't take Neisha's constant pressure to "get out there." The truth is she isn't built to send flirty messages to men whose profile pictures feature them posing in front of flashy cars . . . or toilets. Or to meet up with some random guy and then see him naked and vice versa. She can't stomach waking up to a stranger and not knowing how either of them feels and the awkwardness (or worse) that could ensue. Enduring an epic dry spell was preferable. But now, at last, comes the chance to break it.

The ride home and the trip to the bedroom is a blur, but when Cora gets her hands on Lincoln and runs them along the muscles up and down his back, the memories of its contours return to her as fast as her habit of overthinking. Which means that instead of surrendering to whatever pleasure awaits her as Lincoln ever so slowly grazes his lips across her collarbone and then down to her left nipple to her belly button, Cora doesn't say *Take me* or *Please* or *I want you*; she says, "Lincoln . . . what are we doing?"

"It's called sex, Cora. As I recall, you're familiar." He cups her ass and pulls her hips to his as if offering a reminder.

"You know what I mean."

"We're doing what we should have been doing all along. Being together. Simple as that."

"Oh, Lincoln. It's not simple at all. It's been twenty years. This is a little crazy. We can't just—"

Lincoln reaches up and presses one finger to her lips while another finger plunges deep inside her, which has the effect of both silencing her and causing her to writhe against his palm. "We sure can."

And so they do.

CORA WALKS INTO A BAR . . .

October 2021

The first thing Neisha demanded to know was: What's it like having sex with someone after two decades?

"Are his pubes all gray now?" Neisha asked. *Are yours?* Cora wondered.

For the record, Cora didn't spot any stray grays on Lincoln, but there was more hair in some places and less in others than there had been before. A soft paunch had emerged where his taut abs once were, no bigger or smaller than her own extra layers.

Cora couldn't say for sure how different or similar the sex was, though. Maybe because she was in a daze so often when they'd had sex back in the day due to her near constant state of surprise that she was actually having it—she didn't register details, just sensations. But the riding-a-bike analogy held true—their two bodies knew the best ways to fit together and remembered them with ease. The distinction was that it all felt more relaxed, less frantic than she recalled from before, more comfortable. That could be because they were older; sex was softer, slower, easier all around because they were too. Maybe the familiarity was the biggest draw. Though she didn't, to be fair, have a lot to compare it to.

Cora offered Neisha the ultimate verdict. "Well, I can say this: It was better than Carlos."

She'd once confessed to Neisha that sex with Carlos wasn't great so Neisha could help her troubleshoot the issue or at least assure her it had nothing to do with Cora's overall desirability or performance.

"It just comes down to chemistry, Cora, and that isn't something you can force. Doesn't matter how hot he is . . . or you are, which is very, by the way."

Cora had decided to let it go, reasoning sex wasn't an important part of her relationship with Carlos. Who needed torrid passion when it would burn out anyway?

Neisha had a decidedly different viewpoint: "If the dick ain't doing it, it best be done."

"I'll put that on a pillow, Ne-ne."

"I'm for real," Neisha had said. "Life's too short for bad sex. Otherwise, folks can just be shuttled right on to the friend zone. Y'all wonder how I ended up with Tim, a man who collects vintage action figures and draws cartoons for a living? Well, he dickmatized me, that's what happened. That's a scientific phenomenon—look it up. I mean, I grew to love other things about him, obviously, but that first night we were together, he blew my mind in bed. Maybe I was in shock when all his dorkiness disappeared as soon as his pants came off, like Superman coming out a phone booth. Who knows. Who cares? The point is, sex is important. Don't fool yourself."

Five years after that conversation and eight years after Tim and Neisha's first date, their physical connection remains obvious, a little too obvious for Cora, who is currently perched at the kitchen counter of their quaint Studio City bungalow where she has a front-row seat to the casual kisses and playful booty slaps. Witnessing Neisha and Tim's affection and their domestic bliss is having same effect it always does—ginning up both admiration and a jealousy that makes her want to throw up in their copper farmhouse sink. She makes a show of mock vomiting.

Neisha matches the theatrical gagging with an extravagant eye roll. "Oh, stop. Just offering you some inspiration for your next trip to Chitown. Take notes, girl. Tim and I need to start a podcast—*Keep It Hot with the Harmons.* Hey, that's got a ring. Who can I call?"

Cora turns to their daughter, Dylan, sitting next to her at the wide quartz island eating strawberries that Tim cut in precise quarters. At five, Dylan has stronger preferences, opinions, and hot takes than most people have at thirty. Exponentially more than Cora ever did. Because of this, Dylan is her muse and hero. Because of this, Cora is also a little terrified of her strong-willed goddaughter.

"Your parents are a trip, you know that?"

"Yeah, they kiss a lot." Dylan makes loud, smacking kisses, and Cora has a shadowy glimpse of what it must be like to be a mother—to be so utterly delighted by your child, your breath catches. She has some claim to this hint of maternal love; Cora was there, after all, when Dylan was born and she was the first person to hold her after Tim. It meant something. An indelible connection not defined by blood or law or anything but the fierce love between them, the pride and possessiveness Cora experiences when Dylan presses Cora's cheeks between her small clammy hands and says, "You my Cola." The nickname toddler Dylan gave Cora when she couldn't pronounce her *r*'s.

"It's Mommy's birthday tomorrow!" Dylan announces, clapping her fruit-juice-stained hands.

"I know, that's why I flew out here last night, to help her celebrate," Cora says. "And to see my favorite goddaughter, of course."

"Mommy's old now." Dylan turns serious, as if this is a worrying development.

"Watch it, kiddo. Mommy's a little sensitive about turning forty." Tim wipes red juice from Dylan's hands and mouth with a wet paper towel while Neisha is occupied rapidly tapping on her phone. Neisha looks up to clarify that she is not old. "I'm in my prime, babycakes!"

Taking Neisha in, Cora absorbs just how true this is. Her friend is as happy as Cora has ever seen her, and it isn't just due to the antidepressants she started just after moving to LA. Doting husband, precocious daughter, work she loves—doing PR for fashion brands. A stunning backyard anchored by the pond-like oasis that Neisha refers to as the "pool that Pixar built," funded as it was by Tim's *Toy Story 4* bonus.

Time is more of a slingshot than anything else. It has the illusion of passing slowly, and then suddenly, finger snap, you're in your friend's million-dollar house on the eve of her turning forty when you could swear you were carrying a plastic tray across the cafeteria just five minutes ago. All your visions of how life would unfold then were about as substantial as mist, and all your emphatic ideas about how the world worked turn out to be as slippery as sand.

It's as if Cora got to fast-forward Neisha's story and see how it turns out. So focused was Cora on obsessing about her own outcomes at twenty that she didn't consider how satisfying this part would be, getting to witness, from the beginning, her friends build their lives brick by brick, side by side. The payoffs of having friends just keep coming, the ultimate long game.

Then again, the flip side is that it's equally heartbreaking when a friend's path takes a dark turn. Part of why Cora is so tired this morning is because she and Neisha sat by the pool until three a.m. discussing an issue that has taken up much of their time, energy, and brain space the past year: What to do about Kim.

Their worries escalated after Kim texted them yesterday—just hours before she was supposed to get on a plane—to say that she wasn't coming to Neisha's fortieth birthday bash after all. She claimed a COVID scare, which they didn't buy for a second. They knew the real reason: Nathan, or, as Neisha has taken to calling him, Narcissist Nate.

As soon as Tim disappears with Dylan to get her dressed, they seamlessly pick up the Kim conversation where they left off.

"Have you heard from her this morning?" Cora nurses a hope that maybe Neisha has been texting with Kim.

"Nah. Nada. We may just need to fly out to Memphis and physically drag her away from that asshole. Our tough-love conversations don't seem to be cuttin' it."

The first time they'd tried to gently suggest that Nate wasn't right for Kim (or anyone, for that matter) was five years ago, when Kim told them he'd "borrowed" twenty dollars from her purse after their second date.

The three of them were reclining side by side on lounge chairs at an all-inclusive resort. They'd gone to Cabo on a "friendship babymoon," a theme Neisha dreamed up for this getaway, a final hurrah to mark the end of something as much as a beginning. She—all of them—knew everything would change once the baby came. Neisha had a baby-name book open over her massive belly, and they'd just been considering Dylan as an option when Kim changed the subject to her new man.

"You mean he *stole* twenty bucks." Neisha tried to force Kim to admit that's what it was, but Nathan had spun some tale about just needing it to run to the store because he didn't have time to get cash.

Kim was barely out of earshot filling her cup with spa water when

Neisha muttered, "Did I get a college degree with that woman? Because she has lost all sense."

They tried to give Nate the benefit of the doubt and keep an open mind when they met him for the first time some months later, after he and Kim moved in together and they visited their new condo in a swanky part of downtown Memphis. But his first words to them—"So, I finally get to meet Frick and Frack"—dripped with such obvious animosity that no one knew what to say, particularly Kim, who laughed nervously and tried (unsuccessfully) to defuse the tension with an elaborate cheese plate.

The rudeness and the "borrowing" ended up being the least of their concerns about Nate, who has slowly taken over Kim's life, controlling what she eats and who she talks to and periodically unleashing his temper in the form of long, screaming tirades. They grew concerned when Kim started beginning all of her sentences with "Nate thinks . . . " and "Nate says . . . " and "Nate wants me to . . . "

But it was even more concerning when Kim stopped talking about her relationship altogether and went into full-on retreat. They could trace that back to a conversation early last year after the pandemic started and weekly happy-hour Zooms were all the rage. The stress was high, the wine was flowing, and it felt like the end of times was imminent—the stage was set for a come-to-Jesus conversation about their concerns. It was Cora who used the word that set everything off. *Toxic*. Kim exploded on her—Cora had no idea what she was talking about! She was out of line! She was just jealous! "What the hell do you know anyway, Cora? You're some kind of relationship expert when you've been single for about three thousand years. You're hardly qualified to be out here giving anybody advice. Puh-lease."

Cora had slammed her laptop shut and threw it to the other side of the couch as if the MacBook were responsible for wounding her. But it saved her from blurting out, *Well, it's better than throwing myself at every guy who looks my way! At least I can stand my own company!* Her restraint that day probably saved their friendship. As did Cora's willingness to forgive Kim. She did that almost instantly and without expecting an apology (which still hasn't come) because she understood that Kim's reaction came from a deep well of fear and pain, that particular type of bitter defensiveness that erupts when you hear a truth you'd rather not confront. But there was, nonetheless, a tear in their relationship, like a small snag in your favorite sweater. You still loved it, but sometimes you avoided wearing it because it hurt to look at the marred material and be reminded how easily something precious could be damaged.

Last night, in the dark of Neisha's backyard, Cora and Neisha dared voice their biggest fear, and even then they did it in a whisper.

"Do you . . . do you think he's hurting her? Like, physically?" Cora asked, hoping Neisha would find this speculation irrational, unthinkable. Instead, she shook her head slowly. "Yeah, it's possible. He's got her isolated, he controls her—all the signs are there."

This morning, in the cold light of day, their concerns are all the more sobering.

"Should we call her mom?" Cora asks, flailing for impossible solutions to the age-old struggle of seeing your friend fall for a bad man, a slow-motion train wreck you can only stand by and watch, sad, knowing, and utterly helpless.

"What the what? No way. It's why Kim's in this mess, all her mommy issues. Not to mention her daddy ones. Nate's daddy played in the NFL once upon a time and he looks good in a suit—that's all her parents care about. And now he works at the family company, it'd be too messy for them to let themselves see he's the fucking worst. Besides, Jackie's stood by her own man all these years, even with everything he's done."

"You mean the bribery stuff? He's never been indicted for anything."

"That's not what I'm talking about."

"What, then?"

"Kim's dad hit her mom. I don't know how often it happened, but it definitely did at least once. I thought you knew. That's on top of all his womanizing. Malcolm Freeman bedded every woman with two good legs. More like Malcolm Free Dick."

"I didn't know any of that! How did I not know this?"

"I don't know. Kim told me one night—I guess it was after you'd already left school. I lost it when my dad announced he was marrying Misty, and she was going on about how he seemed happy and let him be and not to get involved in my parents' stuff because I'd never win. And then it just came out that she'd caught her dad having an affair with—get this—her high-school math teacher, and when she threatened to tell her mom, her dad said, 'Go ahead.' And that's when she knew it wouldn't matter. He knew it, and Kim knew it."

"Wow. I can't believe she didn't tell me any of this."

"Probably because you always thought she had these perfect parents. You idolized them. And she didn't want to ruin it for you."

"What are you talking about? No, I didn't."

"Of course you did. You did the same with my parents. You romanticized them. Like, it's cool to be married for a long time, but it's also messy AF. You acted like having two happily married parents was some sort of be-all, end-all. This pretty picture in your head, like the Cosbys. I mean, look how that turned out. Need I say more? I always thought you were better off. It was just you and Wes—so much less drama."

This is the downside to long-term friendships—your views can get trapped in time. There's a narrow lane for any growth and change because it's comforting for people to believe you will always be exactly who you were. Naive little Cora. Sure, she probably did idealize having two happy parents once. What kid who didn't have that doesn't at some point? But she knows better now. So the surprise isn't this news about Jacqueline and Malcolm; it's that she didn't know something so essential about Kim. It makes Cora's heart hurt for her friend even more.

"Well, if her parents are no help, then what? Because we have to do something."

"I'm just not sure there's much we can do. It's her life. You can't change people. Or rescue them, especially from their own damn selves. I used to think I could, and man, I've tried, but I also used to think I was gonna be the next Vera Wang, so there you go. We all gotta accept our limits one day. All we can do is hope she wises up before it's too late."

It's too late sits there.

Their biggest fear is that Kim will have a baby with Nate and be tied to him forever. She's been trying, desperately—her infertility is a saving grace, though Kim doesn't see it that way. When she came to them after each disappointment, they were in the tricky position of balancing compassion with their secret relief.

Cora wishes she could unequivocally root Kim on in her journey to become a mother, especially having witnessed the frayed edges of her longing over the years. The first night of their Cabo getaway, Cora found Kim in the hotel bathroom sobbing into a towel after Neisha had shown them an intricate mermaid mural Tim had painted on the wall of their future nursery. When Cora asked her what was wrong, Kim whispered, "It was supposed to be me." Cora didn't have to ask what she was talking about. She knew that Kim felt the same way on the morning they'd walked down the aisle in their bridesmaid dresses in St. Lucia. Neisha was living the life featured on Kim's many vision-turned-Pinterest boards, and it ate at her in ways that she could dare admit only to Cora, who didn't begrudge her these ugly resentments. Probably because if Cora had wanted a picturesque family with 2.5 kids and weekends on the soccer field as badly as Kim did, she'd have had similar trouble battling her envy. It was a relief to be spared all the coveting. Or most of it, at least.

"Okay, we can't keep obsessing about Kim. It's bringing me down." Neisha grabs a bottle of prosecco from the fridge and pops it open. "What? It's my birthday weekend. We can drink before noon. Now get out your phone—I want to see your sexy texts with Lincoln. Can you imagine if we'd had cell phones in college? Thank God we didn't. Do you know how many naked pictures of me there would be on the interwebs?"

Neisha reminds her for the umpteenth time that she and Tim did long distance for a year so she has pointers on "keeping it spicy."

"We're not doing long distance, Neisha."

Cora doesn't know *what* they've been doing exactly over this past month. There's been an endless text stream filled with *Good morning* and *Good night* and *How's your day*? and *Remember that time when . . .* in between. There's been phone sex, for which Cora *does* need some tips, specifically where and how to position the phone so she's not knocking it over at the worst possible moment. They've planned for Cora to continue to go to Chicago every other weekend. But she isn't ready to put a label on anything or reckon with how easy it's been to drop back into the well-worn groove of adoring Lincoln.

"Could have fooled me, but you need to spill. I'm not having you avoid the subject forever. A girl is entitled to some answers."

Cora's response is to announce she'd better shower if they're going to make their IV infusion appointments on time. It's the most LA thing Cora has ever heard of, a service where you get vitamins shot into your arm through an IV to ward off a hangover. But Neisha swears by its benefits and she's footing the bill, so Cora will get over her distaste for needles and be a good sport. Besides, she hates hangovers and they're only getting worse the older she gets.

The West Hollywood bar they arrive at hours later—full of B_{12}, strapped into Spanx, and, in Cora's case, tottering on heels, as unsteady as a newborn deer—is like stepping into Neisha's id. There's faux graffiti splashed on every wall, crystal chandeliers everywhere, and a blinding strobe light behind the DJ. At the entrance is a wall of ivy with a blinking neon-pink sign that reads #SLAY in aggressively large letters. It's a command Cora's not sure what to do with.

The whole scene is trying so hard, Cora is exhausted by its efforts, but Neisha pronounces the vibes "impeccable." Cora knows to keep her concerns that they're quite possibly too old for these particular vibes to herself. Besides, Neisha would never agree. She'll be in clubs with her walker. It's important to have one delusional friend who's convinced she's Peter Pan. She will keep them young in a way retinol could never compete with.

They stop in front of the neon sign to take a selfie—or, rather, eight selfies, until Neisha's happy with her duck lips and the angle of Cora's head tilt. Cora quickly sends it to Lincoln before tucking her phone back in the clutch she's borrowed from Neisha and secretly plans to keep. She's fooled no one with that furtive communication. Cora looks up to find she's caught in the crosshairs of Neisha's glare. "You better not be in the corner texting him all night."

"Never! Tonight's about you."

"I know that's right. Come on—we're off to the bar. Remember, no eating."

"Ne-ne, I can't not eat all night!"

"Well, you shouldn't have worn white!"

"*You're* the one who made this a white party! Like it's P. Diddy 2003!"

"P. Puff Diddy Daddy, my ass. Don't even say his name. Something's very wrong with that man. We're wearing white because Nubian princesses belong in white. I just hope you have a Tide stick in that purse. And don't think you're keeping that bag either, it's my favorite."

They've arrived at the venue fashionably late. Or, as some (Cora) would say, rudely late, but it means Neisha can enter to a waiting throng of admirers as intended. Neisha screams "You're here!" at each guest as though they're the one person Neisha hoped would be there. Cora is reminded of why she adores Neisha. Everyone is a celebrity in Neisha's orbit and they all shine brighter in the light she radiates.

The bartender passes Cora the signature drink Neisha had the venue create for her—a Nejito. Cora holds it up to the light, taking in its shocking shade of blue. "It's the curaçao," the bartender explains. "Your girl said she wanted tropical paradise in a drink."

It tastes like suntan lotion and overly ripe pineapple, so he clearly understood the assignment.

Cora attempts to look busy sipping and fiddling with the little paper umbrella floating in the cocktail. She vows to pull out her phone only as a last resort, but she's banking on someone talking to her soon if she keeps smiling. Sure enough, a woman comes sashaying—that's the only word to describe it—over, leaving a trail of white feathers from a long cape, and says, "You must be Cora."

Before she can answer, there's Neisha squealing again: "Tyyyyyy!" She turns to Cora. "This is my hairdresser, Ty."

Cora has heard all about Ty, how hilarious she is, how many celebrity clients she has, how she makes her own to-die-for sandalwood oil. She's just happy Neisha introduced Ty as her hairdresser instead of her new best friend, although it seems that's what Ty has become. Neisha hardly needs someone tending to her tresses, she's stayed bald since college—her self-proclaimed signature look—but once a month, she goes to Ty for a shave just because she likes to be in the salon. "It's where I get all my good LA gossip. Forget the Shade Room."

Neisha hands Ty her own drink. "Here, have this. I'll get another. Where's your cousin? I thought he was coming too."

"He is. He's just too cheap to valet so he's going to be driving around for the next hour looking for parking. You know how out-of-towners are."

Ty turns to Cora, grabs her hair with authority, flips it up. "Girl, come on. These ends. You were right, Neish. Bring her by the salon and we'll do a trim and my signature conditioning mask."

They nod at each other like that's settled and both turn to talk to other people, leaving Cora and her split ends to fend for themselves. She drifts back toward the entrance, away from the party's center, and pulls out her phone. Lincoln has texted back **Stunner. Always have been, always will be** followed by a long string of emojis she thinks may be some sort of sexual signal. She's trying to decipher what peaches plus kissy face plus prayer hands plus sunglasses means when the scent hits her. She turns so fast, her drink spills, leaving little splatters of blue across her white dress like a Smurf sneezed on her. He's wearing a face mask that says READ MY LIPS, but she'd recognized those eyes with their flecks of green anywhere.

"Cora?"

"Aaron?"

They say, "What are you doing here?" at the same time.

They say, "You go," at the same time.

Cora's mouth is already hanging open, so she forges ahead, breathless. "It's Neisha's birthday party. Her fortieth. I flew into town for it. How are you here? How is this happening?" She looks around wildly like she's being punked, like someone is going to jump out from behind the ox-blood velvet curtains and explain this shocking turn of events to her.

"I don't know. It's wild. My cousin Ty brought me. She's around here somewhere."

"Ty's your cousin? I just met her. She's at the bar."

"Of course she is. That girl can throw back. I'm in town for a couple weeks crashing on her couch and she insisted I come. I didn't know it was your girl's party. What are the chances?"

Cora aced statistics in college and had found it surprisingly enjoyable to apply an orderly numeric system to determining odds and inferring patterns and outcomes. But she can't wrangle any numbers into a formula that makes this mathematically possible as opposed to completely miraculous. A city of four million. Nineteen years. Thousands of miles. Two people. One ridiculous, random bar a six-hour plane ride from home.

"I don't know . . . point zero-zero-six percent? Rough guess."

Aaron looks up in the air, concentrating hard, like he's doing his own calculations. "Is that more or less than the probability of lightning striking us?"

"More likely than lightning, less likely than hitting Mega Millions," Cora says playfully.

"That sounds right. *Feels* like hitting the lottery, though."

No, Cora wants to argue, it feels much more like a lightning strike, given the hot bolt that sears her. The mask hides Aaron's mouth so she doesn't know if he's smiling, but she's assuming he's not because he's spoken with utter sincerity. She remembers his trademark earnestness and, more than that, she remembers this hot/cold feeling.

Aaron reaches out and runs his hand along her forearm. "You have goose bumps."

"Yeah, it's chilly, I guess." It's eighty-two degrees.

He slips his hand into hers and squeezes it and then doesn't let go, so they're standing there in the dark corner holding on to each other. This should feel considerably more weird and awkward than it does. The strange part is how natural it all is and how she doesn't want Aaron to let go. And how much she misses his hand when he finally does some seconds later.

"I'm going to get a drink. Can I bring you a refill of whatever that is?" He looks at the blue liquid in her glass suspiciously.

"Sure, it's a Nejito." Cora could drink Mississippi moonshine at this point and not even taste it.

Cora tracks Aaron across the room like he's a wild animal, either rare or dangerous, but in any case worth keeping her eye on. He stops and turns like he knows she's watching. Neither of them minds. Now that she can properly take him in, he appears a tad thinner than she remembers, but otherwise, he is exactly like his former self in a way that defies time and physics. His hair is in the same twists; he wears the same unusual, exotic scent. He just might be wearing the same jeans he wore back in the early aughts. It would be less disconcerting if he'd changed dramatically instead of not having changed at all.

When Aaron turns away from her to order, Cora pulls out her phone and texts Neisha from across the room.

Aaron's here. He's Ty's cousin!

She watches Neisha read the text, look up, confused and then start typing. The reply comes second later after Neisha has already tucked her phone back in her pocket.

Aaron? The photographer guy?
Your Paris pen pal? Small world.

Neisha's blasé reaction doesn't at all jibe with what Cora is experiencing in the corner of the bar—full-on emotional pandemonium that has her holding on to the sticky wall to steady herself.

It's not Neisha's fault that this development isn't registering as it should or that she thinks of Aaron as just some guy Cora exchanged letters with. Cora was so distant from both Neisha and Kim at that period in her life—they'd had no idea what was going on with her. They didn't understand the impact Aaron had had on her then (or now), partly because she didn't understand it herself. So she wouldn't have been able to properly articulate it. But it was also, in a way, nice not to have to try. By keeping Aaron all to herself, Cora had more ownership; he'd felt more fully and completely *hers*.

The lone bartender is overwhelmed and Cora waits impatiently for Aaron's return. He looks over at her periodically as if to make sure she's still there. Their eyes lock again and again. When he finally returns and hands her a sloshing glass of blue liquid, holding a bottle of water for himself, he stands close, touching his shoulder to hers. The kind of complete violation of personal space that comes from two people who have seen each other naked.

"I still can't believe you're here." She isn't shy about touching him to confirm it once again, briefly pressing her palm flat against his chest.

"I know. 'Of all the gin joints . . .'"

In any other circumstance this would be an outrageously cheesy line, but she forgives Aaron his corniness; it's part of his charm. But also, this isn't just a clichéd reference; it's a call back to them huddled together over his laptop watching *Casablanca* in his wrought-iron twin bed in Paris. Knowing they're silently sharing this memory makes her flush.

"So what have you been up to since . . . since forever?"

"I don't know. Living. Making art."

"Same here. Except for the marking-art part. Ty said you're just visiting. Where's home these days?"

"Eh, good question. I don't live much of anywhere—or maybe more like everywhere? After five or so years in Paris, I was in Berlin for a while, then London. Then Santa Fe because why not. That desert spoke to me, so I made it a home base for now. Got a little house right on the edge of an Apache reservation. It's where I spent most of 2020, holed up avoiding the plague."

"I hear you. Sounds better than being trapped in my one-bedroom overlooking a parking garage. The pandemic's been rough—still feels strange to be out."

"I guess. I don't know. Being a loner, homebody and all, can't say I hated lockdown. It was kinda nice, actually, but you're not really allowed to admit that."

"Yeah, when the isolation wasn't so crippling I worried I'd forget how to talk or shower, it was fine. I did get closer with two friends—my fridge and Google. I tried to find you, actually, on the socials."

She'd googled Aaron over the years more than she would care to admit. These searches never unearthed more than a few images of his latest artwork at various galleries, with no clues about his personal life. This caused her to rage at the internet for disappointing her—its main purpose, after all, is to allow you to satisfy your curiosity about what everyone you ever knew is up to.

"Oh, yeah, that's not for me. I just refuse. My agent's always on me about it. I try to tell her that the more elusive I am, the more people want my stuff. No one cares what I eat for breakfast or wants to see me doing yoga. Or they shouldn't, at least."

"Agent? You're big-time."

"I don't know about all that, but I get paid enough to do what I love. That's why I'm out here in LA, a private showing for this collector. A kiss-the-ring sort of thing. I hate it, but . . . it comes with the territory."

"The territory of being wildly successful?"

How is it possible a shrug could be such a turn-on? "I've done okay, I guess."

As modest as he is corny.

"What about you? You said you flew in for Neisha's party? Where are you laying your head these days?" He pulls down his mask to take a sip from his bottle of Fiji.

"Still in the DMV, as they call the DC area now. Bought an apartment in Silver Spring, so I'm on the Maryland side, but it's still close to my dad in Virginia. I work at a nonprofit."

"Any kids? As I recall, that wasn't in the plan."

"Nope." Usually, Cora worries about how to get just the right tone in this one syllable so she doesn't sound either gleeful or defensive, but she doesn't need to with Aaron. "What about you?"

"Nope, no rug rats, no ring." Aaron holds up a hand to prove this, which prompts Cora to have a powerful flash of a memory of that very hand stroking the soft skin on the inside of her thigh.

"Yeah, as I recall, that wasn't in the plan for you. Something about not believing in marriage?" She smiles to assure him she's teasing, but she recalls her shock when he'd mentioned this—it seemed like such a radical idea at the time, that you could not believe in marriage. To Cora, it was like not believing in college or work; it was something you did, that everyone did, or tried to.

"Something like that." His laughter is impossible to interpret. "What about you? I don't see a ring. Or maybe you slipped it off just for the night?"

"Ha, no. No wedding ring for me either." Recalling Aaron's aversion to anything traditional, Cora is less defensive about this too than she usually is when she's on the receiving end of the scrutiny (constant) about her romantic status and life choices. To be almost forty and never married, no kids, not even an engagement, not even to have lived with a man? These conditions are unnerving to people, and sometimes even to Cora herself. She isn't a wife or a mother or a "boss bitch," which seem to be the only acceptable options available, so what is she?

It helps that she's used to feeling so odd and out of step with whatever people are supposed to be doing, thinking, or wearing and that she's happy enough being by herself. Still, sometimes when she's called upon to serve up her life, as she is now, and present a platter of exciting milestones and meaningful developments, the offering feels woefully meager. *You could have so much more if you were hungrier.*

So she changes the subject. "How long are you in town?"

"Just till Tuesday. What about you?"

"I leave in the morning. Might as well stay up all night. I need to get an Uber to the airport at like five a.m."

"I would offer to drop you off, but you and I don't have the greatest track record with airports."

With the face mask isolating his eyes and drawing all attention there, it makes them all the more powerful. Aaron's, boring into Cora's now, have the ability to bowl her over. She knows from experience that he's not going to break eye contact, so she must do it or fall to the ground.

A sudden dramatic increase in the volume of the music helps disrupt the overwhelming charge crackling between them. Aaron turns to the DJ stand in the corner and recoils at the obscene level of bass. "Ty said this was going to be chill. She and I obviously have different definitions of that. Love my cuz but she's a little . . . intense. And so is this. I'm going to have to get out of here. Ty can get a ride, I'm sure. Any interest in coming with?"

"I wish." It's beyond wishing; it's like Cora's body is made of metal and his is a magnet, and, owing to those laws of physics, she will quite possibly be powerless to stay put when he walks out the door. "But Neisha would kill me if I left. I have to make a toast soon about all the reasons I love her. She made me practice it in front of her earlier and gave me notes. Are you sure you can't stay?"

"It's tempting, but nah. I have an early morning anyway. But it was real cool to run into you, Cora. Real cool."

If it is possible to embrace someone with your eyes, that's what's happening. She clings to it as a sign that their interaction has been something beyond just two old pals randomly crossing paths.

"Yeah, you too." She waits for him to ask for her number or to work up the nerve to give it to him herself. Neither materializes before he says, "Well, take care, okay?"

When he slowly turns away from her, she screams, *Wait!* Aaron doesn't hear her, though, because that scream took place in her mind and it's still echoing there when she floats to the bar in a daze.

"Speak of the devil," Ty says as soon as she walks up. "Neisha was just telling me you and my cousin used to have some kinda thing."

"I don't know about *thing*. And it was forever ago."

Thing is the ideal description because that's exactly what it was—vague and devoid of labels or categorization. It comes down to interpretation, really. Cora and Aaron were pen pals a zillion years ago and they recall their distant, barely there fling faintly and fondly. Or Cora and Aaron have an indelible, enduring connection (one Cora still thinks about a lot and often), and their importance to each another defies their short interlude.

In one scenario, Aaron is a footnote; in the other, he's the whole story.

It all depends on the perspective; it always does.

Ty's eyes roam up and down Cora, carefully this time. "Yeah, you don't seem like his type. It's usually artsy chicks and models. No offense. Where is he anyway?"

"He left." *He said you're a little intense. No offense.*

"That tracks. He's allergic to fun, I swear. Just wants to be at home fiddling with his cameras and watching grass grow or staring into the distance thinking his thoughts. I'm like, 'Boy, you're not too good to get on your damn phone and obsessively scroll IG like the rest of us.' Tell you the truth, I don't know how you even had anything with him. He aloof like a mofo. I love him like he's a big brother, but you never know what's going on with him. It's always like he's up to something. Or thinking some shit about you. So . . . good luck if you're trying to crack that nut, Cora."

Neisha takes it upon herself to interject, "We don't have to worry about Cora here cracking anybody's nuts. She's taken—look at those diamonds dripping from her wrist."

"Oh, that's right, you have a hotshot Barack Obama type, don'tcha? From back in college? Neisha says it's some love-affair-for-the-ages shit."

Cora turns to Neisha. "Love affair for the ages? I thought you said Lincoln was my bad habit?" She obsessed over Neisha's assessment for hours, if not days. Is Lincoln the love of her life or a habit to break?

"Tomayto, tomahto—could still go either way. But when it comes to poor starving artist versus the rich dude who keeps you in lavish gifts, guess who I'm rooting for?"

"What makes you think Aaron's poor and starving?" Cora asks.

There's no more committed or expert eye-roller in all the world than Neisha Harmon. A practice-makes-perfect situation. "Um. Did you see his jeans? Those patches?"

"He's an *artist,* Ne-ne. He doesn't care about fashion." Why is Cora getting so defensive? Also, who cares about his clothes? Even Aaron's own cousin has lost interest in the conversation.

"What about self-respect?" Neisha says.

"Neisha!"

Ty finally comes to Aaron's defense. "Well, I can tell you this—those downright atrocious jeans aside, he's hardly broke. He's stacking paper with his photographs. But I can also tell you he'd never give you a bracelet like that. He'd be going on about little kids getting their hands chopped off to get those diamonds and demand you read some five-hundred-page book about how corrupt De Beers is."

Cora only wishes she was walking on the beach with Aaron talking about child labor and mining and capitalism. She squandered a chance she hadn't expected and will probably not get again.

Neisha snaps a finger in her face. "You good? Because it's 'bout time for cake and the toasts, so I need you here and not thinking about some rom-com scenario where you convince yourself some man you happened to run into is your long-lost love. This isn't *Love and Basketball.* And besides, you've already played that game. Hell, you're smack in the *middle* of that game. So go ahead and put the genie right on back in the bottle."

The problem is, Neisha is asking the impossible.

CORA REMEMBERS WHEN

October 2021

Cora's flight back from LA after Neisha's birthday visit landed at 3:00 p.m.; it was shortly after 4:00 p.m. when she opened the door to her apartment and dropped her bag. At 4:15 p.m. she was climbing on top of a step stool and digging out the container that held the letters Aaron wrote to her almost two decades ago. The blue-and-white floral keepsake box was covered in dust and dented from the weight of the shoeboxes she'd piled on top, but it was still there. By 4:20 p.m. she was collapsed on the bed, hugging the faded bundle of papers and thinking of how close she'd come to burning them years back.

Cora had gone so far as to actually set a fire in a metal trash can she'd dragged out onto her empty balcony. She'd lived in her apartment only a few weeks and she didn't have much furniture yet, not even the little wicker patio chairs she eventually bought. She was still unpacking boxes, and when she found the letters, she decided it was time to get rid of the carefully folded and stacked papers once and for all. Their very presence had haunted her for too long. It was really her feelings for Aaron that had haunted her, and Cora hoped that in burning the letters, she might rid herself of those, too. In the end, though, she watched the flames flicker and crackle but couldn't bring herself to do it.

She still hasn't decided if she'll bring herself to read them. For the past ten days, the box has lived on the kitchen counter, right next to the little tray she has for mail and the pumpkin cookie jar she swiped from her dad's kitchen when she moved out. At least a dozen times, Cora has opened the box and then slammed it right back shut when she sees the envelope on top, addressed to Aaron in her blocky, neat print, a row of

American flag stamps peeling around the edges across the top corner. Her last letter. The one she'd never sent.

Cora glares at the innocent box suspiciously every time she walks by. *Why are you doing this to me? Why can't I stop thinking about Aaron?*

And why do I keep ordering stuff from Amazon that I don't need and can't afford?

This last question comes as Cora hears the delivery guy fumbling outside her front door. Her online-shopping habit had gotten out of control since the peak of the pandemic. Random items she doesn't strictly need and definitely can't afford arrive with problematic regularity: a white-noise machine, socks that look like fish, a jade face roller, an air purifier, an air fryer, an air popcorn maker, a towel to clean your makeup off without soap (never mind she rarely wears makeup anymore, except when she visits Lincoln).

Today's delivery she does need, though—a lace-trimmed silk sleep camisole she ordered two nights ago hoping it would show up in time for her to pack it for her trip to Chicago in two hours. Whenever she changed into her usual sweats before climbing into Lincoln's California King, she could tell from his face that they weren't cutting it. Cora vowed to make more of an effort, which is also why she's now in the bathroom splayed naked on the toilet with foul-smelling hair-removal cream slathered over essentially her entire body. And why she spent fifty-five dollars on a eucalyptus pedicure yesterday, the first time she set foot in a salon in two years.

Cora maneuvers into the shower like a mummy and washes the stinky paste off, then spends five full minutes assessing herself in the mirror. She was never terribly interested in scrutinizing herself when she was in her twenties, which would have been the time to do it. Then again, because of her lack of interest in (or apprehension about) the details of her younger lithe body, Cora has only a vague recall of what it used to look like—its sharp angles and the way various parts jutted and stood firm. This is a mercy, as it saves her from the tiresome practice of cataloging all the differences between then and now, every new ding, drop, and droop.

It's just as well, because there's not much she can do about it anyway. She shaves when she remembers, tries any serum under forty dollars with effective before-and-after photos on social media, and does an

Eight-Minute Abs workout on her bedroom floor via her old thirteen-inch TV/VCR combo every night she's not too tired for it. As far as anti-aging regimens go, it will not work wonders, but it is, at least, manageable.

Finally, Cora slips on her robe and makes her way to the front door to grab her new nightgown. But the oversize manila envelope waiting on the plastic welcome mat is not from an Amazon warehouse at all; it has a return address in Santa Fe, New Mexico. Cora stops and looks both ways down the dim hall of her building as if the sender personally delivered the package and then darted away.

She goes back in and carefully inspects the object in her hands. It's firm and thick with the words DO NOT BEND across it. She holds it up to the light, shakes it, even, weirdly, goes so far as to smell it. She can't prolong the anticipation any longer—she has a flight to catch—so she rips open the seal. A note flutters out and she scrambles frantically to grab it before it slips into the dusty no-man's-land under the refrigerator.

She closes her eyes, takes a deep breath, before she reads.

Hey there, Cora—it was great to run into you. Ty got your address for me from Neisha—I hope that's okay. I wanted to send you this. (see enclosed.) One of my favorite works. I wanted you to see it. Even more, I wanted you to have it. Here's my number: 240-555-0256. Maybe we'll cross paths again.—A.

Cora tucks the note in the pocket of her robe. Her hands are shaking so badly, it takes her multiple attempts to remove the rubber bands around the cardboard protecting the photo. Aaron's work has ranged widely over the years, based on the few examples she's found online. He might have sent her a picture from his global graffiti series, or one of his southwestern landscapes, or a photo from his latest project, portraits of elderly Black people in rocking chairs. What an honor it will be to have his work, especially since she could never afford to buy it herself. It's not a Kehinde Wiley, maybe; it's better. She's already eyeing a space right by the front door where she can hang it so it's the last thing she sees when she leaves the house. Whatever the image is, it'll be perfect there. She will splurge for museum glass and a bleached-wood gallery frame and smile to herself every time she sees it.

Then she slips the glossy stock out of the cardboard and flips it over.

There are precious few occasions in a lifetime when one has cause to full-on *exclaim*, an actual, audible, involuntary "Oh!" For Cora Belle, this is one of them.

A familiar stranger stares at her.

Part of the shock is that she doesn't remember Aaron taking this photo, but she recognizes the backdrop—his attic apartment in Paris. In it, young Cora is draped in sheets that cascade around her. She holds the top of the white sheet just over her chest and looks over her bare shoulder at the camera. She squints at the soft yellow light streaming through the window with such purpose, it's as if she's controlling its direction. A sated half smile is on her face. There's no trace of inhibition as her eyes meet the lens, or the person behind the lens. There's no hint of the girl who hates having her picture taken. It's a reflection of herself that Cora has never—in all her years—seen: Vulnerable. Unguarded. Brave. At home in her skin. A version of herself she was wholly unaware ever existed.

In the early days of photography, people used to be afraid that the startling new technology would steal their souls. Staring at the photo, Cora wonders if there's something to that. It's possible that her soul was stolen in the making of this image. Or maybe not so much stolen as revealed. There it is for all to see. For her to see.

For this reason, she must lie down.

She heads to the couch, holding the photograph tight as if hugging the girl in it. It moves up and down with the rise and fall of her breath, which she tries to slow.

It's just a picture.

Telling herself this has the same effect as reminding herself, *It was just a chance meeting.*

It was just a fling.

It was just a few months.

It was just some letters.

These defenses are the equivalent of putting a palm up to try to stop a hurricane.

The summer that Lincoln interned in DC, he convinced her to go to Kings Dominion, the Virginia amusement park, and ride her first (and only) coaster. The Rebel Yell (as it was called, after the Confederate war cry, until people demanded a less problematic name) climbed eighty-five feet in the air with a slow, clacking anticipation, sat suspended for an agonizing second, then plummeted sharply and jerked through a series of violent turns and drops, and when it was all over, it did it again. Backward.

It wasn't so much the ride itself that disturbed Cora as the way it took hours for her jumbled insides to settle back into position, for her ears to stop ringing, for the ground beneath her to stop swaying. The "thrill" left too much of a lasting mark.

And so she's felt since seeing Aaron, a similar disequilibrium that refuses to subside.

Her phone, lying on the coffee table, alerts her that the Lyft she'd scheduled to take her to the airport has arrived. She doesn't move. A few minutes later, she gets an alert that the driver has left. Still, she doesn't move.

Lincoln is going to be irritated she's missed her flight. He's gotten them courtside tickets for the Bulls home opener tonight. They were supposed to go straight to the arena from the airport. She'd been about to put on the jersey he'd sent her. She doesn't want to wear a Bulls jersey. Not just because she's a Wizards fan, though she is, but because Lincoln always seems to want to dress her, like a doll. She isn't sure how to object without coming across as petty and ungrateful.

Lincoln wants to do nice things for her—is that a crime?

That's what he told her when Cora mentioned that they didn't need to go on elaborate dates when she visited him. He acted as though the Michelin-starred restaurants and the helicopter tours and the courtside seats were for her, no matter how many times she told him she would be just as happy to sit in pajamas all weekend and watch Netflix or take a walk through Grant Park, to order pizza instead of having a private chef hover over them. But Lincoln wanted to give Cora "experiences."

Cora, meanwhile, wanted Lincoln to have the experience of visiting her, which hasn't happened since they've reconnected. With his demanding job and the kids, it's harder for him to get to Maryland than for her to get to Chicago; he's traveling a lot already; he has more space at his place, et cetera. The excuses are reasonable yet frustrating. Cora has stopped pushing, though, because every time she thinks of Lincoln in her little one-bedroom with its IKEA bookcases, it's like imagining Kim's mother strolling the clearance aisles at Kmart in her mink coat. Cora is in no hurry to see her surroundings—and thus all her life choices—through Lincoln's eyes.

Also, there would inevitably be, in the wake of his visit, a period of proposed upgrades. Just like last week, when Lincoln learned that her bedroom TV was the same thirteen-inch TV/VCR combo from her childhood. He threatened to buy her a new flat-screen. She explained she kept the TV because she loved being able to watch her old VHS tapes: *Love Jones, Sliding Doors, Dirty Dancing.* The music video she and Kim and Neisha made when they got their hands on a camcorder one afternoon their freshman year. Even, when she was in a certain wistful mood and beating herself up about her lack of hobbies, her violin recitals. Cora successfully convinced him she didn't need a fifty-inch plasma screen, or a new TV at all.

It didn't go as well when she pointed out that Lincoln always ordered for her when they went out to eat.

"I've just been to all these places before, so I know what's good. I also know what you like. Have I ever steered you wrong?" Lincoln responded, affronted.

"No, you haven't. But that's not the point. I'd just like to be able to make my own choices sometimes," Cora said lightly. "Try something new even, who knows?"

"Right, because you love to try new things. Come on, Cora. I know you, and I know what you like."

But she does like to try new things. Maybe she didn't before, but she does now. It was how she'd discovered sushi and Bollywood movies and the pleasures of dining at a restaurant alone.

One thing that does remain very much the same is how averse Cora is to conflict, so she tries to let slide the small disagreements that flare between them like sparks flying from grinding train wheels picking up speed.

For example, when Cora lamented the distance that had grown between herself and Kim, Lincoln responded with "You need to let her live her life and mind your business." He didn't understand that your friends are your business. Which is why it's so hard with Kim, the responsibility Cora feels to save her, never mind if it's irrational . . . or impossible.

And when Cora suggested it was wrong for him to call his paralegal *honey*, Lincoln railed on that. "People are just too uptight. To go to HR over that? To be all up in arms about that and go to HR? Come on."

They'd even argued about actual arms, as in the gun Cora learned he owned—a gun!—and sometimes carried around in a hidden holster. Lincoln's view: "I grew up with guns, you know that. My mom always had a rifle under the bed. I'm trying to stay safe out here, Cora. And keep you safe. It's Chicago. And I have a license."

As if her apprehension were about its legality.

The situation reached an almost comical apex when, last night on the phone, they almost fell into an argument about . . . arguing. She'd told him that she couldn't remember them bickering in college but she wasn't sure if that was due to the haze of nostalgia or if it was an actual fact and asked what he thought. His response: "I don't know what you even mean. We don't argue now."

It's a pointless exercise to keep shifting between then and now to see how they aligned. But it's also an unavoidable hazard of reconnection. Anytime you put two things side by side, you're going to invite comparison—and that includes the past and the present.

It's an even more pointless exercise for Cora to pretend she has any idea of how relationships are supposed to work, how much arguing is too much, how much time should be shared, what's worthy of sacrifice and compromise. Whatever other maturity and wisdom she's gained over the years, when it came to matters of the heart, most days she feels as clueless as she was when she was flailing along in her twenties. All the worse is the fact that everyone else seems to have gained more knowledge, experience, and credibility when it came to such things by now, like they're all in on a secret. Kim was right about Cora, and maybe that's why what she said sliced so deep—what *did* Cora know after "about three thousand years" of being single?

Well, one thing at least: She's fairly sure that missing your flight to go spend a weekend with your boyfriend qualifies as a serious relationship misstep, and yet her paralysis remains. She has three hours before Lincoln gets to O'Hare and realizes she won't be coming. The right thing to do would be to tell him now, but he'll only insist that she get a later flight.

There's a sudden chorus of wind chimes on the balcony. Cora has six of them hanging in a row. Some might call it a collection; some—her neighbors—might call it overkill. But as much as Cora hates anyone, including Gloria in 208, being unhappy with her, she loves the chimes even more. The wild cacophony of sound they make with even the softest breeze breaks up the noise of her mind.

When and how hard the various chimes bang against each other is controlled by outside forces (nature, the universe, God?), allowing Cora to believe they're sending her messages in a language only she can understand and only if she listens closely enough. The one she receives now is unmistakable: *Call Aaron.*

Cora rises from the couch and lies down on the floor because it's supposed to be grounding—at least according to the teacher in the one yoga class she went to. Then she pulls the note out of her pocket, reaches for her phone, and lets her fingers fly over the screen, waiting for the acceleration in her heartbeat. It doesn't come. Her pulse remains shockingly slow and steady as the phone rings. And rings. And rings.

She imagines what Aaron might be doing instead of answering: Taking photographs. Skipping stones across still water. Kissing a girl who has two long braids down her back. Driving a pickup truck that's kicking up desert dust. Apparently, she can picture Aaron only in the context of a Darius Rucker music video, not in the middle of basic tasks like taking out the trash or washing the dishes.

She hangs up, takes five "box breaths" that Greta taught her, and then dials his number again. This behavior is unhinged, but no more so than lying spread-eagled on her living-room floor and missing her flight. No more so than tracing her hand across the photograph of herself over and over. No more so than allowing wind chimes to guide her. No more so than revisiting her love life in reverse.

This time as the phone rings, Cora's heart does accelerate, but only because she's imagining Aaron thinking she's a stalker. It screeches to a halt for a millisecond when he answers. "Hello?"

"Hey, it's Cora?"

She waits for a response, which is, as far as she remembers, how conversations go, but there's just emptiness on the line. "Hello? Aaron?"

"Yeah, sorry. Sorry. I'm here. Just wasn't expecting it to be you is all."

"You gave me your number."

"Yeah, yeah, I did."

The dialogue is not following the script in her head. Cora is at a loss as to how to get him to say his lines. Or to remember her own.

"Well, I just wanted to say thank you. For sending the photograph. I just got it."

"You're welcome." She knows Aaron to be the quiet type, but this is something else altogether. They aren't going to get very far in this conversation with two-word answers.

"You wrote in your note that it's your favorite photo you've taken. That can't be true."

"Why not?"

"I don't know, you've taken hundreds of photos . . . "

"More like thousands. And this one is my favorite. Easy."

Cora's stomach dips and turns more than it did from the steepest drops and spins of the Rebel Yell. She has no choice but to revert to self-deprecation. "Er, guess you haven't photographed Naomi Campbell."

"I have, actually."

"Get out of here—seriously?"

"Yeah, I do commercial work from time to time. The money's too good to turn down. It was a shoot for some perfume ad."

"That you don't even think that's a big deal is the best part."

"Eh, I just don't love using my work to sell stuff but bills be bills. That sort of thing doesn't matter to me like my 'real' work. That's what's the big deal. The only thing I care about."

"Well, if you ever need to sell my picture, please feel free. It would get at least fifty dollars."

"I would never sell it. Or even show it to anyone. But for the record, it would fetch not a cent less than seventy-five."

"You're probably right. I mean, I *was* young and naked . . . "

"And all sultry . . . "

"Ha! Not the word I would have used."

"Well, you were. Just facts."

"I don't know about that . . . I have to say, it actually kinda threw me a bit, seeing it."

"How?"

"Like, I didn't recognize myself, this smiling, calm, self-possessed stranger."

"The camera captures only what's there. The truth."

Cora braves looking at the picture again, squinting as she does when she looks up at a fierce sun. Her smile—that's what gets her. It was such a terrible, sad, stressful time in her life and yet she was radiant here. It's plain on her face.

"I look happy."

"You sound surprised."

"I guess I am . . . I don't remember being happy then. It was such a dark period." That's a lie. The thing she remembers most about Paris is the feeling of joy, freedom, a lightness she tried not to credit Aaron for . . . or get used to. In the years since, she's convinced herself she imagined it all, their seventy-two hours together—a languid dream sequence. That's why the picture is so striking—it's proof. The Cora she searched for and found across an ocean, in Aaron's arms . . . and lens.

"I recall you being in pretty decent spirits. Your discovery of crepes alone—"

"Oh God, and you challenged me to eat six!"

"Yeah, if I had known you were going to throw up Nutella in a garbage can in the Tuileries, I would have rethought that bet."

"Not my finest hour." Another lie—everything about that trip was her finest hour. Up until the end, at least.

She thinks they've paused in conversation to soak in this memory, but the quiet stretches out and lingers, which gives her some time, but not enough, to prepare for where she senses they're headed.

"I have to say, Cora, running into you . . . it threw me, to steal your words. It brought back some stuff. It took me a minute to . . . to get over what happened between us. You just ghosting me like that. With not so much as a *That was fun, good luck with your future plans.* I waited and waited to hear something from you . . . *anything* . . . and nada. I'm not sure why you did me like that, but I've come to terms with it. You must have had your reasons. And they must have been good ones."

Not *reasons,* plural; there was just the one. And it wasn't a good one. Or so Cora is coming to see now, slowly, painfully, thanks to the hindsight practically blinding her, so bright and hot it could ignite a fire, like the one she lit all those years ago to burn his letters. It was supposed to have saved her from this.

"Tell you the truth, I always assumed it was because of that dude . . . you clearly weren't over that guy. Your ex. Or whatever he was. I guess I thought maybe you'd decided to be with him after all."

"Lincoln."

"Yeah, Lincoln."

Lincoln. Who is waiting for her right now with a fridge stocked with her favorite seltzer, who has sent her roses every Monday for two months, who's said, more than once, "I'm so grateful to God for bringing you back into my life."

"Aaron, I—"

"No, sorry, I don't mean to cut you off, but for real, I'm not saying any of this to make you explain yourself. It's ancient history now. You don't owe me anything. Let's just let it go. Chalk it up to timing."

Aaron says *timing* like it's no more powerful a force than a bunny sneezing.

"It really wasn't about Lincoln, though. Let me at least say that."

It still isn't about Lincoln, which is why she doesn't tell Aaron that they're in touch. Also because patterns are, by their very nature, easy to fall back into.

"Okay, well, cool. You did what you needed to do, and I respect that. All good. I just needed to say that. The past is the past, let's talk about now. You said you work at a nonprofit? Tell me about it."

Retreating to small talk comes with whiplash; it's like staring at the wreckage of your house after a tornado has blown through while eating a turkey sandwich.

"Yeah, it's a literacy program for kids. We provide after-school, in-home, and summer support for kids who need extra help reading, because they have learning challenges or ADHD or English is their second language or whatever."

"Love that. Did I inspire you?"

Cora hasn't made the connection until now, and then she wonders about it too.

"I don't . . . maybe. We do have a lot of kids with dyslexia. It's funny, I was thinking about our letters—"

He interrupts her. "You still have them?"

"Yeah, I do." Cora's eyes float over to the box on the counter.

"Cool—yeah, me too. I haven't read them in a while. What about you? You thought of reading them?"

Only every day. "No. I'm curious, though."

"You know what they say about that . . . dead cats. But sorry, I interrupted you. Tell me about the kids."

"Oh, yeah. So, in the after-school program last week, I had the teens do this exercise where they write letters to their future selves to read when they're old, which to them is, like, thirty. I got the idea from this book, *What I Know Now.*"

"Uh-oh! That sounds like self-help. The addiction continues, I see."

Her laughing blending into his is like when Cora's two favorite wind chimes fall into harmony and make a sound that she thinks of as glitter in the air.

"No, it's not! I swear. More like inspirational, not self-help. Although when I read the kids' letters, it broke my heart a little. They have such big ideas for what they want, which all boil down to being famous one way or another. No one ever says to the future self, *Hope you're enjoying your work as an accountant.* Or *I hope wife number two is working out better for you.*"

"So . . . what would you tell your younger self, Cora?"

"Ahhhhh, an Aaron question!"

"You act like I go around asking people deep questions like I'm Barbara Walters or something. I always asked *you* deep questions because I was curious about *you.* The way your mind worked. You weren't like any girl I'd ever met. I'm willing to bet that's still true."

"That's funny because most of my life, or maybe all of it, I just wanted to be like every other girl. Or what a girl should be. Easy, low maintenance, chill. Pretty much everything I'm not."

"That's everyone's problem, seems to me. Wanting to be someone, anyone, other than themselves. It's an epidemic."

"Not for you. And you're not like anybody I've ever met either."

"Would have been a lost cause for me to even try."

"So I have an Aaron question for you—are you happy?" After all these years, Cora is suddenly emboldened to cut to the chase. "Like, have things worked out the way you thought they would?"

"What even is happy?"

"Oh, boy, here we go!"

"I'm serious. Here me out."

Cora splays out on the floor and places the phone by her side, close to her ear, as if to replicate Aaron next to her. It's an approximation of all the times that they'd sat together eating tacos on the battered wood floor of his studio or lying face-to-face on the old flannel sheet he turned into a picnic blanket at whatever field or park he took her to. The way they said so much between them without having to actually say much, or anything, at all and how that wasn't even the odd part; what was bizarre was how fully she trusted this communion.

The conversation settles into an ease and flow that stretches until the last dregs of light leak from Cora's living room unnoticed. When she grabs her phone—finally—to check the time, she sees hours have passed and that her screen is filled with alerts for missed calls and text messages from Lincoln.

Where are you?

Did you miss your flight?

I just called you twice

There's another flight @ 8:30—call me.

Cora—WTF?

Now I'm worried.

Okay, I'm getting more pissed off than worried. You have to let me know you're alive.

Aaron's in the middle of telling her about a critic who recently described his work as "too Black" but she's having trouble concentrating on these two things at once—their conversation and the onslaught of messages.

"So, any chance you'll be out in LA then?" Aaron says, pausing, which means a response of some sort is required.

"Sorry—what, now?"

"I was saying, I have an event back in LA in December. The twenty-third. Will you be out there then?"

Cora can't tell if this is an invite, hint, or innocent question.

Her phone lights up, again. It's Lincoln, again. Cora can't figure out why she's punishing him, but she is and it's not right.

"Listen, Aaron, that's my other line . . . "

"Yeah, sounds like your phone has been blowing up. Popular girl."

"Ha! Popular? Things haven't changed *that* much."

"You gotta go?"

"Yeah, I probably should go."

"Okay, I get it. It was really nice hearing from you." Cora strains to parse the intonation of his every word, hunting for signs of regret, resignation, or longing beneath the excruciatingly polite sign-off.

"Yeah, you too, and thanks for sending the photo. Though *thanks* doesn't do justice to how much I appreciate it. Truly."

"It was my pleasure, Ms. Belle. You take care."

But neither of them moves to hang up. They just sit there listening to each other breathe until her phone starts buzzing yet again.

CORA CAN'T BE SURE

November 2021

When Wes announces at Thanksgiving dinner that he and Lorraine plan to go on a ten-day cruise over Christmas, Cora's somewhat mortified that her first reaction is *But wait, what about me?* She's never spent a single Christmas apart from her father. Other traditions have changed to accommodate Lorraine—for example, they don't have their usual macaroni and cheese on the Thanksgiving dinner menu tonight because Lorraine is lactose intolerant. And in lieu of their traditional pecan pie is Lorraine's homemade caramel cake, her "specialty" for dessert. They've also moved Thanksgiving dinner (and all dinners) to five p.m. instead of their typical later hour because Lorraine has a lot of thoughts about proper digestion that are largely informed by experts featured on the *Today* show. But at least they're gathered at the same mahogany dining-room table that permanently glistened, thanks to Wes's liberal use of lemon Pledge.

After Lorraine and Wes had been serious for a couple years, they decided that keeping two separate homes was impractical, and there were some tense negotiations over whose place would be sold. Wes and Lorraine were amicable enough, it was Cora who was a tense wreck, imagining her father selling her childhood home—the only one she'd ever known—and moving to the condo in Rehoboth Beach that Lorraine bought after her divorce. Wes's fear of hurricanes and devotion to his prized backyard vegetable garden (both of which had reached irrational proportions) eventually won him the relocation contest. But it was close, close enough that Cora had prepared herself to beg, even though she knew she should have outgrown her fierce attachment to this house by now. And even though she knew eventually the day would come when it was sold, whether she was ready or not.

She, a bona fide adult, should be ready for this too—their first holiday apart.

"Ten days in the Greek isles sounds incredible," she tells them. "I'll be fine."

It helps considerably when it clicks, over the next bite of shockingly dry caramel cake, that being abandoned for Christmas could turn out to be a gift. There's now nothing stopping her from going to Los Angeles for the holidays.

"Maybe you can spend Christmas with Lincoln?" Wes suggests. "I don't want you to be alone."

"He'll be with his kids. He and Naomi do a handoff on every holiday at noon. But it's okay. I might take a trip to LA."

"Oh, is the custody situation why Lincoln's not coming until tomorrow?" Lorraine asks. "Too bad he couldn't come for dinner, but I'm so looking forward to meeting him. I'll save him some cake."

Cora needs to get home to change her sheets and hide the most embarrassing products in her bathroom in preparation for Lincoln's arrival early the next morning.

It took four solid days of her groveling for Lincoln to finally get over her bailing on her last visit to Chicago. He was mainly, and justifiably, mystified by Cora's behavior. *Join the club,* she wanted to say. She refused, though, to lie and claim she'd had food poisoning, which was her first instinct. In the end, she explained that she just got overwhelmed thinking about how quickly they'd grown so close again and what it all meant in terms of their future. With that on top of all the turmoil and uncertainty of the past couple years, Cora had hit something of a breaking point. At the heart of what turned out to be a long-winded, rambling excuse was the truth: Cora is overwhelmed by the crossroads she finds herself at—again.

Lincoln accepted this explanation, which allowed him to swiftly shift from irritation to caregiving mode, and he offered her soothing assurances about all the happy times to come by each other's sides. Furthermore, he'd realized that she was right, it wasn't fair that she was always coming to him. He wanted to see her world and her life—and Wes. He would come as soon as possible, the day after Thanksgiving.

If Lincoln had checked with Cora before booking the flight, she would have told him to arrive on Saturday morning instead of tomorrow. She has plans she cannot—she refuses to—miss. The Friday after Thanksgiving held a tradition that was sacred to her, Kid's First staff's annual day of service, where they make meals out of leftovers and distribute them to homeless people around DC. Cora has arranged for Lincoln to have lunch with Wes while she's busy with that, which she reminds her dad of before taking her leave with the rest of the caramel cake Lorraine has thrust at her wrapped in a cocoon of foil to save Wes from all these sweets "he has no business eating."

Cora has even more trouble than usual falling asleep that night; instead of doom-scrolling Twitter, she rereads the last few texts Aaron has sent her. The most recent one is a picture of a cartoon turkey with the caption *They only like me for my breasts.* It shouldn't make her laugh, let alone swoon, but it does both.

Cora hadn't taken Aaron for someone who would send silly memes, but she hadn't taken herself for someone who would secretly text with two different men for the past three weeks either, so there you go. Cora doesn't respond to the turkey text because she knows that this will spark a flurry of communication between them, which will do nothing for her sleep. Besides, she can't lie in these fresh clean sheets texting with Aaron all night and then have Lincoln sleep in them tomorrow.

Cora gets up to drink a bitter tea that's supposed to make her sleepy. She puts on a satin eye mask and listens to a relaxation meditation. She rubs lavender oil on her wrists. The worse her insomnia gets, the more elaborate her sleep rituals become. Perhaps sleep isn't any more elusive than it's always been; she just needs it more than she did.

Finally, she resorts to a sleeping pill. They usually leave her groggy the next day, but desperate times. She awakens on the couch with an unsightly pool of drool on her good throw pillow and all of thirty minutes before Lincoln's flight lands. So much for taking a shower before she goes. She's about to at least brush her teeth when she sees Lincoln's text.

Don't worry about picking me up.
I'll just grab an Uber when I land so
you can sleep in. See you soon, Bella.

The extra hour gives Cora time to shower (using her expensive body scrub, a gift from her boss), flat-iron her hair, and try on one dress and then another. She opens the refrigerator to behold the bounty of fruits and vegetables that look out of place there. She couldn't have Lincoln seeing it as it usually was, empty but for condiment bottles and a jar of pickles. This fridge, the one overflowing with yesterday's Whole Foods haul, offers the illusion of a woman who can roast a chicken, tell the difference between cilantro and parsley, and feed herself wholesome, gorgeous food even if she is cooking for one. Adulting goals never end.

At the last second, when Lincoln is on his way up in the elevator, Cora grabs the photo of herself in Paris that she'd framed and slides it under the couch. There's a lonely nail on the wall where it hung.

When he arrives, Lincoln is too big for her space; he takes up so much room. Cora's used to seeing him in his airy penthouse with vaulted ceilings, not in her snug living room, which is the same size as his bedroom closet. He looks around with the type of smile one has when viewing a particularly good drawing by a kindergartner. "This is . . . nice."

Cora points out various items and mementos, holding her breath a little each time to see if Lincoln shows the proper reverence for what these objects mean to her and what they say about her. The striped vase from Mexico isn't just a vase but proof that she's a worldly person. The framed tapestry above the sofa isn't just a decoration but a sign she has sophisticated taste.

He says, "Cool birds," taking in the living-room wallpaper.

"They're flamingos. My spirit animal."

While Lincoln mulls over what on earth that means, Cora brews coffee and heats the banana nut muffins she got at her favorite bakery. She's doing this because she's hosting, but it's also nice to be the one doting on the other person for a change, feeding Lincoln, rubbing his tight shoulders, and asking about his flight.

When she gets up to refill their mugs, Lincoln reaches for her cell phone on the coffee table. "Hey, mind if I use this to check the scores real quick while mine is charging?"

"Um, sure."

"What's the passcode?" Lincoln asks this with no hesitancy, making Cora reconsider her resistance at sharing it.

"Fourteen nineteen."

"Your childhood home address? You should probably have something stronger."

The 120 seconds that pass while Lincoln taps on her phone lasts a year. It's hard to hold your breath for two minutes—or a year—but Cora comes close. At last, she has her phone safely back in her hands without a single text message arriving.

On the drive to drop Lincoln off at her dad's for lunch, he asks for the full lowdown on Wes's new wife.

"You haven't seen her, right? I guess not, since you didn't make the wedding."

"And because you refuse to post any pictures on your Facebook. Just a lurker. Ever occur to you that people might want to stalk you the same way you're stalking everyone else? I needed a fix over the years."

"Well, you have a camera roll full of pictures of us now, mister. Including my boobs, and *no one* has that, so you should feel lucky."

"Don't worry, I do. Best screensaver a guy could ask for."

"Lincoln!"

"So, Lorraine—what's her deal?"

"Well, prepare yourself because she is a dead ringer for Mrs. Santa Claus. A Black Mrs. Claus."

"I was gonna say, I didn't see your dad taking up with a white lady."

"Is there a type to take up with a white woman?"

Lincoln just glares at her. "Come on, now."

"Anyway, she's great, other than her unnatural obsession with this new game Wordle. She's going to insist you start playing it. But there are worse things. My dad's never been happier."

"Thanks, no doubt, to some little blue pills!"

"Lincoln Ames, I will pull over and drop you off right here on the shoulder."

Due to the fact that they decided to have sex this morning—twice—

Cora is running twenty minutes behind schedule, so she just pulls over in front of the freshly spray-painted black letters on the curb that read *1419* to drop Lincoln off.

"Funny, I remember this place being so much bigger," he says. He pecks her on the cheek and gets out.

Getting to her boss's house in Chevy Chase takes Cora almost an hour, but it's a pretty drive along the George Washington Memorial Parkway with views of the Tidal Basin and the soaring gothic towers of the National Cathedral; the picturesque skyline reminds her why she's never had the urge to flee her hometown as so many do.

Barbara's sprawling stone mansion is nicer than one would expect someone working as the executive director of a small, grassroots nonprofit to have, but she had a successful career as a literary agent representing DC-based journalists and politicos before she decided to go back to social work school and combine her two passions—kids and books. And her wife, Carla, a very successful children's book author, is the breadwinner. Barbara once joked that Carla essentially made five hundred dollars a word on her long-running picture-book series, prompting Cora to try to create her own plucky young heroine who stumbles into extraordinary adventures, but, alas, the best Cora could do was picture herself in a cape, dealing with the riveting conflict of choosing between Crest and Colgate.

The project is already in full swing, staffers assembling sandwiches in Barbara's blindingly white kitchen, when Cora walks in. "Oh, honey, come here." Whenever Barbara encounters Cora, she immediately pulls her into an embrace that lasts long enough and is tight enough to leave a slight imprint on Cora's cheek of whatever chunky beaded necklace Barbara is wearing.

"I'm glad you're here, but you could have skipped today with your beau in town."

A collective singsongy "Oooohhhh, boyfriend," rises from a gaggle of colleagues Cora universally adores. The organization is so small—twenty-two employees total—that it really is like a family. She's missed seeing them every day since they gave up their office space last year, one of 487 pandemic losses. On the occasions they need to meet as a full staff, they come here or Barbara reserves a room at the Metropolitan Club. Heaven knows, the woman loves a team-building off-site retreat. Cora's hamstrings (and favorite leggings) haven't recovered from 2018's Mud Run.

"No, this is important, I wouldn't miss it," Cora says, slipping into the assembly line to finish making sandwiches. "Lincoln'll be fine with my dad for a while. They've got a thing."

After they've packed a hundred lunches, they split up and go in various cars to cover different areas. Cora, Grace, and Maleka head to Northeast DC, experiencing whiplash as they leave the gorgeous neighborhoods lined with towering oaks and wide, sun-bleached sidewalks and cross over what feels like a literal line to pockmarked streets, corner stores with boarded-up windows, and empty lots strewn with weeds and broken glass. They reach a whole other world in an eleven-mile drive.

Cora stays in the idling car while Grace and Maleka jump out at various points when they see people who look like they could use a meal. Grace, a recent college graduate and a transplant from Iowa, is visibly nervous as she hands a sack to an emaciated-looking woman in hair curlers with a very serious-looking baby, heavy on her hip. Cora wants to tell Grace that poverty itself isn't unsafe, but that would mean acknowledging the discomfort Grace is going to great pains to try to hide.

The woman with the baby walks past Cora's open window and nods at her, says softly, "This is much appreciated." Her little boy has broken into a grin waving the granola bar his mom handed him from the lunch bag. His dimples are so deep, each round cheek looks like someone has pressed a finger into dough. Despite his toothy smile, all Cora can think is, this poor child is doomed. What good is a sandwich, one measly meal, in the end?

Then she remembers a story Aaron told her recently about a volunteer trip he'd taken to the southern border to photograph migrant families as they crossed over so that they would have a record of it and a family photo marking their arrival. He'd blacked out the windows of his car and improvised a makeshift darkroom so he could develop the photos almost instantly.

There was one kid who'd never seen a picture of himself before and he couldn't stop giggling and saying, "That's me! On paper!" Or that's what Aaron, whose Spanish is rusty, thought he was saying. Then another volunteer—someone there from a church organization—marched over to

Aaron and told him what these people really needed was food, shelter, and money, not *photos*. She spat that word, *photos*, like it was nothing.

"The thing is, though, Cora, it's not nothing," Aaron had said. "Any little thing you can do to help someone else matters—so what if it feels small? Who's to judge what might make a difference to someone?"

Cora takes out her phone and snaps a picture of the rows of brown bags in the back seat. She texts Aaron the photo with one line: **It's not nothing.** It's as much a reminder to herself as anything.

She then tucks her phone deep into her bag to prevent herself from checking for his response. Though "out of sight, out of mind" hasn't been a particularly effective strategy for her as of late. The same way she'd become fixated on trying to line up the past and the present, she'd tried to line up Aaron and Lincoln, like she was putting two different puzzles together. It was all she could do to stop herself from actually writing out the pros-and-cons list that was ever expanding on the whiteboard of her mind.

So distracted is Cora by this mental clutter that when she gets home, she's shocked to come upon Lincoln lying on her couch. It was always the plan for Lorraine and Wes to drop him off after lunch on their way to the outlet mall in Baltimore for some Black Friday deals, but it still catches her off guard that there is someone—a man—in her house, making himself quite at home, sprawled on the sofa in his boxers, eating a bag of Lay's.

"How was volunteering?"

"It was okay. Tough but good."

"Forgot to tell you . . . I made a donation to Kids First. Figure five thousand can make a little bit of difference."

Lincoln hasn't looked at her.

"Thank you. That's really nice of you. You okay? Was lunch okay?"

"Yeah. Wes is a trip, as always. And Lorraine's cool people . . . " Having delivered this detailed recounting of the afternoon, Lincoln trails off.

"What's up? You seem . . . quiet."

"A guy can't be a little quiet?"

"Well, not you, normally, no."

"Just had a couple things on my mind. Come here a sec." He makes room for her on the couch. "I just wanna know . . . you love me, right, Cora?"

"Of course." She doesn't have to think about her answer. Cora has always loved Lincoln and so she assumes she still does and that this will remain the case quite possibly forever.

"Okay, okay, good."

There's a follow-up question begging to be asked here, but the most strenuous subject Cora can handle at the moment is what's for dinner. Her dream evening involves three of her favorite things: changing into pajamas, ordering pasta from Sole d'Italia, and watching a British mystery. Four things if you count Lincoln, which she does. Once upon a time, Cora thought that the best part of a relationship was all the new things you could do or try with another person; now she's coming to believe that it's even better when you can do everything you already enjoy but with someone next to you.

A message on Cora's phone waylays these plans. It's waiting for her when she gets her phone out of her bag to order food.

U SHLD NO—L WANTS 2 MARY U.
ASKED ME IF OKAY 2DAY.

This text takes some deciphering, and not just because of her father's nearly incomprehensible shorthand. When it finally sinks in, Cora runs to the bathroom and slams the door. She paces the small space with the quaint black-and-white penny tiles—if you can call taking two steps and turning around pacing. She stops to press her hands against both walls to assure herself that the room isn't actually getting smaller—it only feels like the walls are closing in. One thing's for certain: This is not the right reaction to have upon learning the man catnapping on your sofa wants to commit his life to you.

Cora has tried to slow this train down and she told her dad as much last night at Thanksgiving when he expressed some concern about how fast she and Lincoln seemed to be moving in their second act.

"Well, when you know, you know," Cora told her dad. "That's what Lincoln says."

Lincoln's other responses when Cora broached the topic of the rapid pace of their relationship were "We don't have any more time to waste" and "Too soon? It's been twenty years." Her last line of defense—that she hasn't met his kids yet—will be knocked down in two weeks; they're finally getting together at a place called Jump-N-Jams, which, per the website, involves trampolines, rock walls, deep pits of plastic balls, and "hours of family fun." Cora will slip into a dirty helmet worn by hundreds of others and into the role of stepmother for a day. Both prospects make her more than a little queasy.

"And do *you* know, Cora?" Wes asked her last night, firm hand on her shoulder as she dried the good plates with a tea towel.

"Know what?"

"How long unicorn horns are? Don't play with me. You know what I'm asking."

"Can you ever know anything, Daddy?"

Wes moved his hand to his forehead in the gesture of exasperated fathers the world over. "Good Lord, I need the second drink Lorraine is never going to let me have."

As much as her dad loves Lincoln, based on their conversation last night, this text is not a happy sneak preview, it's a warning, and Cora accepts it in the spirit it was intended. It's not as if Lincoln is waiting for her back in her living room on bended knee but he might as well be, given how her heart has clawed its way into her throat and is now thrashing there. What will it be like when the deed goes down? Which, Cora starts to suspect—quickly connecting dots—might happen on New Year's Eve. Lincoln told her he plans to take her to New York City but has been cagey about what's involved in this trip beyond "some big surprises." Something tells her it's not the Rockettes.

It will take weeks, if not years, and untold hours in Greta's office for Cora to even begin to understand what she does next, what force propels her flying through the bathroom door and back down the hall, where she finds Lincoln half asleep and half hard in his Calvin Kleins.

She hovers over him like a serial killer, only her weapon isn't a knife; it's a dagger of a different order.

He doesn't open his eyes when he mumbles, "You were gone a minute. Stomach good?"

"Look, Lincoln, I have to tell you something."

"Mm-hmm. I'm exhausted, though. Can it wait?" He yawns so wide, Cora sees his back molars, like little cratered moon rocks.

"No, it can't. Lincoln, back in college, when I was pregnant . . . I—I didn't have a miscarriage. I had an abortion." Blurting it out this way at this speed, like one might rip off a Band-Aid, is supposed to lessen the pain. But for which one of them? Cora has no idea.

Lincoln slowly sits up. "Say what now?"

Cora takes the question as rhetorical so she doesn't bother to repeat herself or clarify. She can skip straight to the next step. "I'm sorry I lied to you."

"Da fuck, Cora? I can't believe you would do something like that! Behind my back!"

He buries his face in one of her throw pillows, presumably to scream into it, which she's done countless times with that exact pillow and can speak to its effectiveness. Something to do with the particular density of the cotton filling, she supposes.

While she waits for him to face her again—if he ever does—she wants to say, *You lied to me too*, but it's a weak defense, bringing up his cheating. For one thing, two wrongs don't make a right, and for another, her anger has eased over time. They were so young to be so serious; it was a dumb, impulsive mistake; immaturity was a mitigating factor, et cetera. The unyielding nature of her beliefs around what was forgivable or not—and the illusion of control that came with them—has softened, as absolutes are wont to do.

When Lincoln drops the pillow from his face, he's slightly more composed. "You waited all these years to tell me? Or were you just never going to tell me?"

"Honestly? Probably not. If we hadn't reconnected like this . . . " The truth cleared a place for more truth.

"I'm just shocked, Cora. It just doesn't feel like something you would do."

"That's how I felt when you cheated on me." *So much for two wrongs don't make a right.*

"That was a million years ago. I made a stupid mistake. We were kids."

"Yes, exactly! We were kids. I was a kid. A scared kid, and I didn't know what to do. But I couldn't let you force me into having a *baby*, Lincoln."

"You're telling me you wouldn't do the same thing now?"

"Do you mean get an abortion? Probably—you know I don't want kids. That hasn't changed. Lying about it? Probably not. I was scared I'd lose you, Lincoln. And then I did anyway."

And I might again. Only this time the prospect isn't as terrifying. Cora doesn't know quite what to make of that.

Lincoln is now on his feet and hovering over her. "Wait a second. Who else knows about this—that you had an abortion? Your dad? Your girls? Am I the fool who's the last to know about my own damn business?"

"My dad doesn't know anything except for what you told him—that I was pregnant. Which, speaking of people's business, wasn't yours to tell."

Going on the offensive spares Cora from having to confess to the short list of people who do know, which starts with Neisha and Kim and ends with Aaron. She and Aaron talked about it just the other night when another one of their "quick" phone calls stretched to hours. In typical Aaron fashion, he wanted to know if she still thought about her decision, if she was okay, if she'd read that essay in the *New York Times* by the woman reflecting on the abortion she didn't have decades before but had wanted to. When Cora said she hadn't, he pulled it up and read it to her as she was tucked under her duvet.

Lincoln faces her down now, literally, proverbially. "You're right about that, Cora. I'm sorry. It was my bad. I really thought your dad already knew—y'all are so close. I assumed. And I was worried about you."

"That's what he said."

"It's the truth. But I don't get it, Cora. Why are you telling me this now, out of the blue?"

This is what she's sure will take years to unpack, and she'll never arrive at a clear conclusion. Is confessing to Lincoln an act of sabotage? Is she doing it to test his love? Is it an unburdening? She doubts she'll ever be able to come up with a more satisfactory answer than what she tells Lincoln now. "I don't know . . . I thought . . . as we get closer that . . . you needed to know. No secrets, remember?"

"Well, you got any more of those up your sleeve? Anything else you need to get off your chest?"

The throw pillow she's grasping, the twin to the one Lincoln was holding, wilts under the pressure of her arms. But she knows it's the way she chews on her cheek that's the dead giveaway.

"Shit, Cora, really? Okay, what is it? An OnlyFans account? A gambling addiction? I'm starting to feel like I don't know you at all."

"Never mind . . . it doesn't matter."

"It does matter. You might as well just tell me. Let's go ahead and get it all out, why don't we?"

"I've reconnected with Aaron."

"Aaron who?"

"Aaron Wright. He's the photographer I met the summer my dad had his stroke."

"Why?"

"Why what?"

"Why did y'all reconnect?"

"It was by accident." *Fate.* "We hadn't spoken since he moved to Paris and then we happened to run into each other a few weeks ago. At Neisha's party. He was in LA for work. He's a pretty well-known photographer."

"Really?" Lincoln's scoff sends a trail of spit arcing into the air. "I've never heard of him."

If Lincoln were capable of sheepishness, Cora would have sworn that she caught a glimpse of it at his petty comment. An embarrassment that he should have been above it, been the bigger man. Recovering quickly, he immediately plows ahead to the heart of the matter.

"Hold up. Is there something going on between y'all? Are you sleeping with him, Cora?" Lincoln's features break this way and that way in disgust.

"No! No. We're just . . . friends. Or not even that . . . "

"Then why are you telling me this?"

"I don't know."

"Did you used to sleep with him? What was the deal?"

"Just once."

"Once, huh? And when was that, exactly?"

"After you and I—"

"Wait a minute. Paris . . . " Cora has a vivid glimpse of what Lincoln might be like in the courtroom, putting his arguments and case together in real time, preparing to crucify the opposition's witness. "When you went to Paris way back when, was it to see him?" He almost looks more satisfied than upset to have this gotcha moment.

She's sworn to herself to tell the truth and nothing but the truth, so that's what she does.

"Yeah, actually, I did." The tassel she's been nervously pulling at on the pillow comes out along with this confession.

"And then you came home with some bullshit email, all *I can't do this. I need me time. I have to focus on myself.* What a joke!"

"No! No, it was true. It wasn't about Aaron . . . he wasn't a factor in that. It was about us . . . you were putting so much pressure on me, Lincoln."

"Pressure? Pressure! Oh, so loving you and trying to make it work and trying to make up for my mistakes—that's pressure? Not wanting to lose the first and only person to truly love me is something I'm supposed to feel bad about? I see. I also see how you're trying to turn the tables here to make me the bad guy. We started out with *your* lies, not mine!"

"There is no bad guy, Lincoln." She included herself in this but was too defeated to bother with any more of a defense.

"Exactly! And if there was, I ain't the one. Now, let me guess, you're going to tell me Aaron's not a factor now either. Not that I care about that buster. If we're in a may-the-best-man-win type scenario, I'm not trippin'. But damn, Cora. This is a lot. Too much. Like, twenty years and all this just comes tumbling out? That's some shit, I tell you. Don't order me anything to eat. I'm going to bed." Lincoln's jumped to his feet and is moving away from her as fast as he was just moving his mouth.

"I'm sorry. I just didn't want there to be secrets!" She's not sure he heard her down the hall until he calls back.

"Famous last words, huh, Cora?"

CORA IN LA-LA LAND

December 2021

How Not to Fall in Love with the Wrong Person in Ten Easy Steps.

Cora, in all her eager foraging in self-help aisles, has never found a book that would deliver on this promise and spare so many women. Forget diet, exercise, productivity, tidying up, and not giving fucks—it's love that dooms you every time.

"You should have seen her, Cora. He wore her down to a shell of herself." Neisha shakes her head as she recounts her weekend in Memphis helping Kim move out. Or, as they refer to it: Operation Exhale.

As it happened, Neisha's return flight landed at LAX around the same time as Cora's arrived, though they had to cross five terminals to find each other. Whenever Cora visits, their first stop is always Luxe Nails because Neisha sees regular manicures as a way of life. Reclined side by side in the pink chairs facing the ocean is a suitable place to bask in the relief that Kim is at last out of Nate's clutches. And to discuss everything that Cora needs to discuss with Neisha face-to-face. In due time.

"I can't believe it got so bad. But I guess she had to hit rock bottom before she would leave," Neisha says with a sigh so loud and deep, the receptionist at the salon's front desk looks over to make sure she's not throwing a fit about her service.

Rock bottom was Kim learning that Nate had gotten another woman pregnant.

"Well, at least she's free now, finally. I sent her a plant for her new place." Nothing says *I love you and I hope you can get over spending five precious years of your life with someone who I'm convinced is a sociopath* like a ficus.

"She needs an exorcism. But a plant's nice too. She wants to talk to you, you know—like, really talk. Last night she was boo-hooing about how she feels bad that she's been MIA."

"You mean ignoring me?"

"You gotta cut her some slack. Homegirl's been a hot mess. She's been hiding from everyone. She's just gotta regroup before y'all can get into it."

"There's nothing to get into. She said something messed up. But I already let it go and forgave her—she just won't let me do it to her face. I wish I could have been there for her this weekend."

Whatever distance there is between Kim and Cora, the unspoken rule is you show up when it matters—period, full stop—and Cora was ready to get on a plane. After much discussion, though, she and Neisha had decided there was a fine line between feeling supported and feeling ambushed, so it was better if it was just Neisha to the rescue. Neisha was the one you wanted in a crisis, anyway. You could count on her to take charge, take names, and take no prisoners. Also, take revenge. After Kim's bags and boxes were loaded in the car while Nate was at work, Neisha went back upstairs and peed on his toothbrush. Cora found this too delicious to be properly scandalized, though she did offer a halfhearted, "I can't believe you did that," when Neisha called her from the bathroom and told her what she'd just done. But, of course, Neisha being Neisha, Cora could believe it. And she fully supported it, because despite karma's formidable reputation, there was often too little of it doled out—sometimes you had to take matters into your own hands.

"Don't worry, Kim and I talked about you enough—it was like you were there," Neisha says.

This comes as no surprise. Two of them are constantly gossiping with each other about the third in ex parte conversations, analyzing various developments and evaluating the emotional weather of whoever is in the hot seat at any given point. And so it's gone for twenty years of friendship. Rather than being irritated, Cora accepts their devoting so many hours to talking about her behind her back for what it is: a measure of their love and affection. If you don't judge, you don't love; it's come to be the defining philosophy of their trifecta.

"So, what's the verdict on all my life choices as of late, Ne-ne?"

"That depends on the biggest decision you have to make!"

The gyrating massage chair hides Cora's startled shudder. "How did you—what are you talking about it?"

"Bridesmaid dresses! I'm telling you right now, I'm not wearing yellow or pink. Or orange."

"Neisha! You're getting way ahead of yourself."

"What? You said Lincoln forgave you, right? For your little bombshell. If you'd asked me, I would have told you to take that shit to the grave. But you didn't ask me. And I'm trying to be less of a bossy bitch these days and mind my own business. You're not the only one making breakthroughs in therapy, ya know."

"Um, since when? You literally just bossed me into getting this blue nail polish."

"Whatever, it looks good. Now, back to Lincoln."

"Yeah. He's forgiven me . . . just like that. It's been business as usual, like nothing ever happened."

Cora didn't think she would survive the strained silence after she let it all out with Lincoln, like dumping out her purse so she could weed out all the dirty tissues, gum wrappers, and loose change and put the contents back in an orderly way. Though that was a considerably more satisfying and conclusive project.

That next morning, Cora had come very close to making a panicked escape to the gym she'd joined but never went to before she remembered she'd thrown out her one pair of running shoes after the 2018 Mud Run destroyed them. She sucked it up and dealt with the tension as best she could by shopping for new sneakers on Zappos. Around noon, Lincoln said his first sentence to her: "I'm going to need some time, Cora, but let's salvage this weekend."

Salvage was a modest goal; she was in. For lack of a better idea and because the November temps had reached a balmy sixty degrees, Cora had suggested an afternoon at the National Zoo. Turned out standing together, bundled against the cool wind, with hot chocolates in hand, watching two pandas lick each other did wonders to dissolve tension. Cora had half a mind to put that in the zoo's Yelp reviews.

By dinner that night, Lincoln had returned to holding her hand. All that time, all that weight of the secret she'd kept from him, Cora would never have expected her eventual absolution to be so anticlimactic, her greatest transgression reduced to "water under the bridge." "What's done is done," Lincoln told her over cheesecake, leaving Cora with a strange sense of resignation that the sentiment came too easily. Forgiveness, like so much else, was more valuable the harder you had to work to get it.

Neisha gives her a side-eye. "And this a bad thing, that Lincoln's willing to move on? And that he still wants to marry your ass?"

"That was a little bit of a false alarm, remember?"

When Cora was able to talk to her dad about his bomb drop of a text, while Lincoln was in the shower the next morning, she got some clarity. Lincoln had only casually mentioned that he wanted to marry Cora, and only after Wes specifically asked about Lincoln's "intentions," at which point, her father had taken it upon himself to tell Lincoln he might want to "slow his roll a little." It clicked why Lincoln had been so quiet when she returned home from volunteering, why he'd needed the assurance that she still loved him. Her father's reaction must have sown some doubts.

"False alarm, my ass—my money's still on that man proposing to you on New Year's Eve like he's Morris Chestnut in a nineties rom-com. Lincoln knows what he wants, I'll give him that. I can only imagine the rock he's gonna get you. What do you think? Four carats? Five?"

"I don't care about the ring." Though Cora has imagined its weight on her finger. Of course she has.

"I don't get why you're not more excited. You're hitting the jackpot—literally. He still has his hair and that bubble booty and, best of all, he's richety-rich rich."

"I don't think that's why people get married."

"Ha! Are you kidding me? Why do you think they have a name for it?"

"A gold digger I am not."

"I know, I know. But let's not forget, you love Lincoln. You've been loving him longer than my new intern has been *alive*. You might as well get married and get it over with."

"That's so romantic."

"You know what I mean."

"I don't even know that he still wants to marry me. After . . . everything."

"Cora. You could shoot someone on Park Avenue, and he'd still want to be with you. Did you reschedule meeting the kids?"

The big trip to Climb Zone had been sabotaged, as Lincoln put it, by Naomi, who insisted the kids had the flu and it would be too disruptive for them to make it across town to Lincoln's place. Lincoln had described to Cora the vicious argument that followed in painful, stomach-churning detail. The names called, the curses thrown, the accusations made. "You can't keep my kids from me, Naomi, and you can't keep them from meeting my girlfriend either!" His nostrils flared in anger as he recounted the conversation, and no amount of reassurance that it was okay helped. Cora might have mimicked Lincoln's outrage and convincingly conveyed disappointment when mostly she was relieved to have the reprieve from meeting his kids for at least a few more weeks.

"Yeah, we're going to do it in January. MLK weekend."

"Well, you know they'll love you, just like Dylan does."

"That's what Lincoln says."

Lincoln had assured her of this over and over again in a way that had the contradictory effect of making Cora worry she hadn't been concerned enough about her likability in the first place. But it was something else he said in that conversation that hit Cora harder than any meet-the-kids anxiety: "You know, it's incredible how God works. I got to have the children you never wanted. It's all His plan."

It gave her pause to cede her life choices to God's hand, but all she could manage for a response was "Yeah, wild."

Neisha is staring at her hard, a suspicion she deserves. "Okay, for real, what is going on with you, Cora? I know when something's up. Are you constipated?"

"No, I . . . "

Cora doesn't know how to tell Neisha about Aaron, doesn't even know where to begin. The aughts? Last month? Last night when he said, "It's strange how much you can miss someone you never see. Is that crazy?" That was the very nature of missing someone, but she knew what he meant. And she didn't find it crazy, not one bit.

The photograph is as good a starting point as any, but Cora struggles to explain its significance. When she stutters something about it capturing her soul, Neisha rightfully looks at her like the chemical fumes from the acetone must be getting to her. Cora skips ahead to the texts and calls they've had since she ran into him at Neisha's birthday party, skimming over the specifics—how Aaron calls her most mornings when he goes for a walk because he says it's nice to start the day with her and how they've fallen asleep together on their phones more than once because ending it together is nice too. Then Cora gets to the reason why she's in town.

"Aaron's here in LA too. He invited me to this black-tie gala, a showcase for his work, Thursday night. I'm thinking about going." (She'd had a dress sent to Neisha's place just in case this still felt like a good idea in forty-eight hours.)

"Wait—so you're not here to spend the holidays with me?"

"*That's* your takeaway from everything I just said?"

"I'm still processing. This is some Real Housewives–level drama right here. Because it sounds like you've been in love with ol' dude for two decades, and I had no idea. Hell, maybe even you had no idea? Make that make sense."

An impossible task. Since when did these things make sense?

"I can't, Ne-ne, that's the problem. But for the record, I *am* here to see you. *And* Aaron. He and I are actually meeting up later this afternoon. At the beach."

"Hold up. Is that why you're wearing your lucky sweater?"

Cora looks down at the green cashmere pullover with rainbow stripes as if she forgot she was wearing it. *Oh, this?*

"And wait a minute . . . take that hat off." Cora obeys. "Yep, that's a fresh blowout you're trying to hide under there. I see you."

For the next two hours, Neisha grills her about her love triangle, but even that isn't enough time to dissect and analyze, so they add a stop for mojitos, and she continues to alternate between being entertained and exasperated.

"I just wish I could pop some popcorn and pull up at this cute li'l beach meet, but I gotta get all the way to the east side to pick up Dylan from soccer, so you're on your own. I would leave you with some wise words, but you got a girl speechless. First time for everything."

With that, she peels off in her Mini Coop, leaving Cora standing on the boardwalk with her tote bag, an iced coffee, and a low-grade headache from her nerves or Neisha's lectures or both.

She has an hour or so before Aaron arrives, but this is by design; Cora needs some time alone overlooking what's been her happy place since she was a little girl—the ocean. Whenever her father took her to Ocean City or Rehoboth or any of the beaches that dot the mid-Atlantic, she'd bound across the parking lot as fast as her legs would carry her, with her bag of plastic shovels and snacks slapping at her sandy calves, closing the distance between herself and the shore as fast as possible. She tried to explain to her dad that she just felt different by the water. And her dad said, "Looks like you found your happy place. Everyone needs one of those, somewhere that makes you feel big and small at the same time, far away and close to yourself, and like you can breathe better there than you can anywhere else." These were all abstract ideas to a five-year-old, but Cora knew what he meant by the feeling inside her, the same warmth and lightness that spreads through her now. She observes the way the waves catch the sun, making it look like a million diamonds are scattered across the surface, and the ring of imposing gray mountains that edge the water and cut into the blue sky, exuding pure majesty without even working that hard.

No emotion has a shorter shelf life than awe—as impossible to force as it is to maintain. So Cora looks around now and makes a point of soaking it all the way in. This involves opening herself to consider such things as the mysteries and vastness of the universe, subjects she can normally happily and easily avoid, distracted by trips to Whole Foods and getting the oil in her car changed and remembering to dust the baseboards. That's what adulthood is, a million and one tasks to divert you from contemplating the point and purpose of it all and tricking your into believing clean baseboards might be it. But not today.

The meditative crash of the frothy waves (a sound her white-noise app tries in vain to approximate) and the views are the ultimate antidote to this crushing mundanity. Alone with the Pacific, she finds it impossible to think about her to-do list or her grocery list or if she remembered to pack a razor. It all fades away, making room for the big ideas these sweeping vistas invite and inspire: life and death, love and loss, romance and heartbreak.

And, as planned, it's the ideal setting for what she is finally about to do.

Cora pulls a small blanket from her tote and spreads it out, working against the wind. Then she digs to the bottom of the bag for the bundle she carefully tucked there. Her plan had been to start from the beginning, to read the very first letter, but she abruptly changes course and tears open the sealed letter in the envelope.

Taking in how much her handwriting has changed over the years sends a ripple through the hairs on the back of her neck like she's seen a ghost, which in a way she has. The ghost of Cora past, who sat at her little white desk in her childhood bedroom hours after returning from Paris, scribbling furiously.

Dear Aaron—

I don't know how to begin this letter, because I also don't know how to end it—yep, there I go again, thinking about the last part first.

Actually, I want to start with the memories from this weekend . . . I want to write them all down so you'll have them too. (Okay, that's not how memories work, but whatever.)

When you kissed me on the staircase and I didn't have time to think about what we were doing and if we were "just" friends and if this was going to be awkward and where we were going to sleep. Crazy how one kiss can complicate . . . or simplify everything.

Sitting on a patch of grass in the Luxembourg Garden at dusk, eating cheeses whose names I'll never be able to pronounce and you saying, "Wait for it, wait for it," and then the sun suddenly hitting the trees at an angle that created this unreal light, like it had set fire to the tips of every leaf, and you said, "Incredible, right? I've been wanting you to see that."

Climbing the Eiffel Tower in the rain and feeling like there might just be actual clouds waiting for us at the top. Looking over the edge and grabbing your arm to steady myself. You reminding me of

the expression for the phenomenon of wanting to throw yourself off high ledges: l'appel de vide.

Seeing the Mona Lisa—how tiny it is! I couldn't wrap my mind around that. It's so hard to let go of how we expect things to be even in the face of proof. That painting will always be giant to me.

Walking around Paris trying out my terrible French by telling everyone how excited I was to be there, not realizing that the translation of je suis excite is "I'm horny." How hard we laughed when we realized what I'd been saying.

It was all so perfect, until . . .

You ruined it.

Or at least that's how I felt when you told me you weren't coming home. I was angry at myself for getting carried away with a fantasy of my own creation. And I was mad at you too.

For tricking me into falling for you. (Maybe that's not fair.)

And for making it seem so easy to see if we could work, like six thousand miles was not a big deal. (Maybe that's not fair either.)

And for making me wonder if you even truly meant those things about making it work. (Okay, I know that's not fair.)

And for making me have feelings for you even though I promised myself I was never going to do that again with anyone.

And for making me so scared that this wouldn't work.

And for making me so scared that it could.

I guess what I'm saying, in case it's not clear is . . .

I AM willing to try if you are. You're right, what you said . . . this doesn't have to be over before it even truly started. You're right . . . we don't have to say goodbye—so I won't.

xo, C

Cora had stood by the red barn-shaped mailbox at the end of the driveway forever, staring at the letter she'd just placed in its hollow metal guts; long enough for the oppressive scent of honeysuckle from the nearby bushes to cling to her clothes. But not long enough for the mailman to arrive and retrieve it before she snatched it back with shaking hands. Cora just couldn't do it. She had her reasons, the biggest one being her fear. Taking leaps hadn't worked out so well for her. Nor had love.

There is no more torturous exercise than agonizing over what could have been. So Cora doesn't bother wondering what might've happened if she'd been brave enough to send this letter. Because she wasn't. And in the end, that was all that mattered. And there is nothing she can do about it except lie on her back facing the cloudless sky, dig her feet in the warm sand, and let the regret wash over her until she's drenched in it, like too-thick lotion you can't rub in.

Actually, there is something else she can do. Not make the same mistake twice.

When Aaron appears, it's as a shadow across her closed eyes.

You.

It's what Cora thought when she first saw him, in 2002 in a café she hadn't set foot in before or since. It was a sense of recognition that felt so profound and so ridiculous at the same time, Cora couldn't make sense of it; it was like drops of rain falling from a cloudless sky. But now—now she understands the message and where it came from: some primal place within her that she knows now (with wisdom? Experience? Greta's interventions?) she should trust.

The uneven sand is only partly to blame for Cora's being so off-kilter as she gets to her feet that she trips into Aaron's arms, which is just as well because that's where she was headed anyway. They stand there holding each other. If a hug and a slow dance had a baby, that would describe their lingering embrace. Her favorite part is that neither of them has said a single word. *Hello* is too insignificant a sentiment relative to this moment to waste their breath.

They both take a step away from each other, reluctantly.

Aaron looks around. "You got a good spot."

"Is there a bad spot to be had?"

"Good point."

As they get settled on the blanket, he digs into two deep pockets in his utility jacket and pulls out two cans of rosé. He opens one and hands it to her.

"What are we drinking to?" Cora asks.

"I don't know—you tell me."

"Epiphanies?"

He gives her a confused smile as he taps his can softly against hers. "Okay, then."

She watches Aaron's Adam's apple bob up and down as he drinks and wonders if she's ever found a neck more attractive.

"Are you ready for the show on Thursday?" Cora's plan is to steady herself and buy some time with small talk, allowing the alcohol to make its way into their systems and for her to gather herself. It was such a long way from *Hey, long time no see* to *I think we're meant to be together.* (Isn't it always.) She has no clear map for how to get from here to there.

"Yeah, I have to go to the gallery later and check on the final installations, but I'm happy with how it's coming together. I was up pretty late, so I'm wiped."

That explained the dark circles. Cora's trying to be careful not to eye him up and down and even more careful not to touch him because it's possible she won't be able to stop. But she senses a fragility in him that makes her want to reach out and rub his back.

"I'm excited to see your work."

"Well, to warn you, these gatherings can be painful—stuffy small talk, warm chardonnay."

The breeze picks up and the letter she tucked in her bag slips out and is carried off by the wind. Cora jumps up and chases it, grabbing frantically like she's on the verge of losing a irreplaceable possession, which is exactly the case. She seizes it out of the air after a few feet and stumbles back to the blanket, panting heavily from the exertion, or maybe she's been breathing this way since Aaron arrived.

"Is that your paycheck or birth certificate?" Aaron asks, laughing.

"Actually . . . it's a letter I wrote years ago. To you. I didn't exactly ghost you before. Well, I did, but only because . . . here, just read it." She thrusts the paper at him.

"Nah, I'm good. I don't think I want to do that. Like I said, water under the bridge."

Cora was hoping that Aaron would read the letter and, as agonizing as it would be to watch him, it would do the work of reminding him of their connection, the magical time they had together and all the reasons why they should consider taking another shot. In other words, the letter would do for him what it had done for her—make clear she'd made a grave mistake.

If he won't read it, Cora will have to make the case herself, in real time, a much more unnerving proposition. She channels Greta. *Ask yourself: What's the best that can happen, Cora?* It's a tactic Cora is supposed to use in order not to catastrophize. Cora usually argued that her fears were a good warning system; a little caution never hurt anyone. Then one day Greta asked her to consider the possibility that "instead of keeping you safe, your fears can keep you small." And Cora has pretty much not stopped thinking about that ever since, especially in the past hour. That and when Greta said, "A little courage might not cost you as much you think."

So Cora readies herself, with the help of a fortifying swig of wine. The backdrop is utterly cinematic: the empty beach, the agreeable sun, the two seagulls frolicking over the waves. The stage is perfectly set for a big moment . . . except for how pained Aaron looks. He's been lying on his side, but he turns, restless, as if he can't get comfortable.

"You okay?"

"Yeah, yeah."

"You wanna get up and walk?"

"Nah, nah, it's just . . . "

"What?"

"Nothing . . . nothing. Just slept funny. Ty's couch might as well be made of concrete."

Cora is helpless to come up with a smooth transition. There's something to be said for just blurting out what she needs to without wasting another second. And before she loses her nerve.

"Okay, well, I'll just tell you what the letter said. I wrote that wanted to be together, to try. But then I didn't send it because . . . I don't know. I was afraid? I just froze. And now—now you're suddenly back in my life. It feels like that wouldn't have happened unless it was supposed to. Like you wrote to me a long time ago, people come into your life for a reason. So . . . I guess what I'm saying is, do you want to hang out?"

"We are hanging out."

"No, I mean, like . . . what if we . . . had a second chance? Like really tried to . . . be together."

"Oh," he says.

Oh.

In books, it's always stomachs that flip or flutter, twist or turn, but this "Oh" sends Cora's other organs into a frenzy. Her liver? Her spleen, perhaps? She's not certain of its exact location, but the roiling happening inside her seems to involve multiple body parts.

"Umm, I don't know if that's a good idea, Cora."

"Is there someone else? Some model?"

"What? Model? No, nothing like that. It's just . . . bad timing, I guess."

She doesn't know why he winces as if in pain when Cora's the one in agony. Despite her nerves, the real reason she's here today, with him, is that she believes in their connection and that conviction has only grown. There is so little Cora has ever believed in—not God, not Santa Claus, not the Easter Bunny, not magic, not ghosts, not even herself sometimes—but she, someone who has never excelled at faith, believes in *this*. It doesn't seem possible that she got something so critical wrong.

"I don't understand . . . we've been talking and texting. There's . . . something here?"

"True. I love having you back in my life. And what we had was . . . special."

Transformative, magical, profound . . . but *special*; okay, Cora supposes that works too.

"But I think . . . it's too late, Cora."

"What do you mean?" Or, really, *How can you mean that?*

"We had a moment and . . . we missed it. You had your reasons then, and I have mine now. Let's just leave it at that. It's just . . . for the best this way." Aaron winces again as he abruptly gets to feet. "I gotta get back to the installation . . . but, uh, I'll see you. If you still want to come to my thing. No pressure."

Cora spares herself from watching him walk away and instead turns back to the water, willing a ferocious tide to come in and swallow her whole, to wash her and her humiliation out to sea. But then she will miss the opportunity to call Greta and tell her how wrong she was. It does cost you something to have courage and the price is so very high.

Cora's whole heart.

CORA PUTS IT ON THE LINE

December 2021

Dear Lincoln—

We need to talk . . .

I want to try to explain . . .

I've made a mistake . . .

I don't think I can . . .

So, how's your day . . .

Cora has rewritten the opening sentence forty times, never mind the 3,977 words that follow. Even though all those thousands of letters strung together can just as easily be reduced to two: *I'm sorry.*

When Neisha appears at the doorway to the guest room, Cora slaps her laptop closed.

"Good to see you've stopped crying. That's progress."

"I can't make any promises."

"Oh, honey." Neisha crawls into bed beside Cora in her pink satin bonnet. Cora has lost just about everything she once owned in college but for a few CD mixes and videotapes. Neisha's satin bonnet, in contrast, has had the staying power and endurance of Janet Jackson. "What are you doing, working?"

"Sort of. Working on an email to break up with Lincoln."

Neisha snatches off her bonnet for no reason except that this moment apparently called for some sort of spirited gesture. "Excuse me? Again? That was bad enough twenty years ago, but now you know better. Hiding behind an email is not the move, sis. But, more important, you want to end things? Girl, no. No. No."

"You're the one who said I needed to make a decision 'like yesterday,' remember?"

"Yeah, well, I didn't think that would mean kicking Lincoln to the curb! You need to think about things long and hard before you do that. There's no coming back this time."

"All I do is think. I'm tired of it." In what is perhaps an unnecessary emphasis of this point, Cora throws herself across the queen bed and pulls a pillow over her head for good measure. Neisha's pillows are from the Hyatt Hotel collection, but she can already tell it's not satisfying to scream into. Too much memory foam.

"But I don't get it—didn't the choice sort of get made for you? You can just move on from whatever this mind fuck with Aaron is . . . was."

Cora might have been able to fend off tears had Neisha not added that last word. *Was.* All that memory foam is, at least, absorbent.

"One doesn't have to do with the other. Even if I can't be with Aaron . . . it doesn't mean I should be with Lincoln by default."

"So you're just going to break that man's heart because . . . "

You have to have a good reason to break someone's heart, it's true. Facts, evidence, justifications, receipts . . . *a case.* Cora's recurring dream won't cut it, but it's what she keeps returning to.

Its persistence is all the more disturbing because Cora rarely sleeps deeply enough to dream. In it, she and Lincoln are walking hand in hand in a park of some sort, or it's more like a desert that stretches around them. And with every step she takes, these thick ropy vines shoot up from the sandy ground, snake up higher and higher, and wrap around her feet, then her ankles, then her knees. She looks to Lincoln to stop this from happening, but he walks on, oblivious. It gets harder and harder to move forward, dragging the angry tentacles, but she keeps trying, even as she loses ground, until eventually Lincoln's too far ahead for her to reach. And she's alone.

Cora hasn't mentioned this to anyone, not even Greta. It started a few weeks ago, after Cora had worked up the nerve to ask Lincoln *why* he loved her during one of their video calls. She had her phone leaning up against the kitchen counter while she calmed herself by chopping carrots for soup, feigning a casual indifference. *Just curious, no big deal.*

"Why do I love you? So many reasons. I just don't have them all listed out like you . . . don't be mad, but back in college I found your list of things you liked about me."

Cora had her back to the phone when he said this, so she didn't have to worry about the state of her face.

"I know I shouldn't have looked, but it was right there. My own mama couldn't come up with that many nice things to say about me. So maybe at the start of things, I was into how much you were into me. But then . . ."

She turned around at that point so she could focus on whatever redeeming words came next.

"You're just so supportive, Bella. And kind. You always just want to be there for people, for me."

It wasn't lost on her that he could have been describing a golden retriever, but Cora didn't want to be overly sensitive. It reminded her of an article she'd read that said that men often say they love how a person makes them feel, what they do for them, while a woman usually describes the unique characteristics of their beloved. Now she can't unsee this. The same way she's having a hard time unseeing herself as a loyal pet.

If you'd asked her what she most appreciated about Lincoln—then and now—she would have said his tenacity and will, his unwavering conviction that he could create for himself whatever future he wanted. And yet, she can't escape the feeling that she's at the mercy of that will. She's being moved into position, a cardboard cutout to fit in the hole he's outlined. Or a goldfish acquired in haste to replace the old one (Naomi) and dropped into the bowl quickly so that no one will even notice the difference. She was back to pet analogies. Not a good sign.

Cora is about to tell Neisha her *Little Shop of Horrors* dream because friends have to listen to detailed accountings of your dreams, no matter how tedious, the same way they're obligated to talk you out of bangs every four months, but she doesn't get the chance because Dylan bounds in the room and jumps in her lap. "Colaaaaa!"

It is almost—almost—enough of a reason to have a child: to have someone be this thrilled to find you in a room. Cora nuzzles her face in Dylan's afro, drinking in the scent of cherry and cocoa butter.

"How's my favorite godchild feeling today?"

Dylan stops to give it serious thought before she answers. "Fashionable!"

She's quite pleased to have sent her mother and auntie into a fit of hysterical giggles.

"That's *your* daughter."

"She so is."

"What are you guys talking about, Mommy? I don't get it." Dylan wants to be involved in every conversation, the more grown-up, the better. She's constantly aggrieved at the unfairness that she hasn't always been around. It used to be that every time Cora told a story about "when Mommy and I were young," Dylan would demand to know why she hadn't been there for it.

"You weren't born yet," Cora would tell her.

"But where was I?"

At which point, Cora, flummoxed at trying to explain existential metaphysics to a four-year-old, would tell her to go ask her mother. A fallback she plans to deploy when Dylan comes asking about wet dreams.

Dylan, whose favorite color is sparkles, gets distracted by the field of sequins on the dress hanging on the back of Cora's door.

"When are you going to put it on, Auntie?" Dylan asks, running her palm down the sequins.

"I don't know . . . maybe never."

"Oh, she'll be putting it on soon, Dylan." Neisha turns to face Cora.

"But you just said . . . about Lincoln?"

"Right, but you still need to go tonight and see what's up. If nothing else, you can give Aaron a hug and slam that door shut once and for all. Then you walk away slowly in that gown and have him eating his heart out. Actually, your butt isn't your best asset. Maybe you *back* slowly away. You've always had great boobs, and that dress has a serious plunge."

"Neisha!"

"What? It's true. God gave you boobs and no ass—take it up with Him. I was jealous of yours over here in the itty-bitty-titty club. Well, maybe not so much now because . . . " Neisha extends her hand in a wide arc over her belly in the universal sign of *I'm pregnant*.

Cora barely starts to let out a shocked squeal before Neisha puts a finger to her lips in the universal sign of *Shut up*, nodding at Dylan. "We're telling her on Christmas."

"Telling who what?" Dylan asks, sensing that she's missed something in the conversation while she was busy going through Cora's purse for the watermelon-flavored lip balm she likes to slather on her lips.

"Telling you to mind your own business, Ms. Fashionable. Come on, let's get you ready for soccer and leave Auntie Cora here to go pluck her eyebrows. Yes, that's a hint."

Cora goes back to being spread-eagled on the bed, staring up at the massive chandelier hanging above it. Neisha's number one rule of decorating seems to be *Have a chandelier in every space, including the bathroom.*

Cora should see about her eyebrows; she should return Lincoln's many calls; she should google the address for the event tonight and see how long it will take her to get there if she goes. But instead, Cora gets out her book—Jasmine Guillory's latest—because she needs to believe in an uncomplicated happy ending, even if they're only possible in fiction. She's about to settle into the read when Neisha rushes in. "Something's happened!"

Neisha is known for dramatic entrances and has a baseline level of agitation, so Cora's first thought is that there's been a shocking development on *Below Deck* or maybe Neisha finally surpassed fifteen thousand followers on TikTok.

"Ty just texted me—she's taking Aaron to the ER. He collapsed or something."

Cora is upright, alert, her mind instantly and completely cleared of everything else. "What's wrong with him?"

"That's all I know, and I don't want to bombard Ty with texts. They're on the way to Cedars-Sinai. Or maybe they're there by now."

Cora barely takes a breath but somehow Neisha knows what she's going to ask before she says it. Neisha always knows. "Yes, girl, you should go."

"But—"

"Cora, just go, okay? I'm calling you an Uber now."

Rumpled at the end of the bed is the lucky sweater she stripped off yesterday, irrationally angry that it had somehow failed her. In her rush, she puts it back on, along with yesterday's jeans, which still have sand stuck in the cuffs. There's no time to think about clothes or signs.

When she arrives at Cedars, jogging through the electronic double doors, she immediately begins sweating and panting taking in the smell of antiseptic, the stiff waiting-room chairs, the signs about wearing masks, the white coats, and the pink scrubs.

Cora turns right around and goes back outside to text Ty that she was here from a small bench near the ambulance bay. This buys her a minute to collect herself, staring at the clouds and box breathing for her life, while she waits for Ty to come get her and usher her through the labyrinth of the ER to where Aaron is.

Ty doesn't come outside; just hollers loudly for Cora from the emergency room doors and motions her in, greeting her with a quick, surprise hug and a face mask to put on.

"He's okay," Ty says as they walk through the packed waiting room. "He just needs to take better care of himself with his condition. Boy, is it a shitshow here—some dude has been screaming about canned peaches and the illuminati for a solid hour. Look, Aaron's right over there." Ty points down the hall to a row of exam rooms behind a bustling nurses' station. "Third on the right, past the guy who's screaming. I'm gonna run and get some coffee right quick while you're here."

Cora does her best to ignore the commotion as security guards surround the naked man, who has his gown open and is pacing in dirt-caked bare feet, ranting about pyramids with eyes. She finds Aaron reclining on a hospital bed, hands by his sides, eyes closed, as centered as ever. Like he's doing a meditation. She thinks of iconic soap opera scenes and pretends she can lean over, softly kiss his forehead, and make him wake up.

It's a disappointment that no kisses are required; his eyes flicker open as Cora sidles up to the bed. "Cora? What are you doing here?"

"A better question is, what are you doing here? Are you okay? What happened?"

"That's three questions."

She can't see his mouth behind the mask, but his eyes have a glint that reassures her as much as his joke does. "Well, you can still do math, so I guess you're going to live. Really, though, are you okay?"

"Yeah, yeah, fine. I fainted, I guess. Got dehydrated. I worked all night on the final touches for the show. I'm just run-down. Only reason I'm here is Ty made me come. Where is she?"

"She went to get coffee."

"Oh, good, I get a little break. I was just pretending to be asleep so she'd stop talking."

"Are you sure you're okay, Aaron? Ty mentioned something about . . . a condition?"

"Leave it to Ty to put a man's private business out there."

"You don't have to tell me."

"No, it's okay. I do have a thing . . . " The way he's turned somber and the pause that follows gives Cora both the time and a reason to catalog every terrible disease she's ever heard of. She knows whatever he has will involve fatigue, pain, weight loss—all symptoms, she realizes now, she'd noticed without registering.

Aaron makes an effort to sound lighter as he goes on, which is probably meant to reassure her, but it has the opposite effect. "It's called autosomal dominant polycystic kidney disease. Lotta words to say my kidneys are failing. Though I prefer *struggling*. It's fairly manageable with meds if I'm careful, but I'm on the transplant list. And I hope my number gets called before my number gets called, ya know?"

"How long?" Cora asks.

"How long do I have to live?"

"No!" She's appalled that he thinks she would ask that. But now that he's planted that idea, she's overcome with a wave of such wooziness, she might end up in the empty bed across the way. "No, I meant how long have you had this?"

"Got officially diagnosed a few years back. But for the record, I'm not dying anytime soon. I don't plan to, anyway."

"Does it hurt?" Cora pats his body as if feeling for broken parts, which has the pleasant, unintended consequence of making Aaron laugh.

"I'm in one piece, Cora. Right now I'm just tired. I need rest and plenty of fluids, that's all."

This sounds credible enough, but Cora is familiar with the lengths people will go to to protect you from their pain. If only Cora could break away and compile a full dossier on Aaron's illness, spend an hour or two on WebMD and the NIH website doing a deep dive into medications, studies, treatments, trials; she could even ask a doctor or two running around the ER.

"Is this . . . is this why you don't want to date me, Aaron?" There is perhaps not a more appalling place or moment to ask such a question, but Cora can't help herself. The timing feels urgent.

Aaron shifts his head so he's looking up at her. "I could never just date you, Cora."

"What does that mean?"

"I mean, if we did this, I know I would be all the way in. I knew that from the jump."

"For real?" The surprise, though, is that this doesn't come as a surprise. It's the disarming jolt of noticing something that's been there all along, hiding right there in plain sight, as big truths tend to. "And . . . and that's a problem?"

"Yeah, because it's not fair. I decided a long time ago I wasn't going to be anyone's charity case. Or burden. All the doctors, the medical bills with my shit insurance. Dialysis. The stress. And it's hereditary. I didn't want to get into the issue of kids with anyone."

"First of all, I don't want kids. You know that."

Cora recalls that when she'd told this to Aaron, he didn't question her or push back or protest. He didn't say, *"But you'd be such a good mother,"* like so many did. He'd said, "That's cool, I get it," with such ease and openness she didn't know what to do but thank him for that reaction. If only all our choices, revelations, and opinions were met with such a refreshing absence of judgment.

"And besides," Cora went on, reaching for Aaron's hand to give it an imploring squeeze. "You don't get to decide that, what's fair to me or not."

"Well, how about this: You're better off with Lincoln." Aaron holds her eyes.

"How do you even know . . . ?" Then: "Ty." They both say it at the same time.

"Gotta say, it threw me that he was in the picture. Still? Again?"

"I'm sorry, I didn't—"

"You owe me no apologies, Cora. But like I said, Lincoln's a better bet. Solid."

"Unfortunately, my heart isn't Vegas."

"I just mean—"

Cora puts her hand up to cut him off because she knows what he means. She's *supposed* to be with Lincoln. He's good-looking, rich, confident, successful, adoring. He's her first love. Her longest romance. Her biggest champion. He's the easy choice, the safe choice. And she's spent months, if not most of her life, trying to convince herself that he's the right choice. There is no reason to believe he isn't. Except there is.

Sometimes when she's with Lincoln, Cora gets a glimpse of herself in a mirror or a store window or the reflection in his shiny new Tesla, and she thinks, *Who is that?* But when she's with Aaron, when she reads her letters to Aaron, which she finally did last night, all the way through, twice, she thinks: *There I am.* It has always been easier to try to be who Lincoln wants her to be than to be herself. It's easier to think love requires work, focus, effort, vigilance, that it is an assignment to be aced. It's much harder to accept it when it shows up in another form—easy, effortless, natural. So hard, in fact, that Cora didn't recognize it until now, when it might be too late.

In the end, if there is a case to be made for her choice, this is it. If there is a lesson to learn, here it is. It took only twenty years.

"If you don't have feelings for me, that's one thing, and I'll have to accept that. But . . . "

She pauses, not because she's nervous about what she's going to say but because she knows, unequivocally, that her instincts are right and true, and she needs to let that revolutionary sensation sink in. "I think you're my person, Aaron. And—and I think maybe I'm your person too. And I think we knew that back then and never stopped knowing it." She steps forward so that her thighs are pressing against the side of the bed, imploring him to hold her eyes. "Tell me I'm wrong."

"You know how I feel. But—"

Cora refuses to let him continue. There will always be *buts* and *what-ifs* and *if onlys*. The important point is that she was right all along except about one thing: that nothing scared Aaron. She recognizes his running away from her at the beach for what it was—fear. And *that,* out of everything, she can deal with. You might even say she was an expert.

"No *buts*, Aaron. We've run out of excuses. Timing, distance, illness, other people . . . it was always something. But I want to be with you. Or at least, I want to try."

"Is it really as easy as that, though, Cora?"

"I can't believe I'm saying this, but yes. I don't want to make the same mistake again—getting in my own way. I don't want to spend any more time wondering what could have been, Aaron. Because we could find out. I want to find out. Don't you?"

In the quiet that follows, Cora doesn't for a single second wish she could take any of it back. She waits patiently and calmly for whatever happens next. It is this: Aaron takes her hand and places it over his heart, which is beating fast and wild. In the steady, rapid thud against her hand, she has her answer.

"Good," Cora says. "That's settled, then."

Finally.

epilogue | CORA LIVES WITH HER CHOICES

January 2022

The breakup happens just after midnight. It isn't how Cora intended to start 2022, in tears, with confetti still swirling in Times Square and the sound of thousands of New Year's Eve revelers drifting into the suite overlooking Central Park Lincoln had booked them.

Neisha had convinced Cora not to send the email, to "pull on big-girl panties" and face Lincoln. As much as she wanted to hide behind a screen, Cora couldn't argue that he deserved at least that. She just couldn't settle on the right time to bring it up. Until she didn't have to. When Lincoln turned to her and said, "You don't want to do this, do you?" it was as simple as quietly shaking her head. This time, there were no demands for explanations, no accusations or entreaties—he spared Cora the drama of it all. Or maybe he was sparing himself.

In the morning, Lincoln is gone. He packed his bag in the violet light of early dawn while Cora pretended to sleep. This act became harder when she felt him watching her, just before he opened the door of the hotel room. And then closed it softly behind him.

He left a note on the bedside table: *It will always be you, Bella.*

When he was in the bathroom last night, Cora had tucked a note away for him too, in his leather duffel bag. In the pocket next to the one she'd found the ring in. She couldn't bear to open the velvet box.

She wrote: *I'll always be grateful to you for teaching me how to love. And be loved.*

There's something so fitting about the symmetry of their last words to each other, she could cry. So she does. But the fit of tears comes and goes like a passing train, and in its wake is an unfamiliar lightness Cora can only take as confirmation that she's made the right choice.

A part of her fears that she'll always wonder what the other path would have looked like, but that's unavoidable—there will always be the house you didn't buy, the job offer you declined, the city you left behind, the man who wasn't right for you after all.

All the lives you would have had if you'd decided differently. Every choice comes with the loss of everything (and everyone) else you let go by making it.

Cora's body tells her she's gained something too—a calm she hasn't experienced before, one that makes everything to come, all the unknowns, far less scary than it would otherwise be. Still, Cora can't help wanting to race ahead to see how it all turns out. Like she did with the Choose Your Own Adventure books she loved as a kid, she wants to determine how the plot of her life unfolds. *Turn to page 46 if Cora moves to Santa Fe. Turn to page 110 if Aaron and Cora go back to Paris.*

She stands, wraps herself in a plush white bathrobe, and looks out on Central Park, a rectangle of bare trees stretching fifty blocks. She lets herself pretend she can see all the way to the end of the story.

She will call Aaron when she gets home this afternoon, and they'll make all the plans they've been waiting to make until Cora "finishes her business" with Lincoln. These plans will include much more than spooning together and whispering into the night, which is what they limited themselves to on the night of Aaron's event ten days ago. He got out of the hospital and rallied, barely, for suits, small talk, and canapés with Cora by his side in the gold gown he called "sublime." By the end of the night, though, he was too exhausted to act on the passion building between them. That was just as well; it was the right thing to do, to talk to Lincoln first, and, not for nothing, the buildup and fevered anticipation is a delicious reward for their virtue.

A couple months from now, Cora will join Aaron to see a specialist at the Mayo Clinic. She annoys the doctors with the four-inch-thick dossier of research she's amassed about Aaron's condition, but the two of them leave with hope.

By the end of April, before her one houseplant—a peace lily—has had a chance to bloom, Cora will ask Barbara if she can work remotely and she'll move to Santa Fe because her life with Aaron can't start fast enough now that they've waited twenty years.

That summer, Wes will come to visit them armed with more information than anyone would want on the history of the Santa Fe Trail. His first morning, they find him crouched on the kitchen floor fixing the dishwasher, and Cora starts to run over and tell him to stop, it's not even his house, but Aaron holds her back. "Let him—he just wants to feel like he can still take care of you."

This makes Cora love both of them even more.

The same thing happens when she and Wes are scrambling eggs and he says, "I'm so proud of you, baby girl."

"For what?" she asks. "I haven't done anything."

"You followed your heart. You took a chance on love. You moved across the country. I don't know, Cora, it sort of felt like you were floating through your life, and now you're seizing it. Seizing your happiness. That's all I've ever wanted for you."

Neisha and Kim will arrive with champagne and homemade chocolate cupcakes for Cora's fortieth, and they will spend a full forty-eight hours getting their fill of reminiscing and chili con queso. When Kim tries to apologize, Cora will remind her: "We don't need to do that, remember? Also, I know." There's a moment when Cora goes inside to refill their spiked lemonades and listens to their laughter carry from the porch. That simple, perfect sound and the weight of all the memories they've shared will give her the same chest-bursting feeling that being with them in their cozy dorm room did—the astonishment of friendship, no less miraculous than starlight. *My girls for life.*

In the fall, when Lincoln announces his run for state senate, Cora will send a donation with a note: *Second Black president isn't too shabby.* She will spend more time on his campaign website than she should, gazing at his kids and his new girlfriend, who looks every bit the politician's wife, down to the gold brooch. She'll remember Lincoln saying that everything worked out like it should. She'll remember, too, that although her first heartbreak left its mark, so too did that smile. Lincoln, impossibly young, in his green bookstore uniform, grinning, isn't just an image she'll carry forever but a feeling.

One day, a year or five down the road, Aaron and Cora will sit on their back porch overlooking a field of scattered succulents, a playground for the lizards that scamper around—her new happy place. It's an uneventful day and that's exactly the point. Aaron has started new meds that are working so far, and the gallery he's opened was packed that afternoon with kids on field trips that Cora helped arrange as part of her art-in-schools volunteer project.

Cora had once dreamed of what a certain type of blissful romantic intimacy would look like—her feet in Aaron's lap as she read; knowing exactly what two dishes they were going to order at a restaurant and share and who would get the last bite of what; asking, "How was your day?" every evening in a way that's both mindlessly routine and utterly sincere. Day after day, when a version of this happens, Cora will feel amazed that she somehow orchestrated it all. This leads to a heady discovery: Having certain dreams come true can make you believe you deserve the credit for your happiness, that you yourself can be more powerful a force than fate or luck.

One particular day, Aaron and Cora will brush their teeth side by side, kissing through foamy mouths, eat fish tacos for dinner, and end the day on the back deck Aaron built by hand playing a game they love called Pente, lazily but competitively. Out of nowhere, Aaron reaches for her arm and sweeps his lips across the back of her hand. It's partly consolation for beating her, again, but it's also much more. It's how he tells her, *I love this, I love our life.* And so, naturally, Cora bursts into tears. This is not so unusual that Aaron is alarmed. He's smiling; they both know love makes her emotional.

"Oh, Aaron. Do you ever think how we might have missed out on all this?"

"Nope. Because we didn't. We're here." It encompasses so much.

"You knew this is how it would end up?"

"End? I keep telling you, this is just the beginning."

At that moment, Aaron will take her hand and hold it to his heart, their secret, silent way of saying *I love you*, and Cora Rose Belle will marvel at the fact that she was ever scared at all.

ACKNOWLEDGMENTS

In the pages of this novel, Cora quips that a relationship is too much to take on alone. So is a book. I'm incredibly grateful to everyone who cheered me on and read early drafts and supported the publication with such enthusiasm. Also, to those who let me borrow from their lives, however loosely.

I sometimes joke with my partner that I still identify as a single woman after spending so many years as one. Likewise, even after all this time being an author and writing three books, I still identify as an editor, having spent decades working in the publishing trenches. This means I have a special level of gratitude for my publishing partners and colleagues, including and especially the entire team at Atria, who are some of the nicest, smartest people in the business. Laura—you grabbed the baton with such passion and grace; thank you. And Falon—publicist extraordinaire. I kid that we have an author/publicist love story for the ages, except it's not a joke. When I see your texts and emails, always full of good news and good cheer, I get the same giddy buzz of a first crush.

Dana, Libby, Kate, Natalie, Jimmy, Zakiya, Kayley, Tracy, Lisa . . . and so many others at Atria and in the book-making journey—thank you too.

On behalf of all authors, I want to use this space to say to all my publishing brethren: I see you, see how hard you work, how much you believe in words and stories and the people who tell them, all your unsung, behind-the-scenes efforts. When a book is successful, it's not just the author's success but the publisher's as well, and I've always just wanted to make the team proud.

And speaking of unsung, behind-the-scenes heroes: Agents are always grinding away, quietly (or loudly!) advocating for their clients, and I'm grateful to Pilar and Byrd and the formidable crew at UTA for having my back. And Sue Armstrong at C & W.

Readers, all of you out there who keep bookstores afloat and motivate authors to write and take time to offer the most fascinating, impassioned reviews on Amazon, Goodreads, and TikTok—you're the absolute best. Without you, the whole enterprise falls apart. If you've made it this far in the book, it means you've spent time and money on this story, and maybe that deserves the biggest thank-you of all.

At the heart of this book is a love story—well, two of them, really—but it's also a story of the power of friendship. Neisha and Kim are a composite of the circle of friends I hold dear. These women (and Rakesh) have been by my side for a lifetime and have guided me to myself over and over. In so many ways, they have been and always will be the true loves of my life. I'm not worried that they need a special shout-out in these pages to know how much I appreciate them because I try to remind them as often as I can. But they deserve the ink, so—TO THE BESTIES: I LOVE YOU.

A couple of them—Felicia and Kara—were early readers of this book, and showing them the first raw pages involved as much trust and vulnerability as shedding violent snotty tears after a memorably terrible breakup. They handled both scenarios expertly. They offered stellar notes on the draft (*More sex*), which matched their always stellar life advice (*He wasn't right for you*)—how right they were on both counts. I also appreciate Andrea Robinson and Brenda Copeland for reading initial drafts of the opening pages and helping me find Cora and the story.

I want to thank my writing partner, Jo Piazza, for helping me transition from editor to author—it's not a leap I would have taken on my own. I missed you in the Google Doc, but your voice was in my head rooting me on: *We got this; We never miss a deadline; We do all the things; Is it time for French fries?*

I have two truly standout parents, but I'm also very much a daddy's girl. I feel lucky that to create a beloved dad in Wes, I could so easily draw from my own experience, having had the good fortune to be raised by a man who was the gold standard for fathers. He taught me many things—to appreciate books, to tell a good joke, to swim, to swing a bat, to laugh at myself, to give to others, to show up, to work hard. He also taught me how to love and, even more important, how to know who was worthy of mine.

He also taught me a great deal about the power of love and friendship; both have been guiding lights in my life and sustained me when he passed away. Miss you forever, Daddy.

ABOUT THE AUTHOR

Christine Pride is a writer, editor, and longtime publishing veteran, having held editorial posts at various Big Five imprints, and has published many bestselling and critically acclaimed novels and memoirs. In addition to writing fiction, she does select editorial work, proposal/content development, and teaching and coaching.